# DEATH TO THE EMPEROR

*By Simon Scarrow*

**The *Eagles of the Empire* Series**

*The Britannia Campaign*
Under the Eagle (AD 42–43, Britannia)
The Eagle's Conquest (AD 43, Britannia)
When the Eagle Hunts (AD 44, Britannia)
The Eagle and the Wolves (AD 44, Britannia)
The Eagle's Prey (AD 44, Britannia)

*Rome and the Eastern Provinces*
The Eagle's Prophecy (AD 45, Rome)
The Eagle in the Sand (AD 46, Judaea)
Centurion (AD 46, Syria)

*The Mediterranean*
The Gladiator (AD 48–49, Crete)
The Legion (AD 49, Egypt)
Praetorian (AD 51, Rome)

*The Return to Britannia*
The Blood Crows (AD 51, Britannia)
Brothers in Blood (AD 51, Britannia)
Britannia (AD 52, Britannia)

*Hispania*
Invictus (AD 54, Hispania)

*The Return to Rome*
Day of the Caesars (AD 54, Rome)

*The Eastern Campaign*
The Blood of Rome (AD 55, Armenia)
Traitors of Rome (AD 56, Syria)
The Emperor's Exile (AD 57, Sardinia)

*Britannia: Troubled Province*
The Honour of Rome (AD 59, Britannia)
Death to the Emperor (AD 60, Britannia)

**The *Berlin Wartime* Thrillers**
Blackout
Dead of Night

**The *Wellington and Napoleon* Quartet**
Young Bloods
The Generals
Fire and Sword
The Fields of Death

Sword and Scimitar
(Great Siege of Malta)

Hearts of Stone (Second World War)

**The *Gladiator* Series**
Gladiator: Fight for Freedom
Gladiator: Street Fighter
Gladiator: Son of Spartacus
Gladiator: Vengeance

*Writing with T. J. Andrews*
Arena (AD 41, Rome)
Invader (AD 44, Britannia)
Pirata (AD 25, Adriatic)

*Writing with Lee Francis*
Playing With Death

To the memory of Glynne Jones, a gentleman in every sense. After a long and rich life, his death leaves a huge hole in the lives of those closest to him, as well as those of us who were privileged to count him as a friend.

Farewell Squire Jones, with great respect and affection from The Varlet.

# BRITANNIA AD 60

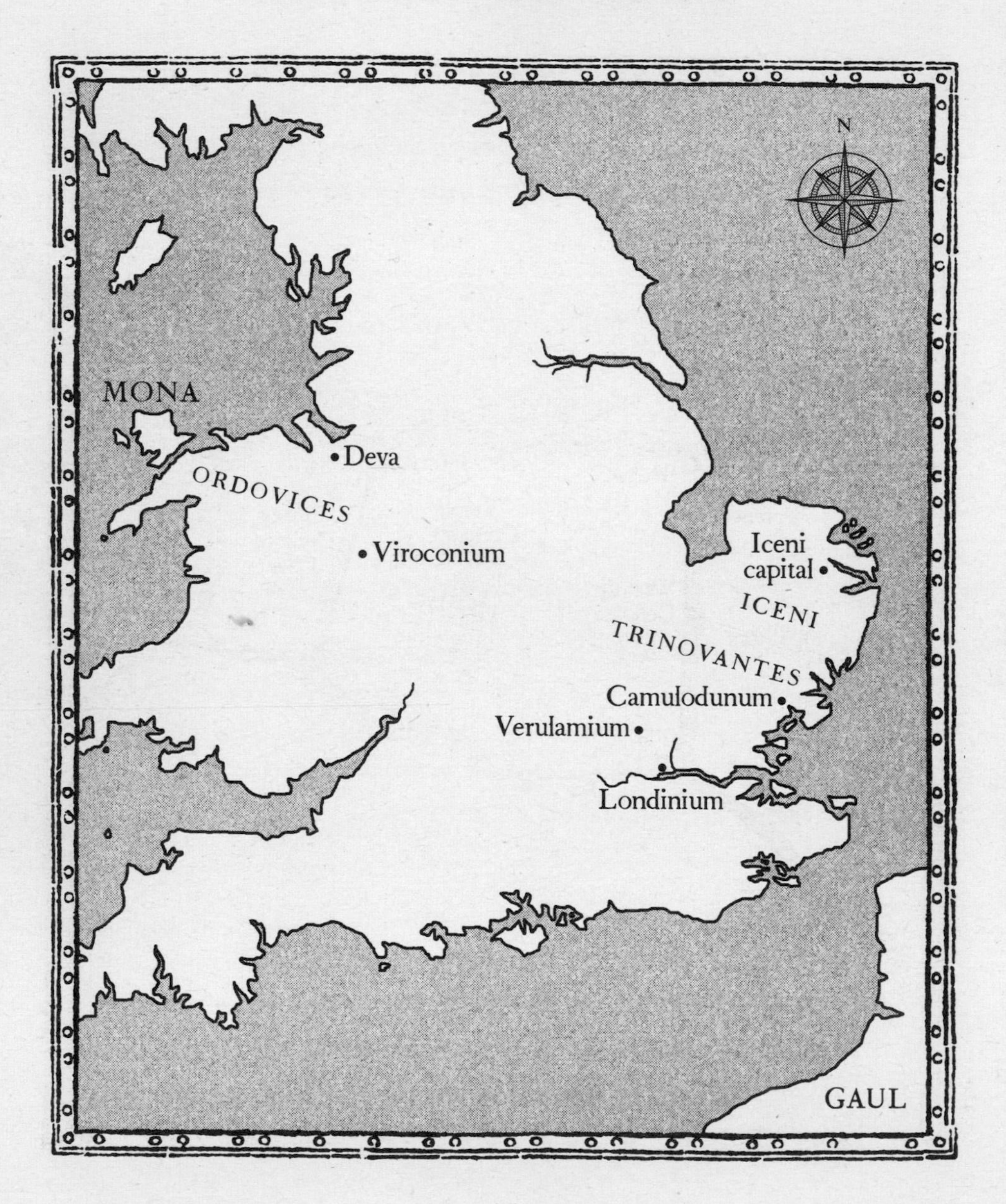

# CAMULODUNUM AD 60

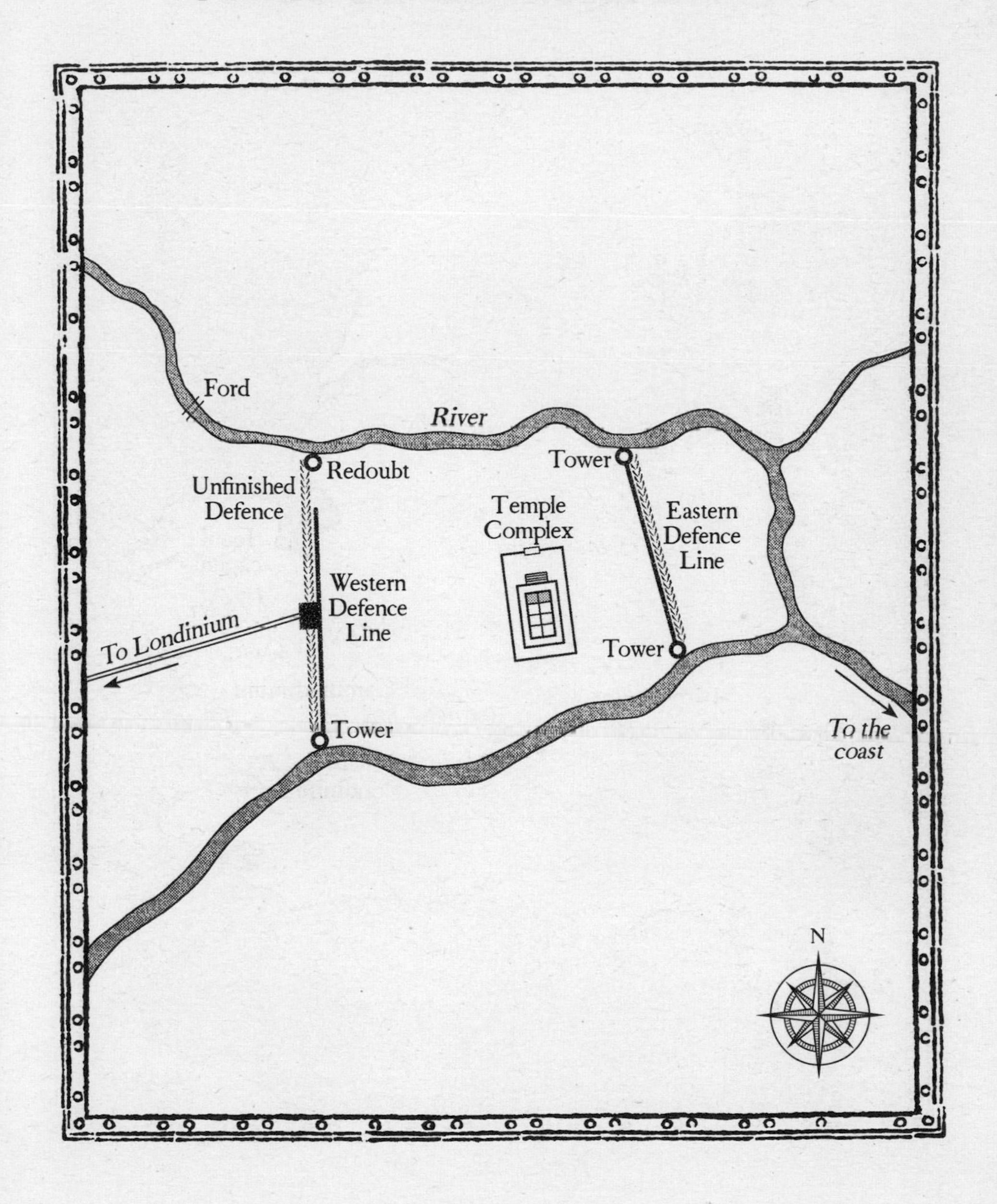

# CHAIN OF COMMAND

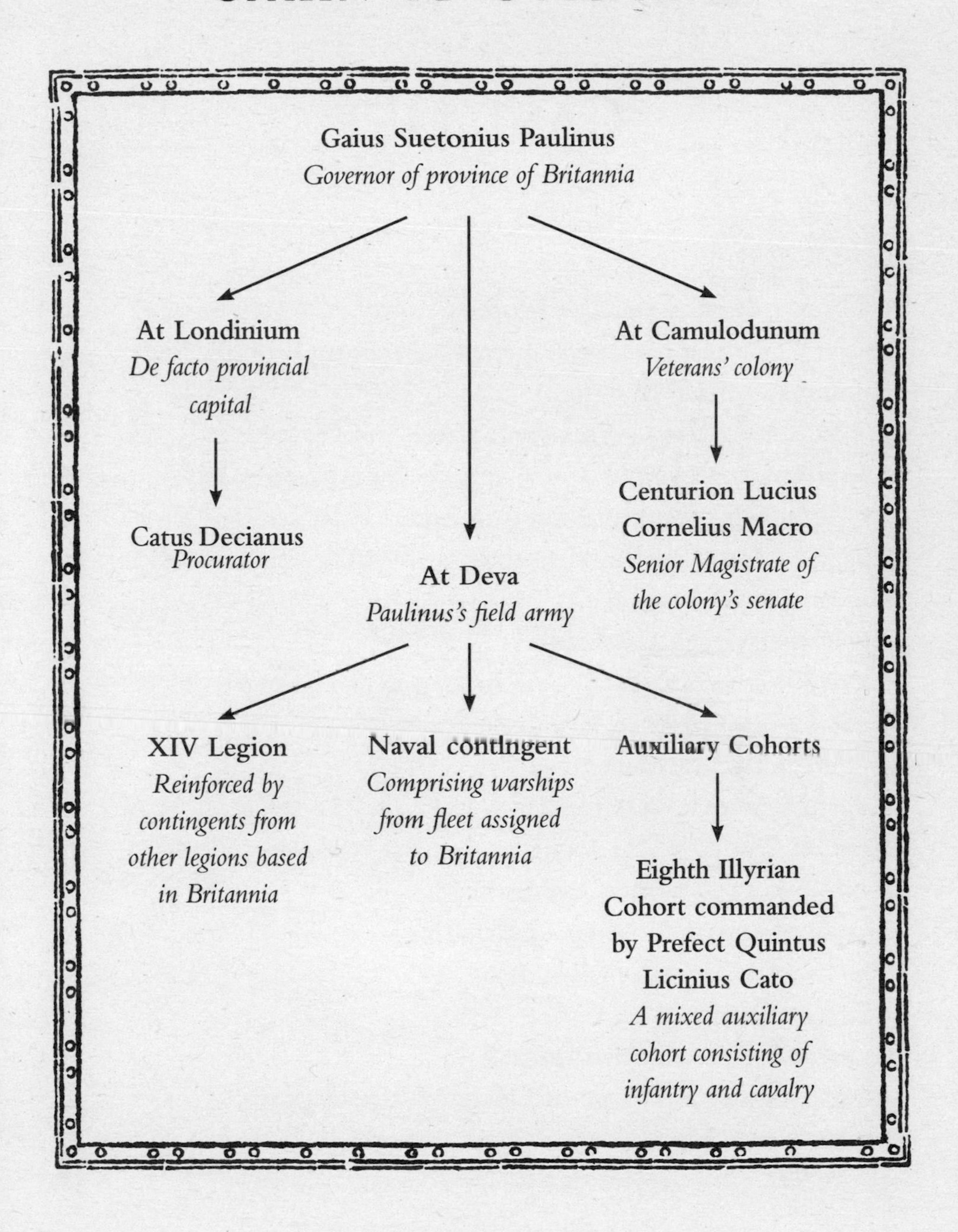

# Cast List

*Centurion Macro*: a hero of Rome
*Prefect Cato*: best friend of Macro; an accomplished soldier
*Petronella*: wife of Macro
*Lucius*: son of Cato by his dead wife
*Claudia Acte*: lover of Cato and former mistress of Emperor Nero, who thinks she died in exile
*Cassius*: a ferocious-looking mongrel with a ferocious appetite
*Parvus*: a mute boy
*Apollonius*: Greek freedman
*Catus Decianus*: procurator of Britannia
*Suetonius*: governor of Britannia
*Portia*: mother of Macro
*Gaius Hormanus*: slave drover
*Boudica*: Queen of the Iceni
*Bardea*: older daughter of Boudica
*Merida*: younger daughter of Boudica
*Syphodubnus*: cousin of Boudica
*Bladocus*: Druid
*Pernocatus*: Trinovantian hunter
*Attalus*: officer in charge of Decianus's bodyguard
*Fascus*: foot soldier
*Thrasyllus*: commander of the Tenth Gallic Cohort

**Eighth Cohort**

*Galerius*
*Minucius*
*Annius*
*Vellius*
*Decius*
*Flaccus*
*Tubero*
*Rubio*

**At Camulodunum**

*Ulpius*
*Vulpinus*
*Flaminius*
*Varius*
*Tertillius*
*Silvanus*
*Caldonius*
*Balbanus*
*Adrastus*
*Venutius*

# PROLOGUE

## *Britannia, November* AD *60*

The king died shortly before dawn.

Outside the royal round hut, his retainers sat quietly around a large fire. At another time they would have been drinking and talking loudly in good cheer, interrupted by bursts of song amid the revelry. But this last night they had sat in a sombre mood, their muted conversation confined to brief exchanges about the future of the kingdom after Prasutagus had passed from this world. It was known that he had recently changed his will and named the Roman emperor Nero as his co-heir, alongside his queen. The news of this had struck many of his people as an act of betrayal.

By what right had Prasutagus gifted half the Iceni kingdom to a despot who lived in a city far away beyond the sea? Moreover, Nero was the ruler of an empire whose legions had put down a minor uprising and killed many of the tribe's warriors only a few years earlier, when Scapula had been governor. Roman soldiers had looted villages and abused the women. Roman veterans, based at the colony founded at Camulodunum, had seized the lands of farmers and the estates of nobles bordering the territory claimed by the colony. All of this was a cause of great shame to the proud people of the Iceni. Now they did what they could to assuage the burden of humiliation by refusing to trade with Roman merchants and rebuffing any contact with the invaders as far as possible.

As much as the king's advisers had shared the feelings of the people with respect to the will, they had come to accept, as had Prasutagus, that an accommodation was needed with Rome if the tribe was to have any control over its destiny. The critical issue was the treaty that had followed the invasion some seventeen years ago. In exchange for accepting Roman protection and recognition of his rule of the tribe, the king had agreed that Rome would have the right to crown his successor. At the time, he had been assured that it was a mere formality, but he and his advisers had come to learn that the status of 'client king', as the Romans referred to it, was little more than a precursor to the annexation of the kingdom, after which Rome would rule directly.

The king and his council had hoped that naming Nero as his co-heir would placate the appetite of Rome and at the same time be taken as a token of Iceni loyalty to the Empire. Some had warned that this was a false hope, and pointed to the example of other tribes who had come to regret treating with Rome. The matter was made more worrying by the notification Prasutagus had received from the governor in Londinium that the silver gifted to the king at the time the agreement was made was not in fact a gift but a loan. Rome intended to foreclose, with interest, the moment Prasutagus died. Much of the coin had been used to buy grain to feed the people after the crops had failed these last two years, and little remained to repay to Rome's moneylenders.

The knowledge of all this weighed heavily on the minds of those gathered around the bier in the royal hall upon which the king's body lay. He had been too weak to rise from his sickbed these last ten days, and his wife and queen, Boudica, had hardly left his side as she nursed him as best she could. It had been a pitiful time. In his prime, Prasutagus had been as tall and powerfully built a warrior as there had ever been in the Iceni tribe. His flowing straw-coloured hair had framed a broad, good-humoured face, and his clear blue eyes had twinkled, adding to the sense that here was a man who enjoyed life and easily communicated such a sentiment to those fortunate to share his company. He had been loved by most of his people, and those who might not have loved him respected him. The illness of the last year had eaten away at him so that now he was barely recognisable even to those who knew him best. Little more than skin on bones, with sunken eyes and mottled skin, his features frequently twisting in agony at the pain racking his failing body.

Boudica had exhausted every attempt to cure him, and the tribe's Druids had proved powerless. Casting aside her distaste, she had even paid for a Roman medic from Londinium to come to the Iceni capital. He too had failed. In the end, all she could do was try to comfort her dying husband and make offerings to the gods to ensure that he was welcomed into the afterlife.

She had sat through the night listening to his shallow breathing becoming more laboured, until it was little more than a faint wheezing rattle. At last it had stopped. She waited a moment before pressing her ear against his skeletal chest, but there was no heartbeat. With a sigh, she raised her head and kissed his limp hand tenderly before laying it across his breast and turning to face her daughters, other family, nobles and members of the royal council.

Drawing herself up, she announced, 'King Prasutagus is dead.'

No one moved nor spoke. Then her younger daughter,

Merida, closed her eyes, covered her face with her hands and began to sob. The older, two years senior to her sister, had inherited her father's strong features, and at sixteen was already betrothed to a nobleman with a coastal estate. She approached her mother and embraced her.

'Oh, my sweet Bardea,' her mother whispered in her ear. 'What is to become of us now? What is to become of the Iceni?'

'The Iceni will endure, Mother. We always have.'

Boudica increased the pressure of her embrace, moved by her daughter's simple expression of conviction. 'Yes, of course.' If only she understood, she thought. Our tribe stands at the very edge of oblivion. Our fate is no longer ours alone to decide. Our future will be settled far away in Rome. The kingdom of the Iceni would continue or fall on the whim of the boy emperor Nero.

She released her daughter and held her at arm's length, regarding with approval the firm set of her jaw and the taut determination not to give way to grief. The tears would come later, in private, as would her own. But there were other matters to deal with first. She indicated Merida and spoke softly. 'Tend to your sister. She was ever her father's favourite, as you are mine. Take her to your hut and comfort her.'

'Yes, Mother.'

'I'll be along once I have dealt with the royal council.'

They exchanged a brief look and Bardea nodded. They had discussed this moment and what must follow several days earlier, when the king had taken to his deathbed.

Boudica watched as her daughters left the hall, her heart aching with concern for what the future might bring for them. Nothing was certain any more. All the tribe's traditions, reaching back across unnumbered generations, might be swept away in the days to come, if Rome acted with callous disregard for the people of the Iceni. What would become of Bardea and Merida in a world that no longer had a place for princesses? Who would protect them when the royal household had been stripped away?

As they disappeared through the entrance to the hall, Boudica nodded to the commander of the king's bodyguard, and he quietly ordered the two warriors on duty to close the doors. The soft thud of timbers caused some to glance over their shoulder before they fixed their attention on their queen. She was solidly built, with broad hips and shoulders, and her height gave her a physical presence that was matched by her commanding personality. Although in her middle years, with a slightly creased face, her gaze was shrewd and penetrating. The long red hair tied back with a simple leather band made her stand out from the other women of the court.

A keen intelligence combined with the learning she had acquired in childhood thanks to the tutor her noble father had brought back from Gaul meant that Boudica was one of only a handful of her people who could speak and write Latin. As such, she had been the right arm of Prasutagus throughout his reign, and as his health began to fail, she had assumed his authority to ensure that the Iceni were ruled wisely and for the most part fairly.

She had won the trust of the people and the majority of the royal court, but now that the king was dead, there would be some who aspired to take his place. Boudica knew who they were and why most of them should not be trusted with power, particularly at such a delicate time. A headstrong noble boldly asserting the ambitions of the Iceni might anger Rome and bring down her wrath on the tribe. The ease with which Roman soldiers had put down the uprising a few years earlier had been a salutary lesson for the Iceni. The defeat had been made more humbling by Rome's insistence that the tribe's warriors surrender their arms. The only permitted weapons were to be used for hunting, and the armour and swords, passed down from father to son and treated with reverence, had been handed to the Romans. Not all, of course. Caches had been hidden, buried beneath their huts or secreted amid the treacherous waterways and marshes that the Romans were loath to enter. There was a feeling in the tribe that a day would come when the swords of the Iceni warriors would be drawn again. That day was not now, Boudica resolved.

She studied the faces of the nobles, warriors and members of the king's council, marking the mix of respect, calculation and expectation in their expressions. Then she looked back at the body of her husband, the man she had soon come to love after their arranged marriage. She already felt a keen ache of longing for him, and smiled sadly as she recalled his hearty laughter and the affection that was always present in their private life, away from their roles as rulers of the Iceni. She closed her eyes and drew a deep breath, pushing aside thoughts of the past and forcing her mind to focus as she turned to the others in the hall.

'We have lost our king. The question before us is to decide who should succeed him. Although I am your queen, it is our custom that the king's council and the nobles have the ultimate right to choose our next ruler. I will say it now, before all gathered here, that I would be honoured to rule in the stead of Prasutagus. You know my worth. I have proved it this last year as our beloved king was stricken by the illness that has finally taken him. It was also his express wish that I inherit the kingdom.'

'Alongside the Roman emperor,' a voice interrupted.

Her gaze swung towards a stout noble to the right of those gathered before her. He wore a gold torc around his neck fashioned to look like a two-headed snake. The breadth of his chest and shoulders made up for his lack of height, and a fringe of fair hair ringed his bald head. A plaited moustache drooped either side of his thin lips, which now lifted slightly in a sneer.

'My cousin Syphodubnus, you know the reasons why Nero was named. You were in the council when the will was agreed.'

'I didn't agree, if you recall. And I wasn't the only one.' Syphodubnus glanced round at the other nobles, and several nodded and muttered their support.

'Nevertheless,' Boudica continued, 'the king asked the council to vote on the matter, and the result was clear and we are bound by the decision.'

'Who says so? No oath was sworn before a Druid. I say we are not bound to abide by the terms of the will. Prasutagus is no more. Maybe his successor will choose to renounce the agreement. Maybe the new king will have the courage to stand up to Rome and salvage the honour of the Iceni.'

Boudica felt her guts twist with anger and disgust. Her husband's body was still warm, and yet this long-standing rival was already intimating that Prasutagus had been a coward and betrayed his people. Clenching her jaw to prevent herself from expressing her outrage at this disrespect, she stood still, aloof and silent, glaring at Syphodubnus for a few heartbeats before she responded.

'It's clear that you think yourself worthy of taking the place of my husband. Is that it?'

Syphodubnus smiled before assuming a more imperious expression. 'If it is the choice of our people that I should rule, then that is a decision I would honour with my life. If I were to become king, it would be my sworn duty to restore the prestige of the Iceni and keep the kingdom out of the clutches of Rome.'

Several men voiced their support for this ambition, and Boudica's quick glance identified them as his cronies, nobles and leading warriors who had followed him in the failed uprising of a few years earlier. They had made great play of what they called their heroic struggle with Rome. In truth, it had been a conflict doomed from the start. Too few had rallied to the standard of Syphodubnus when he had appealed to his people. Rather than waiting to put the matter before Prasutagus and his court and let the Iceni decide as a whole, the noble and his faction had marched against the invader. It had been a rash move.

Boudica raised a hand to command silence, and only lowered it when the last of Syphodubnus's followers had fallen quiet.

'You speak of the prestige of the Iceni, yet it was you who brought shame upon our people by the ease with which you were defeated. You were not even brought low by the Roman legions. All it took to crush your force was a handful of their auxiliary cohorts backed up by levies from the other tribes of Britannia. Second-rate soldiers at best,' she added scornfully.

'At least we fought,' Syphodubnus shot back. 'Fought and won honour for our people.'

'Honour?' Boudica laughed bitterly. 'What did you achieve? You raided a few farms, burned a handful of villas and massacred a few patrols. Then, the moment the Romans gathered enough troops to counter the threat, you bolted to the safety of a fort in the marshes. How long did you and your brave warriors hold out? Do remind us all . . .'

Syphodubnus glared at her, his face draining of colour.

'Nothing to say for yourself?' Boudica prompted. 'Then let me say it for you. You lasted precisely two days while the Roman commander waited for you to respond to his offer to surrender. And then, when you didn't, he ordered his men forward and it was all over in a moment. You and your warriors threw down your swords the moment the gate was smashed in. It was fortunate that so few were killed and that the Roman governor chose to be lenient, but it still cost us most of our weapons and armour, as well as compensation for the damage caused to Roman property and the conscription of two hundred of our best young men into the Roman auxiliary units. To add to our injury, the Romans now have a string of outposts guarding our frontier.' She paused to let her words sink in. 'And you have the gall to call that winning honour for our people. Pah!'

'If the tribe had followed us, we would have triumphed,' Syphodubnus retorted. 'If Prasutagus had mustered the Iceni warriors, we would have crushed the Roman auxiliaries.'

'But you never gave him the chance,' she replied. 'It was over before there was time for the king to summon the tribal council. In any case, even if we had overcome the auxiliaries, we'd then have had to face the legions.' She looked at some of the older men standing before her. 'Only a few of us have seen the legions in action. Those of us who have know that it would be foolhardy for the Iceni to wage war on them. The legions would crush us as they have every tribe that has opposed them in battle. Even the great warlord Caratacus could not defeat them, and was hunted down, captured and taken to Rome in chains. You, Syphodubnus, are not old enough to have seen this.'

'Perhaps age makes cowards of those who fear Rome,' he sneered. 'Perhaps it is time for younger men to wield the swords of the Iceni. If I am chosen to succeed Prasutagus, I swear I will give Rome something to fear. We will inspire the other tribes to rise up and cast out the invader. And when that is done, we will be the most powerful tribe in the land.'

'Bold words from one who faltered at the first step,' Boudica scoffed. 'Do you think my husband did not harbour the same dreams as you do? Yet he had the good sense to know what could be achieved and what was impossible. Yes, there may come a day when the other tribes grow weary of living under the Roman yoke and rise against the invader, but that day is still distant. Until then, we must hide our anger; we must keep our blades sharp but hidden. We must make Rome think that the Iceni are loyal enough to be safely left alone to govern our own affairs and pay the tribute that is due. If we rise before we are ready, before the other tribes find common cause, we are doomed to defeat, and next time Rome will not be so lenient. They will butcher our warriors, burn our farms and seize our treasure, and those who survive will be sold into slavery. In time the very name of our tribe will be obliterated and no one will remember that we ever existed . . . Is that what you wish for?' Boudica opened her arms as she appealed to the men before her, then fixed her attention on Syphodubnus. 'Is that what you desire? Do you wish to lead our brave young warriors to death and destruction?'

She saw the first glimmer of doubt in his expression, and then just as quickly the return of the defiant and arrogant posture, and she realised that she had failed to persuade him. He was still too young for that measure of experience that permitted wisdom. Very well, she decided. He must be prevented from becoming the successor to Prasutagus.

'The will of my husband is clear and has been affirmed by the tribal council. I am your queen. Your loyalty is mine by right.'

'But you are a woman,' Syphodubnus protested. 'A tribe such as the Iceni should be ruled by a warrior.'

'And who is to say that a woman cannot be a warrior? I have

fought at my husband's side. I have wielded sword and spear and shed the blood of my enemies. My own blood has been spilled in combat. Can you say as much, young man? You are an unblooded warrior, thanks to your swift surrender.'

Syphodubnus grimaced and emitted an audible snarl as she continued.

'I have proven myself in battle. And so the Iceni is ruled by a warrior, just as you say it should be.'

'We shall see. It is my right to put the matter before the council and let them debate whether the will is legitimate or not.'

'And you are free to do so when the council next meets.'

'But that is months away. Why wait? We could decide here and now. The council is gathered. There is no need to delay.'

'The council is here to witness the passing of our king, to honour his memory and pay their respects to a warrior whose renown you will never match, Syphodubnus. We will grieve and bury him, and then I will rule the Iceni until such time as the council decides that another should take my place. And that they cannot do until the winter gathering, according to our custom. Is that not so, my lords?'

She looked directly at one of Prasutagus's oldest and most respected advisers, the Druid Bladocus, who nodded and filled his lungs before speaking clearly.

'It is true. Until then, I swear by all the gods that I will be loyal to Queen Boudica. That is my oath.'

'And mine!' cried another man. More took up the cry, drowning out the few voices that raised a protest.

Syphodubnus saw that he was outnumbered, and his youthful features creased into a bitter frown. As the cries died away, Boudica turned to him.

'The Iceni have spoken. You have no choice but to accept.'

'For now.'

'But you do accept?' Boudica pressed him.

'Yes,' he hissed.

'Then say it. Speak the oath of loyalty to your queen.'

Syphodubnus folded his arms and looked pained for a moment before announcing in a flat tone, 'I swear by all the gods of our tribe to be loyal to the queen.'

'Then it is done,' Boudica concluded. 'Now we must tell the people that Prasutagus is no more and that I will rule in his place.'

She gestured to the two warriors guarding the entrance to the hall, and they opened the doors and took up position on either side as the members of the royal council and nobles turned to file outside into the large open space bounded by a palisade. The crowd that had gathered around the open fires rose to their feet expectantly. The first glimmer of dawn was stealing up from the eastern horizon as a light drizzle began, beading the cloaks, tunics and hair of the tribespeople.

Boudica was the last to leave. She looked down on her husband one final time and whispered, 'My love . . . I fear you go to a peace I shall not know while I live.'

Then she drew the woven cover over his face and turned towards the doors. Despite the significance of the moment, she was already looking ahead. While she had thwarted Syphodubnus's ambitions for now, there could be no doubt that he would plot against her in the months to come, despite his oath. He was too dangerous a man to be entrusted with the fate of the Iceni. Yet he was cunning enough to play on the tribe's desire to restore the golden age described in song and legend. Boudica knew that her people, like most Celts, preferred to wallow in sentimentality rather than deal with hard and unpleasant truths. Make no mistake, she thought, Syphodubnus is the enemy within. He would have to be watched closely.

Then there was the matter of the enemy without. Despite the treaty between the Iceni and Rome, there had always been tension, and she could sense that it was coming to a head. Her fate, the fate of her family and the fate of the Iceni depended on how Rome responded to the news of Prasutagus's death. She could not shake off her foreboding about the future. At best the Romans would use the situation to increase their influence over the Iceni. At worst, they would resolve to annex the tribe and reduce it to a region of the new province they had carved out on the island.

As she emerged from the hall and stepped up onto the bed of her husband's chariot, Bladocus called out to the throng: 'The king is dead! Behold Boudica – queen of the Iceni! May our gods preserve her and bring her prosperity in peace and victory and spoils in war!'

War . . . May the gods spare us from that, Boudica silently prayed with all her heart. She gazed into the mid distance as the crowd called out her name again and again and the drizzle gave way to rain borne on a chill wind blowing in with the dawn.

# CHAPTER ONE

## *Camulodunum*

'Keep the bloody point up!' Centurion Macro growled as he parried aside another weak blow from his opponent and delivered a sharp tap to the shoulder as a rebuke for the youngster's poor effort. 'How can you possibly become a legionary if you fight like that? Shit, I've seen newborn kittens who look more threatening! Try again. This time strike at me like you mean it.'

He took a pace back and lowered himself into a crouch, weight instinctively balanced so that he was poised to spring forward or aside instantly, the result of over thirty years of soldiering. Raising his wooden training sword, he inscribed small circles with the blunted tip.

'Now, Lucius,' he instructed. 'Get it right this time.'

Opposite him a thin boy, some eight years of age, with a mop of unruly dark curls, gritted his teeth and adopted a similar stance as he readied himself to attack. His dark eyes narrowed and he glared back at Macro. They stood on the gravel to one side of the small tiled pond in the courtyard of Macro's house. Two women and another man were watching from the chairs arranged around a wooden table at the end of the garden. At the man's feet curled a huge dog with wiry hair, its long head stretched out between its front paws. They were warmed by the logs burning in an iron-framed basket set before them, and yet they still needed cloaks. Like most of the Romans who had come to settle in the new province of Britannia, they were not used to the clammy cold of the island's winters. Macro and Lucius, by contrast, wore only simple tunics, and had worked up a sweat as they exercised in the courtyard.

'Give it to him, Lucius!' one of the women called out cheerfully. She was a firmly built woman with a kindly round face, brown eyes and dark hair.

Macro frowned at her. 'Thanks for the loyal support, wife.'

Petronella laughed and flapped a hand dismissively.

He was about to respond when the boy let out a shrill cry and charged at him, thrusting at his midriff. The centurion parried the blow easily and made a riposte, aiming at the centre of the lad's chest. Back swept the smaller training sword and rapped against Macro's weapon as Lucius rushed in to strike at his opponent's stomach. Despite his heavier frame, Macro moved fluidly out of the way and the point of the boy's sword cut through the air at his side. He was about to slap the boy on the shoulder again when Lucius brought his heel down on the exposed toes of Macro's leading foot.

'Ah!' the centurion cried out in surprise as much as pain, and hobbled back a step. 'Why, you cunning little bastard—'

'Mind your language!' his wife shouted.

Before Macro could respond, Lucius had darted back a pace and lunged at the centurion's chest. The point landed squarely just beneath his ribcage, a sharp prod that merely injured his pride for a heartbeat before he grinned and lowered his sword. 'That's it! Well done, Lucius!'

The youngster's ferocious expression relaxed into a look of proud delight, and he turned to the bearded man seated at the table. In his mid thirties, the latter was slender and had the same dark curls as his son. His face bore a vivid diagonal scar from brow to cheek, but it did not mar his sensitive good looks. He returned the smile, and then his mouth opened to give a warning, but he was too late. Macro slapped Lucius on the wrist with the flat of his training sword, just hard enough to cause the boy to drop his own weapon.

He yelped and scowled at the centurion.

'Never turn your back on your opponent while he's still on his feet,' Macro admonished him. 'How many times have I told you that, eh?'

There was a serious tone to his voice, and Lucius lowered his head as he rubbed his wrist and muttered, 'That hurt.'

'That's as nothing compared to the hurt you'll feel from the sword that'll be stuck through your spine if you ever do that in a real battle.'

Lucius pressed his lips together and his chin trembled in wounded pride. Macro saw that he was on the verge of tears and did not want to let the boy embarrass himself. He ruffled his hair affectionately and spoke softly. 'No harm done, lad. No shame in making mistakes when you're only just learning how to use a sword. I was the same when I started out.' He glanced towards the table and grinned. 'Your father was one of the most hopeless recruits ever to join the Second Legion. More of a danger to himself and his comrades than the fiercest German warrior that ever breathed. Ain't that the truth, Cato?'

Cato grimaced. 'If you say so, my friend.'

'And look how he turned out,' Macro continued as he placed a hand on Lucius's shoulder. 'Risen through the ranks from optio to prefect, and on the way he's served as a tribune of the Praetorian Guard and picked up more awards for bravery than most soldiers do in a lifetime. One of the finest officers in the army, without a doubt. So you keep practising, young

Lucius, and one day you may achieve as much as your father has, eh?'

The fair-haired woman beside Cato looked at him warmly, then reached over and planted a soft kiss on his scarred cheek. 'My hero.'

'Enough of that, Claudia.' Cato recoiled with a frown. It was not in his nature to take praise easily. 'Just do your best, son. No one can ask more of you than that.'

The boy came to the table and squatted beside the dog to stroke it. The animal wagged its tail happily, then suddenly lifted its head and licked his face.

'Oh Cassius! Stop.' The boy laughed as he rose and sat on one of the spare stools, his feet not quite reaching the ground. He looked up at Cato. 'If you are a good soldier, Father, then what are we doing here in Camulodunum? Surely you should be on the frontier, fighting the barbarians and the Druids for the emperor.'

There was an exchange of glances amongst the adults. The truth was that Claudia had been Nero's mistress before being sent into exile on Sardinia. She had since left the island to be with Cato and they had been forced to come to the furthest corner of the Empire to keep her safe. The veterans' colony of Camulodunum was a quiet backwater where the chances of her being recognised and reported were small. But not small enough that they could risk letting Lucius inadvertently reveal the true reason behind their presence there.

'Your father is resting between campaigns,' said Petronella. 'He needs to be ready for when the emperor next needs him. Besides, he wants to spend more time with you. You like it here, don't you, Lucius?'

The boy thought a moment. There were other children at the colony his own age to play with, and in the summer there was fishing on the river and hunting in the woods that surrounded Macro's farm, half a day's journey away. He nodded. 'I suppose so. But it's getting cold again.'

Macro sighed. 'Aye, too true. The bloody winter in this province was made by the gods to test us. Cold, damp and clammy. The roads turn to thick mud that'll suck your boots off, and we're stuck with eating salted meat and whatever fresh vegetables we can store.'

'Keep going,' Petronella said archly. 'You're doing a fine job of cheering the lad up.'

Cato reached for his cup of warmed wine and took a sip. 'Ah, come on, Macro. It's not so bad. You've done well enough out of it.' He gestured to the house around the courtyard. It had once been the legate's quarters when a legionary fortress had been under construction. The work had been abandoned when the decision had been taken to establish the colony on the site instead. There were still many former military buildings in the settlement, although much of the rampart had been demolished and the defensive ditch filled in. Amid the existing buildings there was much new construction, including a forum, a theatre, an arena, and an imposing temple complex dedicated to the imperial cult.

'You have the finest place in the colony, Macro. You've also a profitable farm in the country and you are the senior magistrate of the colony's senate. To cap it all, you enjoy the greatest of fortune in having Petronella for a wife.' Cato raised his cup to her and bowed his head gently. 'I'd say you were sitting pretty. A fine end to your military career, my friend. You've earned it. You can live out your retirement in peace and in comfort.'

Petronella smiled, then took her husband's brawny arm and hugged it.

'I suppose so,' Macro said. 'Though I can't help missing the old life some days.'

'You're bound to. But you couldn't serve in the army forever.'

'I know,' Macro said sadly.

There was a pause before Claudia cleared her throat. 'It is peaceful here, but it might be wise not to take it all for granted.'

Cato turned to his son. 'Why don't you go and see if your friends want to play?'

The boy's gaze shifted to the wooden training swords lying on the table. 'Can I take those with me?'

'As long as you're careful,' said Cato. 'I don't want to hear about any broken bones or bloodied noses. Understand? And take Parvus with you.'

Before Cato could change his mind, Lucius snatched the swords and trotted off towards the kitchen block at the rear of the house. He emerged a moment later with a lanky boy a few years older than himself. Parvus was a mute whom Macro and Petronella had rescued from the wharves of Londinium the previous year and adopted into their household. The four adults stared after the boys as they ran back through the courtyard and disappeared into the corridor that led to the front of the house. Macro chuckled. 'I dare say there'll be a few kids going home with bruises and grazes before the day is out.'

Cato nodded and smiled faintly before turning to Claudia. 'I don't think it's wise to discuss certain things in front of Lucius. He's a good boy, but children have a way of repeating things they overhear.'

'I know. I'm sorry.' She folded her hands. 'But you know as well as I do that the future of the province hangs in the balance. I heard Nero say it many times when I lived at the palace. He hates this island. It's a constant drain on the treasury and he'd rather spend the silver on entertainments in Rome, keeping the mob happy. It's taking far longer than expected to subdue the tribes that haven't accepted Roman rule. Every year the legions and auxiliary cohorts need fresh recruits to replace the losses they've sustained.' She shrugged and shook her head. 'Truly, I don't know how much longer he'll put up with it.'

'He'd be a fool to abandon Britannia,' Macro growled. 'We've paid for this province with our blood. At least us soldiers have. If Nero throws all that aside, there'll be many here, in the ranks as well as the colony, who'll be thinking it's time we had a new emperor. Besides, most of the work has been done. The lowland tribes present no threat. They've been conquered or disarmed and have signed treaties with Rome. The Brigantes in the north are under our thumb and the only remaining hostiles are in the mountains to the west. The new governor's made it clear that he's going to see to them. Ain't that right, Cato?'

The younger man nodded. 'That's the news from our friend Apollonius in Londinium. Suetonius is concentrating men at Deva to strike into the mountains. It'll be tough going. Macro and I were part of the previous attempt. It didn't end well.'

'That's because the campaign started too late in the year,' Macro interrupted. 'If it wasn't for the weather, we'd have done for those bastards in the hill tribes. We'd have taken Mona and put an end to the Druids too.'

'But we didn't,' said Cato. 'And now that they have a victory over Rome under their belts, they are going to be even more difficult to subdue. If anyone can do it, Suetonius is the man. He has experience in mountain warfare. Did fine work in Mauretania a few years back. I imagine he was hand-picked for this job.'

‘Or he pushed himself to the front of the queue.’ Macro grinned. ‘One last chance to put the seal on his reputation. You know what these aristocrats are like. Anything to add lustre to the family name and outdo the deeds of their ancestors and their political rivals.’

‘Will this Suetonius need to call up the reserves?’ Petronella asked.

Macro took her hand and squeezed it affectionately. ‘Not likely. There’s too few of us here to make much of a difference if we were recalled to the ranks. In any case, we’re needed here. The governor knows the value of having a small force of veterans around to ensure that none of the local tribes are tempted to play while the cat’s away.’

Claudia gave a wry smile. ‘I thought you said the lowland tribes posed no threat.’

‘So they don’t,’ Macro replied firmly. ‘The Trinovantes around Camulodunum are as meek as lambs.’

‘I’m not surprised,’ she said. ‘They’ve been harshly treated by the veterans at the colony, so I’m told. Their lands have been seized, and some of their men taken away and forced to serve in the auxiliary cohorts, while I’ve heard that many of the women have been violated.’

‘There’s always a little trouble early on,’ Macro countered. ‘The lads of the colony are used to soldiering. It takes a few years before they get the hang of being civilians.’

‘And in the meantime, the tribespeople just have to put up with it?’

‘That’s how it is,’ said Macro. ‘We’ve conquered this place, just like we’ve conquered lands from here to the deserts of the east. Once they accept their lot, the tribes will be content with being part of the Empire.’

‘I wonder.’ Claudia turned to Cato. ‘What do you think?’

Cato paused to collect his thoughts. He wasn't as convinced as Macro about the security of this part of the new province. The year's harvest had been poor, and that wouldn't be taken into consideration when the tax collectors made their demands on the local people. Hunger and poverty caused discontent, and while the Trinovantes seemed docile enough, it was hard to imagine that the indignities and suffering they had endured at the hands of their newly imposed Roman masters would not cause bitter resentment, even if they were careful not to show it. If Governor Suetonius and his legions were campaigning across the far side of the province, it might tempt the hotheads amongst the local tribespeople to take advantage of the situation. Macro and the veterans at the colony were tough enough and able to put down any small-scale flare-ups, but a concerted uprising would present a real danger to the Roman inhabitants of Camulodunum.

He considered a moment longer before he responded to Claudia's question. 'As long as there are legions in Britain, I doubt there will be any serious trouble in this area. The Iceni have had a taste of what defying Rome means. They'll not be anxious to repeat the experience. As for the Trinovantes, who knows? The bigger worry is what happens if Nero does decide to withdraw the legions. There are tens of thousands of Romans and other people from the Empire who have settled here. They'll be easy meat for any tribes that decide to attack them. The choice will be between staying and trying to defend what they hold, and abandoning their homes, their property and their future here and fleeing back across the sea to Gaul.'

Claudia turned to Macro and Petronella. 'If Nero pulls the legions out, what will you two do?'

Macro glanced at his wife, but she did not meet his eyes. 'I'd not want to give it all up. Everything we own here, and the half-share in my mother's business in Londinium . . . I just don't know. I hope it never comes to that.'

'I'll drink to that,' said Cato, keen to put his best friend at ease. 'It's hard to believe Nero will abandon Britannia. To give it up now would be a dangerous blow to Roman prestige. You can imagine how the mob would react to that, not to mention those senators who keep telling them how invincible Rome is.'

'See?' Macro nudged Petronella. 'The lad's got a handle on how it is.'

'There's another reason why Nero will be reluctant to pull the legions out,' Cato continued. 'If he withdraws them to Gaul, that will give the governor there a significant number of extra soldiers. Those who command powerful armies might be tempted to use them for political ends. So it's safer to keep those legions tied down here in Britannia.'

Macro tutted. 'You have a devious mind, lad. A cynical mind.'

'I'm a realist.' Cato shrugged. 'We've both been around long enough to know how the Empire works. You know I'm right.'

Macro reached for his cup. 'All this talk about politics has made me thirsty.' He lifted the jug, but when he poured, only a thin trickle dribbled into his cup. 'Shit . . . I'll have to get some more from the kitchen.'

As he rose from his stool, Petronella cocked an ear towards the kitchen block at the far end of the courtyard. 'What's all that about?'

Macro frowned. Animated voices were coming from inside the building. 'I'd better see to it.'

He trudged off, jug in hand, and disappeared inside. The others continued to listen as the exchange grew in volume, until it was suddenly cut off by the centurion demanding silence.

'Sounds like trouble among the servants,' Claudia commented.

Petronella shook her head. 'They get on well. There's two Iceni girls, and the stable lad is a local. Never heard a cross word between them. We'll soon know what's up when Macro comes back.' As they waited, she changed the subject. 'It'll be Saturnalia soon. Will you still be living in Camulodunum then? You are welcome to join us.'

'We'll be here for a while yet,' Cato answered. He had rented a modest villa at the colony. It overlooked the river and was south-facing to take advantage of what sun the province provided. There he and Claudia lived quietly while raising Lucius. The boy's education was provided for by a man claiming to be a Greek scholar who had crossed from Gaul to set up a small school. His accent was not one that Cato had ever heard a Greek intone, but he was competent, and Lucius was learning to read and write and the basics of figure work. A more refined education awaited him in Rome, once Cato deemed it safe to return to the capital.

If any hint that Claudia had been traced to Britannia reached Londinium, it had been arranged that Apollonius would send them a warning. The Greek freedman had once served as a spy for Rome before he encountered Cato, and the two men regarded each other with respect if not friendship. Macro had disliked him from the first and treated him with suspicion, but Apollonius had won Cato's trust and had now found himself a useful post at the Governor's palace at Londinium.

'It's a peaceful backwater,' Cato continued. 'And that suits us.'

'We'd be delighted to share Saturnalia with you.' Claudia smiled. 'You must tell me what we can contribute to the occasion.'

The sound of footsteps across the gravel interrupted the exchange, and they turned towards Macro. The centurion wore a concerned expression, and there was no freshly filled wine jug in his hands.

'What's happened?' asked Cato.

'Bad news, I'm afraid.' Macro resumed his seat. 'Morgatha's just returned from the market. She encountered an Iceni fur-trader who's come from the tribal capital. Prasutagus is dead.'

Cato shook his head sadly. Both he and Macro had known the Iceni king well. They had fought alongside him shortly after the invasion, when the tribe was a firm ally of Rome. His queen, Boudica, was also counted a close friend. The last time they had met, less than a year ago, Prasutagus had looked sickly, a distant shadow of the powerful warrior he had been in his prime.

'There's more,' said Macro. 'It seems he named Boudica and Nero as co-heirs in his will. I doubt that's going to end well for the Iceni.'

'Why is that?' asked Claudia.

'Nero doesn't strike me as the kind who will settle for half of something when he can have all of it.'

'Then surely this is a good thing for the province. It will give Nero a stronger stake in Britannia. More reason for him not to pull the legions out.'

'Or he'll just decide to loot the Iceni kingdom for all its worth and then abandon the island.'

Claudia turned to Cato. 'What do you think?'

'I'm not sure how this will play out,' said Cato. 'It'll take time for word of the king's death to reach Rome, then for Nero to reflect on what course of action to take and send the response to the governor in Londinium. If the weather is kind, Suetonius will receive his instructions early next year. About the same time as the renewal of the oaths. The Iceni contingent will be there along with the other tribes and representatives of the Roman settlements to swear their loyalty to the emperor and Rome. That's when they'll find out what Nero has decided.'

'And what do you think he will decide?' Claudia pressed him.

'I suspect Macro's right. The emperor will want it all, whatever Prasutagus's will says. If that happens, there'll be trouble. We know the Iceni.' He nodded towards Macro. 'They're a proud lot with a strong sense of tradition. Fine warriors. We were lucky that they sided with us at the start, and lucky that it was only a handful of them who rose against us when Scapula was governor. If Nero plays this badly, he may provoke them into open rebellion. They'll fight like lions to protect their lands, and I fear it will be a bloodbath.'

# CHAPTER TWO

They had been tracking their prey all morning, and the noon sun hung low in the grey sky as flurries of snow blotted out the horizon. A short distance ahead of Macro and Cato was a Trinovantian hunter on foot, wearing a fur cape over his brown tunic and leggings. Cato was holding the bridle of his mount as they waited for him to inspect the ground. The hunter paused some thirty paces away and crouched as he examined a gap in the entanglement of gorse bushes that spread out on either side. There were many animal tracks in the snow fanning out from the gap, and it was hard to pick them apart and identify what creature might have made them.

'We may have lost him,' Macro muttered as he rested the thick shaft of the boar spear against the horns of his saddle and reached for his canteen. He took out the stopper, tilted his head and took a swig before offering it to Cato.

The prefect's eyes were on the hunter, watching as the man scrutinised the disturbed snow. He took a sip and handed the canteen back before shifting his spear to his spare hand. 'I don't know. Pernocatus seems to be on to something.'

The hunter was tracing his fingers over the snow and then over the dark stem of the gorse bush to his right before he touched the surface delicately and then stared at his fingertip.

He turned towards his Roman companions as he held up his hand so they could see the red smear.

'Blood. The boar came through here,' he announced in guttural Latin.

Pernocatus had hired himself out to Roman hunters ever since the colony was founded, and had picked up the invaders' language well enough to speak it fluently. He was held in high regard amongst the veterans for his skills as a tracker, and when they closed in for the kill, his adeptness with spear and bow was as good as that of any bestiarius in the Empire.

The three-man hunting party had encountered the boar an hour or so after dawn, and there had been barely a chance to ready their spears before the beast charged through them and bolted. Cato had been lucky to land a glancing blow that had torn through its shoulder; not enough to cripple it, but enough to make it bleed and leave a trail to follow across the countryside. The blood spots had become less frequent as the wound had begun to clot, and they had almost given up when they had seen a handful of small splats in the snow close to the path leading to the gorse thicket. Cato was angry and frustrated with himself. It was the sign of a poor hunter to wound a creature and let it escape to suffer. He owed it to the animal to finish the job.

Macro indicated the thicket ahead of them. 'Well, if the bastard's in there, we can't get close to him.'

Cato looked round. The gorse extended fifty paces on either side and looked to be as much across, beyond which rose the boughs of a copse of pine trees. The track through the dense mass was narrow. Reluctantly he agreed with his friend. There was no way they could ride through the thicket, and if they went on foot, they were bound to snag their cloaks and get caught up. If the boar charged them at that moment, there would be no chance to evade it. Still, there was one last trick they could attempt to provoke it.

'Pernocatus, you stay here while the centurion and I ride round and see if we can find where the track comes out on the other side. If we locate it, I'll call out to you. Then you make as much noise as you can. Use your horn. Beat the gorse. If the boar makes a run for it, we'll be waiting for him.'

The hunter tilted his head to the side doubtfully, but nodded. 'As the prefect commands.'

There was something in his tone that struck Cato as being slightly off, a hint of obsequiousness that was uncharacteristic, and he feared that he had offended the man with the brusqueness of his order. Sometimes it was hard to take the soldier out of the man, he mused regretfully.

'Let's get moving,' said Macro, lifting his spear and holding the shaft out to the side. 'Before he gets the frights and bolts.' He urged his mount into a trot and rode off around the line of gorse. Cato handed the reins of the hunter's horse to Pernocatus with a nod and cantered off after his friend.

As he had anticipated, the thicket was not large, and there was a clear gap between the far side and the pine trees. They found the place where the trail left the thicket easily enough, but leaning from his saddle, Cato saw no sign of blood.

'He's still in there.'

The two Romans scanned the tangled undergrowth for movement or sound that might indicate the presence of the boar, but there was nothing. Cato readied his spear and Macro followed suit, then they took up position each side of the trail.

'Ready?' asked Cato.

Macro nodded.

'Pernocatus!' Cato called out. 'Begin!'

The strident note of the hunter's horn cut through the cold

air. The sound startled some birds, who burst from cover with a shrill chorus of panicked tweets, wings moving furiously as they fled towards the pine trees and disappeared. After a few more blasts of the horn, the hunter began to shout, and Cato could make out the faint crackle and snap of twigs breaking as they were beaten on the far side. Then they heard it, the snort and throaty squeal from somewhere between themselves and Pernocatus. A moment later, there was the rustle of dry vegetation as the boar drove towards them, charging down the trail.

'Here he comes!' Macro shouted, his eyes wide with excitement as he lowered the broad iron blade of his spear and held the shaft poised to strike. Cato did the same, keeping a firm grip of his reins and clenching his thighs against the saddle.

The boar burst out of the thicket and both men spurred forward. It was a huge, shaggy beast with a darker line of bristles growing along its spine towards its large head, where curved tusks protruded either side of the snout. Macro was faster to react, and he leaned forward and lunged, the point of his spear driving into the boar's flank. The beast's jaws parted as it uttered a pained cry, then it swerved away from the spearhead, in towards Macro's mount, and collided with the pony's hind legs. Macro swayed, forced to drop his spear as he snatched at the saddle horns and held on tight to avoid being thrown off. His pony staggered in between the enraged boar and Cato, blocking the target for his friend.

'Shit!' Cato hissed through gritted teeth as he pulled hard on the reins and tried to work his own mount round to strike at the beast. Before he could get a clear sight, however, the boar turned and rushed back into the gorse, tearing along the narrow trail in the direction of Pernocatus. At once Cato grasped the danger facing the other man, and quickly turned to Macro. 'Get your spear and follow me!'

Without waiting for a reply, he urged his pony into a gallop along the edge of the thicket, the blood pounding in his ears. There was always a risk in hunting, particularly with prey as deadly as wild boar, and that was why only the most reckless faced such a beast alone. As he steered his mount around the spiky tangles of gorse, he heard Pernocatus cry out in alarm.

'He's here!'

Swerving round an outlying clump of bushes, Cato caught sight of the hunter a hundred paces away. He was on foot and facing the boar, a dagger in his hand. The beast, flanks heaving with exertion and surrounded by swirls of exhaled breath, stood between Pernocatus and his mount. As Cato kicked his heels in to force his pony to increase its pace, he saw the boar charge, kicking up gouts of snow as it sped towards Pernocatus. The hunter's pony reared in panic and turned to flee. Pernocatus lowered himself into a crouch and held his position until the last instant before throwing himself aside and slashing at the boar as it swept past. Despite its bulk, some five feet in length and as high as a man's midriff, the beast was nimble, and it slithered to a halt and swerved round in a heartbeat, ready to charge again.

Cato tightened his grip on the shaft of his spear, but as he raced towards the confrontation, his mount stumbled. The sky and the frozen landscape spun around him as man and horse tumbled into the snow. The impact drove the breath from his lungs, and he released his grip on the spear and rolled aside to get clear.

As he came up onto his feet, gasping for air, he saw that Pernocatus had released his dagger and somehow grasped the boar's tusks, and was desperately trying to keep himself from being impaled as he wrestled with the beast. But it was an unequal struggle, and the hunter was battered and tossed as the boar hurled its weight around and tried to dislodge him. Cato glanced round in the calf-deep snow but could not see his spear.

His ears were filled with the ragged snorts of Macro's pony as the centurion rushed past him, braced firmly in his saddle as he leaned forward, right arm bunched up in readiness to thrust. The boar made a frenzied, twisting leap and tossed Pernocatus aside. The hunter flew through the air and landed heavily several feet away. Swinging its head from side to side, the beast turned and caught sight of its prey again, and surged forward, tusks lowered, as Pernocatus scrambled away through the snow on hands and knees.

'No you bloody don't!' Macro roared. The shout and the blur of movement on the periphery of its vision caused the boar to hesitate and half turn towards the new threat, exposing its flank. Macro leaned out, tugging the reins to avoid a collision, and slammed the broad point of his spear into the animal's shoulder. The force of the impact drove the boar off its feet, and it landed on its side, twisting the shaft from Macro's grip so that it swayed from side to side above the beast's body as it writhed, bright flecks of blood spraying across the snow.

Macro swung his leg across the saddle horn and dropped to the ground, then sprang forward and grasped the shaft in both hands, using his weight to pin the boar down as it snorted and squealed desperately. Pernocatus had retrieved his dagger and darted in to slash at the animal's throat. Cato, back on his feet, spotted his own spear and snatched it up before rushing to help his friends complete the kill.

It was over before he reached the scene. With a last flailing of its trotters and a violent spasm, the boar slumped to the ground in defeat, blood pulsing from its wounds. After a final few pants, it stopped breathing and lay limply in the gore-streaked snow. For a moment longer Macro continued to grip the spear shaft, leaning his weight on the weapon to keep the body pinned down. Pernocatus stood to one side, blood dripping from the tip of his dagger. Cato drew up and regarded them both anxiously until he saw that they appeared to be uninjured. All three were breathing hard.

At last Macro eased up, twisting the shaft from side to side as he pulled it free. He shook his head. 'Fuck me, that was close.' Then he gulped a breath and laughed in nervous relief. His companions instinctively joined in before stepping back to regard their kill.

'He's a big brute,' said Cato. 'Biggest I've seen.' He glanced at the hunter. 'Lucky escape.'

Pernocatus thought a moment before stepping towards Macro and extending his arm. 'You save me, Centurion.'

They clasped forearms and Macro puffed his cheeks. 'I was lucky, friend. A heartbeat later and . . .' He drew a finger across his throat.

The hunter grimaced and stared at him fixedly for a moment before bowing his head. 'I owe you my life . . .'

'Right place, right time, that's all.' Macro grinned. 'Could have happened to any one of us.'

Cato saw the pained look that flitted across the hunter's face. He realised that there was more weight to his words than Macro realised. A debt was owed and Pernocatus regarded the matter with utmost seriousness.

The man leaned over the boar's head and cut into the gristle around the snout, sawing and pulling at the tusks. When he had cut both free, he held them up for Macro. 'These are yours. Your kill. Your prize.' When Macro hesitated, he wiped his dagger clean on the side of the carcass and sheathed the blade before reaching into his tunic and drawing out a thick leather cord from which several tusks hung. 'Bring you good fortune, Centurion.'

Cato wondered about that, given the hunter's close escape from death a moment ago.

'Ah . . . thanks.' Macro smiled diplomatically, which was no small achievement for him. No doubt being the senior magistrate of the colony had enhanced that side of his character, Cato thought.

Once the tusks had been tucked away in Macro's sidebag, the three men set about the business of butchering the carcass. The boar was too large to sling across the back of a pony and would need to be cut up into more manageable chunks. Fortunately, the hunter and the two soldiers were familiar with the messy task and set to it efficiently. Macro had made the killing blow, so was given two of the haunches, while Cato and Pernocatus had one apiece. With the meat loaded across the saddles, they cleaned the worst of the blood and fat from their hands by rubbing them in the snow. Then they retrieved their spears, took up the reins of their ponies and turned back towards the colony on foot.

It had taken over an hour to render the carcass, and labouring through the snow made for slow progress, so it was not until late in the afternoon that they crested the low ridge that overlooked Camulodunum, some mile and a half away, lying under a thin haze of woodsmoke. The sprawl of buildings – a mixture of repurposed military structures, civilian dwellings with shingled roofs, and thatched huts – surrounded the centre of the settlement, where the temple, theatre and other civic edifices were in the process of construction. The walls of the sacred precinct had already been erected, as well as the stepped pediment and the first few feet of the enclosure. The round bases of the columns were in place, and stonemasons had cut the fluted sections that would be raised into position once a crane had been set up.

'The temple's going to be quite a sight when it's finished,' said Macro with a hint of pride. 'Hope I live long enough to see it.' He glanced at Pernocatus and grinned. 'You're young. You'll be sure to see it. I envy you.'

'Envy?' the hunter said.

'Aye, who wouldn't want to see such a fine building rising above the surrounding countryside?' Macro continued. 'A tribute to Roman engineering and civilisation. It'll still be standing long after the rest of those buildings and huts have gone.'

Cato sensed the hunter's discomfort at Macro's words, and he could understand the cause. The cost of the temple and the rest of the public buildings was falling mostly on the shoulders of the Trinovantes. Their taxes had been increased by Macro's predecessor as senior magistrate. A poisonous bequest indeed, thought Cato. The resentment of the natives towards their Roman overlords was apparent enough, and the recent poor harvest had made the tax burden more onerous still. Human nature being what it was, most of the Trinovantes blamed the current incumbent – Macro – regardless of the fact that their suffering was nothing to do with him. No doubt Pernocatus shared the feelings of his people, even as he seemed to enjoy the company of the two Roman officers and appreciated the silver they paid him to act as their guide. Now that Macro had saved his life, a further obligation weighed on him. Cato tried to change the subject.

'I'm hungry. I can already taste roast boar.' He smiled at the others. 'And we've enough here to feed us until Saturnalia.'

'More than enough!' Macro grinned as they began to descend the slope towards the colony.

Away to the east, nearly two miles from the far side of Camulodunum, Cato spied a distant column approaching along the track that led towards the lands of the Iceni. There were twenty or so riders, two wagons drawn by horses and several figures on foot at the rear. Too many men for a merchant and too few to constitute any danger to those in the colony. Nonetheless, his curiosity was piqued and he pointed them out to Macro.

'Could be a military detachment. There's an outpost on the border with the Iceni. They might be coming for supplies. We'll know soon enough. If they're here for long, they could join in the celebrations. The gods only know, we could use some diversion from the endless bloody cold of the winter in this province.'

Halfway between the ridge and the colony, a track branched off to a small group of huts where Pernocatus and his extended family lived. Once the land around them had been their farm, but now it had been appropriated by a retired Roman officer, one of the centurions, who had taken it as part of his retirement bonus. Pernocatus and his folk still worked the land, only now they did so in exchange for a fraction of the produce they grew, and the owner sold the rest to grain merchants in Londinium. This was one of the reasons the hunter was obliged to offer his services to Roman officers. The coins he was paid allowed him to buy back some of the grain to support his people through the harsh winter.

The three of them halted at the junction and Cato took out his purse and counted out the coins to meet the fee they had agreed. Pernocatus took them with a nod of thanks and slipped them into his sidebag.

'One other thing,' said Cato as he lifted his boar haunch off the back of his pony and offered it to Pernocatus. 'As Macro said, we have more than enough for our needs. Here. Take it.'

The Trinovantian hesitated. Like all those who had once been warriors in his tribe, he was a proud man and found it hard to accept charity from a Roman.

'You've earned it,' said Cato. 'We'd never have been able to track the beast down without you.'

'As the prefect wishes,' the hunter responded. He accepted the meat and secured it over his saddle so that one haunch hung from each side. Then he tapped two fingers against his forehead in the manner of the Britons and turned to lead his mount down the track towards the huts.

'We'll hunt again after Saturnalia!' Cato called after him. Pernocatus waved his spear in acknowledgement but didn't look back.

Macro whistled softly. 'There's gratitude for you. Why did you give him that? It was most of your share.'

'I've got plenty left. Claudia and I aren't going to go hungry. Unlike some of the locals.'

'So that's it.' Macro shook his head. 'You can't afford to show pity to everyone you meet, lad.'

'It's not pity. It's respect. These lands once belonged to his people. For generations beyond memory.'

'And now it belongs to Rome. By right of conquest. You think the Trinovantes didn't take it off someone else at some point? Do you think if the positions were reversed he'd have given you his share of the meat?'

'He might.'

Macro led his horse back down the main track. 'Sometimes I really don't understand you, Cato. You've been a soldier, what, some seventeen years now. You're the reason Rome has an empire. It's us soldiers who won it for Rome. We fought for it, shed blood for it and now we get to enjoy our spoils.'

'That's true,' Cato responded, following his friend. 'But it's not about that for me. It's about the men I serve with. They've been my family all my adult life. It's them I fight for.'

Macro nodded. 'I know that. I understand, and you're right . . . That's why I miss it. I'm happy enough with my lot. I've got a fine woman, a good home and top seat at the colony's senate. But so help me, I miss the army. It's a shame that it's all over for me now. No more fighting. But at least there's hunting to be done. Jupiter's bollocks! That boar was a monster! For a moment there, I thought he had the three of us bang to rights.'

Cato smiled. He was glad for Macro that he had found his place in Camulodunum, where he could live out his days with Petronella in peace. Many soldiers did not survive to see such times. If death did not claim them at the hands of the enemy, then injury or sickness usually did. It was Macro's dogged toughness, and not a little good fortune, that had seen him reach this point. Cato was still on the active list and would likely be recalled and given a fresh command someday. He hoped Fortuna would be as kind to him as she had been to Macro, and that he too would live out his retirement, with Claudia at his side.

By then, Lucius would have reached manhood, and Cato wondered what the future had in store for his son. He would have more opportunities than Cato himself had enjoyed. Even though he had risen to the equestrian class of Roman society, that would be as far as he was likely to advance by virtue of his humble origins. Lucius would start from a higher base and might one day aspire to become a senator, maybe even a consul. The prospect thrilled Cato; to have come so far in two generations! At the same time, there was a niggling frustration about the limit placed on his own ability and ambition. The best he could hope for was to become the imperial prefect of

Aegyptus. The province was the main supplier of grain to Rome, and as such was ruled by a man directly appointed by the emperor, lowly enough in rank not to use the position to challenge him. Meanwhile he would have to endure the prospect of watching lesser men secure senior political and military appointments for no better reason than the accident of birth that accorded them greater opportunities to win power and wealth than were afforded to the son of a slave. At least Lucius would be able to do the things he himself was denied, Cato comforted himself.

They walked on in happy anticipation of returning home. The watchman on the colony gate raised a hand in greeting as they approached. Even though the gatehouse was almost all that remained of the original defences of the fortress, there were certain niceties to be observed. People came and went from the colony through the gates just as they would at any other Roman settlement surrounded by a ditch and a wall.

'Good hunting, Centurion?' he called out.

Macro stood aside to reveal the meat hanging over his saddle. 'As good as it gets, friend. Boars don't come much bigger on this island.'

'Only in Sardinia, sir.'

'Bollocks.'

'It's true,' said Cato. 'I've seen them. Some of them are monsters.'

'Bah!' Macro made a dismissive gesture as he passed between the posts and entered the colony. Cato shared a glance with the watchman and both men rolled their eyes.

Dusk was gathering over Camulodunum and the smells of the evening meals that were being prepared filled the cold air, sharpening the appetite of the two officers as they made their way along the main street to Macro's house in the centre of the settlement. Coming the other way, they saw the group of travellers they had spotted earlier. They could see now that they were mounted warriors, large men in thick cloaks with long Celtic swords worn at their sides and shields hanging from their saddles. Behind them rumbled the wagons, crude vehicles with solid wooden wheels.

Near the head of the mounted party, a woman rode alone with the hood of her emerald cloak drawn over her head. An imposing figure, sitting tall in the saddle even after a day's travel, when some of her escort were slumped forward wearily. She called out a curt word of command as she drew level with the entrance to Macro's house, and the party came to a halt. As Macro's stable hand emerged from the covered gateway, she addressed him in fluent Latin.

'Boy, fetch your master and tell the magistrate that we need shelter for the night.'

Macro drew up and waited for Cato to come alongside him. 'Bloody hell, you know who that is?'

'Unmistakable,' said Cato. 'Boudica, queen of the Iceni.'

# CHAPTER THREE

Although the daylight hours were short, the inhabitants of the colony made the most of them as they celebrated Saturnalia at the close of the year. Bright strips of cloth and boughs of holly were hung above the doors and windows of the dwellings, and the air was rich with the aroma of cooking as neighbours vied to outdo each other. The festivities began at dawn with the sacrifice of a lamb on the altar at the unfinished temple. The colony's priest assigned to the imperial cult pronounced that the entrails were propitious and that the gods were pleased with the offering and had blessed the day's celebrations.

A schedule of races, wrestling bouts and a display of gladiatorial combat was provided by a travelling lanista for a modest fee, which was all the small colony could afford. Consequently, the three pairs of gladiators who faced each other in the turf arena outside the settlement were well past their prime. The veterans jeered and laughed as clumsy blows were traded, and since the fee only covered fighting to the first blood, there was little drama in the display. The only serious wound arose when a retiarius lost his grip on his trident and managed to skewer his own foot. The crowd sitting on the raked rows of simple wooden benches roared with laughter as his opponent punched the air to claim victory, while the lanista hurried forward with a small medical chest to treat the injury.

In the afternoon, under a clear sky, the feasting began. People moved from home to home to honour the small shrines of the household spirits before sampling the food and wine laid out for them. Mindful of the evening feast still to come, most of the adults ate and drank sparingly, but the children gorged themselves, shouting excitedly as they chased each other through the muddy streets. As the light faded, the inhabitants drifted back to their homes for the final stage of the celebrations.

In the hall of Macro's home, two rough-hewn tables had been set up, with benches and stools beside them. He had not bought any slaves yet, so it was the servants and guests who would be treated as masters of the household that evening, according to custom. Parvus, the two Iceni serving girls and the stable hand were joined by Boudica, her daughters and her bodyguards, nearly thirty souls in all. It was the first time that Macro had met the queen's children, and he was struck by the difference between the two girls. The younger, Merida, was tall and blonde like her father had been, while the older, Bardea, was shorter and sturdier, with dark hair and features.

Macro and Petronella had been roasting the boar over a charcoal fire since midday, and the rich scent of the slow-cooked meat coming from the kitchen block was mouth-watering. As the last of the daylight faded, Cato, Claudia and Lucius arrived with the dog, bearing baskets of bread and honeyed pastries. Cato was pulling a small handcart containing two jars of wine packed in straw to protect them from the jolts of the rutted street. Cassius's nose lifted to savour the aroma of the roasting boar, and he padded cautiously towards the counter where Petronella was cutting the cooked meat into manageable portions.

'Shoo!' She glared at him. 'You'll have some scraps later if you're good.'

Cassius backed off and then craned his neck to one side to keep the meat in view.

Lucius set down his basket of bread with an exaggerated sigh. 'Can I go and join Parvus, Father?'

Cato shook his head. 'You know you can't. Tonight you must serve Parvus and the others. Just like the rest of us.'

Lucius frowned. 'I don't want to.'

'It's only one night of the year.' Claudia smiled encouragingly. 'It won't harm you.'

'But I don't want to,' Lucius repeated haughtily. 'They're our servants. They're there to do what we tell them. I don't care about Saturnalia!'

Cato placed the basket on a shelf, above the reach of Cassius, and squatted in front of his son so their faces were on the same level.

'Listen, there's a good reason for Saturnalia. It reminds us that whatever our place in the world now, it could change at any time, for any reason. Take me. I am the son of a slave. Now I own slaves at our house in Rome. For that I thank Fortuna, and Saturnalia reminds me of how much I have to be grateful for. It reminds me that but for a twist of fate, I might be a slave or a servant, and those who serve us might be my masters. So tonight, you will wait on Parvus and count your blessings, my boy.'

'I still don't like it.'

Cato stared at him a moment before he spoke again. 'You want to be a soldier when you grow up, don't you?'

'Yes.'

'You want to be an officer? You want to lead men?'

'Yes, Father.' Lucius lifted his chin imperiously.

'Then you need to learn what Uncle Macro and I have known ever since we were given men to command. A good leader looks after his horses and mules before his men, and his men before himself. He feeds his soldiers first before he looks to his own hunger. If you don't understand that, Lucius, then you will never be a good leader. Do you understand?'

The boy's gaze fell to the floor, and Cato gently lifted his chin so he could not avoid his gaze. 'Do you understand, Lucius?'

'I . . . I suppose so.'

'Good man.' Cato stood up again and gestured to the samianware bowls on the counter beside Petronella. 'Now why don't you take a plate of meat and some bread to Parvus to get the feast started? Show him how a good leader looks after his men, eh?'

Lucius nodded, stiffened his spine and heaped a generous portion of meat into the bowl along with a ladle of fried onions and two small loaves. Then he left the kitchen and made for the hall.

'He's a good boy,' said Claudia as she kissed Cato on the cheek. 'He'll make you proud one day.'

'He already does.'

Macro looked up from the spit he was still turning. 'You two going to help us, or just play lovestruck like a couple from a cheap theatrical romance?'

The role reversal was regarded with bewilderment by those of Boudica's bodyguard who were not familiar with the Roman custom. At length, the servants and the guests had been fully sated, and Macro and the others helped themselves to what remained of the food and took their places at the bottom of one of the tables, next to Boudica and some of her men.

'Hope you've had enough to eat,' said Petronella.

The Iceni queen had barely cleared half her bowl and looked tired and strained. She tried to smile. 'You have done us proud. A true Roman feast.'

'Oh, this is nothing like the feasts back in Rome,' Claudia intervened. 'But it's as good as it can get here in a frontier on the edge of the Empire.' She nodded at Petronella. 'You've done wonders with what is available. I've never enjoyed such succulent meat from a boar.'

Boudica turned to Macro and Cato. 'I have to say, your Saturnalia is an odd custom.'

'You have nothing like it amongst the Iceni?' asked Macro.

'No. We have a warrior caste, and the rest are farmers and some slaves. It is their duty to provide for the warriors as well as themselves. Everyone knows their place and what is expected of them. The Iceni would never play such games as you do.'

'I see. A pity.' Cato indicated the burly men of her bodyguard sitting nearby. 'But what place is there for warriors in your tribe now that the Iceni and Rome are at peace?'

'Peace . . .' Boudica repeated the word with a look of distaste, as if she had just eaten something horribly sour. 'We agreed an alliance with Rome. We have honoured our side of the treaty. My fear is that your emperor may not do the same when we present Prasutagus's will to the governor in Londinium. I've learned that some of Rome's emperors have a habit of promising one thing and doing another. When we swear an oath of loyalty along with the other tribes at the ceremony to mark the new year, I hope that will be enough to satisfy him.'

'I hope so too,' Cato responded.

'And if it isn't?' Boudica regarded him closely. 'What do you think he will do?'

There was an awkward pause as Cato struggled to frame

a response in diplomatic terms. 'It all depends on how the governor interprets the situation. But whatever he does, the matter will have to be referred to the emperor for the ultimate decision.'

'So I understand. And what do you think Nero will decide?'

Cato hesitated again, and this time she leaned closer and touched his arm. 'For the sake of the friendship we have and for the times we have fought side by side, be honest with me.'

'There are rumours – more than rumours – that Nero and some of his closest advisers are considering abandoning Britannia. I am not so sure I agree. It would look like a defeat however it is presented. But a rumour is often enough to make people act. I know that a number of tribes in Britannia have been loaned money by powerful men in Rome. They will want to call in the loans if there is any question of the new province being abandoned. The emperor will give orders for his soldiers and officials to loot the island of as much portable wealth as possible before they withdraw. If Nero does decide to keep the province within the Empire, he will be under pressure to make it pay its way. His officials will find any and every means they can to raise taxes and appropriate land and wealth. Against such a background, I fear for the future of you and your people. The death of Prasutagus may be the pretext needed to annex the land of the Iceni and confiscate its wealth. I pray that I am wrong and that the will is honoured and Rome continues to treat you like a loyal ally. With all my heart.'

Boudica eased herself away with a sad, worn expression. 'If it comes to that, how do you imagine my people and I will react?'

'In your place, I know how I'd react,' Macro intervened. 'I'd fight it. What else would anyone with a sense of honour do if they were treated like that? But it would be foolish. There could only be one outcome. For all their bravery, the Iceni cannot hope to defeat the legions. They'd be crushed and would lose everything along with their lives. Those spared would be sold into slavery. In ten or twenty years, no one would remember they ever existed.'

Cato mentally winced at his friend's frank appraisal.

The Iceni queen sighed. 'So the choice is submission or death. If that is what is presented to my people, then regardless of the outcome, they will choose to fight. And I will choose to lead them in that fight. There is no question of abject submission for the Iceni. Our pride, our traditions, our honour will not tolerate it.'

'You speak as the queen. You speak for the nobles and your warriors. But do you speak for the common people of your tribe? I think not. Do you imagine their day-to-day lives will change much if Rome annexes your lands and sweeps away your nobility? All the ordinary people care about is putting enough food into their stomachs to survive. In the end, what difference does it make if they are ruled by you and your nobles, or Rome?'

'I think I know my people better than you, Cato. They are the Iceni. They are proud of that. They are proud of our traditions. That may not feed their hunger if the crops fail, but it nourishes them nonetheless. They would rather die standing against Rome than grovel on their knees in submission.'

'Brave words.' Cato shook his head. 'It breaks my heart to think that they might be put to the test.'

'Then let us hope that does not happen. Cato, you are a good man. A man of honour. A man who is held in high regard amongst your people. If you could speak on our behalf, if you would explain the debt Rome owes us for the times we have fought with you . . .'

'And what about the times when some of your people fought against us?' asked Macro.

'They were hotheads misled by fools. They were renegades. Prasutagus denounced them at the time.'

'He may have done,' said Cato. 'But to Roman eyes, the actions of some Iceni warriors were the actions of all the Iceni. The betrayal of the alliance by the few was seen as a token of a wider betrayal. It may not be fair, but that is how it is understood from Rome's point of view. One thing Romans are very good at is nurturing a grievance. Particularly over something they see as a breach of faith. As Carthage once discovered to its cost.'

Boudica gave a dry chuckle. 'The Greek who taught me your tongue also taught me something of your history. I must say I find it surprising how many times Rome was guilty of a breach of faith, especially given how resentful they are when the tables are turned.'

'It's true,' Cato conceded. 'Great empires tend to have a flexible notion of morality with regard to their actions. I am merely trying to warn you how Rome may play this. Pointing out the hypocrisy of hypocrites achieves little in the end. It will not advance your cause and may only result in resentment, however unjustified that may be. You will be at a double disadvantage because you will be seen as a barbarian, and because you are a woman. I know the tribes of Britannia are proud of their women and hold them in high regard, but that is not the way of Rome. It is our tradition to be fearful of any woman who wields political power. You may be treated with disdain, but that will be motivated by fear, and frightened men will go to extreme lengths to put women back in their place, as they see it.'

'There's a reason for that,' said Macro. 'That wildcat Cleopatra seduced Caesar and Marcus Antonius – two of the greatest Romans who ever lived, in my opinion. That nearly did for the Empire.' He took a breath and continued. 'Women—'

Petronella coughed and looked at him meaningfully as she arched an eyebrow.

'Women . . . some women, er, can create mischief. But most are wise, and it is often best for men to heed their words and keep their mouths shut and their thoughts to themselves.' Macro smiled at his wife. 'How am I doing so far?'

'Not bad. Still room for some improvement, my love.'

Those at the end of the table smiled at the moment of light relief, and Boudica turned her attention to Cato again. 'On the off chance that the governor has not been educated to the same degree of perspicacity as Centurion Macro, I fear I may need a Roman at my side when I face him to defend my husband's will. Someone who understands the Roman way of thinking and who also has some sympathy for the Iceni's position. As I have already said, I think that man is you, Cato. I ask you as a loyal friend, as someone who fought your cause only a year ago. I ask you as someone who understands right from wrong and what common justice demands. Will you come with me to Londinium and speak on behalf of the Iceni?'

Cato felt a moral compulsion to stand up for this ally of Rome, to whom he and Macro were also personally indebted. He feared that Boudica and the Iceni would be given short shrift by Governor Suetonius and the scheming provincial procurator, Catus Decianus. The latter in particular. It was Decianus who controlled the province's purse strings and who acted as an agent for the rich moneylenders in Rome who had made lavish loans to the rulers of those tribes allied to Rome in the early years of the invasion. Neither of the two Roman officials had been in Britannia long enough to understand the sensitivities of the Celtic tribes they ruled. There was a danger that they might inadvertently provoke the Iceni, even if they didn't deliberately set out to humiliate them. Although that was equally possible, given the cross-currents of imperial policy under Emperor Nero.

He sensed that the future of the province hung in the balance. If Rome mishandled the prickly pride of the natives, there would be conflict. If it was a costly conflict, it might convince the policy-makers that Britannia was a province too far and it would be wiser to pull out, whatever the damage that might cause to Roman prestige. On the other hand, if Governor Suetonius and Procurator Decianus could be persuaded to treat the Iceni with respect, they would cement the alliance with a powerful tribe and have one less threat to face in pacifying the rest of the island. The lives and livelihoods of many were at stake, and it was Cato's bounden duty to do what he could to keep the peace.

He looked into Boudica's enquiring eyes. 'I'll do it. I'll come with you to Rome to speak for your cause. The gods grant Governor Suetonius the wisdom to listen to us.'

# CHAPTER FOUR

'Are you sure this is wise?' asked Claudia as she handed Cato the carefully folded equestrian toga to complete the contents of his travel pack. He placed the white woollen garment with the narrow red stripe running along the hem in the leather bag and flipped the cover over before buckling it securely.

'I have to do this. It's a debt I must repay to Boudica and the memory of Prasutagus. If it were not for them, I would probably still be an optio, or a junior centurion at best. Or even dead.' He held her shoulders before kissing her. 'You'd do the same in my place. I know you would.'

'I hope that's true,' she replied. 'In any case, you saved my life. I know what it means to be indebted to someone for that. I understand that you must do this. I just ask if it is wise. There are already people in Londinium who know you are in the province. There may be some recent arrivals who might be curious about why you have chosen to live in a veterans' colony so far from Rome. If you draw attention to yourself, you may draw attention to me. If it is discovered that Claudia Acte did not die in Sardinia after all and Nero gets to hear of it . . .'

She did not need to complete the sentence. From what she had already told Cato about her days as the mistress of the emperor, it confirmed the impression he had formed of Nero as a vain, capricious and jealous young man. He had reluctantly sent Claudia into exile because he had been obliged to by his mother and the senatorial faction that backed her. He had claimed to love her nonetheless. If he learned that she was now Cato's lover, it was likely that his immature possessiveness would cause him to send assassins after them to track them down and kill them. She was right to be wary.

'I will keep out of the way as much as I can and only speak to the governor when Boudica presents the will and asks for Rome to honour its terms. I will come back here as soon as it's done. Meanwhile, look after my son.'

'Of course.'

They embraced and kissed again until Cato felt something thrusting its way between their legs and backed off with a start. Cassius looked up at them, tail wagging as he whined softly.

Claudia laughed. 'He knows you are leaving.'

Cato shook his head and played with the animal's one good ear. There was not much left of the other, lost in some canine fight before Cato had found him while campaigning on the eastern frontier some years earlier.

'And look after my dog. Try not to spoil him.'

'It's not me you have to worry about. It's Parvus. The boy spoils him rotten. I dare say Cassius will have moved into Macro's household by the time you get back.'

He hefted his travel pack and strode out into the short covered walkway that ran along the rear of the small house they were renting. There was a large room that took up most of the building, with three rooms at the rear and a small wing with a kitchen and a room just large enough for the elderly Trinovantian couple who kept the place clean and did the cooking. A pony was hitched to the rail beside the gate at the rear of the enclosed yard. Cato slung his pack across its back and secured the straps to the rear saddle horns. He checked the saddle and reins and turned to Claudia.

'I'll be back soon.'

She smiled and nodded.

He paused for a heartbeat, but knew it would be better not to prolong the parting. He grabbed the saddle horns and pulled himself up, swinging a leg over before dropping into the saddle in one neat motion. As he turned the pony towards the gate, he saw that Lucius was standing there in his path, hands on hips as he glared at his father.

'Uncle Macro says you are going to Londinium.'

'Yes.'

'Why can't I come? Uncle Macro's going too. So is Petronella. Why do I have to stay here?'

'I need you to protect Claudia and Cassius while I am away.'

Lucius glanced at his father's lover. 'She doesn't need protecting.'

Cato felt his heart sink at the resentment in the boy's tone. He had hoped that Lucius had grown to regard Claudia with more affection in the time the three of them had been together. He looked at him with a stern expression. 'Claudia needs protecting. Cassius too. I picked the best man for the job and that man is you. Was I wrong? Are you not up to the job, Lucius?'

He knew his son well enough to know that the boy would be proud of being chosen and ashamed of falling short of the standard his father expected of him. But Lucius still struggled with the idea of missing out on a trip to Londinium. He had friends in the colony and had come to regard it as home, but the prospect of seeing the bustling streets and markets of the province's largest town vied with his pride at being the man of the house in his father's absence.

'Take me next time?'

'I will. I promise.' Cato smiled fondly. 'I'll see if I can bring you back a present.'

The offer sealed the deal, and Lucius stepped aside and offered a salute as his father rode by and out into the street. Cato returned it, then turned to wave one last time to Claudia before urging his pony into a quick walk towards the west gate of the colony.

Macro and Petronella were waiting, along with Boudica and her party. As the Iceni queen saw Cato approaching, she gave the order to move off and fell in behind the four warriors at the front of the small column. The Romans took their place at the rear, and a moment later they had passed through the gate and were following the Iceni along the road that led to Londinium, some four days' march away.

Cato glanced at Macro. 'You didn't have to come with me. The governor may not like what I have to say. I'd rather you kept out of it. You've got a good thing going for you here as senior magistrate of the colony. Best not get yourself on the wrong side of Suetonius.'

'I've been in worse positions,' Macro replied. 'Besides, apart from standing up for Boudica and her people, it'll give me a chance to look in on my mother and see how business is going.'

Macro's mother, Portia, ran a very profitable inn and brothel in the heart of the thriving port. Macro had invested some of his savings and owned a half-share in the enterprise. Between that and the bonus and land grant he had received on retiring from the army, he was a man of considerable wealth and status these days. But all of that depended upon the continued presence of the legions in the province. He had a vested interest in ensuring that there was no conflict between Rome and the Iceni.

It was a cold day, and a biting wind was blowing in from the north-east, bringing a band of dark cloud with it. More snow, Cato feared, as he pulled his cloak tightly about him and drew the hood over his head. He hunched forward and looked between the pointed ears of the pony towards the two wagons rumbling along the frozen ruts ahead. Through the flaps of the goatskin cover he could see the furs piled within, as well as the small chest containing silver and jewellery, the tribute that Boudica hoped would placate the Roman officials when she presented the will, after swearing an oath of loyalty along with the rulers of the other tribes gathered at the governor's palace. Perhaps it would be enough, he reflected. Perhaps he would not have to plead her case. Then there would be no trouble and the Iceni would be able to live at peace with their Roman overlords.

Behind the column, Camulodunum slowly slipped into the distance and then was lost from view as the road dipped down the far side of a low ridge. Overhead, the skies darkened, and by noon the snow was falling heavily, covering the road so that the travellers could only make out their route by the cambered line stretching across the winter landscape.

It was Petronella who spotted them first and called her husband's attention to the group of men marching along a track that angled towards the main road. The drifting snow had slowed their progress, and now it was certain that they would not reach the imperial way station before nightfall. Nor was there any sign of an inn or other habitation.

'What do you make of them?' she asked.

Macro drew back his hood and Cato followed suit, and the two soldiers squinted into the light breeze, blinking away the snowflakes that gently impacted on their faces.

The other party was no more than a quarter of a mile away, some twenty or so figures. With the exception of one rider, the men were on foot, with some large dogs on leashes. Half of them carried spears and appeared to be guarding a line of a dozen men with hands bound behind their backs, linked together by a rope that looped through an iron bracket around their necks.

'Slave traders?' Macro mused.

'Most likely,' said Cato. 'Looks like we might have company when we camp for the night.'

'Not sure I fancy that,' Macro grumbled. The slave trade, while very profitable, was an enterprise that was regarded with disdain by most Romans. The same was true of running gladiator schools or moneylending. The aristocrats who engaged in such business did so via lesser mortals who managed their affairs. Happily for the senators and members of the equestrian classes, this arrangement allowed them to reap the profits while continuing to regard the source of their gain with aloof contempt.

Macro scrutinised the approaching figures. 'It's a pretty low trade for any self-respecting man to be engaged in.'

'And yet you have been happy to accept your share of the proceeds from the sale of prisoners taken in battle,' Cato pointed out. 'Sauce for the goose and all that.'

'Rubbish,' Macro shot back. 'Making a little money from it is not the same as being part of it.'

Cato grunted. 'That's one way of looking at it. What do you think, Petronella?'

They exchanged a look and chuckled. 'He's got you there, Macro,' she said. 'Can't hold your nose with one hand while holding the other out to catch the silver.'

'You're supposed to be on my side.'

'I'm your wife, not your slave. I have a mind of my own and I'm happy to keep it that way.'

'Gah!' Macro shook his head. 'You're trouble, you are.'

'And you love me for it.' She leaned across from her saddle and kissed him clumsily.

The other group was keeping level with Boudica and her entourage, and Cato saw that they would reach the junction of the two routes at the same time. As the distance closed, he urged his mount forward to draw level with the Iceni queen.

'We've got company. Have you seen?'

'Not the kind of company I prefer to keep.'

'We can hardly ignore them. It's almost dark and we'll need to stop. They'll be doing the same.'

'They can do what they like as long as they keep their distance from me.'

'I'll deal with them,' said Cato. 'It'd be best to avoid trouble in case they're heading for Londinium and make a complaint when they get there. We don't want anything to complicate matters between you and the governor.'

Boudica nodded. 'You speak to them then.'

He dipped his head in acknowledgement and turned his mount to cross the short distance between the two groups, making for the mounted man leading the party.

'Greetings, friend!' he called out as he trotted up, blocking the man's way and forcing him to raise his hand to halt those behind. In the gathering gloom, he saw that the rider was tall and well proportioned. He wore a felted skullcap below which strands of grey hair projected, and had a broad, lined face and deep-set brown eyes. His cloak was striped in the eastern fashion, and a long cavalry sword hung from his hip.

'Friend, you say,' he observed. 'What manner of friend would that be?'

'A fellow traveller on the road to Londinium. Prefect Quintus Licinius Cato.' Cato edged his pony closer and extended his arm.

'Prefect, eh? A soldier, then?' The man's tone was suspicious. 'What unit?'

'None at present. Between commands.' It was a safe enough answer. 'And who might you be?'

The man spat to one side before taking Cato's forearm. 'Gaius Hormanus. No rank to speak of. Not since I was an optio in the Second.'

'The Second Legion?' Cato released his grip and withdrew his arm. 'Then we might be old comrades. I joined as a recruit nearly twenty years back. My friend there was a centurion.' He pointed to Macro. 'We'd be glad to share a flask of wine around the fire tonight, if you will.'

Hormanus smiled for the first time, revealing a set of good teeth. They marked him out as a man in prime condition, even for his age, which Cato now put at late fifties, sixty at most. 'Wine? A drink with old comrades? Now there's an offer a veteran such as myself can't turn down. I'll have to deal with that lot first, mind.' He jerked his thumb back at the men following him.

'Slaves?' asked Cato.

'Not yet they aren't. Will be once we reach Londinium. Debt defaulters from the Trinovantes. Half failed to pay the tax that was due, the rest couldn't repay their loans. So their debts will be met by whatever I can get for them in the slave market in Londinium. Less my commission.'

Cato cast an eye over the chain gang being guarded by Hormanus's men. The prisoners were a mixture of ages, but all were dressed in the simple woollen tunics of tribal farmers. A few had cloaks, but they still stood shivering along with the rest. A pitiful sight, but not uncommon in many of the provinces of the Empire. He turned his attention back to Hormanus.

'We'll be camping for the night soon. You are welcome to stop nearby. We'll be safer together if there are any brigands about. Once we've set up, Centurion Macro and I will come over to share some wine by your fire, if that's agreeable.'

'Most agreeable.' Hormanus grinned. 'I'll look forward to it. So what's your story, Prefect? How did you and the centurion come to be on the road with that bunch of barbarians?'

'It's the queen of the Iceni and her retinue on the way to the oath-swearing ceremony.'

'Ah, royalty. I dare say that's the reason you popped over, to make sure we made camp near you rather than with you, eh?' Before Cato could respond, the older man raised a hand. 'It's all right, sir. I'm used to people turning their nose up at what I do for a living. I dare say even your Iceni friends there think their shit smells better.'

'Something like that,' Cato conceded. 'Sorry, brother. Not much I can do about it. Until later, then.' He nodded his head and tugged the reins of his pony.

'Make sure that wine's a good one!' Hormanus called after him, and laughed.

The two groups made camp a short distance apart on the edge of a pine forest. Boudica had beds for herself and her daughters made up in one of the wagons, while her men foraged for dry wood to make a fire. Their own accommodation was more modest: simple leather shelters supported by poles cut from the nearby forest. Cato and Macro had brought an old army tent with them in case they were caught out in the open, and quickly set it up a safe distance from the Iceni fire but close enough to enjoy its warmth.

Soon an iron tripod had been erected over a smaller fire, and a large pot hung from the chain, heated by the flames. Snow was melted before Petronella and some of the Iceni began to add barley and cuts of salted meat. They worked cheerfully together, with Petronella attempting to converse in the snatches of the tribal tongue she had picked up from those Iceni who lived at the colony. Inevitably there were misunderstandings, mime shows and roars of laughter, arising from the warm conviviality of coming together after a day's travelling to share a meal.

As the stew began to cook, Cato and Macro took one of the canteens of wine they had brought with them from Camulodunum and crossed the open ground to join Hormanus. The slave drover and his men also had a couple of old army tents, but had contented themselves with one fire, over which they were roasting a joint of pork. The aroma was appetising, and the prisoners watched hungrily as the meat sizzled above the glowing embers.

Hormanus was sitting on a log, warming his hands, as they approached, and he smiled as he rose to greet them. 'Welcome, comrades!'

Macro introduced himself, and all three sat down on the log facing the fire. Macro took out the canteen and removed the stopper before passing it to Hormanus. The slave drover sniffed the spout and raised an eyebrow appreciatively. 'Smells like the good stuff.'

'As good as it gets in Camulodunum,' Macro responded. 'Which ain't too bad at all.'

'How so?'

'There's a trader who brings a good haul of wine from Gaul when he makes the crossing. Of course we don't see him over the winter, so we have to stock up.' Macro regarded the flask sadly. 'We went through most of it at Saturnalia. That's almost the last drop of the Narbonensis.'

'No worries, Centurion, I'll be kind to it.' Hormanus winked and took a swig before passing the canteen back. 'Ah! A good drop, that is!'

Macro and Cato took a mouthful each before the canteen was stoppered up.

'Cato says you served with the Second Legion,' said Macro.

'That's right. Started out in the ranks and ended up as optio of the Second Century, Ninth Cohort by the time I was paid off. That was fifteen years back.'

'You were in on the invasion then? Like the prefect and me.'

'Aye. Mad times, eh? That ambush in the wood, and the battles over those two river crossings before the last affair outside Camulodunum. It's a fucking miracle we survived that lot.'

'Too right.' Macro nodded as he recalled the bitter struggles of the early days of the invasion. 'Can't say I remember the name of your centurion at the time.'

'Tintillius. Well, him and then the new boy, Vendosius, after some Dubonni bastard piked Tintillius. I had hoped for his spot, but they promoted Vendosius from another century. Shame. Would've been nice to have made the centurionate before I was discharged. Nice bonus payment and a few privileges that go along with it. I bet you've done well out of it, eh, Macro?'

'Centurion Tintillius?' Macro frowned. 'I think I remember him. Tall chap? Lost the end of his nose.'

'That's the one! Hard bastard, but a good soldier.'

Macro glanced at Cato. 'You remember Tintillius?'

'I was just an optio at the time. Didn't get to spend any time down the centurions' mess,' Cato replied. In fact, he did recall the name. Tintillius had a reputation for taking every bribe he could get from his men in order to skip duties or be given leave. It was certainly a perk of the rank enjoyed by many centurions, but few did it on the scale of Tintillius. Cato doubted if many of his men had shed a tear over his death.

'The Second used to be a good legion back then,' Hormanus mused. 'One of the elite formations. If it hadn't been for us, things might have gone very differently. I dare say the invasion would have faltered and we wouldn't be sitting here now sharing a drink.' He looked meaningfully at the canteen, and Macro handed it over.

'Used to be a good legion?' Cato queried. He had been keeping his head down after settling in Camulodunum, and news of any kind was slow to reach the colony.

'Aye.' Hormanus took a second swig before returning the canteen and wiping his lips with the back of his hand. 'The Second's little more than a training unit these days. They take in fresh drafts of recruits off the ships from Gaul and try to turn them into legionaries. The losses we've been taking in the fight with the mountain tribes mean there's a constant demand for replacements. The best men from the Second were the first to be transferred to the other legions. Now there's a handful of decent men left at the fortress at Isca serving as drill instructors. I get down that way from time to time on business and have a drink with the old hands. The legion's in a sorry state, they say. In no condition to fight.'

'It's a damn disgrace.' Macro frowned. 'To let a fine reputation go to the dogs like that.'

'They'll recover,' said Cato. 'Once the Silures and the Ordovices and their Druid masters are defeated, the Second will no longer have to be a training formation. The men will gain experience and the legion will be fighting fit again. You'll see.'

'I hope you're right, Prefect.' Hormanus shrugged. 'But from the barracks talk I've heard lately, we've got too few men, let alone good men, to be sure of ending the fighting in the mountains any day soon. Even if the new governor's the expert in hill fighting they say he is.'

There was a brief silence as the three soldiers stared into the flames licking up from the fireplace, reflecting on the challenges facing Suetonius. Then Hormanus gestured towards the other camp.

'What's the story with you two and the Iceni woman? How come you're travelling with that lot?'

'The queen,' Cato responded with emphasis, 'may need us to speak in her support when she goes before the governor.'

'Why would you speak up for one of them barbarians? They'd happily stab us in the back first chance they get.'

'We're honouring a debt,' said Macro. 'If it wasn't for Boudica and her men, it's likely the prefect and I would have been killed in that fight against the crime gangs in Londinium at the start of the year.'

Hormanus's eyes widened. 'You were caught up in that? Sounded like open war on the streets, from what I've heard.'

Cato nodded. 'Took some tough fighting, and the queen and her men were at the heart of it.'

'So we don't take too kindly to people bad-mouthing the Iceni,' Macro added.

Hormanus raised his hands. 'No offence meant, brother. It's just surprising to see a couple of Romans willing to risk travelling with a band of natives in this part of the province. That's all.'

'We're quite safe, I can assure you,' said Macro. He nodded

towards the Iceni. 'As it happens, I'd trust that lot with my life.'

'Fair enough, it's your funeral, friend.'

Macro stared at the veteran for a moment before glancing at Cato. 'I think we should get back. Before our supper gets cold.'

He stood up without waiting for a reply, and Cato followed suit. 'Safe travels, Hormanus.'

'And to you,' the veteran replied, and nodded to Cato. 'And you, sir.'

As they trudged away from the slave drover's camp, Macro muttered, 'How the fuck are we supposed to keep any of the locals on our side if people like him treat them like the enemy all the time?'

'It's usually the older hands who adapt to change slowest,' said Cato. 'We've seen that often enough. He meant no harm.'

'Maybe, but he came close to causing himself some.'

Petronella was sitting chatting with several of the Iceni warriors, and the convivial mood around the cooking fire was warmer than the discussion Macro and Cato had just concluded. They sat on their rolled-up sleeping mats and gratefully accepted the steaming mess tins she handed to them.

'Have a good chat with your friend there?' she asked.

Macro grunted and took the spoon from his pack, hunching over his mess tin.

'That good, eh?'

'He was an old sweat with all the views that go with that,' Cato explained. 'Macro took exception to something he said about our Iceni friends.'

'Did he?' Petronella kissed the top of her husband's head.

He looked up. 'What was that for?'

'I'm just counting my blessings that you haven't turned into an old sweat like him. And if you do, I'll push you under a wagon and be done with it.'

'You're a hard woman to please, my love.'

She wagged a finger at him. 'Just don't ever change, eh?'

Cato smiled at the two of them, happy that his friend had found a woman to match him. His thoughts returned to what Hormanus had said about the losses the Romans had suffered in their war with the mountain tribes. Suetonius faced greater challenges than he had supposed. In a political climate in which those in Rome were reconsidering the wisdom of invading Britannia, the slightest setback on the battlefield might settle the fate of the province.

# CHAPTER FIVE

'Because it's my fucking tent!' Macro snarled, and turned over, pulling most of the covers with him. Petronella wrenched them back and stuck her knee into her husband's spine.

'You're having that dream again. Wake up, you old fool!'

Macro stirred, blinking as he stared at the goat leather of the tent above his face. There was enough light in the hour before sunrise for him to see by. He thought about turning back towards Petronella and snuggling up for a little more sleep before they had to rise and pack for the day's ride. Then he felt the uncomfortable sensation in his bladder and realised he could not put off relieving himself.

'Bugger it,' he muttered as he eased back the fur and woollen coverings and made his way on hands and knees past his wife. Beyond her, Cato was curled up, still asleep. The tent had been cut down from an old army section tent that had once held eight men, and now was just about big enough for half that number. Pushing the flaps aside, Macro stepped out in his bare feet, wincing at the morning stiffness in his joints.

'Getting too old for this lark,' he muttered as he paced a decent distance away from the tent and the Iceni shelters before lifting the hem of his tunic. As he pissed, he looked over the snowy landscape in the thin light that imparted a blue hue to the scene. A sudden movement caught his eye as a fox cautiously emerged from the treeline no more than a hundred paces away, freezing as it caught sight of him.

'Well, hello there, Peeping Tom,' Macro grinned. He tucked his manhood away and raised his arms. 'Boo!'

The fox burst into motion, racing over the open ground a short distance before swerving in the direction of the slave drover's camp. Macro's grin disappeared. Hormanus's tent, the shelters of his men and the chain gang they had left out in the open had disappeared. A glance round the immediate surroundings found no sign of them. An uneasy feeling gripped him. It was too early for them to have already gone on their way. Besides, he would have expected Hormanus to wait around long enough to say farewell. Something was wrong.

It was then that he realised he was the only one up and about. Where were the two men who should be doing their stint of sentry duty? He scanned the camp and saw two dark bundles beneath the bed of the larger of the Iceni wagons.

'Sleeping on the job,' he growled, and paced his way across to them. 'Oi! You two! Wake up, you lazy bastards!'

When they did not stir, he crouched between the solid wheels and gave the nearest man a vigorous shake. The Iceni warrior did not respond, and as Macro withdrew his hand in readiness to deliver a kick, the warrior toppled onto his back where he had been lying. There was a jagged tear in the flesh at his throat, and his eyes stared unblinking at the pale sky. A look at the other man told the same story.

'Shit!' Macro cupped a hand to his mouth and bellowed across the camp. 'To arms! Get up!'

The first sleepy figures emerged from the Iceni shelters, looking at him in confusion as he ran past barefoot.

'Don't just stumble about like sheep! To arms, you bloody fools!'

By the time he reached the tent, Cato had already crawled out, boots on but unlaced, his short sword in his hand as he quickly looked over the camp.

'Where are the others?' he asked. 'Hormanus and his crew?'

'They fucked off in the night.' Macro pointed in the direction of the bodies under the wagon. 'After they'd knifed two of Boudica's lads. Or so it looks like.'

As Cato's gaze snapped in the direction of the wagon, Petronella pushed through the tent flaps and pressed a cloak and Macro's boots into his hands. 'Get those on. You'll do no good if you're too frozen to think.'

The two men quickly tied their boots as the Iceni warriors armed themselves and formed a protective ring around Boudica's wagon. She climbed out a moment later, accompanied by her daughters, pulling a thick fur coat about her shoulders as she spoke to the commander of her bodyguard. Macro and Cato trotted over, the latter sheathing his sword now that there seemed to be no immediate danger.

'What is the meaning of the alarm?' Boudica demanded.

'The sentries are dead.' Macro pointed to the other wagon. 'I saw they were missing when I rose at first light.'

Boudica led the way and squatted to examine the bodies before glancing up, a look of alarm on her face. Rising, she hurried to the back of the wagon, snatched the flaps of the cover aside and rummaged through the furs, then let out a cry of rage.

'The chest, it's gone . . . They've stolen the annual tribute.'

'We have to find Hormanus,' said Cato as he glanced towards the road fifty paces away. 'They can only have a few hours' head start on us. They have one horse; they can't have got far.'

'No, look.' Boudica pointed to the horse lines, and Cato saw that some of the Iceni mounts were missing. He thought swiftly.

'They've taken their prisoners with them, and the chest will slow them down, even if they divide the contents between them. There's still a chance. Have your best men ready the remaining mounts. They're to take nothing with them other than their swords. We'll ride lighter than Hormanus and his men. There's every chance we can run them to ground and recover your treasure.'

'I hope so,' Boudica responded bleakly. 'I fear for the future of my people if we fail to present the annual tribute to the governor.'

Cato had already grasped the implications, and he turned to Macro. 'On me.'

He led the way at the trot, through the camp back to the road. There had been little snow overnight, and the tracks from the previous day were clear; the deep ruts of the wagon wheels amid the churned hoof marks and footprints. He stood atop the slight camber and looked back in the direction of Camulodunum. There was no sign of any fresh marks. He turned towards Londinium. It took no more than a heartbeat to make out the impressions of wheels in the compacted ice. He squinted down the road, tracing its course towards a low ridge some two miles away. There was no sign of movement, other than a thin trail of woodsmoke some distance north of the road.

'They've got a good head start on us.'

'Maybe.' Macro scowled. 'But we'll catch 'em. And when we do, I'll feed that bastard Hormanus's balls to that dog of yours.'

By the time they returned to the Iceni camp, the riders had saddled their horses. True to Cato's orders, they wore only their cloaks over their tunics and sword belts at their waists. No shields or armour. One of Boudica's men had prepared the mounts of the Roman officers, and Petronella had fetched Macro's sword belt. She hurriedly fastened it around his midriff as he swung his cloak about his shoulders and fastened the clasp. A moment later, the flaps of Boudica's wagon parted and she dropped to the ground wearing strapped leggings and a bright green cloak over her tunic. Her red hair had been tied back in a simple ponytail and she too wore a sword belt. The warrior commanding her bodyguard spoke in a mildly reproachful tone, and she snapped at him and strode towards the horses.

Macro opened his mouth to speak, intending to dissuade her, but was silenced by a look of ferocious intent.

'There's no time to waste,' she announced, and swung herself onto a horse. 'Which way did those Roman thieves go?'

Cato swallowed his pride at her word and nodded towards Londinium. With a brisk jerk of the reins, Boudica gave a sharp cry and urged her mount into a canter. The rest of her men and the two Romans scrambled onto their horses and set off after her, swinging left when they reached the road. Petronella, Boudica's daughters and the handful of Iceni warriors and servants that remained watched them go until they were no more than distant blots against the winter landscape.

'Right then.' Petronella turned to the others and indicated the tents and cooking pots. 'What are you lot waiting for? Let's get the wagons packed and get moving.'

One of the men indicated the bodies still lying beneath the larger wagon, and Petronella sighed sadly. 'Put them with the furs. The queen can oversee their burial when we catch up with her.'

It was two hours after sunrise, by Cato's reckoning, when they came across the first bodies. Two of the prisoners from Hormanus's chain gang. Both of them at least fifty years old and thin and frail-looking. Like the murdered Iceni warriors, their throats had been cut. They had been abandoned at the side of the road, just before it entered a forest with thick undergrowth between the bare limbs of the trees. Cato got down from his horse and kneeled by them, removing a leather mitten so that he could feel the cheek of the nearest prisoner. The flesh was cold to the touch.

'Must have been here a while,' he said as he stood up. 'I imagine we'll find more bodies as we continue on their track.'

'Why kill them?' asked Boudica.

'They were holding Hormanus back.'

'Why not let them go?'

'They might have known something that could have helped us. They might have understood a little Latin and overheard the thieves' plans. Could be any reason. They were killed just to be sure.'

Macro leaned forward in his saddle for a closer look. 'Why keep any of them if there's a danger of being held back? Surely if Hormanus is aiming to escape pursuit, the best thing to do would be to get rid of all the prisoners. It's what I'd do in his place.'

Boudica shot him a sour look. 'Lovely people, you Romans.'

'Hormanus is greedy,' Cato reasoned. 'He thought he could get away with the silver *and* his prisoners. I'm surprised we didn't come across the bodies sooner.'

He remounted and scanned the undergrowth on both sides of the road ahead. Like most roads built in the early years of the invasion, the engineers had cleared the land for twenty paces on either side to make it harder for anyone to launch a surprise attack. As the province had become more settled, the need for such a safeguard diminished, and scrub had begun to grow back so that only a narrow margin remained.

'What do you think?' asked Cato, nodding at the way ahead.

'I think he'd be a fool to ambush us.' Macro hawked and spat to one side. 'We outnumber him two to one.'

Cato eased his mount into a trot as he led the way into the forest. A mile further on, they found the rest of the chain gang on the road, still bound together and killed in the same manner. He slowed as they passed to see if there was any sign of life, but Hormanus and his men had done their job effectively, and none of the prisoners stirred as the horses trotted by. A short distance beyond was a large clearing, where they encountered a crossroads. The remains of a timber signal tower stood nearby. The ditch was overgrown and most of the stockade had collapsed. The corner posts still stood, along with the sturdy logs that formed the first eight feet of the tower. Above that, the framework was bare, and what was left of the platform had been taken over by crows' nests.

They stopped at the crossroads, where the snow was heavily disturbed. Fresh hoofprints went off towards Londinium, but also in both directions on the road that crossed the main route.

'Clever,' Cato conceded as he glanced about him. 'They mean to divide us.'

'Or they've decided to split up and go their own ways,' Macro suggested. 'In the hope that we'll go after just one group of the bastards.'

'I don't want any of them to escape,' said Boudica. 'All that they've stolen has to be recovered.'

'I agree,' said Cato. 'I don't know where the other road leads.'

'I do.' Macro pointed south. 'Trading post on a river that way. At least ten miles. I settled a property dispute there last summer. North goes to one of the auxiliary forts guarding the border with the Iceni. There's a small civilian settlement there. Too small for any of Hormanus's lot to disappear into. Those making for the river could find a boat to take them across, or head out to the coast. We could easily guess the wrong direction and lose 'em. I'd say their best bet is to get to Londinium. It's large enough for them to go to ground without attracting attention. Plenty of people pass through. A few more faces aren't going to be noticed. That'll be the route Hormanus has picked, if I'm any judge of the man.'

The riders were split into three parties. Cato and several of the warriors continued along the road towards Londinium, while Macro's party turned north and Boudica and the remaining horsemen headed south. It was agreed that if no trace of the thieves was found, the three groups would return to the crossroads by nightfall.

As he rode at a steady canter, Cato considered the odds. Depending on the number of men Hormanus had kept with him, he and his Iceni warriors would have the advantage, just as Macro and Boudica would in any skirmish. That was reassuring. The Iceni were good riders and knew how to get the best out of their mounts, whereas it was likely that the men they were chasing were not. That was another advantage. Enough to keep him hoping that Boudica's tribute would be retrieved for her to present to the governor.

The sun reached its modest winter zenith and the sky assumed a steely grey hue as the afternoon began. As the road left the forest, the landscape opened up, dotted with clusters of native huts and a handful of small Roman farming estates. The riders paused at an inn beside the road, where two men in aprons were butchering a pig that hung from a frame. Offal steamed in a wooden tub to one side.

Cato raised a hand in greeting. 'Speak Latin?'

'As well as any lads from the Aventine,' the older of the two men chuckled. 'What's up, friend?'

Close to, Cato could see the eagle and numeral tattoo on the man's forearm that marked him out as another veteran who had settled in this part of the province, and he gave an informal salute to reassure him that he was part of the brotherhood of Roman soldiers, despite the fierce-looking tribesmen riding with him.

'We're looking for a party of riders who passed this way earlier today.'

'That'd be Claudinus and his lads, then. Sure, they stopped by here not more than an hour ago. Long enough to buy some food and fill their canteens.'

'Claudinus? Is that the name he gave?'

The other man nodded and wiped the back of his bloodied knife hand across his brow.

Cato briefly described Hormanus.

'That's him. Another veteran, I'd say. Same as the lads with him.'

'How many of them?'

'Six all told.'

'Did they say where they were headed?'

'Why do you ask, brother?'

'They're thieves and murderers.' It was bluntly said. Cato knew that the code of the legionaries did not brook stealing from each other, and that those who did were held in contempt and punished without mercy.

'I see . . . Verulamium, he told me.'

It was as likely to be as much a desperate deception as the lie about his name. But it still caused Cato some doubt. What if Hormanus was playing a double bluff by revealing his destination and that was where he fully intended to go? But there was still time to chase him down before he reached the fork where the roads headed towards their respective destinations.

'My thanks, brother.' He swept his arm forward as he forced his mount into a trot and then a canter, picking up the pace of the pursuit.

They were careful to ride along the edge of the road to avoid any hidden ruts that might trip up their horses, and from where they could clearly see the tracks left by Hormanus and his men. Shortly afterwards, they passed a small settlement, and now the prints left by the thieves were joined by those of other travellers. Cato cursed silently as it became harder to distinguish those of the men he sought. Then, as the road crossed a low rise, he saw a horse lying on the road. It was still alive, and it shifted and whinnied in pain as he approached. He could see that its right front leg was twisted and misshapen, and realised that it must have stumbled and broken the limb. There was no sign of the rider.

As he made to move on, there was a shout of protest from behind, and he turned to see one of the Iceni gesturing at the injured beast.

'There's no time for that.' Cato stabbed his finger in the direction of the road, and put together some of the Iceni words he had learned since arriving in the colony. 'We go. Now.'

The warrior shook his head and slipped from his saddle, joined by one of his companions. He advanced on the horse, talking softly, before kneeling beside its head and gently placing a hand on its muzzle. The beast's eyes widened in what seemed to Cato to be a fearful expression, and it snorted as its flanks heaved. The warrior continued to talk soothingly, and the horse became calmer. Then, glancing up at his companion, he gave a quick nod. The horse's throat was cleanly cut in an instant. Both men stepped back hurriedly as the blood gushed and the animal's legs flailed violently for a few heartbeats, before its strength began to fail and it went limp.

The two Iceni remounted without a word, but Cato saw the tears that glistened in the first man's eyes before he roughly cuffed them away.

'Let's go.' He spoke more gently this time, and they set off once again.

The rider had not got far and was limping when they first caught sight of him. He turned as he heard the thud of hooves, but made no attempt to escape. Instead, his shoulders slumped in resignation, and he released the small leather pouch he had been carrying, which landed heavily at his feet. The horsemen closed around him in a loose circle as Hormanus's man, heavily built, with cropped hair, leaned on his good leg.

'Where is Hormanus?' Cato demanded. 'And the rest of the silver you stole?'

'It's with the boss and the other lads,' the man replied in a defiant tone. 'You'll never catch them. You don't even know which direction they went.'

'Londinium, for certain,' Cato replied. 'Where else would murdering scum like that try to hide with their loot?'

The man's expression gave nothing away. Cato dismounted and handed the reins to one of the Iceni before stepping forward and regarding the man closely. 'Is that the silver, in the pouch?'

'My share of it.'

'I'm surprised your friend Hormanus didn't kill you and take it when your horse fell.'

'I'm sure he would have done.' The man laughed bitterly. 'But I had fallen behind. He didn't see it happen.'

'Lucky for you.'

'I think not. I don't have any doubts about what your Iceni friends intend to do to me.'

Cato looked round and saw the steely expressions on the

faces of the Iceni warriors. His gaze returned to the thief. 'I'll have that pouch.'

'Be my guest. Come and get it.'

Cato placed his hand on his sword hilt. 'Try any tricks and I'll gut you.'

Keeping an eye on his prisoner, he leaned forward and retrieved the pouch. He felt the coins shift within, and the weight was reassuring. Backing off, he handed the pouch to one of the Iceni, who opened it and glanced inside before hanging it securely from a saddle horn.

'What's your name, brother?' Cato asked, hoping to win some of the veteran's confidence as a prelude to getting the information he needed.

'Legionary Junius Bellocatus, First Century, First Cohort, Twentieth Legion. At least, I was.'

Cato looked him up and down. Bellocatus had served in the most senior century of his legion. He would have received a handsome bonus on discharge. It was hard to believe that one of the Empire's elite had fallen so low as to become a slave drover's henchman, let alone a murderer and thief. He found it difficult to keep the disgust out of his voice when he spoke again. 'Jupiter's cock, what happened to you, Legionary Bellocatus?'

'Same as the others with Hormanus. We fell into the clutches of a con man. You know how it goes when there's a large number of men taking their discharge bonuses. The crooks smell the silver and come running, using every trick in the book to part us veterans from our life savings.'

'That's as maybe. But there's a long road between being the victim of a trickster and turning your hand to robbery and murder.'

'Easy to say when you haven't had to endure it.'

'It's not too late for you, brother. Hormanus was the one responsible. Tell me where to find him and I'll do everything I can to see that you are treated leniently.'

Bellocatus snorted with derision. 'You must take me for a fool. I'm a dead man. I've nothing to gain from helping you.'

'Except going to your death with a clearer conscience. You owe Hormanus nothing. You're going to die because of what he chose to involve you in. Why not make him pay for it, eh?'

'Hormanus said you and your friend served in the legions. Then you know how it goes. You don't rat on your comrades. I'm saying nothing.'

Cato accepted that he was not going to get any information out of the thief, and he climbed back into his saddle and looked round at the Iceni. 'He's all yours.'

There was a chorus of rasps as the warriors drew their swords and edged their mounts forwards. As Cato steered his horse in the direction of Londinium, he heard Bellocatus's last words. 'Twentieth Legion! Till the day I die!'

The battle cry was cut off by a series of thuds and grunts as the Iceni hacked at him without pity, avenging their two murdered comrades.

Daylight had almost gone by the time Cato reached the camp that had been set up by the crossroads. While the Iceni saw to the horses, he took the pouch of silver coin to Boudica and handed it over.

'We caught up with a straggler,' he explained. 'Then we found an auxiliary patrol a few miles further on. They hadn't seen any sign of Hormanus and his men. He must have got off the road somewhere and we missed him. The light was starting to fade, so we came back. How did you fare?'

Boudica sighed. 'We lost the tracks, then doubled back to a stream we had crossed. We followed it for a while, but found nothing before I gave the order to return here. I suppose they left the stream somewhere further along before making to rejoin the rest.'

'They pulled a similar trick on me,' said Macro. 'Lost them in a pine forest when they left the road.'

'What happens now?' asked Petronella as she squatted beside her husband and pulled her cloak more tightly around her body.

'We'll continue to Londinium. That's where Hormanus is most likely to be. Not for long, though. If he's smart, he'll try and find passage on a ship to Gaul and get as far from Britannia as possible before he enjoys his loot. However, there won't be many skippers willing to risk crossing the sea in winter. We'll ask around the wharf district and see if anyone knows anything about him.' He looked to Boudica, who was staring at the pouch in her lap. 'There's still some hope.'

She shook her head and tapped the pouch. 'Your governor will laugh when I present this as tribute. He'll demand to know where the rest is.'

'Then tell him about Hormanus,' Macro suggested. 'Tell him to have the man hunted down and the silver retrieved.'

'You think he will listen to the excuses proffered by a barbarian woman?' she responded icily.

'Maybe he will listen to us,' Cato said.

'And you think that will make a difference?' She lifted her face to the night and closed her eyes in frustration. 'Do you not yet understand? The Romans mean to crush the Iceni and take our land. They will use the failure to pay tribute as the excuse they need to carry out the deed. I will enter Londinium as a queen and leave it as a slave. So ends the kingdom of the Iceni.'

# CHAPTER SIX

There were loud noises of celebration coming from the Dog and Deer inn as Macro and Cato led the way towards the yard at the rear. The inn and attached brothel, co-owned by Macro and his mother, Portia, was the cornerstone of the growing business empire she had worked hard to establish in Londinium. She now also owned a bathhouse, a block of small shops close to the forum and a warehouse by the river from where she ran a wine-importing business. She was a thin, frail-looking woman with the sharpest of business minds and, when the occasion required, the sharpest of tongues. Some merchants were inclined to underestimate her on first meeting, to their cost.

The yard had changed out of recognition since the last time Cato and Macro had visited Londinium. The neighbouring buildings had been demolished to enlarge the space, and now a six-foot wall with a shingle tile gatehouse fronted the street, an armed watchman standing in a small shelter to one side.

'Open up!' Macro called out as they approached.

The watchman, burly enough but simple-looking, stepped out in front of the gate and stuck a thumb in the wide leather belt about his midriff, swinging a studded club from a strap around his right wrist. 'Who says so?'

It was three days since the murders and theft, and the spirits of Boudica and her people were at a low ebb. Their Roman friends shared their mood, not helped by a change in the weather. The temperature had risen slightly, bringing with it a penetrating rain carried on a cold easterly wind. The snow had turned to slush and melted in patches across the countryside. The travellers were soaked through and shivered as they picked their way through the muddy streets of the town towards their destination. There were many other tribal rulers, representatives and retinues in Londinium for the annual oath-swearing ceremony, and the town felt more than ever like a frontier outpost, where Roman civilisation mingled with the more primitive garb and rough tongues of barbarians. At least that was how it might seem to a tourist from Rome. More seasoned men like Macro and Cato had lived amongst the peoples of Britannia long enough to understand and appreciate the ways and traditions of the tribes. A different kind of civilisation, but civilisation nonetheless.

Macro increased his pace to advance ahead of the others. 'I say. Centurion Lucius Cornelius Macro. Open up.'

The watchman hesitated a moment, before recognising the name and the inherited brusque manner at the same time and bowing his head quickly. 'Yes, master!' He ducked back into the shelter, and a moment later, there was a dull grating sound and the gates opened inward.

The watchman stepped aside to let them enter the yard, regarding Boudica and her followers with a mixture of surprise and suspicion. The riders dismounted, and while the wagons were driven to the far corner of the yard, Macro looked round.

'The old girl's made quite a few changes. Business is doing well.' He smiled as he contemplated the rise in value of his half-share.

'I'd lay off the "old girl", if I was you,' Petronella cautioned as a door at the rear of the inn opened and a rake-like figure in a fur-trimmed cloak stepped out.

'Here's trouble,' Macro muttered.

'My dear Petronella!' Portia held out her arms and the two women embraced briefly. 'I see you've brought my son with you, and that nice boy Cato.'

'Hello to you too, Mother,' said Macro as Cato smiled a greeting.

'And so, so many friends . . .' Portia looked over the Iceni warriors unsaddling the horses and removing the yokes and traces of the mule teams that had drawn the wagons. Then she saw Boudica emerging from amongst her men and abruptly her manner changed to one of deference. Successful businesswoman and Roman as she was, Portia was inclined to be in awe of anyone with a regal title.

'Queen Boudica, you are most welcome to my humble premises. It is a pleasure to see you again.'

'The pleasure is mine,' Boudica replied, forcing a weary smile. 'My retinue and I need quarters for the next few days. If that is not too much trouble.'

'I would be honoured.'

Macro noted the calculating expression that flashed across the older woman's face. 'As our guests, Mother.'

'Guests?'

'Take their lodgings and food out of my share of the profits.'

'As you wish. The queen and her daughters can have the best room in the inn, and I'll find quarters for you, Petronella and Cato.' She turned to Boudica. 'The best room is mine. It's cosy and warm, being above the kitchen. The roof doesn't leak and it's at the far end of the building away from the brothel, so it should be nice and quiet.'

'Sounds delightful.' Boudica smiled. 'You are too kind.'

Portia's gaunt face flushed with pleasure, and she turned to call out to her handyman and occasional lover. 'Denubius! See to it that my room is prepared for Queen Boudica, and move my things into your room for now.'

'My room?' Denubius looked pained. 'Where shall I go, mistress?'

'It's an inn,' she replied tersely. 'There are other rooms.'

His shoulders slumped as he turned and made his way back inside to do her bidding.

'Now, I imagine there's plenty of news to exchange.' Portia smiled. 'But I expect you will need to change into some dry clothes and have something to eat and drink first.' She glanced up as the rain began again, splashing circles in the puddles in the yard. 'Let's get inside.'

'She's in a real pickle, poor love, and no mistake,' Portia sighed once Cato had explained what had happened on the road from Camulodunum. She was sitting beside the brazier in her office, an extension to the inn in one of the neighbouring buildings that she had bought out. Cato, Macro and Petronella were seated on stools opposite, holding beakers of heated wine. 'They should protect travellers along that road,' Portia opined. 'That's what we pay our taxes for. You should speak to the governor about it. He'd listen to someone of your rank.'

'I doubt it,' Cato replied. 'Suetonius is too busy with preparations for the coming campaign. He'll not want to repeat the mistakes of the governors who came before him. This time he'll complete the job and put an end to the hill tribes and the Druids. But he's going to have to scrape together every soldier he can find, and provision the expeditionary force as it passes through the mountains. No small task. He won't have time to deal with guaranteeing the safety of those on the road. We'll just have to look out for ourselves.' He took a sip of wine, noting that some spices had been added, and raised an eyebrow approvingly before he continued. 'As for Boudica, you are right. She is in trouble now that almost all the tribute has been stolen.'

'That's why I suggested she stay at the Dog and Deer,' said Macro. 'Otherwise the cost of looking after her escort would have eaten through what is left. I knew you wouldn't mind.'

'I don't mind it coming out of your end, son.'

'Mother . . .' Macro gave her a reproachful look. 'I don't mind paying for them, but do you have such a short memory? It was thanks to Boudica's help that we managed to bring down the Londinium gangs.' He gestured at the room. 'Do you think you'd have been able to build the business as you have since then if the gangs were still taking almost every spare sestertius in protection money? Her people shed their blood for us. The least we can do is share a little hospitality in return, eh?'

Portia considered this for a moment and nodded reluctantly. 'All right then, I'll give you a good rate to set the costs against. After all, as you say, we owe them. Besides, with those heavies of hers around, it'd take a brave man to cause any trouble at the inn, or try to steal anything from the yard.'

'You are the very epitome of kindness, Mother.'

She made a face before turning back to Cato. 'And how is that dear little boy of yours?'

'Not so little any more,' Cato said with a touch of sadness. 'He's growing up fast and naturally he wants to be a soldier like his uncle Macro.'

'A fine role model,' Portia said wryly.

'Fine indeed,' Cato responded with feeling. 'I just wish I'd spent more time with him in his early years. The army exacts its price as far as family life is concerned.'

Petronella nodded emphatically.

'What about your new lady?' asked Portia. 'I imagine she's finding living in a veterans' colony a bit of a challenge after the imperial palace. I'm not sure I would be keen to make the trade down.'

'You might if you'd been Nero's mistress. But the less said about that the better. So far we seem to have avoided any unwelcome attention. Claudia's happy enough in Camulodunum for the present. She's getting on well with young Lucius. He doesn't remember his mother, which is a good thing. The three of us will keep our heads down until it is safe to return to Rome.'

'And when do you think that will be?'

'When Nero has gone.'

'You could be waiting for some years then. He's only a young man.'

'True, but so was Caligula. He didn't last even four years in the job. I get the feeling Nero may be cut from the same cloth. And then he has the added problem of what to do about Britannia. Those around him are divided on the issue. Whether he chooses to keep the legions here or pull them out and abandon the province, he will make people unhappy.'

'Well, he'd make me bloody unhappy if he abandoned Britannia.' Portia spoke forcefully. 'After all the money and effort I've put into building up the business. If that little prig puts an end to the province, he'll have me to answer to.'

Macro rolled his eyes. 'I am sure the prospect causes him to lose sleep.'

'Laugh as much as you like, boy, but it's your livelihood too. How long do you think your veterans will last at the colony when the barbarians come sweeping down on you once there are no legions to fear? Think about that before you make any more cheap cracks at my expense.'

Cato did not want any chippy tensions to sour the reunion, and cleared his throat noisily to distract mother and son. 'We're in the lap of the gods these days, Romans and Iceni alike, and there's not much we can do about it. All we can do is live the life we have as well as we can for as long as we are permitted.'

Macro shook his head and drained his beaker. 'Very philosophical of you, lad. You should scrawl that bollocks on the side of the Senate House when you get back to Rome. That'll set 'em thinking. Well, I ain't for letting other people make decisions for me. If it comes to it, I'll fight to hold on to what's mine in this province, whatever Nero and his cronies decide. I'm here to stay.'

He rapped his beaker down on the edge of his stool to emphasise the point. Portia nodded approvingly and reached forward to top it up.

'Well said, son. You have your moments.'

'Gods preserve us,' Petronella muttered. 'They're as mad as a box of Gauls, the pair of them. Tell 'em, Cato. If the legions go, the province goes. And if that happens, then we should go too, as quickly as we can. I'm not hanging around for the bloodbath when the tribes turn on the Romans who are pig-headed enough to stay put.'

'Petronella's right. There's more to life than money in the bank and a property portfolio.'

Macro tutted. 'You're full of the aphorisms tonight, lad. Let's hope that silver tongue of yours does the job when you go and speak up for Boudica and her people. I've a feeling more is hanging on it than just the fate of the Iceni.'

Cato took a thoughtful sip and nodded. 'I fear you are right, brother.'

* * *

Early the next morning, Cato and Macro donned plain cloaks over their tunics and concealed their sword belts beneath the thick woollen folds. After a hurried meal of porridge, they set off for the wharf and warehouse district to try and track down Hormanus and his gang. Despite the cold showers that fell fitfully from a grey sky, the streets were crowded. Besides the retinues of the allied tribes who had journeyed to Londinium to attend the oath ceremony, there were those who had come to witness the spectacle, and pedlars and street vendors who welcomed the opportunity to trade trinkets from elsewhere in the Empire for furs and jewellery.

When the two Romans reached the wharf running along the bank of the Tamesis, they saw that there were perhaps twenty seagoing cargo ships moored along the wharf, and several more riding at anchor on the river. They worked their way along, asking the captains and crew if they had been approached by a man seeking passage to Gaul. They offered a description along with the name Hormanus and the other name he had given in an attempt to throw the Iceni pursuers off his tail. As Cato had anticipated, there were only a handful who were contemplating setting sail before winter was over, and none of them had seen Hormanus and his men.

Retiring to one of the drinking holes on the main road leading up from the river, the pair considered their next step over a jar of wine that was overpriced and over-watered.

'He's here,' Cato insisted. 'I'm sure of it.'

'Maybe.' Macro looked down wearily into his cup. 'But if he is, he hasn't made any attempt to get out of Londinium by sea.'

'Then we'll have to start working the inns, brothels and bathhouses. We'll let it be known there's a reward for information. Someone will be happy to sell him out for a handful of silver.'

'Unless that someone tries to get him to pay them more to keep silent.'

Cato smiled grimly. 'Do you think Hormanus is the bargaining type? He'll agree a price to save his skin and then knife the happy informant the moment their back is turned. If I was an informant, I'd play it safe and take the ready money rather than risk dealing with a murderer and thief.'

'Fair point,' Macro conceded. 'The trouble is, we don't have much time. The ceremony is the day after tomorrow. If the coin isn't returned to Boudica by then . . .'

'Quite.' Cato drained his cup, stood up and slid some bronze coins onto the table. 'We've no time to waste. Let's get going.'

They bought some paint and brushes from a building supplies merchant in the forum and spent the rest of the day painting notices on the walls of plastered buildings around the town. The message was brief: *A hundred sestertii will be paid at the Dog and Deer for information on the whereabouts of the veteran who calls himself Hormanus. Wanted for murder and theft.*

The equivalent of half a year's pay for a legionary should be enough to attract the attention of any literate passer-by, Cato reasoned. They also announced the reward in a number of drinking places across the centre of town so that the message would swiftly radiate out to the rest of Londinium.

As dusk closed in across the sprawling settlement, they returned to the Dog and Deer, where Boudica was waiting impatiently.

'Any luck?'

Macro sat down on a bench beside the brazier in the kitchen. 'No news of him along the wharf. Nor in any of the places we stopped by to ask for information. If he's here, he's dug himself in somewhere nice and quiet while he waits for his chance to escape.'

'Why wouldn't he just stay in Britannia?' asked Petronella, who was busy stirring a pot of stew over the cooking griddle.

'The province is a small place,' explained Cato. 'There are only three large Roman settlements: Londinium, Verulamium and Camulodunum. He'd be a fool to try the last, and Verulamium is too small for him to go unnoticed. If he's anywhere, it's here.'

'You seem very sure of that,' Boudica remarked. 'If you're wrong, then all hope is gone. Even if you're right, we have only one day to find him and get our tribute back.'

Cato was about to offer some encouragement, but the words died on his tongue. They would be empty platitudes and would do little, if anything, to raise Boudica's spirits.

The next day, a handful of chancers presented themselves at the Dog and Deer demanding payment in advance of revealing where to find Hormanus. Once it became clear that their intention was to take the reward money and run, Macro kicked them out and threatened to do to them what he planned to do to Hormanus if they ever showed their faces at the inn again. Meanwhile, Cato was doing the rounds of the inns, brothels and bathhouses, asking for information, without result. He began to wonder if he had been mistaken in his assumption that Hormanus was hiding in Londinium. What if he had continued past the town and made for Verulamium after all? Or perhaps he was holed up in some abandoned native hut in the heart of one of the forests that covered much of the countryside between the colony and Londinium. If that was the case, there was no chance of being able to save Boudica and the Iceni from the consequences of failing to provide the tribute due to Rome.

He returned to the Dog and Deer late in the afternoon,

footsore and frustrated as he reported his failure to Macro and learned that the offer of a reward had proved futile.

'How has Boudica been today?'

'How do you think?' Macro responded. 'Not happy. She spent the morning at the banking houses in the forum trying to secure a loan to cover the tribute, but it seems word has got round that the Iceni are in trouble. In any case, the agents acting for investors back in Rome are calling in more loans than they're issuing. There's clearly a feeling that the province's future is uncertain. She tried her hand with some of the other tribal leaders in town, too, but it's been a tough year and most of them have struggled to raise enough to pay their own tribute. The only ruler who is flush is that arse-licker Cogidubnus. He's been living off the import taxes he levies for trade passing through his port at Noviomagus Reginorum, and most of that has been squandered on the palace he's having built. Boudica's come up empty-handed.'

'Where is she now?'

'With her people, outside. Mother's brought them a hog to roast and they're busy preparing a charcoal pick to cook it. She threw in several jars of her cheapest wine too. Doing her best to keep their minds occupied, bless her. It's uncommonly generous of her, and she ain't even going to take it out of my share of the business profits.'

Cato gave him a thin smile before stroking his jaw thoughtfully. 'I fear it's going to feel more like a wake than a feast the ways things are going. Let's pray the gods look favourably on Boudica when she faces the governor tomorrow.'

# CHAPTER SEVEN

The first day of the new year dawned with a marked improvement in the weather. A serene azure sky stretched across Londinium, and the sun bathed the town in a warm honeyed hue.

In the huge open courtyard of the governor's palace, servants and soldiers were overseeing the final preparations for the oath ceremony. Areas were being marked out for each of the tribal contingents due to attend, as well as places for Roman civic officials and the commanders of most of the legions and auxiliary cohorts in the province, with a final section roped off for the common people of the town. An altar had been erected on the stone dais in front of the pillared main entrance to the palace, the fluted sections of each pillar shipped over from Gaul thanks to the lack of local material suitable for the construction. The men of the governor's bodyguard, hand-picked soldiers from the legions, were putting the final touches to their appearance, polishing helmets, shield bosses and the medals on their harnesses. The standards of the legions and auxiliary cohorts that had been placed in the underground shrine and safe room beneath the building were now being set up in front of the palace, the gold and red of their falls burnished by bright sunshine.

Outside the walls of the courtyard, street vendors were arranging their wares, wine and snacks ready for the crowds that would be drawn to witness the procession of the governor and his bodyguard and lictors to the temple of Roma. There Suetonius would seek divine approval from the augurs before returning to the palace to receive the oaths of loyalty and the payment of tribute. It would be a public display of the authority of Rome and the loyalty it demanded from those who served the Empire and those who were ruled by the Empire. On this day, similar scenes would be played out across the breadth of the Roman world, from the frozen forests of Germania to the searing deserts of the eastern frontier. All would turn to Rome and acknowledge her seemingly invincible power.

The yard behind the Dog and Deer was also bustling, as the Iceni dressed in their finery and the warriors put torcs on their wrists and around their necks, awarded to them for brave deeds – their equivalent of the Roman soldiers' medallions. As Cato regarded them, wine cup in hand, from the rear door of the inn, he noticed a telling difference between the two martial codes. The Roman army awarded decorations to units as well as individuals, gold or silver crowns or wreaths added to the unit's standard, whereas the Celts only rewarded individual warriors. It reflected the different fighting styles and perhaps went some way towards demonstrating the greater power of a trained body of men over fanatical raw courage. Man for man, the best of the Celtic warriors had the edge over their Roman adversaries. They tended to be bigger, raised to fight from an early age and revelling in their warrior prowess. Combat was seen as a test of the individual, and that encouraged the wild rush tactics the Celts often favoured and which shattered on the tight shield wall of the legions. It was not until the wily

Caratacus had rejected the old ways and instead turned the Celts' efforts towards harrying Roman supply lines and isolated outposts that Rome's advance across the island was effectively contested.

Boudica had emerged from her room before first light to oversee her retinue's preparations, and as Cato watched, she took out the leather-cased royal standard of the Iceni and began to work the cover off. When at last it was free, she unrolled the long strip of bright green cloth with a yellow hunting dog running at full stretch along its length. Then, raising it vertically, she set it up against the side of her wagon, the folds rippling gently in the faint breeze.

'Stand still!' Petronella ordered as Macro stepped into the yard. 'How do you expect me to get you ready if you keep wandering off the moment my back is turned.' She glanced at Cato for support. 'Was he always like this in the legions?'

Macro shot him a warning look and Cato cleared his throat noisily to temporise while he came up with a diplomatic response.

'He was a stickler for proper appearance, starting with himself.'

'Then why,' Petronella poked her husband in the chest, 'can't you be bothered to be the same now? You're the senior magistrate of a veterans' colony. A man of importance. Not some squaddie setting off for a stag do. You need to have more regard for your appearance.'

Macro winked at Cato. 'Save me, lad.'

'You're on your own, Centurion,' Cato replied, tipping the dregs of his heated wine into the yard. 'I value my life too much to cross words with your lady.'

'Whatever happened to leave no man behind?'

Cato turned to go inside, muttering to his friend as he squeezed past, 'Not too late for the pair of us to re-enlist.'

'Just give the word, brother,' Macro whispered.

Boudica led her retinue and her Roman friends towards the gateway of the palace courtyard, taking her place at the end of the line of tribal groups waiting to be admitted and escorted to their positions. As they passed by, there were exchanges of greetings as old friends were spotted, good-natured jeers from some old adversaries and bitter looks from enemies. At another time, and with a few jars of wine or beer inside them, there would certainly have been a punch-up or two, but Roman officials had made it clear that there was to be no violence between the tribal contingents for the duration of their stay in Londinium. So Boudica and her companions shuffled forward under the banner of the Iceni as they made their way towards the gate.

Cato was aware of the stiffness of her posture and the fixed expression on her face, and guessed at her inner turmoil as she contemplated the outcome of her failure to pay the required tribute, as well as the governor's decision on how to carry out the terms of Prasutagus's will. Her mood communicated itself to her retinue, who fell silent as they slowly approached the gateway.

In the distance there was a sudden blare of trumpets and a loud cheer from the crowd as the augurs announced that they had read the entrails of an unblemished white goat and the omens were propitious. The gods were content to allow the ceremony to go ahead. With their blessing Suetonius would soon be returning to the palace to conduct the main business of the day. The centurion at the gate looked up in alarm and began to process the tribal contingents more quickly in a bid to get everyone inside the courtyard and in place before the governor made his entrance.

When Boudica's turn came, the officer held his wax tablet open, with his stylus poised in the other hand.

'Tribe?'

She drew herself up and addressed him haughtily. 'We are the Iceni.'

'Iceni . . .' He nodded and ticked an entry on his tablet. 'Name?'

'My name is Boudica. My title is Queen. You will address me according to my rank, Roman.'

The centurion looked up with an amused expression. 'To the right, fourth block along on the front row.'

Boudica glared at him silently as Macro stepped forward. 'Centurion Lucius Cornelius Macro, senior magistrate of the colony at Camulodunum. Stand at attention!'

The centurion snapped his shoulders back and stared over Macro's shoulder as the latter closed up on him and spoke in the low, menacing voice he had once used to address lowly recruits. 'That's more fucking like it. You will address me as "sir", and my friend here as "Majesty". Understood?'

'Yes, sir.' The centurion's gaze shifted to Boudica and he gave a curt nod. 'Majesty.'

'Now you will escort the queen and her retinue to their place, and if there's any more of your bloody insubordinate nonsense, I'll be sure to take the matter up with your legate. Are we clear?'

'Yes, sir.'

'Right then. Name?'

The centurion hesitated, and Macro leaned closer, almost nose to nose.

'Centurion Gaius Menapilus, sir.'

'Noted. Now run along and do your duty, Centurion.'

Menapilus turned to bow to Boudica. 'If you would follow me, er, Majesty?'

As the Iceni party entered through the gate, Macro arched an eyebrow at Cato. 'Not lost my touch, eh?'

The two Roman officers made their way into the courtyard. With his advantage in height, Cato could see that the Roman officers and officials were to the left of the passage passing through the crowd, which was lined with legionaries standing to attention, shields and javelins grounded. The tribal rulers and their retinues were to the right. The space roped off for the commoners of Londinium was empty. They would only be allowed to enter once the governor and his escort had taken their places. He bade Macro farewell and went to stand with Boudica and her people, inconspicuous enough in his plain brown cloak, tunic and felt cap. He would not be mistaken for one of the Iceni, and a curious onlooker might wonder what he was doing amongst them, but he was confident he would not be recognised as a senior Roman officer by the casual observer. It would avoid any awkward questions about why someone of his rank was not sitting with his peers on the dais.

The last of those taking part in the ceremony took their places, and there was an expectant hush as they listened to the sound of the crowd cheering Governor Suetonius growing louder as he approached the palace. As the first of his bodyguards, marching either side of the imperial standard, entered the gateway, the air was filled with the shrill blare of horns sounding from the bucina men either side of the entrance. A moment later, Suetonius entered on horseback, the very image of Roman power. His breastplate gleamed in the sunlight and the bright red cloak swept back over his shoulders was embroidered with a gold oak leaf design. Red leather strips, edged with more gold thread, hung from his shoulders and from around his waist. Below his knees he wore red leather boots topped with tassels. He was mounted on a gleaming black stallion with a saddle made by the finest leather-workers of Hispania. An ivory-handled sword hung from the baldric slung across his shoulder.

He rode down the avenue lined by his legionaries and dismounted at the foot of the dais before climbing the short flight of steps to the cushioned seat in front of the altar where the tribal tribute was to be laid. His lictors formed up in front of the dais while the standard-bearers of the units of the army of Britannia formed up behind and grounded their staffs. Suetonius turned to face the crowd and surveyed it sternly for a moment before he slowly raised his arm and the bucinas fell silent. The crowd was still, and the only noise was the hubbub of the common people in the streets outside the palace.

Cato watched as Suetonius lowered his arm and drew a deep breath before beginning his address.

'Loyal citizens of Rome! Loyal soldiers of the emperor! Loyal allies of the Empire, I bid you welcome in the name of Nero. Long live the emperor! Long live Rome!'

'Long live the emperor!' the soldiers, officers and veterans echoed in unison. 'Long live Rome!'

One of the Iceni warriors muttered a phrase in his own tongue that Cato had long since come to know: 'Death to Rome.'

Around him, the representatives of the tribes joined in a more ragged and muted chorus of 'Long live Rome', thanks to an unfamiliarity with Latin and the ceremony in many cases. Cato mouthed the words from habit. Suetonius waited for the sound to die away before he continued.

'We are gathered in this place to swear our annual oath of loyalty to the emperor, the Senate and the people of Rome. It is a sacred oath that binds us to the service of the Empire. It is an oath that we give freely that we may partake in the protection afforded to us by Rome in exchange for our loyalty, our service and our tribute. We swear this oath to the emperor as the living embodiment of the spirit and genius of Rome, as ordained by Jupiter, Best and Greatest. Long live Nero!'

Once again the crowd repeated the phrase, and the roar echoed off the walls of the courtyard and the palace behind the governor. Suetonius nodded to the standard-bearer holding the image of the emperor, a golden representation of his face surrounded by a concave sunburst in silver. The standard-bearer stepped up onto the dais beside the governor and Suetonius held on to it with his left hand as he offered his right to those gathered before him.

'Let the oath-taking begin!'

The senior legate of the four legions that formed the backbone of the army in Britannia stepped forward. Going down on his knee in front of Suetonius, he clasped the governor's hand between his own as he bowed his head and intoned, 'I, Petillius Cerealis, commander of the Ninth Legion, the Hispania, do hereby swear to obey the emperor and to serve him, the Senate and the people of Rome. This I swear on my life and on the reputation of my family. Long live Nero. Long live Rome.' Then he stood, saluted the governor, turned on his heel and marched back to his original position.

One by one the other legates swore the oath, then the prefects of the auxiliary cohorts who could be spared from their commands to attend the ceremony. After them came the tribunes serving with the legions. When the last of the military had sworn, then came the turn of the civilian officials, starting with the procurator, Catus Decianus, and the rest of the governor's staff, followed by the senior magistrates of the colony at Camulodunum and the other towns of the province where a local senate had been set up. Cato felt a catch in his throat as he proudly watched his best friend approach the governor to swear his oath in a loud, clear parade-ground tone. Macro had served Rome loyally for the best part of thirty years and had fully earned the honour of being the senior magistrate of the colony.

Cato saw Boudica glance towards him and give a brief smile. He was touched by the gesture, pleased that she recognised the significance of the moment and shared in the pleasure of seeing Macro enjoying his honoured position in society.

As the last of the Roman officials returned to their place, the first of the tribal representatives were called to present themselves to Suetonius. Some of them were kings, some were chiefs attending in lieu of their ruler. Apart from Boudica, there was only one other queen present – Cartimandua of the Brigantes, a northern tribe whose loyalty to Rome had been sorely tested by factions hostile to their queen's alliance with the invaders.

A well-built man in his twenties with flowing blonde hair and beard stepped forward. He was wearing a toga, with a blue cloak of Celtic design hanging from one shoulder in a carefully calculated display of Romanisation combined with a gesture towards tribal conventions. He kneeled and intoned the oath taken by the tribes, speaking in barely accented Latin.

'I, Torbellinus, king of the Atrebates, offer my submission to Rome, to the emperor and the Senate. I offer my unconditional obedience to those whom Rome has placed in a position of authority over me, and the Atrebatan people. I swear on my life and the blood of my people to be obedient to the laws Rome sees fit to impose on us and to honour our obligation to pay the taxes levied on my people to the authorities commissioned by Rome to collect taxes on behalf of Rome. I also swear to pay an annual tribute in return for the protection of myself and my people as enshrined in the terms of the treaty agreed between Rome and the Atrebates.'

As he concluded, Cato sensed a stirring in the ranks of the tribesmen around him. The oath demanded of the tribes was more oppressive than any he had heard before. From the angry muttering that surrounded him, it was clear that the tribal contingents realised this as well. Boudica moved towards him with a furious expression.

'What is the meaning of this? Why has your governor changed the oath?' Her eyes narrowed suspiciously. 'Did you know about it, Cato?'

'No! I swear by all that I hold holy, I knew nothing about it.'

She stared at him for a beat. 'I pray that you are telling the truth.'

She turned away and spoke to her retinue in a calming tone, and they fell silent. Elsewhere in the immediate crowd, the murmurs continued as the second oath was taken without any objection from the tribal leader. The third went the same way, and Cato realised that Suetonius had ensured that the most compliant tribes went first to set the tone for those that followed. One after another they pledged their unquestioning obedience as the other tribes looked on with open disgust. Then there was a brief pause, before the governor turned to the Iceni and called Boudica forward. She hesitated, aware that what she did next would weigh heavily upon her reputation and that of her tribe.

Cato understood her predicament. If she took the oath,

those tribes who resented its terms would regard her as a coward or a collaborator. The Iceni were one of the most powerful and respected of the tribes of Britannia. They had maintained a degree of independence from Roman influence, and harboured many warriors from other tribes who were quietly biding their time in the fading hope that a rebellion might one day set the spirit of resistance alight again. If Boudica refused to take the oath, Suetonius would view that as an act of civil insubordination that could not be tolerated. Especially if her example encouraged others to follow suit. Rome would be sure to send soldiers back into Iceni territory to police it and stamp out any sign of rebellious spirit. Gone would be the chance to plead her case over the stolen tribute, or press for favourable treatment of Prasutagus's will. It was an impossible situation, and she was damned either way. Cato shared her sense of abject frustration, despair and anger.

Why was Suetonius doing this? he asked himself. Surely he must understand the burden he was placing on those trying to keep their unruly people loyal to Rome? The only reason he could conceive of for changing the terms of the oath was a need for the governor to smoke out those tribes he felt he might not be able to trust at his back as he concentrated his army to lead them against the last of the mountain tribes and Druid strongholds defying Rome. While it might achieve that, at the same time he risked incurring the bitter hostility of those tribes that resented the new oath.

He saw the agonised expression on Boudica's face as she drew herself up and paced slowly towards Suetonius. A tense silence filled the courtyard, so that it was possible to hear her footsteps on the gravel. She went down on one knee before the governor and reached out to enclose his hand in hers as she spoke.

'I, Boudica, queen of the Iceni . . .' Her voice was low and strained, and she paused to clear her throat and draw a deep breath before she resumed clearly. 'Queen of the Iceni, offer my submission to Rome . . .'

Cato felt his throat tighten in pity and admiration for her courage in putting the lives of her people above the pride that ran through her like rock. How many others would have failed this test? he wondered. Around him, the Iceni retinue and those in the other tribes who had not yet sworn the oath looked on as if they were mourners at a funeral.

Once she had finished, Boudica withdrew her hand and returned to her feet. She refused to meet Suetonius's gaze as she turned away and rejoined her retinue. There followed a sullen procession of the remaining tribal leaders before the governor offered his final remarks.

'Soldiers of Rome, Roman citizens and allied client rulers! We have today reaffirmed our loyalty and obedience to the emperor. The sacred oaths have been given and we are bound as one. Let us look forward to another year of order and prosperity in the province. The year in which I will finally put an end to the barbarians who still hold out against Rome. Once our standards are flying over the island of Mona and the last of the bloodstained sacred groves of the Druids have been torn down, the people of Britannia shall finally know the peace that Rome brings.'

He raised his arm in salute and waited for the traditional acclaim that greeted the conclusion of the ceremony. But while the Romans and their most loyal tribal followers cheered heartily enough, Cato noted that those around him remained silent.

As the cheers died away, the procurator ascended the dais to make an announcement.

'The governor will retire to the audience chamber of the palace, where the presentation of tribute will take place.'

Cato glanced at Boudica and saw the haunted expression in her eyes. For the queen of the Iceni, the moral torment of a moment earlier only marked the beginning of the day's distress. The worst was still to come.

# CHAPTER EIGHT

'You were with the other officer, weren't you?' Centurion Menapilus regarded Cato warily as they stood to one side of the audience chamber.

The tribal retinues were filing in, each party bearing small chests or richly woven bags containing their tribute. It approximated to the weight in silver and gold defined by the procurator's staff as a suitable amount for each tribe. The calculation was based on the census that the Roman officials had carried out in the province. Occasionally bribes were discreetly paid to those carrying out the census to reduce the taxable value of a settlement. There was only so much latitude available to them, though, since if the subsequent census resulted in a marked increase in value, those responsible for the initial figure would be vulnerable to prosecution.

'That's right, and I need to speak to the governor as a matter of urgency.'

'It's always urgent,' Menapilus sighed. 'If you gave me a sestertius every time a petitioner said that—'

'Look here, I'm not interested in your aphorisms,' Cato interrupted. 'It is urgent. I must speak to Suetonius at once.'

'You've got a pretty high opinion of yourself. Who did you say you were?'

'I didn't.'

'Right, and I should just tell the governor that some nameless person off the street needs a quiet word in his ear and I thought that would be fine and dandy? You're going to have to try harder, friend. At least tell me your name.'

Cato clenched his jaw in frustration. The fewer people who knew he was in Londinium the better. Then he had an idea. Pulling off one of his mittens, he removed the iron ring that signified his membership of the equestrian order of Roman aristocracy and held it up for the centurion. 'See this?'

Menapilus squinted briefly and then regarded Cato in a more respectful manner. 'All right, you have my attention, sir.'

'Good. Take it to the governor and tell him I must speak to him now. Before the tribute session begins.'

The centurion knuckled his brow in salute and disappeared through the door at the rear of the audience chamber, where legionaries of the governor's bodyguard stood on either side.

Cato folded his arms and shifted his weight from one foot to the other as he regarded the tribesmen filling up the chamber. The Iceni were not there. He had asked Boudica to wait with her people outside while he asked to speak to Suetonius, in the hope that the Iceni queen would be spared the indignity of failing to produce the tribute and be allowed to plead her case in private.

Menapilus reappeared in the doorway and beckoned to him. Cato hurried over and slipped between the two guards, entering a small anteroom where benches lined the walls and a clerk's stool and table stood to one side of the entrance to the governor's office.

'Best be quick. His nibs was not best pleased when I told him you had to see him.'

Cato nodded in gratitude and stepped inside the office, closing the door behind him.

The governor was leaning against the edge of his desk. The procurator sat on a stool to one side, a wax tablet open on his knee.

'Yours, I believe, Prefect.' Suetonius tossed the iron ring to Cato who slipped it back on his finger before removing his felt cap. He saw Decianus's eyes widen in recognition, even though he now had a beard and it was two years since they had last met. 'What are you doing here?' continued the governor. 'I thought you left Londinium a year or so ago, after that fight with the crime gangs. I assumed you'd gone back to Rome.'

'I've been at the colony in Camulodunum, sir.'

'Hardly the place for someone of your rank or class. That's by the by. What's this business that is so urgent it can't wait? Spit it out.'

Cato described the theft of Boudica's tribute and the largely fruitless hunt that had followed. 'So you see, sir, they cannot pay what they have been assessed for. Not for a while, at least.'

'That's too bad,' Decianus commented.

Cato ignored the procurator and kept his attention on Suetonius. 'I thought it was important for you to know, before the queen is forced to hand over the little she has left in front of the other tribes and your officials. She's already in a tough situation, having had to provide the example for the other tribes over that new oath they were obliged to swear.'

A knowing look passed between the procurator and the governor, and the latter smiled with satisfaction. 'Just as we intended, Cato. The Iceni are an arrogant lot. They need to be put in their place, and for the other tribes to see that.'

'I understand,' Cato responded coolly. 'My concern is that you may humble them beyond breaking point if Boudica fails to pay the full tribute and you threaten to take action to recover the balance. That would not go down well with the other tribes, who already feel humiliated by the oath. The Iceni have risen against us once before. It would be unwise to provoke them again.'

'Provoke them?' Decianus said with derision. 'Who gives a shit about their sensitivity? The Iceni are a client kingdom. They need to understand their place in the new order now that Britannia is a province of Rome.'

'That's enough.' Suetonius shot him a stern glance. 'Cato is right to point out the danger. They're a prickly lot, these Britons. They need to be handled carefully, particularly as they have to be kept quiet while I put an end to the mountain tribes. Very well, Prefect. What do you suggest?'

'Let Boudica plead her case before you in private, sir. Hear what she has to say in her own words and come to some workable arrangement over the tribute.'

'I've already made an allowance for the poor harvest when King Prasutagus petitioned me a year ago. The Iceni have been treated with considerable leniency, but there are limits.'

'The Fates have not been kind to Boudica and her people,' Cato countered. 'And the issue of limits cuts both ways. They've had to make sacrifices to gather the tribute. If you demand too much too quickly, I fear they may rise up again.'

'If they do, they will be put down again. More harshly this time, to ensure the lesson is learned.' Suetonius let his threat hang in the air a moment before he changed tack. 'Why have you come here with them from Camulodunum? You couldn't have known that you'd need to intervene for them over the tribute.'

'I had another reason,' Cato explained. 'Besides paying the tribute and taking the oath, Queen Boudica also wishes to petition you over her husband's will.'

'Will?' Decianus scoffed. 'These barbarians don't even have a written language. How could they draft a will?'

'They had a Roman lawyer draw it up for them, just in case,' said Cato. 'It is a legal document.'

'That remains to be seen.' Suetonius gestured towards him. 'What is your involvement in this matter? Why are you here with them, looking like some itinerant trinket salesman?'

'Boudica asked me to speak for them, if that was required. She needed someone who was familiar with Roman law and the drafting of wills. I've had plenty of experience of the latter in my role as a commanding officer.'

'I've never been terribly keen on barrack-room lawyers,' said Suetonius. 'I'm even less keen on one of them choosing to represent the interests of a bunch of barbarians.'

'The Iceni are our allies, sir,' Cato insisted. 'They have sworn the oath. They are entitled to be treated fairly in return, wouldn't you agree?'

'I might agree, but I am not sure about this business over a will. I'll have to see what it says and then discuss the matter with Decianus here before we report back to Rome for a final decision on its legality. Very well, I'll hear what the Iceni queen has to say. She is to present herself to me here in the office once the other tribes have handed over their tribute.'

'Yes, sir.' Cato was relieved. 'Thank you.'

'Don't thank me too quickly,' said Suetonius. 'I have another task in mind for you. But we'll deal with the Iceni business first. Now, is there anything else?'

'No, sir.'

'Then you are dismissed. Go and report back to this barbarian queen you are so anxious to help. Bring her back here once we're done with the others.'

★ ★ ★

'Something other in mind?' Macro frowned as they sat with Boudica on one of the benches in the anteroom. The queen held the saddlebag containing what was left of the tribute in her lap. 'What do you think he meant?'

Cato shrugged. 'No idea. But I didn't get the impression I'll be too pleased when he tells me. Anyway, one thing at a time. We're here to help our friends.'

Boudica forced a smile. 'I'm glad my people and I still have friends amongst the Romans. Honourable ones at that.'

'Not all of us are like that snake Hormanus,' said Macro.

'I know. But he's not alone. Too many of your people treat us like servants or see us as dupes for their sharp practice. And back in Rome, your masters think us mere barbarians, one remove from cattle.'

Her words stung Cato. Not because they were offensive, but because they carried the truth of the relationship between the emperor and the most distant of those he ruled with a diffidence that was proportional to their proximity to the capital.

'That will change in time. Once the province is finally at peace and able to enjoy the full benefits of our civilisation.'

'What makes you think we want that? Do you not think we are not happy with our own civilisation?'

'I imagine so,' he conceded. 'But it is likely that Rome is here to stay, and Romans and Iceni must find a way to live alongside each other for all our sakes.'

'Then let's hope your governor feels the same way.'

She turned away and looked up at the latticed window high on the opposite wall. Outside, the sun was setting, and the last warm glow on the wooden window frame was fading.

The scrape of the latch on the door to the governor's office drew the eyes of all three. Decianus stood there regarding them coolly for an instant before he spoke. 'The governor is ready to see you now. But who is this?' He stared at Macro, and there was a flicker of anxiety in his eyes.

'Ah, so you do remember me,' Macro said as he stood up. 'Last time I saw you, or rather your back, was when you abandoned me and the lads from Camulodunum to fight our way out of the hornets' nest you had stirred up.'

That had been a year earlier, Cato reflected, when the procurator had led a small column of veterans on a punitive expedition against a Trinovantian settlement responsible for the murder of a tax collector. It was Decianus who had drawn first blood, and then, when the tribesmen had turned on Macro and the veterans, the procurator had fled the scene with his mounted bodyguards. The others had had to retreat on foot, harried every step of the way. It would be a long time before the cowardice of Decianus was forgotten by the old soldiers of Camulodunum.

The procurator winced and beckoned to them before hurriedly withdrawing out of Macro's reach. Inside the office, the governor had taken off his armour and sat at his desk in a red military tunic and sandals. A slave was busy adding fuel to the brazier that heated the room, fanning the glowing embers until the flames burst into life and began to consume the split logs that had been added to the iron basket.

Suetonius glanced towards him. 'Get out.'

The slave bowed deeply and backed away a few steps before turning to leave through a small door in the corner. In the opposite corner, Cato saw a neatly stacked pile of chests and bulging bags of sturdy cloth. Beside them was a wide table on which a large waxed slate ledger and a stylus lay close to an oil lamp stand. At the other end stood a pair of scales.

'Let's get on with this,' Suetonius said. 'It's been a long day and I'm tired. I'll be leaving Londinium at first light, and I want this matter resolved before I go.'

Boudica approached his desk, flanked by Cato and Macro. The governor frowned at the latter.

'I remember you. The senior magistrate from Camulodunum. Centurion . . .'

'Macro, sir. Centurion Marcus Cornelius Macro.'

'Yes. Why are you here with these others?'

'They are my friends, sir. I stand with them.'

'Queen Boudica seems to have a few friends amongst my officers. I do hope you recall which side you are on.'

Macro took a sharp breath and Cato interceded. 'Since Rome and the Iceni kingdom are allies, sir, I imagine we are all friends.'

Suetonius was silent before he gave a nod. 'Quite so. And I am anxious that we remain that way, though that may well depend on the outcome of this meeting.' He sat back and looked at the saddlebag in Boudica's hands. 'I take it that is the tribute owed to Rome.'

'It is.'

'Decianus.' The governor gestured. 'If you please.'

The procurator took the saddlebag and placed it on the table before opening the ties and folding back the hem to reveal the gleam of silver coins. He reached in to pick one at random, and scored it heavily with his stylus before nodding with satisfaction. He then heaved the bag onto the scales and set the measurement with counterweights, pausing to let them settle before turning to Suetonius. 'Less than a quarter of what is required, sir.'

'Less than a quarter,' the governor repeated as he stared at Boudica. 'How do you propose to make up the shortfall?'

'I can't,' she replied. 'My nobles had to hand over almost

everything they had to trade for the silver you demanded. Your grain merchants paid far below the usual rate for the grain, and your traders did the same for furs and jewellery.'

'I am not responsible for the deals your people struck,' Suetonius replied.

Cato felt his temper rise. Rome demanded payment in coin, while most of the tribes were accustomed to paying taxes in grain, or gold and silver torcs and suchlike. The situation was often exploited by greedy traders, who paid well below the odds for the goods the tribes were obliged to sell to obtain the coin required. Sometimes the traders and the tax collectors were the same person, paying silver for goods and then taking it back in taxes, and profiting from both transactions. Such unscrupulousness was of little concern to the likes of Suetonius and Decianus.

He took a half-step forward to intervene. 'Sir, the Iceni honoured their obligation to gather the tribute. It would have been handed over to you today had it not been for the theft of the silver by a Roman slave drover. The Iceni have met their obligation in good faith. They should not be punished for the actions of our own people.'

'Assuming the theft did occur,' Decianus interrupted. 'These natives never cease scheming to avoid their taxes.'

Cato turned on him. 'I was there, remember? I witnessed it. Are you accusing me of lying?'

Decianus hesitated before responding, not willing to challenge the word of an officer of Cato's rank. 'Of course not, Prefect. You are a man of honour. Your reputation is well known. However, it's possible that this Hormanus was acting in concert with the Iceni to fool you into thinking a theft had taken place.'

'That is nonsense,' Cato scoffed.

'Really? Did you inspect the other bags that were supposed to contain silver?'

'No,' he conceded. 'Why would I?'

'Then you admit that you don't know for certain that there was ever coin in them?'

'Why would I doubt it?'

Decianus gave him a look of pity. 'Perhaps you are too honourable. Too trusting. A wiser man might have wanted to make sure.'

'This is bollocks!' Macro fumed. 'We were travelling with Boudica as friends. You don't go rummaging about in your friends' baggage on the off chance things aren't as they seem. For fuck's sake . . .'

'There's something else you seem to have overlooked,' Boudica said quietly. 'The Romans cut the throats of two of my warriors before they made off with the tribute. Do you think I'd permit that as part of this conspiracy you are trying to paint?'

'It's possible,' Decianus countered. 'It might have crossed my mind if I were in your position.'

'Then I give thanks to our gods that my people have never had to be ruled by a man with as little integrity as you.'

'How dare you?' Decianus snarled. 'You forget yourself, woman.'

'I am a queen,' she replied calmly. 'You will call me Majesty from now on.'

'Majesty? I will do no such thing. You—'

'That will do.' Suetonius slapped his hand on the desk. 'Quiet!'

There was a strained atmosphere for a few beats before the others in the room turned towards the governor and waited for him to continue.

'I don't doubt the word of Prefect Cato. I don't doubt that the tribute was stolen by this man Hormanus and his gang. Whatever fanciful speculations the procurator may spin about the deed.'

Decianus opened his mouth to protest, but thought better of it.

'Nonetheless, the theft of the silver is not my concern. It is your responsibility to pay the tribute, Queen Boudica, and you have failed to do so, whatever the reason. It is for you to make good the shortfall.'

'And if I can't?'

'You must. That is all there is to it. That matter is closed.' He made a sideways gesture with his hand. 'There remains the question of the will you wish me to consider. You have it with you, I take it?'

Boudica was still for a moment, struggling to take in the abrupt dismissal of her hopes for leniency over the loss of the tribute. Then she reached into the folds of her cloak, bringing out the leather tube containing the document and laying it on the table in front of Suetonius. He regarded it before speaking again.

'To spare me having to read through it all, what are the terms of the will?'

'My husband reaffirms the alliance of our people and Rome. He acknowledges our gratitude for the protection Rome has offered us in exchange for the alliance. As a gesture of gratitude, he confers upon Emperor Nero the honour of being co-heir of the kingdom of the Iceni. I am named as the other co-heir.'

'The honour?' Decianus gave a dry chuckle. 'The honour of inheriting half a spread of crude huts peopled by barbarians scraping a living from bog land. I am sure the emperor will feel humbled by such an honour.'

'Be quiet,' Suetonius ordered. He focused his attention on Boudica. 'Your husband chose to leave half his property to Nero. I dare say the emperor may choose to take such a decision at face value and demand his share in full. But that is not what you hoped for, I dare say. Your husband imagined that Nero would be flattered but would have little interest in inheriting half a tribe in some faraway province, and that your life and those of your people would continue unchanged. Am I correct in that assumption?'

'I hoped your emperor would be grateful for the honour bestowed upon him and would look favourably upon my people and treat us in the same spirit of generosity.'

Suetonius smiled shrewdly. 'I imagine you would hope that. Then we must both wait until the will is sent to Rome for the emperor to consider and let us know how he chooses to respond. In the meantime, we must return to the question of the unpaid tribute. I will give you three months to make good. If in that time you fail to do so, I will send Decianus to your capital to draw up an inventory of the land and possessions of your tribe, and then we will seize property to the value of the sum required to fulfil the tribute that was due.'

'Three months?' Boudica's voice rose to a shrill, angry pitch. 'It took us twice that time to amass the original tribute.'

Suetonius raised his hand. 'I have made my decision. How you deal with it is your concern. The matter is closed. You may leave us now.'

Macro looked at Cato and shook his head.

'Sir, if I may?'

'The matter is closed,' Suetonius repeated. 'Do not test my patience if you want to avoid me making the terms even less palatable.'

Boudica turned away in disgust and strode from the room.

Macro hesitated, and was about to follow her when the governor addressed him.

'Not you. Remain where you are. I've not finished with you, or Prefect Cato. We've important matters still to attend to, gentlemen.'

# CHAPTER NINE

Cato's instinctive response to the command was to fear that Claudia Acte's true identity had been discovered and that they were about to be arrested and returned to Rome to face the wrath of Emperor Nero. He could not think of any other reason. He glanced at Macro, who gave the slightest of shrugs before they both turned back towards Suetonius. The governor had observed the wordless byplay with a look of amusement.

'Why is it that my subordinates think they are in trouble when I ask them to remain after others leave a meeting? Could it be they suffer from a guilty conscience? On reflection, that is usually the case.' He paused and then laughed. 'Relax, gentlemen, you are not in trouble. At least not in the sense you might have been expecting.'

His words did little to calm Cato's unease. Some sixth sense made him feel certain that he would not welcome whatever the governor was about to tell them. Suetonius turned his gaze to Macro.

'As senior magistrate of the closest centre of Roman power, it falls to you to assist the procurator in drawing up an inventory of the Iceni kingdom and ensuring that the rest of the tribute is forthcoming.'

'That's assuming Queen Boudica does not gather what is outstanding, sir,' said Cato.

'That's precisely what I am assuming, Prefect. Unless you care to explain how she is to find what is needed?' Suetonius's challenge went unanswered, and he nodded. 'We can agree on my assumption then. Centurion Macro, you will be under the command of the procurator and carry out that duty.'

Macro shook his head. 'With respect, sir, I won't do it.'

'Won't do it?' Suetonius frowned.

'I refuse to serve under that coward.' Macro jerked his thumb in the procurator's direction without deigning to look at him. 'He was responsible for the deaths of a score of good men and ran from the fight he'd started. If he'd been a soldier, he'd have been executed for desertion in the face of the enemy.'

'But he's not a soldier, Centurion. He's a civilian official and he was carrying out his duty in the incident you are referring to. Yes, I've heard his side of it and I am satisfied that it would not have affected the outcome if he had remained with you and your men. As it was, he raised the alarm the moment he reached an army outpost, though sadly too late to be of much use.'

'You're telling me,' Macro growled. 'Like I said, I will not serve under him; if I did, I couldn't be held responsible for what might happen to him.'

'That's enough, Centurion! I will not tolerate threats made by those who serve under me. I don't much care for whatever personal grievance you may claim to have; I have no time to waste over petty differences. You are still an officer in the reserves, as well as the senior magistrate of the colony. As such, you are obliged to obey any order I give you. And I am ordering you to assist the procurator in ensuring that Boudica and her tribe meet their obligations. For the duration of that duty you will obey him just as you would any other officer placed in a position of authority over you. Is that perfectly clear, Centurion? Or would you rather I stripped you of your rank and found someone else to assume your responsibilities and privileges?'

Macro breathed deeply before he replied. 'It is clear, sir.'

Out of the corner of his eye, Cato saw Decianus fold his arms with a look of satisfaction.

'Very well.' Suetonius sighed impatiently. 'The matter is resolved. I have no further need of you or the procurator. You are both dismissed. Centurion, I'd be obliged if you would refrain from beating the daylights out of Decianus the moment you are outside the room. And Decianus, I'd not be very understanding if you made any attempt to goad Macro or abuse my trust in placing him under your command. Are we clear, gentlemen? Don't vex me any further. Now get out.'

Decianus made for the door first, anxious to put some distance between himself and the man whose life he had endangered. Macro made himself pause, fists clenched, before he nodded a salute to the governor and left the office, closing the door firmly behind him. Suetonius shut his eyes and breathed deeply before opening them again to address Cato.

'I have enough to deal with without that sort of thing.'

'Then it might have been better to find someone else to serve under the procurator, sir.'

'I warn you not to weigh in on the matter, Prefect. My decision has been made and those two will do their damned duty or have me to answer to.'

'Yes, sir.'

'So now we turn to my reason for holding *you* back.'

Here it comes, thought Cato, and he clasped his hands tightly behind him.

'You may be surprised to know that I was aware of your record before I was appointed governor of Britannia. Those senators who have a military background tend to share their opinions about the merits and failings of those who have served under them. Your name came up on a number of occasions. Legate Vespasianus, for example, has a particularly high opinion of you. Courageous, resourceful and talented were the words, as I recall. Indeed, Vespasianus even ventured the opinion that you might rise to become the Prefect of Aegyptus one day. Would you agree with that judgement?'

It was not just professional modesty that prevented Cato from assenting. He felt he was being tested. Suetonius was ready to judge him according to the next words he spoke. He was also relieved that the conversation so far had not steered towards the identity of Claudia, and was keen not to give the governor any reason to regard him with disfavour.

'I serve at the will of my superiors, sir. I aim to do my duty to the best of my ability and in the best traditions of the service. If my superiors deem that I have performed to expectation, then it pleases me.'

'I bet it does.' Suetonius grinned. 'Come now, Cato, let's not be coy. I too take pride in what I have achieved. There is nothing wrong in doing so. There should be no false modesty between us. It is no accident that I got this command. Even though I had won some renown for my victory in the Mauretanian campaign, it was by no means certain that I would be picked to govern Britannia. I had to call in every political favour I was owed and gift my villa in Baiae to Nero to get my hands on this prize. And prize it is. When I have defeated the Druids and broken the back of armed resistance in this land, my name will be on everyone's lips throughout the Empire. No political post will be beyond my reach and my family name will rank amongst the most respected in Rome.'

He paused, then leaned forward as he fixed his eyes on

Cato's. 'You could have a share of that glory. The gods know you deserve it after all you have done in the service of Rome. It's time for you to put your skills and reputation to the ultimate test. I need an outstanding officer at my side when I lead the army into the mountains. I need someone who has fought there before; who knows the ground and can anticipate the dangers facing us. I need someone who has won the respect of the men. I need an officer with the ambition and determination to see it through and ensure that he plays his part in my victory. I believe you are that man, Cato. You have achieved much for someone of such lowly origins, I think you will agree?'

A back-handed compliment if ever there was one, Cato mused. Then he saw that his superior was waiting for a response.

'What exactly is the position you are offering me, sir? Chief of your staff?'

'No. That post is already filled. He's a good organiser, but no field commander. I have something more in keeping with your abilities. The unit I have chosen as the vanguard for the army is the Eighth Illyrian auxiliary cohort. They're one of the larger formations, with a complement of over a thousand, including a mounted contingent. The men were hand-picked for the job by the previous commander, recruited from the mountain tribes of Illyria, and they have been trained hard over recent months. A choice command, as I am sure you realise. Now it's yours.'

'I wonder what the current commander will say about it. Him, and his men.'

'Not much. Prefect Rubrius died ten days ago. Riding accident. A simple fall, but it broke his neck.'

'A sad loss.'

'True enough, but a fine opportunity for his successor. Do you accept?'

Cato did not reply immediately. It was indeed an opportunity, and one he would have grasped without hesitation under different circumstances. However, it would mean being parted from Claudia and Lucius for several months, and he knew from previous experience of the mountains and the enemy tribes that held them that the campaign would be hard fought. Moreover, if the victory was as resounding as Suetonius hoped, he would be singled out for public attention the moment he returned to Rome. He would find it hard to hide Claudia away if he was in the limelight, and if she was recognised and exposed, it would endanger all three of them.

On the other hand, the ultimate prospect of the command of the garrison and province of Aegyptus was sorely tempting, and not only because it would place him far from unwanted attention. The post would make him rich enough to buy the privacy he needed once his tenure was over. Then it would be a question of living in seclusion until Nero had forgotten his former mistress's breach of the terms of her exile, or until he died and was replaced by a new ruler or regime. The republican in Cato still hoped for the day when supreme power returned to the Senate. Nero and his immediate forebears, Claudius and Caligula, had comprehensively demonstrated the dangers of placing authority in the hands of men who were insane, easily manipulated or simply vain.

'Well?' Suetonius frowned. 'What is your reply, Cato? I would have thought a man of action like you would not need an instant to make such a decision. Are you not a decisive man?'

Cato despised the question. It impelled a naïve answer in the affirmative. In truth, decisions depended on the circumstances. But 'it depends' was not the answer desired by those who posed the question. Ironically, a forthright 'no' – however decisive – was equally unacceptable. He sighed inwardly.

'I accept, sir.'

'Good man, although a touch more gratitude for my generous offer would not go amiss.'

'I do have one condition, sir.'

Suetonius drew a sharp breath. 'You know how to push your luck, don't you? Prefect Cato, you do not get to make conditions. You accept or you decline. If you do the latter, I will not repeat the offer. Nor will I forget your hubris. A man like you needs political patrons. As I pointed out, I know a good deal about your record.' He paused. 'One might also question why a man of your rank and reputation has chosen to lie low in an obscure backwater of Britannia . . .'

Cato felt his heart quicken. Had Suetonius found out about Claudia? The governor left the query hanging for a moment before he continued. 'I also know that you have made enemies as well as having admirers amongst men of influence. Take Senator Vitellius, for example. There's a man who would just as soon slit your throat as order another jar of wine. I don't doubt that his enmity is a result of professional jealousy or some scheme of his that you might have had a hand in foiling. Nevertheless, he has it in for you, and he is steadily building a powerful faction around himself. He is not a man to be crossed. You will need influential friends to protect you in future. Friends like me. Do we understand each other?'

'With blinding clarity, sir.'

Suetonius nodded. 'So you appreciate that you are not in a position to demand conditions. However, as a measure of goodwill, I am prepared to consider any requests you may have. Well?'

'I will need a second in command. Someone I know well and who I can trust.'

'Let me hazard a guess. Centurion Macro?'

Cato nodded. 'We've served together a long time. There is no man I'd rather have at my side, given the nature of the fighting that lies ahead of us.'

'Macro is not available. I have already given him his orders.'

'With respect, sir, it would be better to deploy him where his abilities can be put to the best use without being compromised by the tension that exists between himself and Decianus.'

'I've made it clear that I have no time for such nonsense. Besides, I have other reasons for ensuring that Centurion Macro remains at Camulodunum. I am under no illusions about the discontent amongst the Iceni that may result from Decianus enforcing the payment of the outstanding tribute.'

'I'd say that was a racing certainty,' Cato ventured. 'Why not put it off until after the campaign is over, sir? It would be better not to march into the mountains while there was any risk of trouble to our rear. Why not give the Iceni another year to gather the rest of the tribute?'

'I don't disagree with your point, Cato. But time is a luxury I don't have. The emperor expects the tribute to be delivered to him in Rome as speedily as possible. He will be as unsympathetic as he is uninformed about the situation here on the frontier. Would you want to be the one who had to explain to him that we did not collect the tribute out of fear of how the Iceni might react? Moreover, if I am lenient with the Iceni today, then other tribes may resent what will look like preferential treatment. What if *they* demand more time to pay? I can't make an example of them all, but I can make an example of the Iceni. They must pay up or face the consequences, and the other tribes will learn the lesson.'

'And what if they learn the wrong lesson? What if the Iceni rise up and inspire others to follow suit? With you and the army away in the mountains, who will there be to face down a revolt?'

'I am not a fool, Prefect. There will be more than enough troops left behind to contain any trouble. Most of the Ninth Legion will remain in the fortress at Lindum, and the Second Legion will hold the south-west of the province. Besides which, there are auxiliary detachments in most of the main settlements, besides the garrison here in Londinium and Macro's veterans at Camulodunum. That is the reason why I will not assign Macro to your new command. He is needed at the colony. I am counting on him supporting Decianus and being ready to lead his veterans against the Iceni should they be foolish enough to cause any serious trouble.'

Cato felt a cold anxiety prickle the back of his neck at the prospect of Macro and his veterans having to defend Camulodunum. The place was almost devoid of fortifications, and there were many civilians and women and children living there, Lucius, Claudia and Petronella amongst them.

'Sir, it's my duty to point out that the colony can muster barely enough men to form a single cohort, none of whom is under forty-five years of age. They're seasoned men, to be sure, but past their prime.'

'I imagine your friend Macro would not be best pleased to hear you describe him thus. Only a moment ago you were telling me there was no better man you'd wish to have at your side in the gruelling campaign we are about to face.'

Cato cursed himself for gifting that argument to his superior and tried to find a way out of the trap. 'It's not Macro's fitness I am questioning, sir. It's that of those he will be called on to lead. The older men and those carrying injuries and illness from their time in the ranks. I fear for the safety of the colony. Besides, there is the wider situation. The Londinium garrison is for the most part comprised of the dregs of the province's auxiliary cohorts. A few hundred men who would be brushed aside with ease if they ever faced a determined enemy. The same goes for most of the other garrisons, since I would imagine you have drained them of their best men to fill out the ranks of the units you will be leading against the Druids and their allies. The Second Legion is a fighting unit in name only. In reality, it's little more than a training formation, taking recruits from Gaul to prepare reinforcements for the other legions. That leaves the Ninth as the only effective formation, and I dare say that too has been thinned out to find men for the campaign.'

Suetonius's silence confirmed his last point. Cato could see that it was impossible to try to change any of the governor's arrangements. He had mobilised his forces and would brook no delay in launching them against the hill tribes. The best that could be hoped for was a swift conclusion of the campaign and a redeployment of the army to its former positions before any serious trouble broke out amongst tribes like the Iceni. Particularly the Iceni.

Neither of them spoke before Cato stirred. 'How long do I have to put my affairs in order? I'll need to fetch my kit from the colony and make sure my son is in safe hands before I take up my command.'

'There's no time for that, alas. I am leaving Londinium at dawn tomorrow. You will be riding with me. The Eighth Illyrian is at Deva. They need to complete their provisioning, bring the remounts up to strength and practise mountain-fighting tactics. It's my intention to march on the enemy no later than the end of March. Winter will be over and the ground should be firm enough for our supply vehicles. You must have your men ready by then.'

'Yes, sir.' Cato was struggling to take in these details while at the same time worrying about leaving his son and lover behind. 'What about my kit?'

'You can draw something from the garrison stores for now and arrange for what you need to be sent on to Deva before the campaign gets under way. As for your people, I am sure you can trust Macro to take care of them.'

Macro was going to have his hands full carrying out the orders of the governor and Decianus, Cato realised. He could not burden his friend with further responsibilities. He must find someone reliable to support Macro in his absence.

Suetonius folded his hands. 'The day is drawing to a close. You have preparations to make. Report back to the palace before dawn, ready to ride.' He nodded towards the door to signify that the meeting was over.

'Yes, sir.' Cato saluted, then turned and strode towards the door with an aching heart, torn between duty and the sacrifices that entailed. He must go to war again and leave without being able to say his farewells to those he loved. But Rome had called on him, and once more he must answer.

# CHAPTER TEN

As night fell over Londinium, Macro helped his mother's handyman to build up the fire, filling the inn with warmth to entice customers in and keep them there. A hearty aroma drifted through from the kitchen at the rear of the inn as Portia oversaw the preparation of the mutton stew that was the establishment's speciality. By the time the early-evening drinkers started drifting in, he was sitting at a corner table in the Dog and Deer waiting for his friend. At length his patience was rewarded as Cato ducked under the lintel and closed the door to the street.

'I was starting to think something had happened to you,' Macro greeted him, then saw the grim expression on the other man's face. 'What is it?'

Cato briefly related what had passed between himself and the governor.

'Tomorrow?' Macro's eyebrows rose. 'Shit. Nice of the old boy to give you so much warning. Did he hint at what condition the Eighth Illyrian are in? New boys or veterans?'

'He holds them in high regard.'

'Sure, that's what he's telling you to tempt you into accepting the command. I'll bet they're a green bunch in need of some good drill.' Macro's tone warmed. 'I'd get them into shape quick as bloody boiled asparagus.'

'Sadly, you won't have the chance. You have your orders.'

'Ah, come on, lad. You know I'm the best man for the job. Any fool could nursemaid Decianus while he deals with the Iceni. Frankly, it's the last thing I want any part in. Have a word with Suetonius and sign me up for the Eighth Illyrian.'

'I can't,' Cato responded with regret. 'I already asked for you. The governor refused.'

'Why?'

'He says you are needed at Camulodunum if there's trouble from the Iceni. I agree with him on that.'

Macro glared at him. 'Bollocks to that. Is this because you think I'm getting too old for proper soldiering? Is that it?'

'No, not that,' Cato answered truthfully. 'However, you are married now, to a fine woman, and I don't think I've ever seen you happier than during the months since I arrived in the colony. You've earned your retirement, Macro. I'd like to see you live to enjoy it in peace with Petronella.'

'Ah, come on. Who do you think we're up against? A bunch of hairy-arsed barbarians and their black-robed maniac friends. We'll have them in the bag and be back in Londinium sharing out the booty before summer begins.'

Cato tilted his head slightly to one side. 'We both know that's not true. Those same barbarians chased us out of the mountains the last time you and I had cause to venture there. We lost a lot of good men in the process.'

Macro was still for a moment before he relented and gave a nod. 'That's why you need me with you, brother.'

'I know it. But we both have our orders and that is the end of the matter.' Cato reached into the sidebag beneath his cloak and took out a small leather tube, which he laid down in front of his friend.

'What's this?' asked Macro.

'Letters for Claudia and Lucius. I'd have liked to say goodbye in person, but this will have to do. Tell them I had no choice in the matter. I've tried to explain it all.' He tapped the tube.

He had chosen to write on papyrus to demonstrate the care with which he had committed his thoughts, prayers and tender farewells in writing. A clerk on Decianus's staff had sold him the materials for five denarii – an exorbitant price, but he was content to pay. He had sat down and carefully formulated each phrase before writing it down by the dim light of an oil lamp.

'If anything happens to me, I'd like you to look out for them, if you are willing.'

'Of course. But look here, Cato, you'll return. I'd bet my pension on it. So let's not have you behave like some maudlin recruit on the eve of his first battle, eh?'

'I know.' Cato's brow creased. 'I can't help it. I haven't felt so uneasy about such an undertaking before. A sense of foreboding. I feel it in my gut.'

'That's my mother's cooking talking.'

'I'm serious, Macro.' He leaned forward earnestly. 'And if something happens to me, I need to know that they will be looked after.'

Macro made a brief pained expression. 'All right. You have my word. Though I don't know what kind of a father figure I'll make for young Lucius.'

'You'll do fine. You guided me when I first joined the Second Legion.'

'That was soldiering. The lad will need a proper teacher for the things he'll have to know now that his father is a member of the equestrian class.'

'I've already considered that.' Cato turned to glance towards the door, and then looked around the interior of the inn.

'I can't see any of Boudica's lot. I'd have thought they'd be in for a drink by now.'

'They've gone. They left the moment she returned from the governor's palace. She said something to my mother about wanting to get out of a place contaminated by Rome as soon as possible. Can't say I blame her.'

'How long ago?' Cato felt a surge of alarm. He had wanted to speak to Boudica and reassure her that he would continue to press her case with Suetonius while he was serving under the governor. It was important for her to know that not all Romans were alike, and that he and Macro would stand up for her. It was not difficult to see how her resentment would smoulder on, threatening to burst into flame should the Iceni be subjected to any intolerable provocation.

Macro thought a moment. 'At least two hours, I'd say. They'd be some miles from the town by now. Too late to do anything about it.'

'Look here, Macro, you know as well as I do how delicate the situation is with the Iceni. A lot hangs on how the procurator handles things. Whatever the governor's orders may be, there might come a point where you have to overrule Decianus and take command. He cannot be allowed to stir up trouble when the army is so thinly stretched across the province. You have to do whatever it takes to keep the Iceni at peace.'

'Do whatever . . . and whoever, you mean?'

Cato pursed his lips and nodded. 'Given what's at stake.'

Macro sat back and puffed his cheeks. 'That's quite a step. Do you really think it will come to that?'

'It may. It's a question of weighing the life of one Roman against those of countless others if there's an uprising. Just make sure you don't get caught.'

It was hard to believe they were discussing the murder of a

procurator, Cato reflected. But the fate of the province and its people hung by a thread. For Britannia to remain part of the Empire, Suetonius had to achieve victory against the mountain tribes and the Druids. He could only do that if there was no danger to his rear. If the governor was defeated, Decianus would be an irrelevance, as the more restless of the tribes would be sure to take the chance to rise up and overthrow the Roman invaders. If the procurator stirred the Iceni into revolt, there would be too few soldiers available to contain them, and if the uprising spread to other tribes, Suetonius and his army would be caught between his enemies in the mountains and the rebels to his rear and be annihilated. In either case, the province was doomed. Its future depended upon victory in the mountains and peace throughout the rest of the province. The killing of Decianus would be a small price to pay to ensure that.

Cato suddenly felt very tired. He shifted uncomfortably. 'I could use a drink while we're waiting.'

'Waiting? What for?'

'I need to call in a favour. I've sent for someone to educate Lucius and protect him until I return from the campaign.'

'I thought that was my job.'

'It is. But as you pointed out, some aspects are better handled by other people. Besides, the boy is a handful. He'll need two pairs of eyes on him.' Cato raised his hand to Portia and indicated he wanted something to drink. She nodded and bent to fill a jug from one of the amphorae in the rack behind her.

'I wonder who you have in mind?' Macro mused, and then slapped a hand to his forehead and winced. 'Apollonius . . .'

'Can you think of a better tutor for the boy?'

'Only if you don't want Lucius to turn out as some kind of conniving professional killer with a tongue as sharp as his blade.'

Cato considered this for a moment and shrugged. 'Useful

skills to have nonetheless, given the world we live in. However, I had in mind a more academically pedagogic role for Apollonius. Between him and you, I'll feel content that my son is in good hands. Ah, there he is.'

Macro looked up to see a slender figure stepping off the street and closing the door behind him. He eased back the hood of his woollen cloak to reveal a bony face topped with fair stubble across his crown. Steely grey eyes glanced round the room before he advanced across the interior to join Macro and Cato. His narrow lips parted into a wolfish smile.

'Centurion Macro, what a pleasure. I saw you at the oath-taking earlier. You cut a fine figure as a respectable local politician these days.'

'And a hearty fuck-off to you too,' Macro responded as his mother came to the table with a tray holding a jug and two cups. Her lined faced creased into a welcoming grin as she recognised the new arrival.

'Ah, Apollonius. Good to see you again. Your usual?'

'Usual?' Macro frowned. 'He's a regular?'

'One of my best customers. He enjoys the food, tips well and is polite. You could learn a few things from him about good manners, my boy.'

'You are too kind.' Apollonius bowed his head graciously. 'I would consider patronising no other establishment in Londinium. It has no equal in wine, food and the congeniality of the landlady.'

Portia patted him on the cheek. 'You flatterer.'

Macro rolled his eyes and snorted in disgust as she hurried off to fetch another cup.

'Well, this is nice.' Apollonius rubbed his bony hands together. 'Three old friends meeting over a jar of wine. I got your message at headquarters, Prefect. What's the occasion?

Are the three of us going to be reunited on some vital new mission against desperate odds?'

'Sadly not,' said Macro as he reached for the jug and poured the wine. 'That's Cato's job. Unfortunately, for me in particular, he has another task in mind for the two of us.'

Apollonius's brow creased in amusement as he turned to Cato. 'Oh? And what task would that be?'

'I'm calling in a favour. I need you to do something important for me while I am on campaign with Suetonius.'

'On campaign? I thought you were lying low in Camulodunum.'

'I was.' Cato explained the outcome of his meeting with the governor.

'A new command? Well, I can't say I'm surprised. From what I've heard, Suetonius has been hard pushed to scrape together enough men, and good officers to lead them, for when he goes up against the Druids. He's lucky to have you here in Britannia.' Apollonius thought briefly. 'Not so fortunate for you, though, given the reason you are here at all.'

'Quite.' Cato looked round, but the nearest customer was two benches away and seemed to be busy chatting up one of the prostitutes.

'So what do you need me for?' asked Apollonius. 'Scouting? Interrogation? Intelligence-gathering?'

'More like the opposite of the last,' Macro muttered, enjoying the faint look of confusion on the spy's face.

'I want you to be Lucius's tutor whilst I am away,' Cato explained. 'The boy has to begin his formal education. Oh, he can read and write, but he needs something more challenging, and you have the required erudition. I have a small collection of histories and poetry that I brought with me from Rome. You can start with those once you join him in Camulodunum.

He will be cared for by Claudia, under the protection of Macro. There's a spare room at the house I am renting at the colony. You can use that.'

Apollonius looked disappointed. 'I am not sure that is the best use of my particular skills, Prefect. I've never been a teacher before. More of a student of life, espionage and the quiet disposal of inconvenient persons.'

Cato leaned a little closer. 'It may come to that. There's another reason I'm asking you to take on the role. No one will question your presence in the colony if you arrive as Lucius's tutor. They might be a bit more curious if you just turn up and stay in my house with my son and Claudia while I am gone.'

'I can imagine.'

'You may not have heard the news yet,' Cato continued. 'The Iceni have not paid their tribute and Suetonius has tasked Decianus with seizing whatever wealth he can find to make up the shortfall. I have my suspicions about the man. He might cause us trouble while the army is in the mountains. It's possible he will provoke the Iceni into an uprising.'

The spy's eyes glinted. 'By accident or design?'

'Quite. Either way, he cannot be permitted to do it. I've already made the position clear to Macro. He's been ordered to support the procurator and will command the veterans' detachment that will accompany him. There will be others with Decianus too. A small staff of clerks and some bodyguards, and some of the veteran contingent may uphold the chain of command if there is a confrontation between Macro and the procurator. That's why I need you on hand. When the time comes, stay as close to Macro as you can. If all goes well, Decianus will do his job and Boudica will be able to restrain any hotheads in her tribe. But if Decianus needs to be reined in and Macro is unable to do it, it'll be down to the two of you to handle the fallout. If necessary, you might be forced to deal with the procurator and any of his men who endanger the fragile peace with Boudica and her people.'

'Deal with?' Apollonius repeated tonelessly. 'Discreetly deal with?'

'The more discreetly the better,' Macro said quietly. 'We need to be able to cover our backs when the governor returns to Londinium and asks questions.'

Cato nodded. 'But let's hope it doesn't come to that. If the gods are willing, Suetonius will defeat the enemy and the army will return to their garrisons before there's any trouble that can't be contained. Otherwise . . .' He paused to look round again and then lowered his voice as he casually topped up their cups. 'Otherwise, the province will be torn apart by any uprising and our soldiers and civilians will be surrounded by tribes baying for our blood.'

Apollonius lifted his cup and took a thoughtful sip. 'You paint a very dark picture, Prefect. And no wonder. I've learned some interesting things while I have been working at the governor's palace. There was a man who arrived from Rome several days ago. An agent representing the emperor and a group of senators who have provided loans to some of the rulers of the tribes in Britannia. He has a taste for good wine, so I brought him here and made sure he was in his cups before I teased the truth out of him.' He raised an eyebrow at Macro. 'Thanks to the quality of your mother's cellar, that was not so difficult. It turns out he has been sent to call in the loans, and he carries an imperial warrant to see that the job is done.'

Cato and Macro exchanged a look. Macro sighed. 'The emperor's in on it then. Looks like he wants the province to fail. The bastard's too cowardly to give the order directly and go back on Claudius's decision to conquer the island. The mob wouldn't like that. Not one bit.'

'Indeed,' Cato reflected. 'So the moneylenders get their investment back, with interest no doubt, the province goes up in flames, and Nero has his excuse to pull the legions out and argue that Rome should never have wasted the men and treasure on Britannia in the first place.'

'What about those of us who'd be left behind?' Macro demanded. 'The veterans at the colony. The merchants and traders here in Londinium, like my mother. And those who have built up farms and businesses. What happens to us?'

'What do you think?' Apollonius replied drily. 'You either stay here and fight for what you have, and most likely perish in the attempt, or you pull out with the legions and take the loss.'

'We'd be ruined,' Macro growled. 'Every last sestertius I have is invested here.'

'You think that worries Nero?'

'It should, if he knows what's good for him. If the army sees him throwing veterans like me and the other lads at Camulodunum to the wolves, they're going to question the value of being loyal to the emperor and those around him. It's not as if the legions haven't mutinied in the past.'

Macro had made a telling point, thought Cato with a growing sense of concern. Since the Praetorian Guard had murdered Caligula and placed Claudius on the throne, it had been clear that the army, especially those units closest to the emperor, had the power to make or break a ruler. Nero, despite his immaturity, would understand that. But was he counting on the discontent of those far from Rome not having much impact on his popularity in the capital? Did he think that putting on a few extra gladiator and chariot-racing spectacles would distract the mob from the shame of the retreat from Britannia? It was possible. The common people were inclined to have short memories, and were easily distracted from bad news by entertainments and spectacular ceremonies. The senators were no better, and those who might be disgruntled would be bought off with lucrative political appointments or lavish gifts. Meanwhile, those who had been forced to flee from Britannia and leave their property behind would have to survive as best they could.

But what if Nero had miscalculated? What if the discontent over the loss of the province spread through the ranks of the legions and the streets and salons of Rome? Mutiny and civil war haunted the Empire, and the prospect of a return to the bloodshed of the age of the Second Triumvirate terrified those with an understanding of history. As dominant as the Roman Empire was, it was ever vulnerable to the ambitions of powerful generals, politicians and their factions. The loss of Britannia might be the spark that caused a new conflagration that might tear the Empire apart. If such a fate was to be avoided, there had to be peace amongst the tribes under Rome's sway while Suetonius secured a swift and crushing victory against the Druids and their allies. Cato felt the delicacy of the moment and the ease with which the fate of Rome could slip either way into continued peaceful order, or division and savage conflict.

'You look worried, lad.' Macro broke into his thoughts.

Cato stirred, and drained his cup. 'I have every reason to be. May the gods preserve us.'

# CHAPTER ELEVEN

The governor's party separated as it reached the huge expanse of open ground where the army was gathered. It was late in the afternoon and sunlight cast long shadows across the burnished landscape. While Suetonius and his staff made for the fortress of the Fourteenth Legion, Cato was directed to the camp of the Eighth Illyrian. The fortress had been expanded to accommodate the contingents drawn from the Twentieth and Ninth legions, and sprawled across a large area. A series of smaller marching camps surrounded it, each protected by a ditch and rampart topped with a palisade. These had been constructed by the auxiliary cohorts that had been concentrated around Deva in preparation for the coming campaign.

In addition to the fortress and the camps, there were a number of other fortified areas, where the supply wagons were parked, stockpiles of food and equipment were massed, and thousands of mules, oxen and cavalry remounts were penned. Sentries patrolled the walkways or kept watch over the surrounding landscape as foraging parties came and went and supply columns trundled into the mobilisation area. The inevitable vicus, a modest shanty town of hurriedly constructed buildings, stood off to one side, set up by the camp followers, merchants, traders, prostitutes and other entertainers ready to exploit off-duty soldiers with money to spend and few places to spend it.

The camp of the Eighth Illyrian was larger than those of the other auxiliary units, as the cohort comprised a cavalry contingent in addition to nearly five hundred infantry. The mounted men were divided into four squadrons, each made up of three troops of thirty riders, and with the extra farriers, drovers and headquarters staff, Cato's new command came to around a thousand soldiers. Auxiliary units of such a size were rare, and were commanded by hand-picked men. The previous prefect, Gaius Rubrius, had been such a man, so Cato had been told. The cohort had already won an enviable reputation since arriving in the province, and his diligent training had improved the unit further still.

For that reason, Cato was keen to prove himself a worthy replacement when he approached the cohort's marching camp ten days after leaving Londinium with Suetonius and his retinue. Reining in a hundred paces from the main gate, he paused to inspect the regular line of the ditch and the rampart, and the horsemen exercising on the open ground outside. Under the watchful eyes of their officers, the riders were weaving between rows of stakes, striking at them from right and left with their swords. Cato could make out the gleam of medals on the harnesses worn by some of the decurions, and wished he was wearing his own medals and armour. It would have made a good initial impression on the men, he reflected regretfully, but there was nothing he could do about that for now.

He felt self-conscious about his appearance. He was wearing a simple military cloak over the tunic and leggings he had drawn from the stores of the garrison at the governor's palace. His sword and the spare clothes he had brought with him from Camulodunum were in the leather bags hanging from the weathered horns of his saddle. There had been no time to buy any kit or other necessaries before setting off, and he would be fortunate if the items he had sent for reached him before the army marched into the mountains. The silver in his purse would barely be sufficient to purchase a suitable helmet and armour. Unless the governor's quartermaster was prepared to advance him some pay, he would face the humbling possibility of having to ask another officer to lend him money to complete the equipment and supplies needed for the campaign.

He had got to know a handful of his companions on the road – the usual mix of young tribunes excited about their first military operation and a handful of more seasoned officers some of whom he recognised from his previous period of service in Britannia seven years before. From the latter he discovered that even though the legions were under strength, there were many still in the ranks with plenty of experience of fighting the mountain tribes. Morale was high in most of the units chosen for the campaign and the naval squadron assigned to support the army. After a succession of governors who had been content merely to defend the territory already subdued, the soldiers of Rome were keen to finish the conquest of the island.

While Cato was gratified to observe their confidence, he knew that even if the Druid stronghold on the island of Mona was destroyed, there were still tribes in the highlands to the north who remained implacably hostile to Rome and would offer spirited resistance when the legions moved against them. Even though the invasion had begun seventeen years earlier, there was still resistance from the tribes of Britannia, and he wondered if there would ever come a time when the province would know untroubled peace and prosperity. In the meantime, its fate was being deliberated by the emperor and his advisers. Their decision might well rest on the outcome of the coming campaign. A victory would buy the province a breathing space, while defeat, or a protracted period of conflict, might tip the scales in the favour of those politicians agitating for the abandonment of Britannia. And so Cato had gone along with the optimism of his companions and offered words of encouragement to those young tribunes who had sought him out around the campfire to ask advice from an old hand.

He smiled at that. He had served for so many years, it was hard to recall what it had felt like to be a raw recruit. The callow and anxious youth who had pitched up at the fortress of the Second Legion shivering from the cold and rain was a stranger to him these days. Indeed, he was now about the same age as Macro had been when they first met. He could recall the nervous respect with which he had once regarded his closest friend and comrade. Macro's grizzled features and the puckered white scars on his limbs and face had made him look fearsome. It amused Cato to think that he himself was now a similar figure of veneration for recruits and the young officers around him. He certainly carried as many scars as Macro ever did, and had the same air of an experienced warrior about him.

Encouraged by that thought, he urged his horse forward again, making for the narrow causeway that crossed the ditch and led into the camp. The sentry at the gate stepped into his path and grounded his javelin.

'Halt! Name and business?'

Cato swung his leg over the saddle horns and dropped to the ground. 'Prefect Quintus Licinius Cato. I've been appointed to command the Eight Illyrian.' He held up the tube containing Suetonius's letter of appointment to reveal the governor's seal.

The sentry looked him up and down before nodding and moving aside. 'You may pass, sir.'

Cato led his mount forward. On the far side of the gatehouse, he paused to take in the neat rows of turf and timber huts and the horse lines. Several large buildings dominated the centre of the camp. The absence of tents indicated that the cohort had been in position long enough to construct winter quarters. The recent thaw had turned the lanes between the buildings and the clear ground behind the rampart into stretches of mud and puddles that squelched underfoot as he made for the headquarters building in the heart of the camp.

Those men out in the open spared him little regard as he passed by. Without any sign of his rank, he could have passed for a lowly messenger or even a civilian come to conduct some business. He made no attempt to call attention to himself, content to make mental notes as he passed by the timber and daub barrack blocks and store sheds with their bark shingle roof tiles. The men looked to be in good shape, ranging from fresh-faced younger auxiliaries to veterans with lined features, with few who seemed either too young or too old. The previous commander had done a good job of weeding out those who might not cope with the rigours of campaigning in the mountains. Contrary to Macro's comments, there did not seem to be any need to get the Eighth Illyrian licked into shape. They appeared tough and ready for action.

The headquarters and commander's accommodation formed three sides of an open square, with the largest building in the centre. Cato approached the tethering rail to the side of the entrance and called out to a passing soldier.

'You there! On me.'

The long-established authority in his voice caused the man to trot across and salute.

'Have my bags taken to the prefect's quarters and then have my mount unsaddled, groomed and fed before joining the horse lines.'

'Yes, sir.'

They exchanged a salute before Cato adjusted his tunic and cloak. He drew his sword and scabbard from his pack and slipped the strap over his shoulder, letting the weapon hang comfortably at his side before reattaching the cloak clasp at his shoulder. Then he strode towards the entrance of the largest building.

The interior comprised an open area that took up most of the space, with a handful of rooms at each end. Several men were working at campaign tables laden with wax tablets and scrolls. Most of the latter protruded from small leather tubes, and Cato recognised them for what they were: military wills awaiting an official seal before being added to the cohort's records chests for safe keeping. Most men made wills before embarking on a campaign. Some chose not to, perhaps fearful of tempting fate, and if they failed to return, their personal effects and kit would be auctioned by their units to raise funds for any dependents they had.

Cato approached the optio sitting on a stool at the end of the row of tables. 'I'm looking for the officer in temporary command.'

'Centurion Galerius? He's in the prefect's office.' The optio looked Cato over before he continued. 'What is your business with the centurion?'

'I'm the new prefect,' Cato explained as he presented the governor's letter of appointment. 'Quintus Licinius Cato, assuming command of the cohort.'

The optio hurriedly rose from his stool and stood to attention. 'Yes, sir. I'll take you to the centurion directly. This way, sir.' He led the way to the middle door of the offices to the right and rapped on the door.

'Come!'

The optio opened the door and stood aside to let Cato enter. The prefect's office was a modest space some ten feet across, with a planked floor and illuminated by a window on the wall at the rear. A simple campaign table, a handful of stools and some chests of documents comprised the only furnishings. A wide-shouldered man with thinning brown hair and dark brown eyes looked up from the wax tablet he had been examining.

'Yes?' His brow furrowed slightly. 'And you are?'

Cato removed the cover from the leather tube as he took two steps to reach the table. Pulling out the scroll within, he handed it to the centurion.

'I am Prefect Quintus Licinius Cato, appointed to replace Prefect Rubrius.'

Galerius nodded as he flattened out the document and read through it quickly, then tapped the governor's seal. 'It would seem your authority is in order, sir.' He extended his hand and the two officers clasped forearms. 'Welcome to the Eighth Illyrian, Prefect Cato. I hereby relinquish command.' His tone was formal and flat. 'I'll have the desk cleared and my papers taken to my old office at once, sir.'

Without waiting for a response, he looked past Cato towards the optio waiting outside. 'Callopius, move this lot next door.'

'Yes, sir.'

As the optio set to work, Galerius waved Cato to the stool behind the table and pulled up one of the spare stools from the side of the room. 'Mind if I sit, sir?'

Cato nodded, and the two settled down to the more informal stage of introducing themselves.

'I'm glad you've arrived, sir. I was a bit worried that the army would march before a replacement was appointed. Never easy to take command of a unit on the fly. As it is, you're only going to have a few days to find your feet before the campaign begins.'

'Can't be helped.' Cato shrugged. 'I was only notified about the appointment the day before I left Londinium with Suetonius. I'll need to draw some officer's kit from stores while I wait for my baggage to arrive.'

Galerius picked up a tablet and stylus lying on the table and made a note. 'Any other requirements, sir?'

'A good horse, the best man you have amongst the headquarters staff to act as my secretary, and the strength returns for each of the centuries and squadrons in the cohort.'

'Yes, sir.'

'I'll also want to meet all the officers and optios here at headquarters when the evening watch is sounded.'

Galerius glanced up at the light coming through the window and Cato read his expression. 'Any problem in assembling them by that time?'

'There's a mounted patrol out on the hills, and a foraging party. I can have the decurion and optio report to you when they return.'

'See to it.' Cato regarded the other man closely before he continued. 'How long have you served, Galerius?'

'Twenty-one years, sir. Ten in the current rank and I've been senior centurion for the last three years.'

'How about your service record?'

Galerius collected his thoughts before he began. 'I started out in the Fifteenth Primigenia when Emperor Caligula formed the legion, sir. We were raised for the invasion of Britannia, but when that was delayed, we were redeployed to the Rhenus. I served on a few sweeps across the river before being promoted to optio. After that, the legion was transferred to Vetera, and I served on a number of amphibious operations along the river before word went out that officers were needed for a new auxiliary cohort that was being formed. I applied, and was accepted and promoted to centurion. Been with the Eighth ever since. The cohort served on the Danuvius frontier before being sent here last summer.'

Cato took this in for a moment. The majority of Galerius's experience, and that of the cohort, appeared to be along the great rivers that formed the northern frontier of the Empire. It was possible they had not been tested in mountain conditions. 'What about Rubrius? How long was he in command of the Eighth?'

'Five years, sir.'

'I see.'

Long enough to have forged a solid relationship with the men and officers, which was something of a mixed blessing, Cato reflected. The cohort had enjoyed a period of continuity, and had been forged into a weapon that could be readily wielded by its former commander. However, that now meant that Cato would have to get used to the arrangements he had inherited and then impose his own manner of command on the cohort in due course. A period of adaptation would be required by his men and himself as they got used to each other. There were commanding officers who liked to change things at once. Some carried it off well, but many only succeeded in incurring the resentment of their subordinates, particularly if the changes appeared to serve no purpose other than change itself.

'A good commander, I expect.'

'One of the best, sir,' Galerius replied frankly. 'His death was a sad loss to the lads. He had been training us hard for the coming campaign. He had the men keyed up and ready to win their unit's first decoration.'

'I see.'

'Sir, may I speak freely?'

Cato regarded the centurion warily. He had only just met him, and was anxious not to let Galerius offer advice that might set a precedent for him second-guessing Cato's decisions. Yet if he rebuffed his advice, that might make him seem arrogant and aloof and create tension between himself and the man who was his second in command.

He cleared his throat. 'Thanks to the suddenness of my appointment, you haven't had the chance to find out anything about me on the grapevine at headquarters. I don't have any doubt that you will rectify that as swiftly as possible.'

The two men shared a smile before Cato continued. 'So let me save you some time. This is by no means my first command. I have served as prefect of a number of cohorts across the Empire. Nor is this the first command I have held in Britannia. In fact, you might say I cut my teeth in this province. The invasion was my first campaign. I fought outside Camulodunum when we defeated Caratacus. I was with the Second Legion when we subdued the hill forts of the south-west. I have fought two campaigns in the mountains where we are headed, the last of which ended in retreat in the depths of winter. I know the mountains. I have fought the tribes who inhabit them, and had I had the chance to fetch my baggage before leaving Londinium, I would have the medals on my harness to prove the years of good service I have given Rome, along with the scars I bear on my body.' He gestured towards the vivid white mark that extended from his brow to his cheek, softening his voice as he concluded. 'Centurion Galerius, I am a soldier through and through and I have earned my rank every step of the way. I will not let the men of the Eighth Illyrian down. You have my word on it. Do we understand one another?'

Galerius was silent for a beat before he nodded. 'That's all I wanted to hear, sir.'

'Good. Then pass the word that I want all the officers gathered here this evening. I'll tell them what I have told you. I don't want there to be any doubt about my commitment to the men of the cohort, or their commitment to their new commanding officer. I will do honour to the memory of Prefect Rubrius and together we will win that decoration for the standard that he promised you.'

'Yes, sir.' Galerius stood up and saluted formally. 'Welcome to the Eighth.' This time there was warmth and sincerity in the greeting.

'Thank you, Centurion. Carry on.'

# CHAPTER TWELVE

As a slave built up the fires burning in the braziers at each corner of the hall at headquarters, the officers of the Eighth introduced themselves to Cato one by one. Besides Galerius, commanding the First Century of the cohort, there were five more infantry centurions: Minucius, a swarthy, slight man about the same age as Galerius; Annius, tall and fair with startling blue eyes, the youngest of the centurions; Vellius, a few years older, overweight and nervous-looking; Decius, a solid, self-assured veteran who reminded Cato of Macro; and then Flaccus, a bearded giant with forearms that looked like joints of ham.

The cavalry contingent of the cohort was commanded by Centurion Tubero, another tough-looking officer who seemed to regard the infantry officers with a degree of aloofness. It was not uncommon for those in the cavalry to behave that way, given that they enjoyed more pay and considered themselves a cut above the trudging foot soldiers. Tubero's squadron commanders, Decurions Ursinus, Albinus and Ventidius, were in their early thirties, spare men with dark hair and tanned skin who had all been recruited from the same tribe in Macedonia.

They seemed as professional a group of officers as any Cato had encountered in the auxiliary cohorts of the army, and yet he sensed an edge to them as they formed their first impression of their new prefect. It was always a test when a commander and his subordinates met for the first time, Cato reflected. He clasped his hands behind his back as he drew a calming breath.

'You men have been fortunate to have a man like Rubrius in command of the cohort when it needed to be prepared for the challenges we face in the coming months. I have encountered the tribes we are going up against and I know how tough and skilled they are when it comes to mountain fighting. I have experienced the hardships of their lands and I have few illusions about the dangers we face together. When I was appointed to replace Rubrius, I was informed how well he had prepared the Eighth Illyrian. The governor himself told me that the cohort was the best auxiliary unit in the army and had been chosen to lead the vanguard into enemy territory. It is a great honour he has bestowed on you, and it is a great honour he has done me in appointing me your commander. Together we will honour the memory of Rubrius. He will look upon our triumphs from the shades and be content that his hard work and fine example have made it possible for the Eighth to win the fame that is ours for the taking.'

He paused to let his words sink in, and was gratified by the keen glow in the expressions of his officers. They had responded well to the emotional appeal of his rhetoric; now it was time to win over their reason. Cato turned to the table and unrolled a large strip of cured goat hide upon which he had marked out a crude map drawn from memory of the disastrous previous campaign he had fought against the mountain tribes and their Druid allies.

'Gather round,' he ordered.

The men shuffled closer, forming a tight ring around Cato and the map. He moved the lamp stand to a position where its light would illuminate the details. 'This is Deva.' He indicated their position. 'To the west, the coastline stretches towards the island of Mona, here. As you can see, there is a narrow channel running between the mainland and the island. That is as far as the Roman army got the last time we tried to destroy the Druids and pacify the mountain tribes. It is a formidable obstacle, but this time Suetonius has ordered the building of collapsible boats to allow us to cross. We will also be supported by a squadron from the navy. While taking Mona is the ultimate goal of the campaign, the governor intends to crush what remains of the resistance amongst the Deceangli and the Ordovices.' He gestured to the areas of the map indicating the lands of the two tribes.

'Suetonius outlined his campaign plan to me while we were on the road from Londinium. It is his intention to divide the army into two columns. The first will make for the coast and follow it to Mona. This column will take with it the boats, artillery and heavy equipment needed for the assault on the island. It will be supplied from the sea as it advances. The column will comprise the Fourteenth Legion and two auxiliary units under the overall command of the legate of the Fourteenth. The second column, the more powerful of the two, will be made up of the legionary contingents of the Twentieth and Ninth legions and the remaining cohorts of auxiliaries, including ours. The main column will be commanded by Suetonius and will march south to Viroconium, here, and then swing west to cross the mountains and destroy the remaining Ordovician strongholds. We will drive the enemy back towards Mona, where we will unite with the other column and finish the job by crossing the strait and conquering the island.'

Cato straightened up as he delivered his conclusion. 'The campaign will be over by early summer at the latest. If all goes according to plan, that is,' he added with a hint of irony, and there were a few dry chuckles from the other officers. 'As we know, plans have an unerring ability to stumble and fall the moment they leave the starting gate. I imagine you have a few points to raise, gentlemen. You may speak freely.'

It was a calculated invitation. His subordinates might not be willing to offer any comment to their new commander that might be taken as a criticism of the governor. At the same time, Cato did not want to appear the kind of superior who refused to hear the reasoned arguments of his officers.

Galerius spoke first. 'From previous experience, it would be unwise to divide our army, sir. It might tempt the enemy to try and defeat us in detail.'

It was the obvious observation, and one that Cato had offered to Suetonius when the governor had first outlined his plan. However, Suetonius had had a ready response.

'The governor has determined that the northern column will be adequately supported by our warships. By the time it leaves Deva, we will have moved well into the mountains and drawn the enemy down on us before they are aware of the advance of the other column.'

Centurion Tubero gave a dry laugh. 'Sounds like we're the ones who are going to be in the thick of it while the others swan around the seaside.'

'They'll have enough trouble making sure the baggage train advances on schedule,' Cato responded. 'But you're right, we'll be facing the stiffest resistance. And the Eighth Illyrian will be the spear point of the Roman thrust into enemy territory. We'll be the first to make contact, and the attention of the governor and the rest of the army will be on us to see how we perform. Suetonius will expect us to clear the way for the column, scout ahead and on the flanks, and pin any enemy warbands in place so that the heavy infantry can finish them off.

'We are the eyes, ears and teeth of the army, gentlemen. The success of the campaign will depend upon how well we perform our duty. If we do it well, the Eighth will win the decoration I know it is thirsting for. Who knows? If our contribution to the victory is mentioned in the governor's report to the emperor, then such a decoration may be the least of our rewards. The members of an auxiliary cohort have all been granted Roman citizenship for outstanding deeds in the past. Have your men think on that. And since we will be the vanguard of the army, it is more than likely that we will have the pick of any booty we come across.'

He let the prospect of the honours and riches to be had tempt the imaginations of his officers for a moment. In truth, he was aware of the danger of the cohort winning too much fame back in Rome. Questions might be asked about its new commanding officer, given that he was still on the active list of the Praetorian Guard and should therefore be residing in Italia. On the other hand, nothing excused like success. If he led the Eighth Illyrian to victory and glory, it would be difficult for Nero and his advisers to make life difficult for him. Rulers needed victories and heroes keep the mob happy, just as a man needed to breathe air. If Cato and his men came out of the campaign well, the reason for his presence in Britannia might be overlooked. Of course, that did not remove the need to continue concealing Claudia's true identity.

One of the other centurions caught his eye and Cato nodded.

'On the question of booty,' Decius began, 'what is the arrangement this time?'

The division of riches derived from a campaign was within the purview of the army's commander. Some used their position to claim the lion's share for themselves and reward the soldiers with crumbs from the feast. Others with an eye to political advancement gifted most of the proceeds to the emperor, or used them to pay for public entertainments and banquets to win over the mob. Those generals desiring a longer military career tended to ensure that their troops benefited the most in order to maintain their morale and, more importantly, their loyalty. In Suetonius's case, the division of the spoils was a much easier matter to resolve, given the poverty of the mountain tribes. There would be some gold and silver jewellery, maybe some coin too. Other than that, the main source of riches would come from the proceeds of selling prisoners into slavery. The rewards would not be enough to tempt Suetonius into claiming for himself more than was wise. His largesse would cost him little while his soldiers would laud him for the prize money that would allow them to drink themselves into oblivion when they returned to Deva.

'The governor has determined that the booty will be shared by all ranks, in proportion to pay levels,' Cato announced. 'I trust that satisfies you, Decius.'

The centurion nodded, and there were murmurs of approval at the prospect of a reward that while not large enough to be life-changing, was welcome nonetheless.

'Needless to say, the booty is going to have to be earned. Since the Eighth will be the first into the fight, we're going to take the first casualties, and maybe the most casualties when the final butcher's bill is drawn up.'

That was the sobering reality facing the cohort, and Cato needed the officers to understand and prepare the men accordingly. He cleared his throat before he continued. 'Make sure that every man who wishes to makes his will. Pass that on tonight. Our column will be marching in a matter of days, and I'll need the wills written, signed, witnessed and delivered to headquarters before we leave. So if you gentlemen have property you wish to leave to wives, sweethearts or both . . .' He paused to let the others laugh at the old joke before looking round. 'Any further questions or comments?'

None of the officers spoke.

'Very well. I know my appointment was made at short notice and that's not what any of us would wish for under normal circumstances. It can't be helped. This is the first chance we have had to size each other up. We'll get to know each other better in the coming days. In the meantime, if there are any matters you wish to bring to my attention, then speak freely to me. In my experience, a good commander needs an open ear as well as a commanding voice.' He lifted the leather tube containing Suetonius's appointment from the table. 'There will be a full parade in the morning when I present my authority to the cohort. That will be all for now. Dismissed.'

Galerius remained as the others left the room before turning to face his new commander.

Cato arched an eyebrow. 'Centurion?'

'Just wanted to say I thought that went well, sir. You remind me of Rubrius. Same direct manner and an understanding of your men. For what it's worth, I think you'll do us proud.'

Cato was not comfortable with the overfamiliar tone of the remark, complimentary as it was. He forced himself to keep his expression neutral as he responded. 'We must do each other proud, Galerius. I lead from the front and I'll not order a man to do anything I am not prepared to do myself. In return, I demand the very best from those under my command. I will not tolerate anything less. Be sure you understand that, and ensure the men do as well; that way the cohort will do what is required of it. Good night.'

Galerius saluted and left the room, closing the door behind him. Cato eased himself onto the stool behind the desk and gazed down at the map. It was as accurate as he could recall from his previous knowledge of the landscape, and he had made a note on the corner based on the itinerary prepared by the governor's intelligence officer. He calculated it would take the column four days to cover the sixty miles to Viroconium. After that, the distances and times were rough estimates. Another eighty miles from Viroconium to the coast, across mountains where every natural obstacle would be stubbornly contested by the enemy, even as they did their best to harass the column. Once the column reached the sea, it would turn north to march the final sixty miles to join the baggage column and naval squadron opposite the island of Mona. It would be hard going, Cato knew. He would do his best not to subject his men to unnecessary dangers, but it was obvious that the Eighth Cohort was going to suffer heavy losses before the campaign was over. He wondered if the real reason that Suetonius had chosen him was not for any reputation he might have earned amongst the high and mighty of Rome, but rather because he was expendable.

Whatever the reason, he was charged with responsibility for the men under his command, and he swore a private oath that he would do his best to lead them to victory and bring as many back to Deva with him as possible. Assuming he was still alive at the end.

Rubrius had not been the kind of commanding officer to indulge himself, and apart from his office, his only accommodation had been the small room adjoining it, where there was a simple wooden-framed bed with a straw mattress, and a stand with a ewer and a sponge. Cato's saddlebags had been placed by the door, and he wearily unpacked his few belongings. The scale armour cuirass he had drawn from the garrison stores he draped across the stool by the wash stand, along with his military cloak. The sword belt he hung from a peg on the back of the door, and the officer's helmet with its faded horsehair crest he set down carefully at the end of the bed. There were items he would need to draw from the cohort's stores the next morning to complete his military kit.

He could not help wondering what the men of his new command would make of their prefect in his tarnished armour and the grubby tunic and cloak he had worn since leaving the military colony at Camulodunum. They might be foolish to judge him so superficially, but judge him they would. They would expect an officer in the finery a man of his social rank could afford, not a figure dressed and equipped from whatever was available from a quartermaster's common stores. Cato knew from his own experience in the ranks that soldiers expected their commanders to come from privileged and affluent backgrounds, and the respect they automatically granted such aristocrats would have to be earned by him.

He wished he knew more about the man he was replacing. He had never heard of Rubrius before his appointment. Had he come from an aristocratic family? Had he been one of those well-groomed men with smooth accents, good looks and an easy charm who considered themselves entitled to the privileges of their class – characteristics that for some reason commanded the admiration of the plebs and the ranks and file of their units? Or had he been like Cato himself? A man from a low social class who had worked his way up through the ranks. It was tempting to find out more about him in order to understand what the men expected of his successor.

He dismissed the thought. He was his own man, with his own way of doing things. He must trust in that and not try to be someone else, the person he thought his men wanted him to be.

He missed having Macro at his side. It was much easier to command when he had such a powerful ally to reinforce his authority and to whom he could speak and ask advice in confidence. But Macro had retired from active service, and it was wrong to resent the fact that his comrade was able to live out the rest of his life in peace. He even missed the company of Apollonius, despite never having been completely at ease with the former spy who had chosen to serve with him in recent years. Apollonius's skill at arms was lethal, and his shrewd intelligence was often useful, even when it was being paraded in the face of others. Now Cato was on his own, far from his friends, his lover and his son and he longed for them all.

By the dim light of the oil lamp hanging from a bracket above the bed, Cato's gaze drifted to the small alcove in the wall that had served as the shrine of the previous prefect. He rose to examine it more closely, and for the first time noticed the small figures of a woman and two children behind the handful of carved icons that Rubrius had worshipped. They were painted with fine dark lines on the pale plaster, and he saw that there was even a dog curled up at their feet. He felt a surge of sadness at the sight. Rubrius's family had probably not heard of his death yet, and even now looked forward to celebrating his return from Britannia. Such were the realities and tragedies of military life across the Empire.

He reached for the likenesses of Fortuna, his personal favourite amongst the gods, and Jupiter, and held the icons to his forehead, closing his eyes as he prayed.

'Fortuna, please grant me the grace of good fortune so that I might be spared from my enemies and come home to my family and friends. May you also grant your favour to the men under my command so that they too might return from war to those they love. Jupiter, best and greatest of the gods, I humbly beseech you that I might serve with courage and devotion to duty and that I do honour to my cohort and the Senate and people of Rome. I ask that you guide my sword and shield to vanquish my enemies and protect me from harm. I ask this not just for myself but for the peace that follows victory. I ask it for all those who have shed blood and given their lives to bring these lands within the embrace of the Empire. I pray that those in Rome whom you have seen fit to appoint to rule us will not betray the memory of those who have died, and that their noble sacrifice will not have been in vain.'

# CHAPTER THIRTEEN

## *March AD 61*

'You could not ask for a more tempting target,' Macro said as he looked down the slope towards the colony.

At his side, Apollonius nodded in agreement as the centurion raised his vine cane and pointed to the main gatehouse. The structure was formidable enough: double arched, with two storeys above and a crenellated sentry platform on top. The causeway crossed a wide and deep ditch that had once run around the legionary fortress upon which the colony had been built. However, a scant twenty feet of rampart and wall extended from either side of the gatehouse before crumbling away to ground level where the walls had been abandoned and scavenged for materials to construct civilian buildings. The same fate had befallen most of the military structures. Those that survived now served as homes, shops and stables.

'What the fuck is the point of a gatehouse if there are no longer walls on either side of it?'

'Well, yes, quite,' Apollonius remarked as his gaze followed the direction Macro had indicated. 'We cannot count on an enemy observing the usual niceties with regard to entering the town in the absence of any other fortifications.'

The dry response missed its mark as Macro scowled at him. 'I'll thank you to contain your humour while we deal with the matter of the colony's defences.'

'My apologies.' Apollonius bowed his head, and both men turned their attention to the layout of the town sprawling across open ground below them. The regular lines of the former fortress had long since been subsumed by the settlement's growth as it overspilled the fortified area and spread out along the routes leading west to Londinium, and north and south into the farmland once owned by the Trinovantes but which was now in the hands of the Roman veterans who had been granted the land by the emperor. The river curved around the northern side of the town before meandering south-east towards the sea. A smaller tributary flanked by marshes flowed along the south of the colony. Neither stretch of water was crossed by bridges as there were fords close by.

With the change of the season, the first cargo ships from Gaul had made the crossing, and now several were moored alongside the wharf, their masts towering over a line of low-lying warehouses. Two hundred paces in from the river was the building site of the theatre and temple that had been begun under the reign of Emperor Claudius. Progress had been slow, and only the stepped pediment and no more than half of the columns had been raised around the inner sanctum. The paved area around the pediment was piled with building materials, and as Macro and Apollonius watched, a team of men in rough tunics was working one of the cranes as an engineer directed the lowering into place of one of the sections of a column. To the south flowed a lesser river that joined the first to the east of the colony.

'It's not just the walls,' Macro continued. 'Most of the ditch has been filled in as well. A man could easily cross the rest of it. Like I said, the place is a tempting target.'

'Assuming there is anyone harbouring hostile intent.'

'Oh, there's plenty of hostile intent about.' Macro pointed to the men hauling the stays of the crane. 'That lot are from the local tribe. Conscripted labour, poorly fed and paid, and being forced to erect a temple dedicated to the emperor who conquered them. You can imagine how well that's going down. Meanwhile, their kin are denied their help working on those farmsteads that are still in tribal hands. That's before we even consider the Iceni to the north. Now that they've been tasked with finding a fresh source of tribute, they're not going to be too happy. And all of 'em know that the governor and most of the province's garrison are marching to the arse end of Britannia, leaving only skeleton forces behind in most of the rest of the province.' Macro thumped his cane into the ground. 'If there's going to be trouble, that's when it'll happen.'

'What do you propose to do about it, Centurion?'

'We need to get our defences in order. There's been too much complacency in recent years and the colony's senate has allowed the place to go to the dogs. I'd have hoped for better from the veterans in charge of Camulodunum. Now that I'm the senior magistrate, there are going to be some changes. The place needs order and discipline restored to it.'

Apollonius made a face. 'It's not a fortress any longer. Hasn't been for a while. It's a sleepy provincial town like any others. I suspect you're going to have a hard time persuading people that there's any need for change. However much it's needed at the moment.'

'Maybe,' Macro conceded. 'I'll deal with them once I've drawn up a plan for the defences.'

'What did you have in mind?'

'The rivers cover the approaches from north and south. There's no bridge to defend, which helps. However, if the enemy have boats, we'll need to use the warehouses as our first line of defence. There's no hope of running fortifications around the rest of the colony. It covers too much ground for that. We'll have to make what use we can of the lines of the original legionary fortress. We can put some defences along the bank of the river to the south, though the marshes should be enough of an obstacle to discourage any attack from that direction. Then we'll fortify the western and eastern approaches. It'll be smaller than the original fortress, but that's as much as we can defend with the men I have available.'

Apollonius considered this. 'That's no more than half the size of the colony. I wonder how those outside the defence lines you're proposing will react.'

'They'll have nothing to worry about unless there's trouble. If there is, I imagine they'll have bigger things to consider, like keeping their heads. I dare say they won't stop to think about where the defence lines are, as long as they're inside them.'

'Fair point. What happens if the new lines can't be held, or aren't completed in time?'

Macro indicated the temple precinct. 'If it comes to that, we make a stand there. The precinct walls are solid enough, and we can raise them a few feet reasonably quickly to create a fighting parapet. We'll also be defending a much shorter line. And if we can't hold that, we can build defences on the pediment as the final redoubt. I hope it doesn't come to that. We might be able to hold the colony for a few days before help arrives. Otherwise our heads will be decorating the lintels of warriors' huts.'

The spy winced at the suggestion. 'I'd rather not end my life as a macabre trophy.'

'Me neither. That's why we need to be prepared. Just in case some madman or Druid decides to take advantage of Suetonius's absence to stir the natives up into a rage.'

'Or some Roman official pushes them too far.'

'Yes.' Macro nodded solemnly. 'That too.'

There was a brief silence as both men recalled the contingency Cato had spoken of before they parted in Londinium.

'If it comes to that,' Apollonius spoke quietly, 'it would be best if you let me deal with the problem. It's the kind of work I have some experience of.'

Macro looked at him in distaste. 'I know.'

Apollonius laughed. 'You soldiers can be so precious. A dead enemy is a dead enemy, no matter how that is achieved. Do you really think it makes any difference if the blade goes in from the front or the back, or who wields it?'

'It does to me. As you know. That ain't going to change.'

'And yet as long as it's me who does what you consider to be the dirty work, you can live with that arrangement.'

Macro shrugged. 'Your words, not mine.'

'But certainly that's what is in your thoughts, am I right?'

'All right, yes. Well done you for reading my mind.'

'Not the most challenging of tasks.' Apollonius's thin lips parted in amusement. 'Which in some ways is a compliment.'

'Oh, sure.'

'No, I am being sincere, Centurion. I have served a number of masters before I met Cato and yourself. Almost all of them were venal, ambitious men with no scruples who lied and schemed as easily as they breathed. I do not recall them ever being troubled by the morality of their actions or the orders they issued to me. I was content to go along with it for no better reason than it paid well and I learned new skills and languages along the way.' He paused. 'Your friend Cato is an interesting exception. He is a man of principle, yet he has a pragmatic streak and is not afraid of being ruthless when he needs to be. I am fascinated to see if he retains his integrity if he rises any further in rank, or whether he goes the way of my former masters.'

Macro regarded the spy. 'It's all a game to you, isn't it? Sitting there and looking on like it's some cheap drama at the theatre.'

'Given what you know of me and the perils we have shared, it's hardly accurate to portray me as a member of the audience, wouldn't you say?'

Macro thought back over recent years and relented. 'You are right. I apologise.'

'Apologise? Centurion Macro, that is an honour indeed. I thank you.'

'Yes, well, don't push your luck.' Macro tilted his head to one side. 'What I don't understand is what's in it for you. It can't be just about wondering how the lad Cato is going to turn out.'

'Oh, but it is. I see many similarities between myself and him. If he can retain his integrity through it all, then I can aspire to the same qualities.'

Macro smiled wryly. 'Bit late for that, I'd say. Given everything you've already done.'

'You're wrong. It's never too late. I just need proof that it's possible.'

'Fuck me but you're a strange one. Why can't you just stop thinking and start living, eh? Be content with food in your belly, a roof over your head and a warm woman at your side.'

'Like you have?'

'It works for me.'

'But I am not you. I never will be. I have different ambitions.'

'Suit yourself. But I don't see them ever making you happy.'

Apollonius chuckled. 'That's for me to find out.'

'Well, good luck with that.' Macro stretched his shoulders.

'We'd better get back to the colony. You can help me draft the plan of the defences so I can put it to the senate when it meets tomorrow morning. They're not going to like the disruption and the cost of the work, but I hope they have the good sense to see that it's for the best.' He looked up at the sky. 'Looks like rain's coming our way. Let's go.'

The rest of the morning was spent drafting the plans for the colony's defences, and then in the afternoon, Lucius and Claudia arrived with Cato's dog, Cassius. It had become the routine for the boy to be taught by Apollonius while Claudia and Petronella worked together at the loom, weaving lengths of cloth as they chatted with Macro, and Parvus sat in the corner with Cassius playing tug-of-war over a length of rope. But that afternoon, Macro was preoccupied with the need to remedy the defences of the colony and the other measures that would be required if there was trouble. At length, Petronella could not suffer his brooding humour any more, and she set down her wattle and turned to him.

'What's on your mind, lover? Is it that business with the procurator?'

The prospect of being part of Decianus's dirty work had been discussed by them a number of times since Macro's return from Londinium.

'It's to do with that, yes. I'm worried about the state of the colony's defences.'

Petronella frowned. 'Do you really think we might be attacked?'

Macro's protective instinct rose to the occasion, and he tried to sound reassuring as he replied. 'Oh, it's just the soldier in me. We like to plan for every contingency, no matter how unlikely, just so we don't get caught by surprise. The walls of

Camulodunum are in a shocking state. It's time something was done about them, if only to make them less of an eyesore. You've seen the ditches. Filled with rubbish. And they stink. We need to get them sorted out. I'm raising the matter when the senate meets tomorrow.'

Petronella stared hard at him and then shook her head. 'You may be a fine soldier, Macro, but you are a terrible liar. I can see how worried you are. This has been on your mind for many days now.'

'I know, I'm sorry.'

'That's fine. I know you want to keep us safe. But you can be straight with me, and the others.' She gestured to Claudia and Parvus. 'Do you think Camulodunum is in danger?'

'I fear so,' he admitted. 'All the conditions for an uprising are falling into place. The governor is determined to win his victory in the west, even if that means weakening his rear. The bad harvest last year has left people hungry, and they've struggled to pay their taxes and tribute. If they're going to strike, they'll do it when we are most vulnerable. That's why the colony has to look to its defences. Before it's too late.'

Claudia eased herself away from the frame and turned on her stool to join the exchange. 'And what if it *is* too late? What happens if the defences aren't ready in time?'

'Then a decision will have to be made. Either we stay and fight, or we abandon the colony and retreat to Londinium.'

She smiled. 'You have the soldier's gift of using orderly language. I doubt it will be a retreat, Macro. We'll be running for our lives. There will be women, children and the old on the road. How do you expect them to keep ahead of an enemy out for our blood?'

'Then let's hope we get plenty of warning. Enough to make sure I can get the people safely away in time.'

'What if you can't, and the enemy natives catch up with us? Are there enough veterans to protect us?'

'Let's hope so,' Macro replied.

The following morning dawned bright and clear, as if to announce the arrival of spring. The members of the colony's senate entered the hall in the old legionary headquarters that now served as the meeting place for the small body of veterans that looked after Camulodunum's administrative needs. There were ten of them in all, besides Macro, all former centurions. Some had been there since the foundation of the colony and resented Macro's elevation to senior magistrate based upon his service in the Praetorian Guard. They settled on the stools arranged in an arc around his seat, and there was a soft hubbub as they exchanged greetings and gossip while light streamed through the windows high in the gables at each end of the hall. The conversation died away as Macro and Apollonius emerged from the small chamber at one end that served as the office of the senior official.

Apollonius stood to one side, a roll of leather tucked under his arm, as Macro settled onto his chair and glanced round at the other members of the senate. Most were grey-haired or bald, and one had a patch over his eye, while others sported scars on their faces and limbs. By the time legionaries had risen to the ranks of the centurionate, they had already proved themselves as men who led from the front in combat and were the last to leave the field in the event of a withdrawal. Courage and devotion to duty were demanded of centurions, and they had rightly earned the reputation as the backbone of the Roman army. These were men to be accorded respect, even if their previous service as soldiers was no guarantee of similar success as administrators. In most military colonies that Macro was aware of, the governance was usually carried out by clerks while the senate members reminisced about the old days over wine. Camulodunum was no exception, but he hoped that he would impress upon them the urgent need to make good the colony's defences.

Clearing his throat, he leaned forward. 'Brothers, I thank you all for attending today's council. I appreciate that we were not due to meet until the end of the month, but I trust you will understand the importance of gathering sooner rather than later after you have heard what I have to say.

'As you are all aware, Governor Suetonius has embarked on a campaign in the mountains to the west of the province at the head of an army comprising most of the troops stationed in Britannia. The men he has left behind to garrison the towns and forts in the rest of the province might be deemed adequate under better circumstances. Rome has already witnessed one uprising by a faction within the Iceni, back when Ostorius was governor and waging war on the mountain tribes. Therefore, we should be on our guard against a possible return of the rebellious elements amongst the Trinovantes and the Iceni.'

'Centurion Macro, if I may?' The man with the eye patch, a veteran of the Ninth Legion, raised a hand, and Macro nodded his assent. 'The uprising you refer to was over ten years ago. Even then it was a small affair. No more than a few hundred of the rascals, who caused little mischief before they were brought to heel. Since then, the only trouble we have had was after the murder of that tax collector last year, and that never posed any danger to the colony. The truth of it is that the tribes you mention have learned their lesson. They know that if they cause any problems, Suetonius will be sure to punish them when his campaign is over. With respect, I don't think there's anything for us to worry about.'

'I sincerely hope you are right, Ulpius. However, you can't have failed to notice the change in attitude amongst the locals. There's something in the air.'

'There always is with their kind. Barbarians live like pigs and smell just as bad.'

There was a soft ripple of laughter, and Macro felt his temper rise a notch.

'Nevertheless, there is cause for concern, and that should focus our minds on the deplorable condition of the colony's defences.'

Macro went over the deficiencies that he and Apollonius had noted during their inspection of what remained of the fortifications. When he had concluded the survey, he turned to the side. 'Apollonius, if you please?'

Apollonius laid down the tanned goatskin and unrolled it to reveal a map of the town, overlaid with the defences that Macro was proposing. He rose from his chair as the other members of the senate leaned forward to inspect the diagram, and used his vine cane to point out the details as he spoke.

'As you can see, the colony has outgrown the original lines of the fortress. Most of the rampart has been pulled down and the ditch filled in. In my view, it would take far too much time to attempt to restore the original structures, so I propose that we restrict the extent of the new fortifications to a size that we can easily defend and which can contain the population of the colony. From the last annual census, I see we have eight hundred and fifty veterans, with four and a half thousand dependents, six hundred and fifty other Roman citizens engaged in businesses, and around two thousand non-citizens, most of whom are from the local tribes. Eight thousand in all. Our priority is the protection of Roman citizens. With the numbers I mentioned, I believe we only need two lines of defences to cover the open ground between the rivers. The wharf and warehouses can easily be fortified if necessary and the southern bank can be screened with stakes. Besides, the ground there is too marshy for any frontal attack. Restoring the ditches and ramparts will mean removing those buildings constructed over the defences. We're also going to need a large construction force to get the work done.'

Ulpius shook his head as he looked over the diagram, and then glanced up at Macro, his remaining eye staring with a piercing intensity. 'This is madness. Your ditch goes right through my house and stable. I'm not the only one. Look there, Stellius. The same goes for you.'

The centurion next to him leaned forward and frowned. 'He's right.'

'Quiet!' Macro ordered. He tapped the tip of his cane while he waited for them to fall silent. 'I understand you may not like this, but we have a duty to the people of the colony to protect them in time of emergency. The senate has failed in that duty for a number of years, and it is time to put that right. Sure, some homes and businesses are going to be pulled down, but the owners will be compensated.'

'Compensated with what?' Ulpius demanded. 'Our reserves would not cover more than a fraction of the sums that would be due. And what about the cost of the labour and materials? Are you going to pluck the silver off some magic tree to pay for it, Centurion Macro? The colony can't afford to do this.'

Macro struggled to contain his rising temper. 'Then we shall have to impose a new tax to pay for the work. The truth is that the colony can't afford *not* to improve its defences. Not if its people value their lives above the protests of penny-pinchers.'

Ulpius clenched his jaw so that Macro could see the muscles working furiously beneath the skin. 'How dare you?' he snapped. 'You forget yourself, Macro. You are talking to men who have fought for Rome. Who shed blood for the people of Rome.' He lifted the edge of his patch to reveal the puckered skin around the void where his eye had been. 'I lost this fighting Caratacus and his Catuvellauni, so don't you dare lecture me about the value of life!'

Several of the other veterans grumbled their support as Ulpius let the eye patch drop into place and leaned back with a thin smile.

'No one is questioning your past sacrifice, nor that of any man in this room,' Macro responded. 'My proposal is intended to make sure that lives are not sacrificed in the future. If we can't defend the colony when we need to, we risk losing everything.'

'It's not a case of *when*, but *if*,' said Ulpius. 'And in my view, the danger of any uprising is remote. We've given the natives around the colony a bloody good thrashing, and they won't be coming back for any more if they know what's good for them. It would be a complete waste of effort and money to prepare for something that is never likely to happen.'

Apollonius chuckled. 'I'm sure the same was said about the possibility of Hannibal marching elephants across the Alps, and yet . . .'

Ulpius turned to look briefly at the spy before addressing Macro. 'Who is this?'

'*This* can speak for himself,' Apollonius said calmly.

Ulpius ignored him as his lips lifted in a sneer. 'Your slave? Or your servant? Either way, you should teach your underlings to mind their business in the presence of their betters.'

'In what regard could you possibly consider yourself my better?' Apollonius asked with an innocent expression.

Ulpius's remaining eye widened as his head turned swiftly. 'What did you say?'

'I believe you, and everyone else, heard me.'

The veteran looked over Apollonius's wiry build. 'I think I need to teach you a lesson.'

Macro managed to intervene. 'This man is my adviser. He is Apollonius of Tarsus.'

Ulpius frowned. 'You say that like I should have heard of him.'

'Let me just say that you should be grateful you *haven't* heard of him. Otherwise you would not have been foolish enough to suggest that you might teach him a lesson. Many have tried. Most have died.'

Ulpius looked closely again at the unassuming figure next to Macro and snorted with derision, but he didn't address Apollonius again.

'We'll need to put it to the colony's senate. You may be the senior magistrate of the colony, but you only have one vote, like the rest of us.'

'That's true,' Macro agreed. 'And that is why I am raising the matter today. If it was down to me, I'd have already given the orders to make a start. I don't believe we have much time to get the defences ready before they are needed. If by some miracle there is no uprising this year, that only increases the odds that there will be one next year, given the burden we are imposing on the tribes of this island.' He paused and let out a deep sigh. 'At the end of the day, the issue is the same one that all Romans have faced throughout our long history. If we want to live in peace, we must prepare for war. Even if you are right, Ulpius, it is better that we rebuild our defences and not need them rather than need them and not have them.'

Ulpius raised his hands dismissively. 'Fine sentiments, Macro. But try telling that to those whose homes and businesses will be demolished to make space for your pet project. Try telling that to the people who will have to endure higher taxes to pay for the work. I say we put it to the vote right now.' He stood, turned his back to Macro and addressed the others. 'Those in favour of Macro's proposal to waste money on new defences for the colony?'

The members of the senate sat still for several beats before one of the veterans raised his hand uncertainly. A second followed suit before Ulpius hurriedly spoke again. 'Those against?'

At once those who had been sitting closest to him raised their hands, and the remainder of those who had not voted yet did the same. Ulpius turned to Macro with a triumphant expression. 'Eight to two against you, Macro. Or three, if you wish to register your own vote. Your proposal is defeated.' He returned to his stool and sat down, arms crossed. 'Was there anything else on the agenda?'

Macro fixed his gaze on Ulpius unwaveringly. 'I pray that you are right and that we never have need of any defences. I pray that we all live long and peaceful lives and die of old age in our beds. That said, I pray that if you and your cronies are wrong, you go to your graves tormented by the knowledge that your deaths, and those of your families, are on your consciences alone. Not that it will be a comfort to me to have been proved right. My family and I will pay the same price for your mistake. Go. Get out of my sight.'

Ulpius and the others turned to leave the hall. The first man who had backed Macro's proposal remained behind.

'What is it, Vulpinus?' asked Macro.

'Sir, I'm the one responsible for entering the details of such meetings for the public record. Do you wish me to set down an account of the discussion and the vote?'

'Yes, damn you. Do your job.'

'Wait,' said Apollonius. He spoke softly to Macro. 'What is the point? If you are proved right, the records will burn with the rest of the colony. Who will ever know? What is the value of such a hollow victory?'

Macro looked at him with a bleak expression before swallowing and nodding. 'You can go, Vulpinus. No need to waste your time on the matter.'

'Yes, sir.' The veteran bowed his head and made his way out of the hall. Macro leaned forward to take a final look at the diagram.

'The bloody fools. They think me too cautious. Too afraid.'

'For what it's worth, I'd rather follow you into danger than all of them put together.'

Macro looked up in surprise at the compliment before Apollonius grinned. 'Of course, I'd much rather I didn't have to follow you into such a situation at all.'

'I thank you for the thought anyway. Now roll that up and let's go and get royally drunk to try and forget this foolishness, for a few hours at least.'

# CHAPTER FOURTEEN

The good weather continued to hold over the following days, with only occasional showers, which swiftly passed before the sun once again beamed down on the colony and the surrounding countryside. Some five days after the senate meeting, Macro was sitting in his courtyard garden in a patch of light, eyes closed as he basked in the warmth and idly listened to the birdsong and the muted hubbub of the sounds of the town: the banter of people passing in the street, the cries of traders, the dink-dink of metalworkers and the rumble of cart wheels. After brooding for two days over his failure to win the other members of the senate round to his view, he had resigned himself to hoping that his fears for the safety of the colony were overwrought.

He heard a sharp rapping on the main door of the house. From the kitchen, where she was baking, Petronella ordered Parvus to see who was at the door. There was the clank of the heavy iron latch before a man's voice spoke. Macro could not catch the words. A moment later, Parvus emerged into the courtyard. He stopped in front of Macro and gesticulated excitedly, grunting and moaning incomprehensibly.

'Slow down,' Macro instructed.

'Peem! Lob a peem abador!'

'People?' Macro groaned at the interruption to his moment of peaceful relaxation. He rose and followed Parvus to the door. Outside he saw Vulpinus standing in front of a small crowd of veterans and Roman civilians who had gathered in the street.

'What's this about?' he demanded. 'Vulpinus, explain yourself.'

'Sir, word has got round the colony about what happened at the senate meeting. I was at the hall when these people arrived demanding to speak to you about your plans to improve Camulodunum's defences.'

Macro gritted his teeth. It seemed that Ulpius had not been content to merely win the vote, he was now agitating the inhabitants of the colony, perhaps with the intention of driving Macro from his position as senior magistrate so that he could claim the post for himself.

'Well, what of it?' he responded irritably. 'The senate voted to save you all from paying more taxes. Might cost you your lives, of course, but at least it won't hurt your purses, eh?'

There were some angry mutterings in the crowd, and then a man in his twenties stepped forward. 'Look here, Centurion, we don't want to be worrying about getting a knife in the back if some natives stir up trouble. I've got a wife and kids. It ain't right that the senate voted to leave us defenceless.'

Others shouted their support for his comment, and the protests swiftly grew in volume. Macro raised his hands and waved them to try and calm the crowd, without success.

'Fuck it,' he muttered; then, drawing a sharp breath, he bellowed, 'SILENCE, damn you!'

The crowd instantly wilted under his glare and their tongues stilled. Macro waited until he had their attention before he continued. 'I can't help you. I can't challenge the vote.'

Vulpinus shook his head. 'Sir, that's what I told them at the hall. But that's not why they're here. They haven't come to demand that you challenge the vote. They've come to volunteer to do the work themselves.'

'What?' Macro's brow furrowed. 'Volunteers?'

'Yes, sir.'

The younger man who had spoken a moment before nodded his head vigorously. 'If those politicians won't look out for us, we'll have to do it ourselves. I'm one of the builders at the temple site. I've got the tools for the job. The same's true of many of the others here. And there are more people across the colony who will help out once we make a start.'

'Aye!' An old man nearby raised his fist. 'We'll show Ulpius and those other bastards.'

The crowd cheered and Vulpinus turned to Macro with a grin. 'What do you say, sir?'

Macro felt a dig in the small of his back and glanced round to see Petronella staring anxiously at the crowd, her hands covered in flour. 'What in Hades is going on here?'

Macro put an arm round her and smiled as he explained. 'It seems that the people of Camulodunum have rather more sense than most of those who represent them.'

She nodded. 'No surprises there, my love. Well, if you're going to get this lot sorted out, the least I can do is feed 'em. We're going to need a bigger bag of flour . . .'

In the days that followed, Macro and Apollonius organised the work that could be done without demolishing buildings: clearing stretches of the original ditch and rebuilding the rampart. Each morning, fresh recruits joined the teams toiling to repair the colony's defences, bringing their own tools or those they had borrowed. Many of the veterans still had the picks from their army days, a piece of kit as valuable to a soldier as their sword. Petronella had taken charge of feeding the workers, and some bakers and innkeepers she had persuaded to volunteer their services set up a field kitchen next to the ditch. The prospect of a good meal in return for labour even attracted a number of local tribesmen. Macro could not help a wry smile at the thought that the same people who were helping to rebuild Camulodunum's defences might one day soon be amongst the ranks of those trying to overwhelm them.

He and Apollonius toiled alongside the volunteers to clear the ditch, stripped to the waist as they shovelled muck, shards of broken pottery and animal bones. Occasionally Ulpius or some of his cronies would pass by with mocking expressions and shake their heads at the spectacle of the colony's senior magistrate up to his knees in filth and streaked with dirt. Macro would look up, returning their expressions of contempt, before resuming his work with renewed intent, mindful that scant days remained before the deadline given to the Iceni to pay the balance of the tribute. As he worked, he hoped that his example and that of those who worked alongside him might shame the other magistrates into reversing their decision. Without a change of mind, it would be impossible to complete the work, since the buildings astride the new ditch that he had planned could not be removed unless the senate agreed to permit it. Besides, there was a limit to what could be done without funds being provided for the necessary building materials. At the same time, there was a palpable sense of division within the town between those who perceived the need to prepare for trouble and those who refused to pay further taxes to better protect themselves.

Towards the end of the month, the weather changed. A thick belt of cloud rolled in from the east, bringing bone-chilling rain. As the cleared stretches of ditch filled with water,

Macro ordered the work to stop until the wet weather had passed. In the meantime, he turned his attention to the construction site of the temple complex. Wearing thick cloaks impregnated with fat to keep the rain out, he and Apollonius inspected the site, where a handful of workers were still attending to the tasks that could be carried out even under the heavy downpour that glistened on the large pieces of masonry and piled roof tiles and turned the churned ground into a sheet of clinging mud that sucked at the men's boots. The precinct wall was near completion, some eight feet tall, constructed of limestone; all that remained was to finish capping it with angled slabs.

'It's solid enough,' Macro noted as he patted the wet stonework. 'But easy enough to scale unless we can make it higher. Of course, it wouldn't last long against a decent ram.'

Apollonius nodded and made a note on his wax tablet before shaking the water off and closing it with a snap. 'Let's have a look at the inside.'

They trudged along the wall through the driving rain until they reached the corner and turned into the full force of the wind. Their cloaks whipped out around them and both men struggled to gather the folds in and hold them tight as they approached the precinct gate. While it possessed an impressive-looking arch, the structure had never been designed with fortification in mind, and the top, some twenty feet above the ground, was flat and afforded no protection to any who might stand upon it. Nor had any gates been hung on the heavy iron hinges fixed to the stone. The two men hurried inside out of the wind and stood with their backs to the wall as they surveyed the site and went over the observations they had made from the hill above Camulodunum at the start of the month.

'On the plus side, there's plenty of material here we can use to build up the defences of the precinct if a time comes when we need to,' said Macro.

'On the down side, those materials are the property of the imperial cult who commissioned the temple,' Apollonius countered. 'If we're to commandeer any of this, we're going to need the permission of the cult's priest in Londinium. How long will that take?'

Macro grumbled something incomprehensible at the rhetorical question before he coughed. 'Fucking rain. Always gives me a bloody cold these days.'

'Sorry to hear it,' Apollonius replied as he fixed his attention back on the piled stones waiting to be shaped before being lifted into position on the pediment. 'If we need to use the builders' supplies, I'd say the possibility of asking permission from the cult is going to be a touchy issue.'

Macro nodded. 'In that case, they can take legal action against me when the dust settles, assuming they can find what's left of me first.'

'Have you had any word on how the governor's campaign is going?' asked Apollonius.

'Last news I got was from a courier bringing me the latest numbers of veterans to be settled here next year. That was yesterday. Seems Suetonius only gave the order to march ten days ago.' He recalled the lie of the land from his memory of fighting in the region and did a quick calculation. 'They won't have penetrated far into the mountains yet. If they're suffering the same weather as us, it'll be slow going. I wonder how Cato's faring with his new command.'

'You wish you were out there with him, don't you?'

'Better than having to deal with the likes of Ulpius and shovelling shit out of a collapsed ditch. I had hoped for less grief when I hung up my sword and retired from the army. There are times when I wish I was back in uniform and with the lads once more.'

'You may need to wield that sword again,' Apollonius said grimly. 'Be careful what you wish for, Macro.' He looked up at the grey clouds, blinking away the raindrops that fell on his face. 'Do you mind if we continue this when the weather has improved?'

'Hot wine time?'

'Isn't it always?'

Macro chuckled and slapped him on the shoulder. 'You're growing on me, spy. We'll make a half-decent soldier of you one day.'

'The gods forbid. I have lived my life out of step with such people. I'm not going to change now.'

They passed back through the arch and headed along the main street towards Macro's villa in the heart of the settlement. Ahead of them in the distance, they could see a column of men on foot led by a party of riders coming through the Londinium gate.

'Not the best weather to be on the road,' Apollonius mused. 'Quite a few of them. I wonder what their business is in Camulodunum.'

Macro's heart sank as he guessed the identity of the new arrivals and their reason for being in the colony.

When no more than ten paces separated them, the rider at the head of the small column reined in and drew back his hood enough to see his surroundings clearly, and for Macro to recognise him.

'Decianus,' he muttered sourly. 'When it rains, it really fucking pours.'

'You two!' Decianus pointed to them. 'Where do I find the chief magistrate?'

Macro approached the last few paces before he eased back his own hood. 'You found him, Procurator.'

Decianus raised an eyebrow and leaned forward in his saddle. 'So it is! Well met, Centurion Macro. I took you for some kind of labourer, wading through this mud in that filthy cloak.'

'What do you want?'

'So terse a greeting is hardly suitable to an imperial official of my rank.'

Macro stared back wordlessly as the rain hissed down around them. With a shrug, Decianus straightened up in his saddle.

'I want shelter for my men, stabling for the horses, and food.'

Macro would have offered almost any other visitor the hospitality of his own home, but he had certain standards and Decianus fell beneath them. 'The administration hall should be big enough for your needs. There's a stable in the yard. As for food, I know where I can get some fresh bread, but it'll cost you.'

'See to it then.'

'Payment in advance.'

Decianus reached under his cloak and brought out a small leather pouch. He tossed it to Macro, who caught it deftly and opened the drawstrings to see the glint of silver within.

'That should cover the bread, and some meat and cheese and wine besides. Have your man there see to it. I need to speak to you. You can show me the way to the hall.'

Macro handed the purse to Apollonius and spoke softly. 'Small fortune there. Make sure Petronella spends as little as possible on these scoundrels and keeps the rest. She can use up the stale bread.'

'I'm sure she will. Do you wish me to join you in the hall afterwards?'

'No. I doubt there will be any surprises.'

As the spy squelched away, Macro turned to Decianus and his bedraggled-looking column of clerks and bodyguards. 'Follow me.'

The hall was filled with the sounds of Decianus's men as they found a place for their kit and set about lighting the braziers to get warm and start drying their clothes. Macro was gratified to see the procurator shiver as he dumped his sodden cloak into the arms of one of his bodyguards.

'Is there somewhere we can speak in private?'

Macro nodded towards the door of the office assigned to the senior magistrate. 'In there.'

Decianus opened the door and glanced round the small room. 'It will do.' He nodded towards the brazier in the corner, with its small stock of kindling and split logs set to one side. 'Better get that going, Centurion. I'm chilled to the bone.'

Macro refused to be goaded by his superior. He went to the door and called out to the nearest of the clerks. 'You. In here. Light the fire for the procurator.' He stepped aside for the man, whose wet tunic clung to him as he set to work.

Once the clerk had left the room, Decianus stood in front of the brazier, the flames illuminating his face and outstretched hands in a soft blood-red hue. Macro regarded the procurator's dome-like head and intense eyes with distaste as he recalled the time Decianus had ridden away from Macro and a band of veterans, leaving them to face a desperate conflict that the procurator had provoked. There was blood on Decianus's hands all right, Macro reflected bitterly as he cursed the governor's orders to obey the man.

'You know why I am here, don't you?' Decianus glanced at him.

'I can guess.'

'It's time to pay a visit to our Iceni friends and hold their feet to the flames to make sure they pay the rest of the tribute.'

'Let's hope it doesn't come to that. Let's hope they have managed to find the sum they owe and then there will be no need for trouble.' Macro stepped a pace closer. 'Trouble you caused the last time you crawled out from behind your desk in Londinium.'

'Still holding me to account for that little skirmish of yours?'

'Good men died because of you. That will never be forgotten, nor forgiven, as long as I, or any of the veterans involved, still live.'

'That's too bad, Centurion. Sometimes mistakes are made, and that is regrettable. But we must both do the job the governor assigned to us now. I'll be counting on your abilities and your obedience in the coming days. It would be best if you did not let me down.'

'I'll do what I must.'

'Yes, you will.' Decianus gave him a hard stare. 'And if you give me the slightest cause for dissatisfaction, you can be sure that will be included in the reports I submit to the governor and the imperial palace.'

'I'll be submitting my own account if I have to,' Macro responded. 'Like I said, let's hope the Iceni pay up and you can go quietly on your way.'

Decianus laughed. 'Do you seriously imagine they will be able to scrape together the sum they owe?'

'It will be difficult,' Macro conceded. 'But if they can't, what then?'

'Then we'll have to execute the will of the late King Prasutagus and seize what is outstanding. In which case, I will need some muscle to back up my demands. That's where you and your veterans come in. I've already got fifty auxiliaries drawn from the Londinium garrison. I need you and a hundred of your veterans to make sure the Iceni don't get silly ideas about disputing any claims I make on their property. A show of force will bring those barbarians to heel and make sure there is no trouble.'

'A hundred? We're going there to settle a bill, not invade the bloody place.'

'A hundred of your veterans is what I am ordering you to provide. See to it.'

'Any other requirements?'

'If I think of any, I'll let you know.'

'And when do you need us ready?'

Decianus gave one of his cold smiles. 'Tomorrow morning will do nicely. Best we get this business over and done with as soon as possible, eh?'

# CHAPTER FIFTEEN

The column had crossed the frontier into Ordovician territory on the last day of March. The sun had come out and shone brilliantly from a cloudless sky. A screen of cavalry patrols from the Eighth Illyrian led the way, scouting the terrain and watching for signs of the enemy. Behind them marched the rest of Cato's new command, the remaining mounted men at the head of the column, followed by the infantry and the modest baggage train of laden mules and small carts carrying tents, feed and rations. A hundred paces behind the rear of the cohort marched the first of the legionary cohorts, heavy infantry burdened by their armour and weapons, while their large shields and remaining kit hung from the yokes braced against their shoulders.

After many months in winter quarters preparing for the campaign, the men were relieved to no longer be cooped up in camp and excited by the prospect of action and the booty to be won. They were in high spirits as they stepped out along the route leading from Viroconium into the hills. Cato remembered his own early days in the army and the thrill of being in uniform and laden down with kit as he marched alongside his comrades, eager to put his training to the test. Nothing then had seemed impossible, and old age and the prospect of death, or worse, a crippling injury, had been far from his mind. Memory of a time he could never regain tempted and taunted him, and he forced himself to revert to the alert, calculating way of thinking he had adopted as habit. More than fifteen years of experience told him that the exhilaration of the men setting out to war would not long survive days of gruelling marching, the discomfort of camping in the open, the inevitable shortening of rations and, once the fighting began, the loss of comrades they had come to regard as closer than brothers.

From somewhere in the ranks of the leading unit of the legion marching behind them, a voice started singing a popular marching song, and within moments, his immediate comrades had joined in before the singing spread to the rest of the cohort. The words and the din of nailed marching boots on the stony track echoed off the rocky slopes of the hills on either side.

Cato turned in his saddle to look back with a fond smile as he spoke to Galerius, who was marching at his side.

'Hear that, Centurion? I reckon our men could do better.'

Galerius laughed and nodded. 'I reckon so, sir.'

He stepped off the track and turned to the auxiliaries striding past, drawing a deep breath and launching into a different marching song. The men quickly joined in and sang along lustily.

> The soldiers of Rome,
> They know no home,
> Across mountain and raging river,
> They come from far and thither.
> On the slate they make their sign
> Then form up and stand in line.
> Become brothers for life

Through battle and strife,
Singing through times good and bad:
'The best fucking job I ever had!'

The auxiliaries roared out the last line and then laughed heartily. Behind them, the legionary cohort responded by singing more loudly, and the men of the Eighth raised their voices again, matching the rhythm to their marching pace as they strove to outdo the legionaries.

Galerius left them to it and trotted up along the line to rejoin Cato. The two officers shared a grin.

'They're in good spirits,' Cato observed.

'Aye, sir. Who wouldn't be on a fine day like this? After all the cold and rain and being cooped up in barracks, at last we're on our way to Mona.'

The mention of the lair of the Druid cult caused Cato's grin to fade as he recalled the Druids he had fought in the past, and their fierce hatred of Rome. The atrocities on both sides still chilled him to the bone.

'Have you fought them before?' he asked Galerius. 'The Druids?'

'No, sir. There were rumours of Druids amongst the tribes across the Rhenus, but I never saw any. I've heard they foam at the mouth like they're possessed by evil spirits, and they can fight with the strength of ten men and use magic against their enemies. But you'd surely know more about that than me, sir, given the years you've served in Britannia.'

'They're fanatics to be sure,' replied Cato, 'but they fight, bleed and die like the rest of us. I've seen no evidence of their magic, but it helps their cause if their followers believe they can cast spells. It helps even more if their enemies believe it too. So let's not put any store in that nonsense, eh?

If you hear such rumours doing the rounds of the cohort, step in and set the men right. I don't want them jumping at shadows. Understood?'

'Yes, sir.'

'Good.' Cato rode in silence for a moment before he spoke again. 'I'm going to catch up with Tubero. You take command here.'

They exchanged a salute and Cato urged his horse into a canter, pulling ahead of the infantry and then the men who had dismounted to walk their horses over the rough track. Half a mile ahead, he could see one of the squadrons on top of a hill beside the track. The cavalry contingent's standard was clearly visible against the sky, marking the position where Tubero would be found. Steering his mount off the track, Cato climbed the slope and reined in beside the centurion and his standard-bearer.

'Good day, sir,' Tubero greeted him. 'You've arrived at an opportune moment. We've sighted the enemy for the first time.' He raised his arm and pointed towards a ridge running parallel to the track, over a mile away.

Cato strained his eyes, scanning the rocks and clumps of bushes and trees scattered across the ground dropping away from the ridge line. Then he spotted them as they shifted their position, several men on ponies.

'I see them.'

'What should we do, sir? I can send a patrol after them. We might take some prisoners.'

'I doubt it. They know the ground and would likely evade any attempt to run them to ground. There's too few of them to do any harm. They'll be doing the same as you, Tubero, screening their forces and reporting our movements to their chiefs. The initiative lies with them for now. Keep an eye on them, and watch for any more. If you sight any party larger than fifty men, send word to me.'

'Yes, sir.'

Cato turned his attention to the track the Roman column was following as it snaked its way into the mountains. Two miles ahead, the ridge above the slope where he'd seen the Ordovician scouts curved gently to the north, closing up on another ridge to the right of the track and creating a narrow defile. Pine trees and thick undergrowth grew close on either side.

'I don't like the look of that.' He drew Tubero's attention to the feature. 'Good spot for an ambush. Send a squadron to occupy the ridge on either side and advance along them to the end. They're to report on anything suspicious.'

Tubero scanned the ridges. 'I don't know about that, sir. Looks like difficult ground for horses.'

'Difficult or not, I want them up there before the rest of the cohort reaches the defile,' Cato said firmly.

The centurion issued the orders as Cato continued to survey the landscape around them. He soon spotted more of the enemy on each flank, watching the Romans from the tops of hills some miles distant. The tiny figures were so still he wondered if they were actually mannequins set up to unsettle them, or lure patrols away from the main column.

Tubero's messengers cantered down the hill towards two of the patrols sweeping the boulder- and copse-strewn slopes on either side. As soon as the fresh instructions were given, the decurions in command of the patrols turned their men and began the arduous climb to the ridges, dismounting from time to time to lead their mounts across ground too dangerous to risk riding over. The head of the Eighth Cohort had drawn level with the hill, and Cato was about to ride down and rejoin the column when one of Tubero's men thrust his arm out and pointed ahead.

'Sir! Down there. The enemy!'

Cato straightened to his full height in the saddle as his eyes followed the direction the auxiliary was indicating. A score of men in light cloaks and leggings and armed with spears had broken cover from a jumbled outcrop of boulders beside the track and were now running back along it towards the ravine. Tubero turned to Cato. 'Sir! The honour of the first contact is ours. What are your orders?'

Cato was watching the enemy racing for the cover of the trees along the sides of the ravine. Twenty or so men on foot were going to be no match for Tubero's squadron of thirty. There were prisoners to be had and interrogated for information before they were bound and sent back to a pen in Viroconium and eventually sold into slavery. It would be good for the men's morale to have so easy a victory, so swiftly, however insignificant.

'Sir?' Tubero pressed him. The enemy were drawing closer to the trees and the chance to take them might be lost if Cato acted too slowly.

'Very well.' He nodded. 'If you can catch them before they reach the trees, then take them. If not, let them go and wait for the column to catch up. We'll not take any foolish risks. Go!'

Tubero's men were watching eagerly, and the moment their centurion raised his arm, they were urging their mounts forward.

'First Squadron! On me!'

Tubero galloped his horse down the slope and his men followed, spilling out on either flank. Cato was tempted to charge with them, but he knew that his duty was to remain in control of the vanguard of the army rather than racing off to join the hunt. In any case, it looked as if the enemy had a sufficient head start to reach the trees before the auxiliaries caught up with them. He trusted that the centurion would obey his orders and call off the chase the moment the enemy disappeared. If not, he would give him a public dressing-down in front of the rest of the officers once the column had stopped and made camp for the night.

The riders reached the foot of the hill and launched themselves across the open ground as they raced to catch the Ordovician warriors. Within a few moments, Cato could see that the race had been lost. The enemy had almost reached the place where the track passed between the pine trees growing in copses on either side, interspersed with bushes and brown patches of fern. Any moment now, they were sure to turn off and race for the cover of the trees to make good their escape. But instead, they continued running along the track, frequently glancing back at the horsemen bearing down on them. A hundred paces ahead of them, the track curved in the direction of the defile and was lost to sight.

Instantly Cato cursed himself for not being more specific in the orders he had given Tubero. There was still a chance that the centurion would have the sense to call off the pursuit, but Cato realised how hard it was for cavalrymen to give up the chase when the enemy was fleeing before them. Their blood was up, and it took a high degree of discipline and self-control to stop. As the Ordovicians ran for the bend in the track and began to disappear one by one, Tubero and his men closed up into a column and continued the pursuit. Cato felt his guts clench with anxiety, fully expecting the trees to disgorge hundreds of warriors at any moment to crash into the flanks of the auxiliaries, but there was no sign of movement in the shadows. His relief was momentary, however, as he grasped the true nature of the enemy's guile.

As Tubero and his men plunged along the track towards the curve and moved out of sight, Cato whispered, 'Shit . . .' Then he wheeled his horse round and galloped down the slope towards the men leading the horses at the head of the Eighth Cohort.

'Mount up!' he cried as he approached. 'Mount!'

The auxiliaries swung themselves into their saddles and readied their shields and reins as they waited for the next command.

Cato made for Galerius, who had halted the infantry a short distance behind the rear of the mounted contingent.

'What's happening, sir?'

There was no time for explanations, Cato decided. 'As soon as I take the cavalry forward, you bring up the rest of the cohort, close formation.'

'Sir, I don't—'

'Just do it!' He turned his mount to the front and kicked his heels in, galloping past the long line of mounted men and slewing to a halt before wheeling to face them. 'You will obey my orders precisely! You will not go in pursuit of any enemy without orders from me! Forward!'

He jerked the reins to direct his horse into a gallop, and the remaining two squadrons of mounted men rippled forward after him, pounding along the track in the direction of the defile. Cato hunched forward, gripping the reins and clamping his thighs against the flanks of his mount as the saddle horns held his waist securely. Ahead, he could see no sign of Tubero's men, nor the enemy, and he felt sick with anxiety. He should have been clearer with the centurion and forbidden any form of reckless pursuit of the enemy.

As the trees and undergrowth closed in on either side of the track, he glanced left and right, but there was no movement amid the shadows from where he had first feared the enemy might launch an ambush. He urged his mount on, reassured by the sound of the hooves of the riders close behind. When he was no more than a hundred paces away from the curve, a riderless horse careered into sight. There was a splash of blood on its flank and the saddle was awry, making the horse unbalanced, so that it swerved and straightened and swerved again as it galloped towards Cato and the riders behind him. Cato just had time to steer his mount aside, but the rider behind was not so lucky. The saddle horns of the oncoming horse caught his and spun both animals round before they tumbled to the side, crushing the rider beneath them. Cato spared the man a quick glance, but there was nothing that could be done for him. The rest of the mounted men hastily jerked their reins to avoid the writhing animals and keep clear of their lashing hooves as they passed by.

Reaching the curve in the track, he saw Tubero's squadron fifty paces ahead, fighting for their lives. Ordovician warriors on foot darted amongst them, thrusting with spears and hacking with their long Celtic swords. Beyond the seething mass, a crudely cut abatis blocked the track. One of the auxiliaries was trying to rip his shield free from the grip of an ambusher, and raised his sword high to strike at the man. But he never got to make the blow, as he was piked between the shoulder blades from behind. The impact caused him to fling his arms wide before he was torn from the saddle and tumbled to the ground, where he was butchered by the tribesmen.

Cato drew his short sword and held it out to the side, ready to thrust or cut as needed. Tubero and several of his men were gathered about the standard, fighting savagely to keep it from the enemy. The distance to the skirmish was closed in a few heartbeats, and Cato raised his sword as he picked his target: a large warrior sporting a gleaming Roman helmet, a trophy from one of the failed campaigns of the past. The man's attention had already been drawn by the thrum of hoofbeats as Cato and the other auxiliaries charged into the fight. Now he turned and braced up, raising his shield and sighting his spear at Cato's midriff as the Roman charged towards him.

With no shield to protect him, Cato gritted his teeth as he closed in. At the last moment, he pulled sharply on the reins and the horse staggered to one side, throwing its rump towards the warrior, who was forced to leap out of the way before he could strike. Cato twisted and slashed with his sword, but his opponent was too fast and the blade cut through the air above the man's bowed helmet. Spurring his horse on, he chose another foe, who was struck down by a blow to the neck even before he realised the danger. More of the auxiliaries were flowing into the struggle now, charging down Ordovician warriors as the balance tipped in the Romans' favour.

On the far side of the skirmish, Cato saw a warrior in a bright green cloak at the head of several men wearing mail cuirasses and helmets. The warrior turned to shout an order, and one of his men raised a horn to his lips and sounded a shrill, baying note that cut across the clatter of blades, the whinnying and snorting of horses and the scrabbling of hooves and feet on the loose stones of the track. At once the enemy broke contact, backing away before turning to run for the trees on the left side of the track. The enemy warrior – their leader, Cato realised – waited a moment and then waved the band of men with him towards the treeline. In a few heartbeats, the enemy had gone; only shadows flitting under the trees could be seen, and then nothing more. The Roman horsemen looked round with raised weapons for a moment in case they came back, but there was no sign of them in the sudden calmness along the track.

Cato patted his horse to calm it and spoke gently before he called out, 'Get the wounded to the rear! Collect our dead!' He looked round. 'Centurion Tubero! On me.'

The commander of the cavalry contingent sheathed his sword and walked his horse over. 'Sir?'

There was no need to ask what had happened; it was all too clear. The enemy had lured the auxiliaries along the track, the abatis was dropped into place, and warriors had burst from cover on either flank and cut them off.

Cato sheathed his own blade and regarded the centurion. 'Your orders were not to pursue them into the trees.'

Tubero was still breathing hard from his exertions, and his face was flushed. 'Sir, I did not pursue them into the trees. They fled along the track and—'

'Do not cavil with me!' Cato interrupted. 'My orders were clear enough. No risks. But you went ahead anyway, and fell into their trap.'

'Sir, we almost had them,' Tubero protested.

'Almost? There was no almost about it, man. They lured you in and you took the bait like the greenest of officers. As a result, you have lost several men.' Cato glanced past the centurion to where his men were laying the casualties off to the side of the track. He counted quickly. 'Eight dead, and others wounded. If I hadn't come up with the rest of the mounted contingent, it's likely that you and all your men would now be dead or taken prisoner. And believe me, being taken prisoner by the Ordovicians and their Druid allies is often a worse fate than death. All because you rushed in.'

Tubero's gaze dropped. He made to reply, then closed his mouth.

'Get your squadron closed up and wait for the infantry to catch up.'

'Yes, sir.'

Cato lowered his voice and leaned a little closer. 'I give my officers one warning, Tubero. If you fuck up like this again, you'll be replaced. I will not have the men of my cohort put in danger unnecessarily. Clear?'

'Yes, sir.'

'Dismissed.'

Tubero returned to his standard and issued orders for his remaining men to mount up in column of twos, except for those who were helping the wounded back in the direction of the cohort's baggage train, and the section picking its way over the fallen enemy to finish off those still alive with quick thrusts to the throat or heart. The mounts belonging to the casualties were rounded up and put in the care of two dismounted auxiliaries.

There was a tense delay as the riders waited for Centurion Galerius and the infantry to reach them. On either side the pine-forested slopes rose up, and Cato felt the back of his neck tingle as he looked for any sign of movement in case the enemy had decided to renew their attack. But all was quiet except for the shuffling and snorting of the horses. The men looked round anxiously, keeping their shields ready while their right hands rested on the pommels of their swords, prepared to draw their weapons the instant the order was given.

At length they heard the tramp of boots, and Galerius appeared, shield held close to his body, leading the six centuries of men around the curve. He halted as Cato trotted back to meet him.

'First blood to the enemy,' he commented as he saw the dead auxiliaries beside the track.

'The honours were even enough.' Cato indicated the enemy bodies still on the track. 'But they gave us a nasty surprise. I hope Tubero and his men have learned a lesson. We're on the enemy's turf now. They know this land and they know how best to fight the legions. We can expect them to attempt such ambushes again, and the officers and men of this cohort are going to need to exercise more caution if we are to avoid making mistakes. The Eighth Illyrian is supposed to be one of the best cohorts in the army. I don't doubt the men's courage, but courage that is not tempered by discipline and caution is dangerous. Particularly when we go up against the warriors of these mountains. Men who are fighting for their very freedom have little to lose. I need you and the rest of the officers to understand that.'

Galerius bowed his head. 'Yes, sir. I'll make sure the word is spread down the chain of command.'

'Very good.' Cato did not enjoy delivering the brief lecture to his senior centurion, but it was important that his message and the reasoning behind it penetrated down to the lowest rank.

He turned away to examine the slopes stretching up to the ridges. The treeline gave way to open rock-strewn ground no more than two hundred paces on either side. Beyond, close to the skyline, he could see the riders of the two patrols he had sent out earlier, remounted and carefully picking their way forward. A mile or so ahead, the ridge to the left gave way to some crags, and he could see distant figures there. Scores of them. More than enough to block the patrol. Shifting his gaze to the opposite ridge, he could make out a similar-sized party. Provided there were not more of the enemy hidden close by, the two forces did not present much of an obstacle to his infantry. If they stood and fought, they would be pushed aside. If they fled, as he expected them to, it would cause a tiresome delay. Which was what the Ordovices intended, he surmised, giving them time to warn their scattered tribespeople of the Roman advance and allowing their warriors to concentrate and give battle. If they could delay and harry the Roman column, and cut their lines of communication, Suetonius would be obliged to leave men behind to protect the supply columns coming forward from Viroconium. With the Roman forces thus weakened, the odds would improve for the Ordovices and their allies.

His thoughts returned to the immediate situation. It would be necessary to clear the forest on either side of the track of any remaining enemy so as not to impede the progress of the main column. Once the defile was passed and the track emerged back into open ground, he could re-form the cohort at the head of the column.

'Galerius, I want the first three centuries to form a line up the slope to the left, the rest of the infantry to the right. When the line is ready, you are to advance until you clear those trees. If the enemy is seen or engaged, I want a report sent to me at once. I'll be advancing with the cavalry up this track in tandem until we reach the far side of the defile and get out of the trees. See to it.'

'Yes, sir.'

The orders were relayed, and the leading men of the First Century wheeled and moved into the pine trees. Cato heard the dull crackle of trampled undergrowth and the snap of twigs and small branches as the auxiliaries climbed the slope. The following two centuries followed suit before the other units moved into the trees on the right. When all was ready, Cato gave the order to advance. The cavalry moved slowly, stopping frequently to allow the infantry to keep up. It was a laborious process, he conceded, but the only way to ensure that the column could pass through the defile without any harassing attacks from the cover of the trees.

The track inclined gently as the ridges closed in on either side. The trees began to thin out, and for the first time, Cato caught glimpses of his men in the open. There was no sound of any fighting and no reports of contact with the enemy. The pace of the advance had picked up noticeably, and he was feeling relieved at the prospect of not delaying the main column's progress. He turned to call over his shoulder.

'First troop, First Squadron, on me!'

He urged his horse into a gentle trot, and the eight men of the troop followed close behind. A mile along the track, there was a steep rise and the defile narrowed, with cliffs and rocks at the top and scree slopes below. Cato hoped that the rising ground would provide a good viewpoint from which to see the route ahead, and perhaps find enough open ground on which to camp for the night.

He spurred his horse to the top of the rise, pulled hard on the reins and stopped abruptly. Two hundred paces ahead, where the defile was narrowest, a crude stone wall had been raised across the open ground. In front of it lay a ditch, though it was not possible to see how deep it was. A redoubt rose in the middle of the wall, perhaps sixty feet across. He could see that the wall was lined with men and bristling with spears and bows. Many helmets glinted in the afternoon sunlight and a long red standard flickered in the breeze. As the warriors caught sight of Cato and his mounted troop, they let out a loud roar that echoed off the sides of the steep slopes on either side.

Cato raised a hand in mock greeting. 'So, my friends,' he muttered, 'this is where it begins in earnest.'

# CHAPTER SIXTEEN

'What are you waiting for, Prefect Cato?' Governor Suetonius demanded. 'Get that rabble out of my way so the column can advance.'

They were standing at the top of the rise Cato had ascended nearly an hour earlier. Nearby, a staff officer was holding their horses. Ten of Suetonius's bodyguards were posted thirty paces forward, facing the enemy's wall. Behind them, just below the rise, the Eighth Cohort was arrayed in a battle line: infantry in the centre, with cavalry on the wings. The cohort's bolt-throwers, mounted on carts, had been brought forward and were being eased into place either side of the two officers. The crew had pulled the leather covers off and were assembling the arms and readying the ammunition. Due to the narrow width of the enemy's defences, no more than a hundred paces from end to end, the men and riders of the cohort were drawn up in deep ranks, waiting for orders.

Cato indicated the ridges. 'I've sent two squadrons to clear the enemy from the crags on each side. It should be done very soon, sir.'

Suetonius squinted in the bright sunlight. 'I can't see anyone.'

'Nevertheless, the enemy do have men up there, sir. Slingers and archers.'

'How can you be certain of that?'

Cato pointed to the grass-tufted ground halfway between them and the wall. The bodies of three auxiliaries and a horse were visible. The horse was still alive and every so often kicked out feebly. 'I went forward with a troop for a closer look. We were lucky the enemy lacked the discipline to wait until we were within range, otherwise we'd have lost more men. If my cohort attempts a frontal attack while the Ordovices still hold the heights, our losses will be heavy even before we reach the ditch.'

Suetonius considered the situation with a frustrated expression. Cato could understand his mood. It was the predicament that faced all commanders advancing into enemy territory: balancing the need to keep moving against taking risks that cost men's lives.

'Very well.' The governor came to a decision. 'We'll wait a little longer, but if there's no sign that your flanking parties have done their work by then, you'll lead your men forward and take that wall.'

Despite his reservations, there was nothing Cato could do but acknowledge the order now that it had been given.

'Yes, sir. As you command.'

Suetonius shot him a close look, sensing the hint of dissent in his subordinate. 'Prefect, it appears you weren't so cautious earlier today when you sent your men into that ambush.'

Cato was tempted to explain that Tubero had exceeded his orders. At the same time, he was aware that he had not sufficiently impressed upon the centurion the need to be wary of a trap. Besides, he considered it unseemly to make excuses for himself by laying the blame on one of his officers. It was his view that when a man took command of a unit, he took responsibility for the actions of those under his command. In the past, he had witnessed commanding officers attempt to duck criticism by claiming they had been let down by their men. It did them no favours. Both their men and their superiors despised them for it, and such behaviour followed them like a bad smell for what was left of their active career in the army.

'It was my mistake, sir. I considered it worth the risk to capture some of the enemy to question for intelligence purposes. The responsibility for the men lost in the ambush is mine.'

'Fair enough. I prefer my officers to take the fight to the enemy rather than exercising too much caution. Just don't make a habit of losing men unnecessarily.'

'Yes, sir.'

The exchange was ended by a cry of alarm from above, and Cato and Suetonius looked up at the crags. An instant later, there were more shouts, then a faint ring of blade on blade and thuds of blows landing on shields. As yet, neither officer could see any signs of the struggle taking place on top of the crags. Then two figures appeared, dark against the sky, an auxiliary trading blows with a warrior, before the latter suddenly doubled over and dropped his sword. The auxiliary drove his thrust further in, forcing his foe back until he stood at the edge. Then, with a powerful wrench, he pulled his blade free and kicked the warrior in the chest. The man staggered, lost his footing and fell, tumbling backwards, limbs flailing, as he plummeted down and was dashed on the rocks at the foot of the crag. More men appeared on the top of the crags – auxiliaries, as far as Cato could make out. There was no more sound of fighting, and the men offered a distant victory cry.

'One down,' Suetonius commented, and turned to the right to look up at the other ridge. There were more figures visible there, this time in the cloaks and flowing hair of the enemy.

Cato scanned the ridge line until he spotted his men. They were over half a mile distant from their target, and he could see the reason for their delay. The ridge on the right was more boulder-strewn and the auxiliaries were forced to pick their way along on foot as they made their approach.

'What in Hades is keeping them?' Suetonius muttered, still looking up at the enemy on top of the crags.

'There, sir.' Cato pointed out the second flanking squadron.

'We can't afford to wait any longer if we're to get through that wall and set up the marching camp before nightfall. You must attack now.'

Cato's first instinct was to try to persuade his superior to wait for the squadron to seize the crags to the right, but he sensed that Suetonius would brook no delay and would insist on the order. He resigned himself to making the best of a difficult situation.

'Yes, sir.' He saluted and turned towards his waiting men, formulating a plan as he did so. A frontal assault was the most immediate, and mostly costly, option. The men on the right flank would suffer a barrage of missiles from the crag as they crossed the open ground to reach the wall. As they closed on the enemy, they would face another barrage from the front. By the time he had reached the officers gathered about the colour party, Cato had discounted any idea of a frontal attack and reached a different decision.

'Suetonius has ordered us to take the wall now,' he informed Galerius and the others.

The centurions glanced in the direction of the enemy and the crags, and Galerius said, 'Ain't going to be the easiest nut to crack, sir.'

'Quite. Especially with the crag above the right flank still in enemy hands.'

'We could use the bolt-throwers to make them keep their heads down,' suggested Flaccus.

Cato had already considered that, and shook his head. 'The angle's too great. Even if it wasn't, they'd have plenty of cover amongst the rocks.' He looked round at his centurions as he continued. 'But there is another way of doing this.'

He turned and pointed to the left of the wall. 'Galerius, I want you to take the first four centuries and advance along the base of the crags. You'll be out of range of the men to the right. There might be the odd lucky shot, but that's all. I need you to force your way over the wall. Maximum effort. Make as much noise as you can while you go about it. The moment you have gained the wall, start rolling up their flank and head for the redoubt.'

Cato looked at the optio in charge of the cohort's small artillery contingent. 'Rubio, isn't it?'

'Yes, sir.' The fresh-faced officer nodded.

'I want you to concentrate your barrage on the redoubt to encourage them to keep their heads down until we're ready to attack from both sides. Once it's taken, the wall will be ours and we can open the way for the rest of the column.'

'Both sides?' Galerius queried.

'That's right. The best way to be sure of completing the job. I'll take the fifth and sixth centuries to the right, along the base of the crags, once your attack goes in and the enemy's attention is focused on you.'

'What about the Ordovices at the top? You'll be at their mercy.'

'They'll have trouble aiming vertically down. They'll throw some rocks for sure, but we'll have to endure that.' Cato saw that Suetonius was getting impatient. 'Right, gentlemen, you have your orders. Go to it.'

The group dispersed, trotting to their respective positions, and the air filled with the cry of commands. Rubio was the first into action, as he ordered his six bolt-throwers to be trained on the redoubt and then shouted the order to shoot. There was a series of overlapping cracks as the released throwing arms snapped forward, discharging the deadly eighteen-inch shafts with their iron heads. The missiles' trajectory was much lower than that of an arrow or light javelin, and most of the defenders on the wall had never seen such a weapon before, let alone been on the receiving end. As a result, the first ragged volley caught them by surprise. Cato saw explosions of splinters as two bolts hit the stonework. Three of the others must have gone high, but one struck a defender in the face and there was a burst of blood as he was thrown backwards off the wall and out of sight.

'Good shooting!' Cato called out in encouragement.

The optio gave the order to continue shooting at will. Cato watched the bolt-throwers for a moment and saw that they were having the intended effect. Only a handful of faces now appeared along the wall, ducking out of sight as the next bolt came hurtling towards them. Meanwhile, the centuries under Galerius's command were filing to the left before forming up in a narrow column close to the foot of the slope leading up to the crags above.

Close by, Centurions Decius and Vellius had nearly completed forming their men into a column, and Cato trotted over to join Decius at the head of the leading unit.

'We'll wait until Galerius has a foothold on the wall before we make our move.'

'Yes, sir.'

Above the continued crack of the bolt-throwers, Cato heard Galerius's commands echoing off the slopes. A moment later, the leading ranks of the column edged forward, with the centurion calling encouragement to his men from the front. There was a loud cheer in response before the ranks fell silent and advanced on the wall. Some of the defenders risked showing themselves and hurled insults at the auxiliaries in a swelling chorus of defiance.

As the distance between the auxiliaries and the wall narrowed, the first slingshot arced over the defences. The enemy were shooting blind, Cato realised, as the lead shot fell short. Galerius ordered his men to bring their shields to the front and angle them above their heads to deflect the incoming missiles. More shot and arrows began to fall close by and on the shields, splintering or piercing the surfaces.

Cato saw the first of the auxiliaries go down, struck on the ankle by an arrow. He moved out of the line and crouched behind his shield as he sheathed his sword and tried to pull the arrow out. A natural reaction, but a nearly hopeless task, Cato knew. It was almost impossible to manoeuvre the barbed head back along the entrance wound; instead, the shaft had to be broken and pushed through.

The enemy had grasped that the bolt-throwers were targeting the redoubt, and now men were prepared to show themselves along the wall on either side, taking aimed shots at the oncoming auxiliaries. Several more men from the leading century were struck down or fell out of formation. Cato saw Galerius's crest dip out of sight as he crossed the ditch. Some of the defenders were hurling rocks, since the target was too close to miss, and the larger pieces drove down the shields of the nearest auxiliaries. Galerius appeared again, half crouched beside the wall as he waved his men up on either side. The century's standard-bearer had halted on the far side of the ditch, ready to be summoned the moment a foothold had been won on the wall and there was less danger of the standard being seized by the enemy. Such a loss would have been a permanent stain on the reputation of not only the First Century but the cohort as a whole, and Cato judged that Galerius was right to be cautious.

Several men stood with their backs to the wall, grounded their shields and cupped their hands ready to hoist their comrades up to attack the defenders. The enemy were massed there, determined to hold firm. Cato could see that some of the warriors further along were moving to reinforce the far flank, and he prepared to lead the second smaller force forward. One of the mounted squadrons was close by, and he paced over and ordered the nearest man to hand over his shield. Thus equipped, he resumed his place at the head of the Fifth Century, beside Decius.

'Now, sir?'

'No. We wait until Galerius's standard is placed on the wall. That will be our signal to go.'

The first of the auxiliaries was raised by his comrades to fight his way over the stone breastwork. He took a glancing blow on his shield before thrusting with his sword. The blow was blocked and then an axe knocked his shield back so that he lost his balance and tumbled into the ditch. At once another man took his place and two more were hoisted up on either side, then Galerius clambered up at the very end of the wall, where he had the best chance of winning a foothold. Cato saw him parry a blow, then strike down his opponent, before he hooked his shield over the breastwork and swung himself up. He was immediately assailed as he fought furiously to hold his ground. With his back covered by the end of the wall, he punched his shield forward and thrust the enemy back, clearing a space for a second man to follow behind him, then another, pushing forward behind their large oval shields.

Within moments there were at least ten auxiliaries on the

wall behind their centurion, while others further along were struggling to get over the top, some wounded and falling or climbing down while others were shoved back to tumble onto their comrades pressed together in the ditch. Cato saw Galerius beckon, and the standard moved forward to the wall.

'That's it,' he said to Decius. 'Time for us to move. We'll double along the base of the cliff to the end of the wall.'

The centurion turned to address his men. 'Fifth Century! At the double pace . . . Advance!'

With Cato and Decius at their head, the century started up the slight slope towards the foot of the crags, kit jingling as their boots pounded across the loose stones and clumps of grass. At once there was a shout from far above, and a moment later, an arrow pierced the ground almost vertically ten feet to Cato's side. They were already close enough to make slingshot difficult, even though a handful of the enemy tried, their missiles smashing into the ground even further off. However, the follow-up century was not so fortunate, now that the enemy were alerted to the advance of the second group of auxiliaries, and three of them were struck down before they reached the bottom of the cliff.

'Keep moving!' Cato called as he increased the pace. He knew that the enemy above must already be changing their choice of missiles with which to barrage the attackers. A moment later he heard the rattle of loose stones, and a rock the size of a man's head thudded down a few paces in front of him.

'Shields up and over!' Centurion Decius shouted.

His men obeyed his order as they continued trotting towards the wall, which was now no more than a hundred paces away. More rocks fell, some deflected outwards as they struck an obstruction so that they crashed down away to the left. The first of Decius's men, three ranks back from the two officers, was flattened by a boulder that smashed through his shield and struck his helmet, driving him to the ground as blood burst from the pulverised metal. Others were also killed outright or wounded by rocks plummeting from the crags.

The ditch was now ten paces ahead, another five across, and then there was the wall, no more than eight feet of rocks fitted roughly together, and above it the heads and shoulders of the enemy as they readied their weapons. The advance had been quick enough to take advantage of the defenders' preoccupation with the action at the far end, and only a handful of arrows and slingshot had been loosed in their direction.

As Cato reached the ditch, he stopped and waved Decius and the first men forward, then called out to the standard-bearer.

'Here! On me!'

Doing his best to cover both of them with the borrowed shield, he watched as the centurion climbed out of the ditch and thrust his men left and right to hoist up those who followed. In the redoubt, some of the enemy who dared to look up in between shots from the bolt-throwers became aware of the new threat to their position, and shouted and beckoned to their comrades to move along the wall to reinforce the few who were in place to meet the second assault force.

'Quickly, Decius!' Cato called across to him, anxious to take advantage of the disparity in numbers.

The centurion glanced at him and then raised his boot into the first man's hands. He was heaved up and steadied by another as he rose above the breastwork. At once he slashed his sword in an arc to force back any defender, swung his other leg over, covered by his shield, and made to roll into a crouch on the far side. He never made it. A warrior wielding a large studded club in both hands swung it savagely down on the side of Decius's head, and he instantly went limp. A moment later his body was heaved back and fell heavily at the foot of the wall.

The men around him froze in shock, and one started to edge back. Panic could spread in a heartbeat, Cato knew. He had to act or the attack would fail before it had barely started.

He turned to the standard-bearer. 'Take my shield and stay put!'

Releasing his grip and thrusting the shield at the man, he rushed forward, scrambling down the outer slope of the ditch and pushing his way through the men in front of him before climbing the far slope on hands and knees until he was standing over Decius's body. The centurion was clearly beyond help, and without hesitating, Cato drew his sword, then thrust his boot into the hands of the auxiliary with his back braced against the wall.

'Get me up there!' he snapped.

The man heaved him up with a grunt, and Cato reached out with his left hand and secured a grip on top of the wall. As he drew level with the final layer of stones, he saw the warrior with the club. Their eyes met briefly, then the man began to raise the club in a two-handed grip. Straining with his left arm to rise more swiftly, Cato punched his sword forward the moment it cleared the wall. It was an instinctive blow rather than a trained one with weight thrown behind it, but the point caught the man under the chin and sank through his bearded throat and up into his jaw. Blood sprayed from his lips as he brought the club down. Cato ducked his head just in time and the weapon slammed onto the stone. He felt splinters strike the side of his nose. At once he looked up and pressed the sword home, swinging a leg over and trapping the club under his torso. His opponent staggered back a step, hands scrabbling at the blade as he tried to pull it out. Losing his footing, he fell back off the walkway, and as the sword came free, Cato swung it left and right to force back the nearest of his enemies.

'On me!' he yelled. 'Get up here!'

There were only two warriors to his right at the end of the wall. One was a man in his forties with his hair tied back with a braided band. He held an axe in one hand and a dagger in the other. His face was thin and his eyes a piercing blue. The youth behind him had the same features. Father and son, Cato decided. As the next legionary scrambled over the wall behind him, Cato called over his shoulder, 'Go left! Left!'

As he gave the order, the axeman came at him, swinging the weapon diagonally at his head. He parried the blow with a loud clatter, and the warrior stabbed the dagger at his midriff. The point caught on the scale armour, but he felt the impact of the blow even through the padding of his tunic beneath and gasped explosively. The two men parted, and Cato held his sword up, ready to deal with either weapon. This time the warrior feinted with the dagger. Cato flinched but did not commit his blade, and as the axe arm swung again, he leaned forward and hacked at the inside of the warrior's elbow. The blow drove the man's arm down, and the axe dropped from his spasming fingers as he looked down in shock at the wound, which had cut through muscle to the bone and rendered his arm useless. Cato punched him on the side of his face with a left hook, then pushed him off the walkway.

The warrior's son was holding a short spear, which he now jabbed feebly forward. Cato saw that he was no older than fifteen. The terror in his expression was clear and his limbs trembled nervously as he made another half-hearted thrust, which was deflected with ease.

Snatching a deep breath, Cato opened his mouth in a wide roar.

The boy shrank back and lost his grip on the spear so that the tip clattered onto the walkway. Cato made to strike, and the boy let out a yelp and leaped off the wall, landing in a heap beside his father. He was up in an instant, torn between the instinct to run and wanting to help his father. Then he crouched and strained to lift his father and pull him away from the wall, crying in a high-pitched voice in his native tongue.

Cato turned to see one of his own men tumbling behind the wall, his shield falling with him. A burly warrior, stripped to the waist, was brandishing a long Celtic sword as he pressed forward to deal with the next auxiliary. Four more Romans had made it onto the wall, and the first of them raised his sword as the Ordovician swung his blade down. It cut through the trim and bit deep into the laminated wood. The soldier went down onto his knees, slashing feebly with his sword but missing his opponent. However, the warrior could not pull his blade free from the shield, and as he wrenched at it furiously, the next man pushed forward, hacking at the man's wrist and almost severing the hand so that it released the sword handle and hung down from a flap of gristle. The Ordovician recoiled, grabbing the hand with his other one and clamping it to his chest as he turned and staggered towards the redoubt. The auxiliary followed him and stabbed him in the back, ripping his sword free and delivering several more savage thrusts before the warrior staggered heavily against the wall, dislodging some of the stones and falling with them into the ditch beyond.

'Push on!' Cato ordered. 'Forward!'

The auxiliaries ahead of him ran into the enemy, leading with their shields and throwing their weight behind them to batter the Ordovices back. Every step taken won more space for the men of Decius's century to scale the wall. Cato leaned over and called out to the standard-bearer.

'Up here! Hurry!'

More auxiliaries streamed over, and then the standard-bearer was hoisted up and stood with Cato.

'Keep it high.' Cato indicated the century's standard, aware of the inspiration it would give to the men of the unit, and the Sixth Century waiting to follow up.

Half of Decius's men were on the wall now, pushing the enemy back towards the redoubt, which was still being bombarded by ballista bolts. Beyond, Cato could make out spear tips and the points of raised swords, and in the distance, the standard of the First Century as Galerius's men fought their way towards the redoubt. The enemy's morale was already crumbling, and several had jumped from the wall to flee. The slope behind the hastily assembled defence dipped down towards a thickly forested area as the ridges opened up again, and it was clear that most would escape that way unless they were prevented from doing so.

Cato turned back to look over the wall and ditch, where Vellius and his men were poised to cross.

'Vellius! Send a man to the artillery battery. Tell them to cease shooting.'

The centurion tapped the brim of his helmet in salute and passed the order to one of his men, who set off towards the battery.

Cato paused a moment to focus his mind and prepare his next orders. The enemy had lost control of the wall, and soon those sheltering in the redoubt would be surrounded and would either have to surrender or die. As for the rest of the warband, they might make good their escape and therefore live to fight another day. It would be better to try and destroy or capture them before they could flee. The Fifth Century was already committed fighting along the wall as well as spilling out onto the ground below. As soon as Vellius was close enough, Cato addressed him.

'Get your men down behind the wall and form a screen on the slope to cut off the line of retreat. Take prisoners where possible. They'll be needed for questioning, and afterwards booty.'

Vellius grinned with approval and instructed his men to form up. Having prepared to close the trap, Cato jumped down and picked up a shield from beside the body of an auxiliary, then hurried towards the skirmish that had formed a short distance from the redoubt. He encountered several more casualties from Decius's century on the way, and a score of Ordovicians, some of them wounded and trying to drag themselves to safety, others lying moaning or silent as they bled. The enemy had fallen back under the initial attack on the extreme end of the wall, but the numbers were more even as those closer to the redoubt had thrown their weight into the fight.

With Decius dead, the century needed a leader at the front of the fight. Cato shoved his way through the middle of the uneven battle line, where the crest of his helmet had the best chance of being seen by the auxiliaries. Over the din of clashing metal and thuds of weapons on shields, he shouted to the standard-bearer to take position behind him, and then called out to the men on either side of him.

'Forward the Fifth Century! For Rome! For Decius! Forward!'

As he pushed on, he came abruptly face to face with one of the enemy, a bulky, bald man with a beard who was armed with a Roman short sword and a round buckler. The warrior punched the buckler towards him, but it was met by the boss of the fallen auxiliary's shield, and there was a brittle clang and then a rasping thud as each man tested the other's strength. As

Cato felt himself being borne fractionally back, he lifted his opponent's forearm and the pressure on his shield eased as the warrior withdrew with a hissed curse. At the same moment, Cato caught a glimpse of the man's blade. He thrust his shield out to deflect it, and the two men stepped apart for an instant.

There was a wary look in the man's eyes as he raised his buckler with a grimace and levelled his sword. Cato was about to lunge when his opponent moved first, the buckler going fast to Cato's left, overlapping the edge of the auxiliary shield. Too late Cato grasped his intention, but before he could respond, the warrior gave a savage wrench that turned Cato's shield and forced him to spin to his right, exposing his left side. At once the warrior thrust his sword, and the point tore into Cato's exposed bicep. He felt the impact of the blow as if struck with a hammer, the tearing of flesh and the grating of the point on his bone, then the searing pain as if he had been stabbed with a red-hot poker. All in less time than it took to draw a breath. His grip loosened on his shield and it dropped to the ground with a thud before tipping forward and striking the warrior's midriff. The latter twisted his sword blade, causing fresh agony, then ripped it free and prepared to make another thrust. Cato's left arm hung uselessly as he raised his sword to block the next attack.

'Get back, sir!' a voice snapped close to his side, and an auxiliary charged between Cato and the warrior and slammed his shield into the man with all his weight. The Ordovician stumbled back and came up hard against one of his comrades, and both men tumbled to the ground. The auxiliary stabbed the warrior in the face, then again in the throat before kicking him to the ground.

He backed up in front of Cato, covering them both with his shield. 'You're wounded, sir. Get to the rear.'

The pain in his arm was searing, and Cato had to grit his teeth. 'My thanks.'

The auxiliary gave a curt nod without looking away from his front, then stepped forward to return to the fight as the Roman line advanced. Cato drew back several paces until he was in open ground, sheathing his blade before inspecting the wound. Blood was coursing from the dark mouth of the tear in his flesh. He felt more dripping from the rear of his arm, where the point had emerged. The limb felt strangely numb, and his fingers refused to respond to his bidding.

The standard-bearer had fallen back with him, and now rammed the iron point at the base of the shaft into the ground.

'Let me see that, sir.' He raised Cato's arm to examine the wound, then reached into his sidebag and took out a strip of cloth. 'Flesh wound, I'd say. Nasty, though.'

He took out some more cloth and folded it to form wadding before pressing it on the arm, then started to wrap the dressing tightly around it. The pressure increased the pain, and Cato ground his teeth and fought off a bout of nausea. To distract himself, he watched the action in front of him. The fight had turned in the cohort's favour on the near side of the redoubt, and the Ordovices were being driven back. To his right, down the slope, the Sixth Century was extending a line to cut the defenders off. A handful had already escaped and were running for the cover of the trees below, while others tried to slash their way through but were quickly cut down by Vellius's men. As Cato watched, the first of the enemy warriors threw down his weapons and fell to his knees in surrender.

As an auxiliary advanced to escort the prisoner to the rear of the century, he was suddenly thrown backwards as if swatted down by an invisible hand. As his body hit the ground, Cato saw the shaft of a ballista bolt protruding from his chest. Another shaft overshot the redoubt, going between two of Vellius's men before arcing into the grass further down the slope.

The standard-bearer had finished tying off the dressing, and Cato pulled free and ran back to the wall, cursing as he used his good arm to help him climb up onto the walkway and rise to his feet. He could see the artillery battery still concentrating on loading and shooting their weapons. Some fifty paces short of the bolt-throwers lay the body of an auxiliary, face down, his shield a short distance to one side. Cato surmised that he was the man sent to Rubio with the order for the battery to cease shooting. He glanced up at the crags above him and saw several of the enemy looking on, some with slings drooping from their hands.

He waved his good arm from side to side and called out to Rubio at the top of his voice. 'Cease shooting! Cease!' But the optio was staring in the direction of the redoubt, watching the fall of shot, and didn't see him.

He was about to try again when there was a loud impact on the stones to his left and fragments of rock struck his side. Cato flinched. Looking up, he saw two of the Ordovicians on the crag whirling their slings overhead while another placed a shot in his pouch. The next two shots were unleashed at almost the same moment. He heard a zip as one went past close by, then saw the body of one of the defenders on the walkway a short distance away lurch as it was struck.

'Rubio! Damn you, Rubio!' He waved again. This time one of the ballista crew saw him and alerted the optio.

Cato cupped his good hand to his mouth and bellowed, 'Cease shooting!'

Rubio barked an order and the crews moved back from their weapons. There was no time for Cato to feel relieved as another slingshot whirred past. He jumped down from the walkway and ran towards the melee relentlessly shifting towards the redoubt. Once he felt he was safely out of range, he turned and saw that the mounted troop advancing along the ridge had almost reached the crag and would clear it of the enemy shortly.

As he approached Decius's men, he could see that the fight on this side of the redoubt was all but over. A handful of the most stout-hearted warriors were fighting to the last, back to back in a small knot surrounded by auxiliaries. The rest of the enemy had fallen or surrendered. The latter were roughly manhandled to the foot of the wall and thrust face down on the ground, where they were left under guard.

There was a movement to the rear of the redoubt, and he saw Galerius trotting towards him with a squad of his men, shields raised as they kept watch on the wall of the redoubt above. Beyond them, Vellius's men were rounding up prisoners, and after a quick scan of the ground, Cato was relieved to see that no more of them had fallen victim to the bolt-throwers.

Galerius nodded a greeting as he approached, then saw the dressing on Cato's arm. 'Are you all right, sir?'

'Does it fucking look like I am?' Cato forced a grin. 'How are things at your end?'

'The wall is in our hands. The bastards put up a good fight, but we got most of them in the end. No more than a handful got away before Vellius put a stop to it.'

'Very good. That just leaves our friends in the redoubt. No point wasting any more lives attacking it. We'll offer them a chance to surrender first.'

'Yes, sir.'

'Have your men pull back and form up in front of Vellius.'

As Galerius trotted back to his force on the far side of the redoubt, Cato saw the last of the warriors resisting Decius's men cut down and finished off under a brief hail of sword blows. A quiet fell across the scene, save for some shouts of alarm from the Ordovicians on top of the crag, and the men with slings turned and disappeared. Cato sought out the plumed helmet of the century's second in command and called him over.

'Form your men up fifty paces back. Take the walking wounded with you and have their wounds seen to.'

'Yes, sir.'

As the auxiliaries pulled back, Cato stood alone on the open ground that was now covered with bodies, shields and weapons. There were many still living who moved feebly, some crying out in agony, some muttering prayers or whimpering. He felt his heartbeat begin to slow as he surveyed the carnage, and then turned his attention to the redoubt. There were a score of men standing in full view now that the bolt-throwers had ceased shooting. One of them hefted a spear and aimed his counter-balancing arm at Cato.

'Wait!' Cato ordered, holding up his right hand.

The enemy warrior hesitated, then his body tensed as he made ready to hurl his weapon. Cato held his ground but braced his feet, ready to spring aside.

There was a shout from further along the redoubt, and Cato saw one of the defenders, a warrior in a green cloak whom he recognised from the earlier ambush, waving to the man who was about to throw his spear. The latter backed down and lowered his weapon. Cato turned his attention to the cloaked warrior.

'It's over!' He indicated the bodies before he continued. 'It is time for you to surrender. There is nothing to be gained by fighting on. Surrender!'

The defenders looked at him blankly, even though Cato was sure they must understand. He drew his sword and mimed throwing it down at his feet. 'Surrender!' Then he turned to point it towards the bodies outside the redoubt. 'Or die!' He jabbed the blade for emphasis before sheathing it and staring back at the enemy leader.

The latter regarded him for a moment, then turned to look at the line of auxiliaries blocking his retreat. His shoulders seemed to sink before he faced the survivors of his warband and began to address them. Cato stood and waited, hoping that no further blood would need to be shed. It had been futile for the enemy to try and block the advance of Suetonius's column with such a flimsy obstacle, and he wondered why they had even attempted it. An early show of defiance, perhaps? A gesture to demonstrate to the Romans that they would be resisted from the very outset? Certainly it had cost Cato a number of men and one of his centurions, and the bruising encounter would dent the morale of the column who had marched out in such high spirits only that morning. Now they would know that they were up against men who would defend their lands bravely against great odds. Perhaps the enemy had won a small victory of their own today.

There was a heated exchange of words from within the redoubt before the voices fell silent and the warrior in the green cloak turned back to Cato and drew his sword. He raised it slowly and pointed it directly up at the sky as he spoke clearly and boldly in his own tongue. For a moment Cato feared that his words betokened a refusal to give in. Then he braced his arm and hurled the sword in Cato's direction. It clattered to the ground halfway between them. Reluctantly the others followed suit, then climbed down from the redoubt and gathered around their leader, who bowed his head and lowered himself to his knees.

'Thank the gods,' Cato muttered.

* * *

By the time the main column reached the defile, Cato's men had demolished a section of the makeshift wall and used the stones to fill in the ditch in front of the gap. Soil was hurriedly packed down and a corduroy of logs laid across the resulting causeway. A cohort of the Fourteenth Legion led the way, the legionaries looking over the site of the battlefield with professional curiosity as they noted the bodies strewn behind the wall, the group of over eighty prisoners sitting close together under guard beside the track, and the weapons and armour being piled up by a section of Vellius's men. The rest of Cato's infantry were resting while the injured were treated. The cavalry had been sent forward under Tubero to guard the engineers, who had already ridden ahead to select a suitable site for the army to sleep that night. Beyond the trees, two miles away, the defile broadened and gave way to a gentle vale where a handful of farmsteads lay, abandoned at first sign of the approaching Romans.

Cato stood beside the redoubt as he concluded his report to Governor Suetonius, who had only seen the action from the far side of the wall.

'The Eighth acquitted themselves well today,' Suetonius commented. 'You and your lads did a fine job.'

'Thank you, sir.'

'Of course, that was after the disappointment of falling for the initial ambush,' he continued. 'That can't be allowed to happen again.'

'No, sir.'

'The orders given to your men must be unambiguous in future, Prefect Cato.'

Cato smarted at the criticism delivered by his superior. He was furious with himself for the oversight, and for failing to account for Tubero's headstrong nature. He had had long enough to get to know his officers and should have anticipated the possibility that Tubero would not be able to restrain himself from going after what looked like easy prey. The fact that the order had needed to be given in a hurry was no excuse.

'I understand, sir.'

'Good. Then you may tell your men from me that their general is proud of them. If the other auxiliary units fight as well as the Eighth, the campaign will be over before the end of summer.' Suetonius gestured towards Cato's arm. 'How bad is that?'

'A flesh wound, sir.'

'How did it happen?'

'Sword thrust, sir.'

'Painful, I imagine?'

Cato kept his expression neutral, even as the wound throbbed, and shrugged.

Suetonius smiled. 'I'll send my personal physician to your tent once the marching camp is completed. He learned his craft treating gladiators back in Capua, so he'll sort that out.'

Cato nodded his thanks. Over the general's shoulder he saw Galerius approaching, wax tablet in hand. The centurion halted a respectful distance away and stood waiting.

Suetonius looked round the scene once again and smiled. 'First blood to us. Let's hope all our victories come as easily, eh? I'll see you down in the camp, Prefect.'

Cato saluted and the governor turned to stride towards the small group of staff officers standing beside the track as two legionaries held the reins of their mounts.

'Into the saddle!' Suetonius called. 'We've wasted enough time here.'

The officers took their reins and mounted, and the governor

led his retinue down the slope before joining the track behind the leading legionary cohort. Galerius approached Cato and touched the brim of his helmet.

'Beg to report, sir. I have the butcher's bill.'

Cato's gaze shifted to the line of bodies beside the road. When the cohort's baggage train arrived, they would be loaded and taken to the marching camp for funeral rites.

'How many?'

Galerius opened his wax tablet. 'Nine dead and eleven wounded from the mounted contingent. Twenty-eight dead and forty injured from the infantry contingent. Most of the wounds are slight, luckily. One optio lost from the Third Century. And Centurion Decius.'

The image of the centurion's pulverised head leaped into Cato's thoughts, and he forced it aside. 'Who do you recommend to replace him? His optio, Metellinus?'

'No, sir. The lad's only recently been promoted. He needs more experience before he makes centurion.'

'Who else, then?'

'Rubio, sir. He's got what it takes. The kind who leads from the front.'

'Rubio, then,' Cato agreed. 'You'd better let him know. Tell him to pick the best man on the bolt-throwers to take over from him. Anything else?'

'No, sir.'

'Dismissed.'

As Galerius paced away, Cato's thoughts turned to the young optio, Metellinus. It looked as if he was going to get all the experience he needed to make centurion before the campaign was over. Provided he lived that long.

# CHAPTER SEVENTEEN

As the procurator's column approached the Iceni capital, Macro noted the hostile expressions on the faces of the tribespeople. At each settlement and farmstead along the route from Camulodunum, the locals had withdrawn into their huts and refused to offer any greeting. In the past, there had been those who wished to trade with Roman travellers, offering furs, trinkets, hunting spears and dogs, but now there was a sullen silence. On a handful of occasions they were greeted with angry insults, mostly from groups of young men at a safe distance. Once, a tall, dignified man, in his sixties Macro guessed, had stepped into their path and berated them bitterly as he gestured to them to turn round. Decianus had laughed and ordered one of his bodyguards to teach the fellow a lesson. A punch to the guts and a blow to the side of his head had driven the native to his knees. He shook his head and stood up shakily before resuming his protest. This time Decianus's man laid him out with a series of blows and brutal kicks. The Romans left him bleeding and moaning as they continued on their way.

Decianus and twenty mounted bodyguards led the way, followed by a small team of clerks with a mule that carried their records and writing materials. Then came the rest of the contingent of men drawn from the garrison at Londinium. The dregs of the army, Macro observed. Mostly unfit and slovenly, they made little attempt at marching in an orderly manner or looking after their kit. Behind them trundled the carts carrying Decianus's tent and other personal baggage, as well as several empty chests intended to be filled with whatever tribute could be squeezed out of the Iceni. At the rear marched Macro and his veterans, the only part of the column that had a genuinely military bearing. Although their weapons and kit were old, they had been maintained well. Their helmets gleamed and their shields were protected from the occasional rain showers by goatskin covers.

Macro had ordered that the colony's standard, awarded at the time of its foundation, be taken from the sanctum under the administration hall and carried at the head of the contingent. One of the veterans chosen for the party, Flaminius, had been the standard-bearer of the Fourteenth Legion for the last four years of his career and now proudly carried the colony standard aloft. Beside him marched Vulpinus, whom Macro had selected to act as his second in command.

The first day's march from Camulodunum had taken them as far as the remains of the fort at Combretovium, now little more than a grassy bank in the shape of a rectangle. It lay close to the border of Iceni lands, and it had worried Macro that the mood of the Trinovantes they had passed was unmistakably hostile. There was a palpable tension across the region that was made worse by the gloomy clouds and frequent light showers that threatened to become a storm but never did.

On the second day, they entered Iceni territory. To Macro it felt more like marching across enemy lands rather than those belonging to tribes who were sworn allies of Rome. That night they had camped by a river, and as the tents were being pitched, he saw a party of riders watching them from the brow of a foothill barely a mile away. Although the men carried hunting spears, there was no gleam of helmets, nor any battle standard or other sign that they were attired for war. Nevertheless, he gave orders that the watch be doubled for the night. Some sixth sense prevented him from sleeping more than fitfully, and he rose on three occasions to make sure the sentries were awake and vigilant before returning to his bedroll.

It was late afternoon on the third day when they came in sight of the Iceni capital. It was recorded as Venta Icenorum on the official Roman itinerary; the local name for the settlement translated as the Vale of the Horse Warriors, or so Macro had once been told by an Iceni cattle trader. Hundreds of round huts spread across open ground beside a river that snaked north-east and was clearly navigable. There were three barges with furled sails moored along a short length of wharf. Close by were several larger huts and a modest hall, surrounded by a palisade. Beside the huts were many pens of varying sizes containing sheep, pigs and some cattle, as well as numerous stables. Horses were grazing in meadows outside the settlement, taking advantage of the fresh spring grass. Here and there smoke curled into the sky from the tops of the thatched huts.

As he gazed down on the bucolic setting, Macro's heart filled with foreboding and pity for Boudica and her people. He dreaded the outcome should they fail to present the tribute due to Rome. His eyes shifted towards Decianus, who had reined in and moved to the side of the track to permit his bodyguards to ride ahead of him. Macro regarded the procurator with unrestrained loathing. This was not the first time he had been obliged to serve under a superior he disapproved of. Some had proved to be incompetent, some cowardly, and a few embodied both failings. Decianus was in a different category altogether. He evinced nothing but contempt for those ranked beneath him and fawning flattery for those above. While army officers, no matter what failings they might have, at least placed the interests of Rome first, even if personal ambition and lust for fame came a close second, Decianus was utterly self-serving and saw those around him as mere tools to be used and discarded in the pursuit of power and the wealth that came with it.

And if he regarded his subordinates as expendable, he considered the Iceni to be little better than animals, dogs to be whipped into submission or beaten to death if they refused to roll over. There was also a cowardly streak in the procurator's character. The anger still burned in Macro, and many of the veterans who marched behind him, when they remembered how Decianus had abandoned them to face the rage of the Trinovantians the previous year. The gods only knew what trouble he would cause Boudica and the Iceni.

'Jupiter, Best and Greatest,' Macro muttered. 'On my sacred honour, I will sacrifice an unblemished lamb to you if you would see your way clear to causing that bastard to slip from his saddle and break his fucking neck . . . Two lambs,' he added wistfully.

'Sir?'

Macro glanced round to see Flaminius at his shoulder, eyebrow raised, smiling slightly.

'I, uh, was just offering a prayer that Minerva and Fortuna grant the procurator wisdom and good fortune in his dealings with the Iceni.'

'I see. Very considerate of you, Centurion,' Flaminius responded. 'I'm sure your sentiments are shared by all of us.'

The gods, as was their way, refused to respond to Macro's request, and Decianus and his column had reached the Iceni capital without event. Ahead of them mothers gathered their children and ushered them out of the path of the Romans. The men, old and young, stood on either side and watched in silence. It was clear to Macro that they and their Trinovantian neighbours had long expected the moment when Rome would extend one hand to demand payment while the other brandished a sword to make it clear what failure to pay would entail.

The sun hung low in the sky and its rays burnished the thatched roofs of the huts in a fiery hue, while long shadows were cast over the muddy thoroughfares of the settlement. The quiet surrounding the marching men was oppressive, and Macro felt icy pins prick their way up the back of his neck as he cast his eyes from side to side looking for signs of danger. As the head of the column approached the timber gatehouse that guarded the entrance to the royal enclosure, a party of cloaked men with heavy boar spears barred the way and forced Decianus's bodyguards to draw up.

The column rippled to a halt and the procurator cupped a hand to his mouth and called out, 'Who dares to bar my way?'

The tallest of the Icenians took a step forward and spoke in clear Latin. 'Who dares to enter the capital of the Iceni uninvited?'

Decianus flicked his reins and trotted his horse closer to the gatehouse. 'I am Catus Decianus, imperial procurator appointed by the emperor in Rome. I need no invitation. I am here to negotiate with your queen, Boudica. You obstruct me at your peril.'

The Icenian looked unperturbed. He turned to exchange a quiet comment with one of his men, and the party laughed. Then he turned back to the procurator.

'Wait here. I will see if Boudica will receive you.'

The man brushed past his companions and paced into the

enclosure. Decianus trotted forward, thrusting his hand out. 'You there! Stop!'

The man's companions raised their spears and took a step forward. There was no mirth in their expressions now, just a steely determination. The procurator's bodyguards reached for their weapons, and Macro's pulse quickened as he saw the first blade drawn.

'Vulpinus, take over. I'm going to the front. If there's any trouble ahead, form the men into a box and wait for me to get back.'

'Yes, sir.'

Macro jogged alongside the carts, passing the men from the Londinium contingent, who looked nervous and fearful. As he reached the bodyguards, he called out, 'Keep your swords sheathed, or I'll have your guts for bootlaces!'

A handful of Decianus's men hesitated and looked to the procurator for orders as Macro strode the last few paces to join him.

'Those men are defying me.' Decianus pointed at the warriors blocking his way. 'Centurion, deal with them.'

Macro forced himself to remain calm. 'We don't want to get off to a violent start, do we?' he said quietly. 'Let's just keep this nice and peaceful, eh?'

'I am the representative of the emperor, the most powerful man in the known world, and I will not be defied by a gang of stinking barbarians. If these men refuse to move, they must be taught a lesson. I will give them a final warning before I order you to cut them down.'

'No one is cutting anyone down.' Macro glowered. 'The only lesson that's being taught today is how to behave diplomatically and not like some aristocratic cunt fresh out of his cradle. Back in Londinium you may well be the emperor's representative, but out here you are the loathsome little bean-counter I've been ordered to nursemaid. We'll get what we came for without any blood being shed and return home safely. If you put our lives at risk, like you did last time, I swear I won't make the mistake of letting you live to regret it. Do we understand each other?'

'How dare you speak to me like that?'

'Very easily, as it happens. Now you'll be a good procurator and behave if you know what is good for you.'

Decianus made to reply, but the words died on his lips as he saw the glint in Macro's eyes. He looked back towards the gatehouse and waited in silence for the return of the warrior who had gone to announce their arrival to Boudica.

They continued to wait as the sun dipped below the rooflines of the round huts and a gloomy dusk settled over the Roman column. At length the man returned and gave a curt order to the spearmen, who ambled aside.

'Queen Boudica will grant you an audience.'

'An audience?' Decianus snorted. He gestured for the column to follow him.

'Just you, Roman,' the warrior countered. 'You and Centurion Macro. The rest wait here.'

Macro was startled. How was his name known? He thought a moment and the answer came. The column had been under observation from the moment it crossed into Iceni territory. His face was familiar to a number of Boudica's followers. It amused him to think that he had been addressed by name, unlike the more terse reference to Decianus.

Decianus turned to him. 'Are they mad? Who would walk into such a place without protection?'

'You and me. Get off your horse and let's go and meet the queen.'

'But . . . is it safe?'

'Only one way to find out,' Macro replied, smiling at the procurator's discomfort. 'Oh, come on, man! Do you seriously think they would do us harm, given the consequences? Show a little backbone and make Rome proud. Let's go.'

He strode towards the warrior at the gate. After a beat, Decianus swung his leg over his saddle horns and eased himself to the ground before indicating to one of his men to take the reins of his horse. He hurried to catch up with Macro and fell into step at his side as they were led across the enclosure to the hall on the far side. Macro looked round as they marched, taking in the men working bellows at a smithy in the far corner. From this distance it was impossible to see if they were making spearheads, arrowheads or something forbidden, such as sword blades. To his right was a line of stables, with horses' heads protruding from their stalls. There was another stable block on the opposite side of the enclosure with wicker screens across the openings, all except the last one. In the failing light he could make out the shape of a war chariot in the gloomy interior.

At the entrance to the hall were two more warriors, armed with boar spears and wearing the blue cloaks of the royal household. One held up his hand and the man escorting them turned to Decianus. 'You'll have to leave your sword here. The queen does not permit you to come into her presence armed.'

'This is intolerable,' Decianus retorted.

'Nevertheless, it is her will, Roman. Your sword, please.' The Icenian held out his hand.

Decianus drew his blade and tossed it on the ground at the man's feet, forcing him to stoop to pick it up.

'What about him?' The procurator indicated Macro.

'Centurion Macro is well known to us, and trusted by the queen. He can keep his sword.'

'Remember what I said outside the gate,' Macro muttered. 'After you, Procurator.'

Decianus led the way under the oak lintel, decorated with ornate carvings of horses, deer and other game. The interior was dimly illuminated by what was left of the daylight coming through a window at the far end, and the guttering, smoky flames of tallow candles in iron stands along the side walls. Beneath the window, Boudica sat on the smaller of the two wooden thrones atop a dais. The other was empty, in honour of her late husband. The light from the window cast a halo over her red hair, which gleamed like fire, while at the same time concealing her features. On either side of her, on smaller chairs, sat her daughters, and behind them her nobles and advisers.

'I welcome you, Romans, in the name of my people,' she announced in a flat tone. 'Approach and explain the purpose of your presence in my capital.'

Macro stepped forward, with Decianus hesitating before following at the centurion's shoulder. When they were within ten feet of the dais, two of the queen's guards stepped forward and indicated that the Romans halt. Macro bowed his head formally. 'Your Majesty.'

'Centurion Macro, I am disappointed to see you in the company of the procurator.'

There was a hint of hurt in her tone, and Macro responded with a measure of guilt. 'Believe me, I would rather not be in his company, but I was ordered by the governor to furnish him with an escort.'

'It was my understanding that you had retired from the army.'

'Retired, yes, but I am still on the list of reserves, as are the men who form the escort. We are duty bound to answer the call if the governor requires reinforcements of the last resort.'

'He is short of men then,' Boudica mused, and turned her attention to Decianus. 'Procurator, explain your presence here.'

Decianus took a half-step forward so that he stood at Macro's side, and tried to affect a dignified air that only succeeded in being haughty. 'Queen Boudica, you know why I am here. I have come to collect the balance of the tribute that was due at the oath ceremony. My purpose is clear, and your duty is to pay over the outstanding sum, in silver or in kind.'

Boudica leaned forward. 'My first duty is to look after the welfare of my people. Only when that duty is satisfied am I obliged to honour my alliance to Rome.'

'The correct term is allegiance.'

Those at her side who understood Latin stirred at Decianus's response, and a moment later the rest did the same as the exchange was translated through whispers.

'That wasn't very smart,' Macro said, loudly enough for the other Roman to hear. 'We're here on their sufferance. Be careful what you say.'

As the light continued to fade outside, the glow of Boudica's hair diminished and Macro could more clearly make out the details of her face. He saw that the Icenian queen was smiling coldly as she responded.

'My people signed a treaty of friendship with Rome, yet you consider us servants.'

'You signed a treaty that guaranteed that Rome would protect you from your enemies in exchange for tribute. We have fulfilled our side of the agreement. You have yet to fulfil yours.'

'It is an empty agreement, Procurator. What enemies would Rome protect us from? You have subjugated all those we ever fought in these lands. The only protection we appear to need is from men like you who would loot our lands on the pretext that you are defending us.'

'However it might appear, the terms of the treaty you willingly entered into are clear and must be honoured.'

'Willingly!' Boudica scoffed. 'Rome came to us with an ultimatum – sign the treaty or be destroyed.'

'Then your people made a wise choice and signed.'

Macro decided to intervene. 'Majesty, it has been a long day's march for the procurator and his men. May I humbly request that we be given permission to pitch camp for the night? We can begin negotiations in the morning with fresh minds.'

Decianus gave Macro an angry look. 'I think—'

'Shut up,' Macro hissed softly. 'Don't think. Don't talk. Just be quiet.'

Boudica sat stern-faced for several heartbeats before she gave a nod. 'Very well. Your procurator is so tired that he forgets himself. Perhaps he will be more inclined to address me in a manner befitting my rank when he has had the opportunity to rest. You have our permission to camp outside the capital. You may return to continue the negotiations in the morning.' She waved a hand towards the entrance at the far end of the hall. 'You are dismissed from our presence.'

Macro steered Decianus ahead of him. 'Let's go.'

They did not look back as they departed, and it was only when the two men were halfway across the enclosure that the procurator addressed Macro angrily. 'What in Hades do you think you are doing treating me like that in front of that barbarian bitch?'

Macro rounded on him, stabbing a finger into his chest. 'You say anything like that again and I will knock your teeth out. Listen, you fool. I know the queen better than any Roman in Britannia. Well enough to know that if you push her too far, you will reap the whirlwind. There was a look in her eye I've not seen before. I'm telling you, we are in great danger, all of us. Bear that in mind when you speak to her tomorrow and keep a fucking civil tongue in your head. Now let's get our men out of here and get the camp set up and under guard before she changes her mind.'

# CHAPTER EIGHTEEN

Macro spent the following dawn worrying about the resumption of the audience with Queen Boudica. He had warned Decianus to choose his words more carefully when he next spoke to her. The procurator had sent his slave to bring a jar of wine from his baggage and had drunk heavily to get over his earlier frustration at failing to put the Icenian queen in her place. Her attitude irked him because she was both a barbarian and a woman. He was also angry at Macro's harsh words and dismissive treatment.

'Do you really think you can address me like that and get away with it?' he had demanded after his fifth cup of wine, his voice already slurred.

Rain pattered on the leather tent and a cold breeze caused the sides to billow gently. At another time Macro would have been content to accept the wine that Decianus had initially offered, even though he despised the man. But not that night. He understood the delicacy of the situation. He was also furious with himself for the comment concerning Suetonius's shortage of soldiers. He had seen the eager look in Boudica's eyes after he had let that slip, and hoped that it had not added fuel to a smouldering fire.

'You forced my hand,' he replied. 'If I had let you continue to bait her, that would have put all our lives at risk.'

'Bait? I was not baiting. I was merely putting that arrogant bitch in her place. She calls herself a queen, but she is like no queen I ever met in Rome.' Decianus took another mouthful of wine. 'Queen of what? A ghastly hovel in the middle of an uncivilised cluster of mud huts that would make the meanest vicus look like a great city by comparison. How dare she treat me with such disdain? I am Nero's representative and I answer only to Suetonius in this benighted province. I shall take great pleasure in humbling her.'

'Whatever it pleases you to think, she is queen of the Iceni and ruler of the land upon which we are camped at her pleasure. Remember that.'

Decianus reached for the jug to refill his cup. Macro's hand closed about the handle first and he placed the jug on the ground by his feet.

'Listen to me. You've only recently arrived in the province. You have spent most of your time at the governor's palace in Londinium and have little idea about the tribes on this island. Little idea about their customs and traditions. These were their lands before they were ours and I have seen how bravely and tenaciously they battled to keep them from us. I can tell you as one who has fought for Rome for over twenty-five years, from the Rhine to Egypt and from Syria to Britannia, I have never encountered a more dangerous enemy than the warriors of this island.'

'Really? Those uncivilised brutes? They are no more dangerous than a pack of wild dogs.'

'You know that's not true,' Macro responded bitterly. 'Or you would know if you hadn't run out on me and the other veterans last year before the real fighting started.'

Decianus's gaze wavered. 'I went for help.'

'All the way to Londinium? We both know what you did, Decianus, and it fucking stinks. You left us to fight our way out. And if you think so little of the warriors of these lands, then how is it that we are still fighting them nearly twenty years after we first invaded? Rome has lost many good men trying to tame this island, some of them friends of mine. When Suetonius has dealt with the last of those still holding out in the mountains and eliminated the Druids on Mona, we shall have peace at last. And I have earned that peace. I have earned the right to call this province my home and I have earned the right to enjoy the fruits of my service to Rome and live the rest of my days without trouble. So I'll thank you not to put all that at risk by provoking Boudica and her people.'

For an instant Macro recalled Cato's words before they had parted ways in Londinium. It was possible that the best way of preventing danger might be to kill Decianus. They were alone in the tent. The nearest of the procurator's bodyguards was too far away to save him if Macro acted quickly and struck before Decianus could cry for help. But a man did not murder one of the emperor's procurators without paying a price, and right then, the price was too high. A better opportunity might present itself, he decided. One where he could strike without being identified as the culprit.

'It doesn't matter if I provoke her or not.' Decianus gave a dry laugh. 'If she pays up, all well and good. If not, and she causes trouble, she will be destroyed. It makes no difference to the report I will deliver to Rome and the recommendations I will make. Now give me back my wine!'

Macro's tired wits were suddenly sharply revived. He topped up the procurator's cup. 'What recommendations?'

'Oh, come on, Macro, this province never had much of a chance of paying its way. It costs Rome far more to maintain the army here than Britannia contributes to the treasury. I've seen the figures. You want to know what I recommend? We loot the place for anything of value and then cut and run.'

'What about us? The Romans who have settled here?'

'Your choice. You leave with the legions, or you stay and try to maintain your peace with the natives.'

'Shit.' Macro leaned closer. 'Then you had better make sure you keep the peace tomorrow. Understand?'

'That depends on Boudica, doesn't it?' Decianus raised his cup and slopped some of the contents. 'To peace.'

As the morning sun warmed the Roman camp, Decianus emerged from his tent, pale but dressed in his finery: a matching green tunic and cloak, both richly embroidered with bright yellow thread. Macro had decided to leave most of the veterans to protect the camp and the carts and baggage while he took ten men with him to accompany the procurator and his bodyguards to the meeting with Boudica.

Decianus called for his horse and was helped into the saddle by his slave. He picked up the reins and positioned himself between the mounted bodyguards and the foot soldiers from the Londinium garrison. Macro and his small party formed up at the rear of the column.

'Forward!' Decianus ordered.

They left the camp and proceeded steadily through the settlement towards the royal enclosure. They were watched in silence by more people than the previous afternoon, as if the entire population of the capital had turned out to line the route. It felt like an ominous sign. They were not stopped at the entrance to the enclosure, and the column marched within and halted in front of the hall.

Macro turned to one of his men, Varius, and quietly ordered

him to take position by the gate and be ready to seal it if there was trouble. Meanwhile Decianus had dismounted and approached the officer in charge of his bodyguard. 'You have your orders, Attalus.'

He waited for Macro to join him before indicating the entrance to the hall. 'Shall we?'

There was a boldness to the procurator that morning that surprised Macro. He nodded. 'After you.'

Decianus strode into the hall with Macro at his shoulder. The sun shone through the opening above and behind Boudica and a hazy beam slanted down to the flagstone floor. Just as before, she was flanked by her daughters and advisers, and burly guards armed with hunting spears stood on either side of the dais. They watched the two Romans approach in silence. Decianus halted some ten feet from the queen and lifted his chin as Macro bowed his head in deference to her.

'Queen Boudica, it was unfortunate that our encounter yesterday took a fractious turn,' the procurator began calmly. 'I put that down to my weariness after a long day's march.'

'I accept your apology,' she replied. 'I trust we can resolve matters today in a better humour.'

'That is my wish too. I also think that yesterday's poor start to negotiations was equally attributable to your misapprehension of the wider situation you and your people find yourselves in. Hopefully that will be made clearer as a result of what happens today.'

Macro felt his pulse quicken. The conversation was already taking an unfortunate turn, and there was a not-so-veiled threat behind Decianus's words.

'Let's waste no time on formalities, Queen Boudica. The governor of Britannia has sent me to collect the balance of the tribute that the Iceni failed to pay in full at the oath ceremony.

I would be grateful if you presented it to me now.'

Boudica gestured to one of her advisers, and the man picked up a small chest at his feet, carried it to Decianus and laid it at the procurator's feet before withdrawing to his place behind the throne. The chest was no more than two feet in length by a foot in depth and another in height, and was made of oak strapped and studded with iron. It was obvious that it could contain only a fraction of the silver that had been stolen by Hormanus. Macro glanced at Decianus and saw that the procurator wore an amused expression.

'What is this?'

'The balance of the tribute that the Iceni can afford to pay this year,' Boudica stated.

Decianus slid back the catch before opening the lid. Macro saw that the contents amounted to a bed of silver coin topped with several gold torcs, brooches and other small items of jewellery. Nothing like enough to fulfil the amount they had been sent to collect.

'Where is the rest of it?' the procurator demanded.

'That is all there is, Roman. If there is a good harvest this year, we may be able to sell some grain to pay a larger tribute next year.'

'That is not acceptable. The governor made it clear that you had until the end of March to make good. Three months to raise the sum necessary. This,' he tapped the box with the toe of his boot, 'this collection of baubles is worth but a quarter of the sum required. I suggest you present me with the remainder at once.'

'That is all that we can and all that we will pay,' Boudica replied. 'You cannot ask for more when it does not exist. Take the chest and be gone.'

'Rome will not be satisfied with such paltry compensation.

If you do not pay in full at once, there will be consequences.'

'You dare to threaten me in my own hall?' Boudica drew herself up on the throne. She raised her arm and pointed to the entrance. 'Take it and go before I have my men throw you out.'

'If that is your response, then so be it.' Decianus turned to the entrance and shouted, 'Attalus! Now!'

The head of the bodyguard bellowed an order, and an instant later the Roman soldiers burst through the entrance, driving aside the two warriors standing guard and knocking them to the ground. Attalus led his men forward at a run, their swords drawn.

'What the fuck are you doing?' Macro demanded.

Boudica stood as her advisers and daughters looked on in shock. The two warriors with spears stepped forward and lowered the tips at the Romans racing towards them. Attalus and his men swiftly surrounded those on the dais.

'Tell them to lay down their weapons,' Decianus ordered.

'How dare you.' Boudica spoke in a clear, flat tone. 'I will have your head for this.'

'You'll do nothing of the sort,' Decianus retorted.

Macro stepped in between them and glared at the procurator. 'What are you doing? This is madness. Are you trying to start a war, you fool?'

'Get out of my way, Centurion, before I have you placed under arrest for insubordination. I've listened to your bleating about the need to respect this rabble long enough. Stand aside, or I will order Attalus to make you.'

Out of the corner of his eye, Macro saw the commander of the bodyguards take a step towards him. He was torn by the need to act to stop Decianus, but it was already too late. The procurator pushed him aside and addressed Boudica again.

‘Tell your men to drop their spears.’

‘I shall do no such thing. I order you to take your thugs and leave my capital at once, if you value your lives.’

Decianus gestured towards the two warriors. ‘Attalus, disarm them.’

‘First section! Take them!’ Attalus snapped.

Eight of his men raised their shields and closed in on the dais. The two warriors defending their queen grasped their spears firmly, and the one to her left thrust at his nearest opponent. The Roman deflected the strike, while another jumped up and thrust his sword into the warrior’s side. The Icenian gasped, and made to turn and strike out at his attacker, but the man slammed his shield forward and he fell at the queen’s feet, dropping his spear as he went down. The remaining warrior let out a ferocious war cry and thrust his spear out as he launched himself off the dais. He leaped onto the shield of one of the bodyguards, and both men crashed to the ground. In an instant, the Romans on either side stabbed their swords into the unprotected body of the warrior before helping their comrade back to his feet.

‘Oh shit,’ Macro whispered. He glanced at the body before turning his gaze to the dais, where Boudica was kneeling, cradling the head of the other warrior as he clasped a hand over the wound to his side. Blood was pulsing through his fingers and Macro could see that he was bleeding out. Behind the queen, her retinue and her daughters looked on with horrified expressions. Some seemed on the verge of throwing themselves upon the Romans, even though they were unarmed.

Macro seized the procurator’s arm and yanked him round so that they were face to face. ‘You fool! You bloody fool! What are you doing?’

Decianus pulled himself free. ‘I’m carrying out my orders,

and you need to do the same, Macro. Don't question me again, or I'll start killing the rest of these barbarian dogs.'

The wounded warrior was coughing up blood and convulsing, and Boudica took his free hand in hers and held it tightly as she whispered soothingly. A moment later, he choked and spasmed, then went limp, his head lolling to one side. The queen was still, then she leaned down to kiss his head before standing up, her long tunic spattered with blood. Macro could see that she was trembling, and she bunched her hands into fists and took a step towards the line of bodyguards standing between her and Decianus. 'I will kill you . . . I will kill you all.'

'Silence!' the procurator shouted. 'You will keep your mouth shut, or those two men will be merely the first to join their ancestors. Nod if you understand.'

She opened her mouth.

'Not one word!' Decianus warned. 'Just nod.'

Boudica's lips closed as her jaw twitched.

'That's better. You failed to pay the tribute when it was due. You failed to make up the shortfall even after the governor magnanimously gave you three months to do so. Therefore I have been authorised to execute your husband's will on the following basis. Firstly, the emperor will take possession of half of the Iceni kingdom as per the terms of the will. Secondly, Rome will take possession of the remaining half of Prasutagus's estate in lieu of the outstanding sum due. The Iceni kingdom will therefore be annexed by Rome and cease to exist as of this moment. In order to ensure the compliance of the Iceni people, I will be taking Queen Boudica and her daughters as hostages and they will return with me to Londinium. As soon as Governor Suetonius returns from campaign, I will return to assess the value of your property and will assign it to the control of Roman settlements to be founded on these lands. That is the fate of the Iceni. If anyone attempts to harm me or my men, or to set the former queen and her daughters free, they will pay with their lives.' He turned to Attalus. 'Seize her, and her two whelps.'

Attalus led the men who had dealt with the two warriors up onto the dais. Boudica's arms were grasped and she was dragged to the centre of the hall. One of her daughters cried out for her and had to be held back by a grey-haired adviser. Other Icenians shouted and gesticulated furiously but kept their distance from the men with drawn swords surrounding them.

Macro's stomach clenched into a tight fist and he felt sickened as Boudica was manhandled past him. Their eyes met and he shook his head helplessly, trying to indicate that he had not known what Decianus had planned. She glared back and spat into his face. He winced as the sputum struck his cheek and eyebrow, and experienced a humiliation such as he had never known before, accompanied by disgust and shame at the actions of the procurator and his own powerlessness to do anything to stop them.

Decianus's bodyguards were wrestling Boudica's daughters away from the retinue behind the throne. Macro saw two men, including the older adviser, beaten with the flats of swords to drive them back while the girls were seized by their hair and dragged off the dais to join their mother under guard in the middle of the hall. Attalus gave the order for his men to back off and then form up around the hostages.

Decianus smiled. 'I believe that concludes the negotiations. Macro, pick up the chest.'

Macro shook his head. 'Do it yourself, or get one of your thugs to pick it up. I ain't having any part of this.'

'You really think so? You reckon those people over there think you are any different to me? Stop behaving like a romantic fool, Macro. You are a Roman officer. You swore an oath to serve Rome and those placed in authority over you. What is happening here is the will of Rome, and not only are you complicit in it, you are obliged to defend it. Now pick that box up, or I will get one of those barbarian scum to do it for you.'

Macro's rage was steadily growing more twisted and tense inside him, like the torsion ropes of a ballista. He needed every grain of self-control he possessed to stop himself from throttling the procurator. With gritted teeth he bent to pick up the chest and tucked it under his left arm, keeping his sword hand free.

'Attalus, let's be on our way,' Decianus ordered.

With the bodyguards closed up around the procurator, Macro and the hostages, the small formation emerged from the hall and made its way over to the veterans near the compound gate. Varius saw them coming and called to the others to form up. They tagged on at the rear of the small column and Macro fell back to join them.

'What's with the women?' Varius asked quietly.

'Not just any women,' said Macro. 'Queen Boudica and her daughters.'

The veteran's eyes widened, then he glanced round as the first of those who had been held back in the hall came rushing out, shouting loudly. 'Oh shit.'

'Quite.' Macro nodded. 'We're in it now.'

As they progressed along the muddy main thoroughfare of the Iceni capital, people began to gather in response to the uproar. When they saw their queen and her daughters being held by Decianus's men, they looked shocked at first, then some groaned in dismay while others began to shout angrily. Boudica paced steadily, her shoulders back and her chin raised, staring ahead like a martyr walking fearlessly to her execution. Behind her, the two girls sobbed and had to be pulled along between their guards. When one of the local men tried to push his way through to the queen, he was struck down by a blow from the hilt of one of the procurator's men. At once Boudica turned to the gathering crowd and called out to them imploringly, and they drew back and let the Romans continue unmolested.

Varius glanced at Macro. 'I heard what happened last year. What if that bastard Decianus runs for it and leaves us to face that lot?'

'He won't,' Macro replied. 'This time he's in the heart of hostile territory, and his only hope of getting out alive is by making sure he keeps the hostages and the rest of us with him.'

'I hope you're right, sir.'

As the column left the settlement and made for the marching camp, Macro saw that Vulpinus had already raised the alarm, and the veterans left to guard the camp were hurriedly forming up as the others approached.

'Centurion Macro!' Decianus called out. 'Come here.'

Macro trotted forward and fell into step beside the procurator.

'I want you to put the chest on one of the carts. I'll have my men guard it after that. Then we will strike camp and return to Camulodunum. We need to get as far from this place as possible today. Do any of your men speak Iceni?'

'I know a few words. I've picked up some of the language.'

'Not good enough. I need someone who can speak to them clearly. I don't want those barbarians to misunderstand the message.'

'Vulpinus can speak their tongue well enough for that.'

'Vulpinus then.' Decianus pointed to the crowd of tribespeople following behind the column. 'When we reach the camp, have him tell them to go back to their mud huts. He's to say that if they follow us any further or try to rescue the queen, it will go badly for her and her daughters. If I see the slightest sign of any warriors pursuing us, I will have her daughters flogged. Got all that?'

Macro nodded.

'Then see to it. Make sure they understand.'

Macro fell back to his men and relayed the order. Vulpinus shook his head. 'He's mad. Does that fool have any idea what a storm he's stirring up?'

'He does, and he doesn't care about it,' Macro replied. 'We're in the hands of the gods now, my friend. Pray that they show us mercy.'

# CHAPTER NINETEEN

As the Roman column moved off along the track leading south, Macro was relieved to see that no attempt was made to follow them. Over a thousand of Boudica's people, by his estimate, stood and watched as she was taken away. Most were silent. Some women cried, while many of the men called her name, or hurled defiant angry insults at Decianus and his retinue. On the procurator's orders, Boudica and her daughters had been placed in chains the moment they reached the camp, and now walked behind the cart that carried the tribute chest. Decianus rode in front of the vehicles, his mounted men riding ahead of him, while the foot soldiers were closed up on either side. Macro and the veterans formed the rearguard, as they had done on the march to the Iceni capital.

Macro regarded the three women with a heavy heart. The shame he had felt earlier was more acute than ever. There was little question in his mind that Decianus's actions heralded a disaster. Even if Boudica and her daughters were held hostage in Londinium, her people were proud enough never to submit to the fate that Decianus had pronounced. They would not let the Iceni kingdom go into oblivion without putting up a fight. One way or another, conflict would break out and the blood of many Iceni and the Romans sent to fight them would be on the hands of the procurator.

In accordance with Decianus's orders, the column proceeded as swiftly as possible to get clear of Icenian territory. The men trudged along the track casting wary glances to either side as they searched for any sign of trouble. Even though the Icenians had been warned not to follow the Romans, Macro was certain that they were out there, at a distance, watching while they decided whether to strike. As the day wore on and there was no sign of pursuit, the tension began to ease in the Roman ranks, and early in the afternoon, Decianus permitted a brief rest stop. As his veterans lowered their packs, Macro approached Boudica and offered her his canteen. She regarded him coldly, and for a moment he thought she might refuse, but then she nodded to her daughters, leaning against the back of the cart.

'Let them have some first.'

The girls eagerly gulped at the water, sharing the canteen between them until it was empty. Macro took it back and slipped the strap over his head.

'How can you stand to let them treat us like this?' Boudica demanded.

Macro looked round to make sure they could not be overheard. 'I had no idea that he was planning to seize you. I swear it by all that I hold sacred. I will find the governor as soon as I can and ask him to have you set free.'

'What about my people? My kingdom? What happens to them if Decianus makes good on his intention to annex our lands? You know the Iceni, Macro. They will die to protect our way of life.'

'That is why I must get you released. You can make them see sense. Make them realise that they cannot win against Rome. If they fight, they will die, you can be sure of that. At the same time, you can plead your case with Suetonius. He will be as keen to save Roman lives as you are to save the lives of your own people.'

She shook her head. 'You are mistaken. You heard how your procurator spoke to me back in the hall. He called us barbarians. He thinks we are little better than animals. That is the Roman view. Do you really think Suetonius is any different?'

'I hope so. Truly, Decianus is not Rome.'

'And yet he represents Rome. He represents your emperor and the Senate and people of Rome. Just like your governor does. And he acts on the orders of Suetonius. No, Macro, I don't think I can expect any help from the governor. The only Romans I have ever truly trusted are you and Cato. We have fought together, shed blood together, and you and I were once close.'

Macro recalled the brief relationship they had shared in the days after the Romans had captured Camulodunum. It had not lasted long, but his desire for her had burned hot in his veins, and there was a flicker of it even now, after so many years. It was a dangerous impulse, and he was quick to push the memory aside as she continued in a wistful tone.

'If things had been different, perhaps I could have been your wife, and these girls, my daughters, could have been yours.'

'I know.'

Her expression hardened and she drew back from him as far as her chains would allow. 'But now? You are dead to me, Macro. Whatever you may say, whatever you may feel, you are part of this.'

'But it is wrong,' Macro insisted vehemently. 'This is not Rome. This is not my doing.'

'Of course it is. How can you say that when you stand there in that uniform? When you have sworn your allegiance to

Rome and the emperor? If you truly think it is wrong, then do something about it. Do something that makes a difference.' She lowered her voice. 'Find a way to get us out of these chains and help us escape. You have a choice.'

Before Macro could consider the matter, Decianus gave the order to resume marching and the men assigned to guard the chest climbed wearily to their feet and moved back towards the cart where he was standing with the hostages. There was no opportunity to respond to her desperate request, and he merely gave a curt nod before turning to rejoin his men as they resumed their position in the line of march. Her words had stung him. Just as his own admission that her abduction was wrong had challenged his conscience.

For the first time, Macro realised that he was entertaining grave doubts about the cause he had served so faithfully and so unquestioningly for most of his adult life. He had been so used to taking the orders he had been trained to obey without thinking, he had never acknowledged his misgivings about the motives driving Rome's ambitions and had blithely accepted that it must be for some greater purpose. He had been too closely bound to the brotherhood of soldiers that had become a second family to him to look beyond it. And now? Now he had a choice. Worse, he was compelled to make a choice, even though every grain of his being wished that he did not have to. He must either continue to blindly accept the world that had made him, or betray it and do the right thing.

The column resumed its march along the track, picking its way through the lush farmland of the Iceni as the sun shone from a clear sky and bathed them in a warmth that was soon beyond comfortable at the pace that had been set by Decianus. Towards the middle of the afternoon, the procurator's foot soldiers began to flag. Most of them were on the strength of the

Londinium garrison because they were either too old or too unfit to serve in an active unit. Boudica's daughters were allowed to sit on the cart, while the queen herself continued stolidly on foot. Macro's veterans, long inured to hardship, kept up as they overtook a straggler, a bulky man in his later thirties whose face was white with exhaustion.

'I'd stay with the column if I were you,' Macro said to him. 'Not a good idea being a Roman on your own in the middle of Iceni territory.'

'I ain't built for this,' the man panted, and then sniffed. His voice indicated that he was suffering from a heavy cold. 'Haven't been out of Londinium for five years.'

His armour was spotted with rust, his leather straps were dull and worn and he was sweating heavily. He undid his chin strap and removed his helmet and liner, revealing thin strands of hair plastered to his scalp. A slovenly soldier, thought Macro. If he had been a legionary, or even an auxiliary, he might have given him a bollocking and shoved him back in line, prodding him with his vine cane to keep him moving. But he was one of the dregs and not worth the effort.

'Perhaps you should have exercised more and eaten less. Good luck.'

They marched on and the man fell further and further behind. As the column crested a ridge, Macro glanced back and saw that he had stopped and sat down on a tree stump beside the track. There was no sign of his shield or helmet, and he realised that the man was discarding his kit. Then the track dipped down the far side of the ridge and the straggler was lost from view. His best chance of survival now depended on Boudica's appeal to her people to leave the Romans alone, but Macro could not help fearing that on his own, and with only a sword to protect him, he might be a tempting object for any Icenians following them to wreak their revenge upon.

They had covered perhaps twenty-five miles by Macro's reckoning and were marching along a slow-flowing river when Decianus gave the order to halt and make camp. Dusk was already gathering, and Macro selected a site in a loop in the river that would protect them from three sides and provide water for the men, horses and mules. The carts were formed up across the open space and the gaps filled with sharpened stakes cut from a nearby copse. Boudica and her daughters were unchained from the cart and sat leaning against the wheels as they rested and rubbed their aching feet.

As the work got under way, Decianus approached Macro. 'One of my men is missing. Fascus.'

'He dropped back some hours ago.'

'You let him fall behind?'

Macro shrugged. 'He's one of yours. Your responsibility. You should keep a better eye on your men. Even if they are a waste of space.'

'I want you to take some of your veterans and go and find him. Before the Iceni do.'

'Send your lads, not mine.'

Decianus folded his arms. 'Centurion, I am giving you an order. And since your men are the only proper soldiers here, as you are happy to point out, they are the best men for the job. Take ten veterans and make sure you return to camp before it gets dark.' He looked up at the sky. 'An hour or so out and an hour back should be feasible. As long as you go immediately.'

Macro gave a mocking salute. 'As you order, *sir*.'

'You don't have to like or respect me, Macro. Thanks to Governor Suetonius, you just have to do as I say, no matter how much it sticks in your throat and how much pleasure that gives me. Now run along.'

Macro no longer felt the urge to punch the man in the face. His hatred and contempt had gone beyond that. He turned away with a leaden feeling and returned to his men. There were angry and weary groans as he outlined the task and picked his party before taking Vulpinus to one side.

'While I'm gone, make sure that a good watch is set the moment the defences are ready.' He jerked his thumb in the direction of Decianus's bodyguards and the Londinium garrison detachment. 'I don't trust that lot to do a decent job, so it's mainly down to our lads if there's any trouble. There shouldn't be, not if Boudica's word carries weight with her lot. Just keep your eyes open until I return.'

'Do you think you'll find the straggler?'

Macro thought a moment. 'Doubt it. Not sure I want to if the other side gets to him first. Ain't going to be pretty.' Then he took his place with the small party of veterans gathered in front of the defences. 'Right, let's get this done.'

He led the way back to the track and turned north, picking up the pace as the stiffness in his legs began to ease. As he walked, he reflected on his last words with Vulpinus. The Iceni had already become the 'other side' in his mind, and he had second-guessed how they would treat Fascus if they found him first. He realised that he had already accepted that a conflict between Romans and the Iceni was inevitable.

Decianus climbed onto the cart containing the chest and watched as Macro and his party marched into the distance and disappeared into the small forest through which the track passed. He smiled at the thought of being without the centurion's presence for a few hours. As much as he enjoyed his power over Macro and felt more secure having a seasoned soldier at his back, he was nevertheless uncomfortable in the presence of competent and respected soldiers. He recalled his brief period of service as a junior tribune some ten years earlier, when he was starting his political career. He had shirked every opportunity to face danger and had earned a reputation amongst the centurions and legionaries of his unit as a coward. He had even discovered that they had a nickname for him: 'Disengagement Decianus'.

That still rankled. At the time, and ever since, he had justified his behaviour on the basis that he was destined for high office. It made no sense to imperil himself on the battlefield, where his loss would be meaningless and the loss to Rome of his future service would be considerable. The likes of Macro were expendable. Men of Decianus's calibre were not. And yet he was troubled by some sneaking sense of inferiority when he compared himself to the centurion. He might be more intelligent, richer and socially superior, but he did not feel himself to be the man Macro was. Macro seemed to be comfortable in his own skin, whereas frequently Decianus was not, and he lived in perpetual anxiety that this was apparent to others.

He caught the scent of the stew that his slave was preparing outside his tent and realised that he was hungry. Kneeling down, he opened the chest and examined some of the jewellery on top of the coins. The latter were a mixture of silver coins struck by the Iceni and those they had picked up in trade from merchants. The designs on the native coins were crude imitations of the first coins that had come to them from the civilised world, and Decianus regarded them with amusement. These barbarians were like children in many ways, keen to mimic the ways of adults in their desperation to be regarded as equals. His faint smile faded as he closed the chest. The governor would not be pleased when he learned how little of the outstanding debt he had collected. The annexation of the kingdom would prove more valuable in the long term, but realising it would be a lengthy and arduous process, with little reward for Decianus in terms of the political capital he might accrue from overseeing the task.

'That is blood money, and you Romans will pay the price for what you have taken with your blood.'

He looked round to see Boudica standing at the end of the cart watching him.

'Really?' he replied. 'Do you truly believe that your benighted tribe of savages poses any serious threat to Roman interests? You belong to the past, woman. You and your people. Civilisation has reached Britannia and you will embrace it or be crushed under the boots of our legions. That is all that the future holds for you. Either way, a hundred years from now it will be as if you never existed.'

'If you do not set me and my daughters free, and if you continue raping our lands, then you will be dead long before I am ever forgotten. Just like that man you sent Macro and his comrades to find. He will soon be on his way to the afterlife as my warriors have their fun with him, and his head will adorn the lintel of an Iceni hut. You can be certain of that.'

Decianus hopped down from the cart and confronted her. Her daughters regarded him nervously from where they were sitting against a wheel. Boudica, however, stood her ground.

He regarded her thoughtfully before he spoke again. 'I wonder what it would take to humble you. To teach you a lesson about the realities of this world and the small part you play in it. You seem to think you are entitled to be treated with the same kind of respect and reverence that is the right of my emperor. Yet he lives in a grand palace while you live in a crude hut. He wears clothes cut from the finest cloth while you dress in little better than rags and furs. He dines on the choicest luxuries while you eat a diet fit for pigs. Everywhere Nero goes he is accompanied by his court, cheered by the mob and worshipped as a god, while you are attended by a tiny retinue of barbarians and grovel before your petty deities.'

'You are a fool to judge a person by their outward trappings,' she retorted. 'You are an even bigger fool if you mock me because I am a woman. Your Roman women may well be meek creatures, little more than slaves, but amongst my people we are regarded with honour, and if called upon to fight we will stand side by side with our men on the battle line. You underestimate me at your peril, Roman.'

'I've heard enough of your boastful prattle.' He slapped her across the face, then again with the back of his hand. Her lip split and blood trickled down onto her chin. With the next blow, his ring caught her on the cheek and cut it open. Boudica gasped with surprise, but refused to cry out in pain as she took the punishment. Decianus stepped back, breathing hard. A short distance away, the nearest of his men and some of Macro's veterans looked up at the commotion.

Decianus turned towards Attalus. 'Fetch one of the mule drivers' whips! It's time this barbarian bitch was taught some manners.'

Boudica's gaze bored into him. 'You wouldn't dare . . .'

Attalus approached holding a coiled drover's whip, and Decianus pointed at the Icenian queen. 'Flog her.'

The commander of the bodyguard called to two of his men to help. They seized Boudica and forced her to bend forward onto the back of the cart, then tied her arms to the rear wagon posts. She struggled violently, but was no match for the men. Attalus took out his dagger and cut a slit in the back of her tunic, tearing the material apart to expose the flesh of her back.

Her younger daughter shrieked in alarm and tried to rush to her mother's aid, but Attalus shoved her to the ground and pointed a finger at her.

'Don't! Or you'll get the same treatment.'

Boudica called to her daughters in a commanding tone, and the older girl slipped her arms around her sister and held her close.

'Begin!' Decianus ordered.

'How many blows, sir?'

'As many as it takes until I tell you to stop. Get on with it!'

Attalus shook out the whip and gave it a flick to test its weight and reach. Then, bracing his feet apart, he swept his right arm to the side and behind him before lashing out with a violent sweep of his arm. The tough, heavy leather shot forward like a striking snake and lashed the pale skin of Boudica's back. She jolted and flung her head back, making a keening moan through her clenched teeth. The muscles on her neck and shoulders were rigid as she tensed herself in preparation for the next blow. As Attalus flicked the whip back in readiness, the first dribbles of blood oozed from the vivid red welt that ran diagonally down from her right shoulder blade. The whip struck her for a second time, and she gasped before setting her jaw and staring fixedly ahead.

Attalus kept up a steady rhythm, lacerating her flesh with a series of red stripes. Decianus's men began to gather in an arc to witness the spectacle. Some passed round wineskins, and there were shouts of encouragement.

'Lay her open! Let's see her bones!'

After twenty blows, Decianus called out, 'Stop!'

Attalus lowered his arm and wiped away the blood that had spattered his face, and the procurator moved forward to address Boudica from the side of the cart. Her back was a criss-cross of bloody red lines and her breathing was ragged as she stood trembling in the cold evening air.

'Have we learned our lesson yet, I wonder?' Decianus mused. 'Let's see. Repeat after me. Rome is my master. Say it.'

She tightened her jaw and stared ahead.

'Say it. Rome is my master.'

Still she refused.

'Say it!'

'Fuck you!' Boudica screamed. 'Fuck Rome! Death to Rome! Death to the emperor! Death to you all!' Her voice faded to a pained groan. 'I swear by Andrasta,' she said softly, 'that I will kill you, Procurator. I will make your death last for days. I will feed your heart to my dogs.'

'You still don't seem to have learned the lesson,' Decianus tutted. He turned to his men. 'Lads, what does it take to tame these wild barbarian women, eh? You can flog the life out of them and they still snap at you like a rabid dog.'

'She needs some more whip!' a voice called out, and there was laughter from the other men.

'No,' Decianus replied. 'I need to keep this one alive. Can't have her bleeding to death. Besides, she'll fetch a good price when this is all over. Her and these whelps of hers.'

'You bastard. Don't you dare touch my girls!'

One of the men holding a wineskin jeered and mimicked her voice as he repeated the comment, and there was another roar of laughter. Decianus joined in briefly, then looked down at Boudica's daughters calculatingly.

'If I can't afford to risk killing you, then maybe there is a better way to complete the lesson. One that causes a different kind of humiliation and pain. Boys! How would you like to sample some Iceni women?'

There was a howl of drunken approval, and the nearest of

the men grabbed the girls and dragged them to their feet. Despite her wounds, Boudica strained against her bonds with all her strength, twisting her wrists to try and loosen them, the veins in her muscles standing out like cords of rope. As her daughters began to scream, she cried out to Decianus to show them mercy, to take her instead. But he merely laughed.

'Why would I offer them a raddled old witch like you when they can have something unblemished?'

The screams and sobs continued as the procurators' men cheered each other on before taking their turn. At length Boudica's strength gave out and she hung limply from the straps. Tears streaked her face as she cried out piteously to the gods of her tribe for mercy and vengeance, while the sun set over the lands of her people.

# CHAPTER TWENTY

Macro was on the point of ordering his men to turn around when they found Fascus. They had been following the track through a forest for half a mile when they came across a small clearing to one side. It was the smell that alerted them first: a heavy odour of roasted meat and woodsmoke. Small flames were still licking up amid the smouldering remains of the fire. Fascus had been tied to a sturdy branch and suspended between two large logs with his torso directly over the flames. From his thighs to his chest the front of his body was burned to a crisp. There was no sign of his clothes, sword or any other possessions. All that remained was a strip of cloth that had been tied tightly about his head to act as a gag.

The veterans stood in a loose arc around the scene, some of them holding their hands to their mouths and pinching their noses to seal out the stench. Macro could feel the taste of it on his tongue as he breathed, and fought the urge to gag. He looked away and scanned the surrounding treeline. There was no sign of movement, but it was possible Fascus's killers were still nearby.

He cleared his throat. 'First four men, ten paces out and keep watch.'

As the assigned men moved off to take their positions, one

of the others gestured to the body. 'What are we going to do with that, sir?'

'That?' Macro rounded on the veteran. '*That* was a soldier once. Not a good soldier, but one of our own all the same. We'll cut him down and bury him here and then get back to camp and report his death.'

'Have we got time for that?'

'We have,' Macro decided. 'Let's get started. Volunteers to cut the body down?'

None of the veterans stepped forward, so he pointed at the two nearest men. 'You help me. The rest of you, start digging the grave.'

The work party set down their shields. They had only brought their weapons with them, and their picks were with the rest of their kit in the camp, so they had to scrape away the soil and cut roots with their swords. As they set to work, Macro approached the body and drew his dagger, trying not to breathe deeply.

'One of you take his feet, the other his shoulders, while I cut the ropes.'

Fascus had been bound in four places: ankles, thighs, midriff and shoulders. Macro began at the ankles, sawing at the coarse bonds where they were stretched over the branch. The first set parted and Fascus's pudgy white legs sagged. It was clear that the body was going to fall onto the embers, so Macro spread them around with his boots before he continued. When the cord around the shoulders parted, the corpse fell face down with a puff of ashes.

'Move him to the grass,' Macro ordered, and the two veterans grunted as they rolled Fascus onto his back. His eyes were wide open and bulging, which surprised Macro. He had expected them to be clenched tightly as the man endured the agony of being burned alive. He bent down and untied the gag, then straightened up with a look of disgust.

'Fuck . . .' one of the other men muttered.

'Explains why they didn't take his head,' Macro commented.

Fascus's lips were parted. Protruding between them was the shrunken end of his penis, forced into his mouth along with his testicles before the gag had been tied to hold them in place.

'There's an object lesson in never letting yourself become a straggler in hostile territory,' said Macro. 'Now help the others and let's get this over with.'

The men had dug down three feet when Macro ordered them to stop and put the body in the grave. The shallow trench was too narrow to fit Fascus's girth, and there was another delay while it was widened about his middle. The veterans hastily scraped the soil back over him, providing a foot of cover that Macro hoped would prevent the beasts of the forest from digging down and worrying the body. Soon there was a mound not far from the ashes of the fire, and he ordered his men to pick up their shields and get back on the track.

In the time spent cutting down and burying Fascus, the sun had set, and there was just enough light to see their way back out of the forest. It would be dark long before they returned to camp, Macro calculated.

They left the clearing behind them and stepped out at a quick pace, eager to get away from the place. On either side the darkness beneath the limbs of the trees was impenetrable, and every noise set Macro's nerves on edge. He only felt a slight easing of the tension as they emerged into open country and continued along the track. No one spoke as their boots softly crunched on the dried mud and shingle underfoot. Whoever had killed Fascus was more than likely out there watching them and tracking them. Perhaps waiting for another straggler to be left behind. If that happened, Macro resolved, he would have to kill the man in order to spare him the same agonies that Fascus had suffered.

Three miles on, he at last caught sight of the glow of the campfires and felt some sense of relief. He was looking forward to his evening meal and having the security of many more men around him. He resolved to make sure that Boudica and her daughters were also fed and made as comfortable as possible for the night. They had endured a terrible day, and would be hungry and exhausted after their ordeal. They were not responsible for the death of Fascus. That was down to Decianus, Macro reasoned. It was he who had enraged Boudica's people and provoked them into taking it out on the hapless straggler. It was also Decianus's fault that he had chosen such unfit men to serve as his bodyguard.

The reaction of the procurator to the news of Fascus's death was a concern. It was possible that he might decide to exact some kind of retribution on Boudica, and Macro would have to make sure that did not happen. Enough damage had already been done, and if there was to be any hope of keeping the peace between Rome and the Iceni, they would need Boudica to persuade her people against further violence.

As the detachment drew closer to the camp, Macro could see men sitting around their campfires and could hear them singing and laughing. He felt reassured by their good spirits. Perhaps there were some with the makings of good soldiers amongst them after all. He glanced back over his shoulder to the men behind him. 'Seems like some of the lads brought wine with them. Get some in while you have a chance, eh?'

There were a few weary grunts of approval, which went some way to relieving the sombre mood.

A hundred paces from the line of wagons, a sentry stepped

out of the shadows to challenge them. 'Halt! Who goes there?'

'Centurion Macro and the search detachment.' Macro approached the man and stopped to exchange a greeting before nodding towards the camp. 'Sounds like they're celebrating. What's up?'

'No idea, sir. I've been on watch since you left. Haven't been relieved yet.'

Macro frowned. Vulpinus should have seen to that by now. He felt the first prickle of anxiety.

'All right, I'll send someone over. Keep your eyes open. The Iceni are close by.'

'Yes, sir.'

The moment the detachment entered the camp, Vulpinus came striding up, his expression taut with concern. 'Thank the gods you're back, sir. I need to speak to you, now.'

'What in Hades is the matter?'

'Sir, please . . .'

'A moment.' Macro dismissed the detachment, and the men wearily made their way over to the campfires of the Camulodunum veterans. He waited until they were out of earshot before he rounded on his optio. 'Spit it out.'

'It happened soon after you left, sir. While I was with some of the men foraging for wood, otherwise I'd have tried to intervene.' Vulpinus hurriedly went over the confrontation between Decianus and Boudica that had led to her flogging and the rape of her daughters. Macro listened with a growing sense of horror. When Vulpinus had finished, he looked down the side of the carts.

'Where are they?'

'This way, sir.' Vulpinus led him to the cart that held Decianus's baggage. The rear of it was empty apart from a bundle beneath a goatskin cover. Macro felt his heart lurch.

'Are they dead?'

Vulpinus shook his head. Walking along the side of the cart, he gently picked up one end of the goatskin and flicked it back to reveal Boudica crouched against a chest with a daughter under each arm. The tunics they had been wearing when they had been taken from the hall that morning were ripped, and the exposed skin of their arms was bruised and scratched. There was a dull clink of chains and he saw that they had been manacled together. All three were trembling. They looked at Macro fearfully before Boudica recognised him by the light of the stars.

'Leave us alone, for pity's sake.'

He raised his hands to try and reassure them, but the younger girl squeezed herself in tighter beside her mother and whimpered, 'Please don't hurt us again. Please . . .'

'I'm not going to. I swear it. I'm here to help.' Macro felt guilty as he spoke the words. After what they had endured, another Roman soldier was not the right person to offer comfort. If only Petronella were there. She would know what to say. She would be a trustworthy presence to deal with their trauma. But Petronella was back in Camulodunum, and Macro knew he must do what he could. If only he had been there to protect them from Decianus and his men. He looked at Boudica and spoke gently. 'Have your wounds been seen to?'

She hesitated a moment, regarding him suspiciously, then shook her head. Macro turned to Vulpinus. 'We need something to see by here. Get a torch lit and remove those chains, then I want you to find two good men to guard the cart.'

Vulpinus hesitated. 'They're hardly in any shape to attempt an escape, sir.'

'To guard the cart from Decianus's thugs, idiot. Then give them water to clean their injuries, and bandages. And find them some spare tunics to wear, as well as food and something to drink. You see to that while I report to Decianus.'

'Did you find Fascus?'

'What was left of him,' Macro replied before striding off towards Decianus's tent.

A dim glow came from the oil lamps that were burning within. One of the bodyguards was standing guard and stepped in front of Macro as the centurion made for the entrance flaps.

'Get out of my way,' Macro barked.

'Sorry, sir. The procurator gave orders that he was not to be disturbed.'

'I bet he did. Out of my way.'

'No, sir.' The guard advanced his spear to emphasise his words.

'I haven't time for this.' Macro snatched the spear from the man's hands, reversed it, and struck him in the groin with the butt. The guard groaned as he folded over and slumped to the ground. Macro tossed the spear aside and pushed his way through the flaps.

The interior of the tent was fifteen feet across, with plenty of space for the procurator's collapsible travel bed, a table and three chairs. Decianus was sitting at the table eating from a silver bowl while his slave stood waiting for him to finish his meal.

He put down his knife and sat back, regarding Macro with a smile. 'Centurion Macro, I wondered if you would make a forceful entrance. I trust you didn't injure the guard outside my tent too severely.'

'You stupid slippery bastard.' Macro approached him, fists bunched. 'Why did you let that happen? Do you understand what you've done? I should tear your fucking heart out with my bare hands, so help me.'

'That would be a foolish thing to do in front of a witness. Why don't you sit down and have a cup of wine whilst you make your report.'

Decianus clicked his fingers and the slave reached into a box and took out a spare goblet, setting it down on the table. Macro swept it away with his fist.

'I'd sooner pluck my eyes out than drink with you again.'

'Your loss.' Decianus picked up his own cup before Macro had a chance to send that flying too. 'Did you find the straggler?'

The shift in subject merely added fuel to Macro's rage. 'We found him. Fascus is dead. They roasted him alive before cutting off his prick and balls and suffocating him with them.'

'Nasty.'

'He's dead because of you. Because you snatched their queen and her daughters. They did that to him and it's on you, Decianus. No one else. His blood is on your hands.'

Decianus examined his fingernails. 'No. I wasn't the one who killed him. That was those Iceni animals. Little better than beasts. Who do you think the people back in Londinium and Rome will blame? A well-connected procurator with considerable promise diligently working his way up through the ranks? Or the barbarian tribesmen with no limit to their savagery?'

Macro's anger was getting the better of him. Even so, he was self-aware enough to know the truth behind Decianus's rhetorical question. But the larger matter still remained.

'How do you think the Iceni will react when they learn that you whipped their queen and your men raped her daughters? The blood of Fascus will be a drop in the ocean compared to the death and destruction they will wreak.'

'And if they are insane enough to go down that road, you can be sure that most of the blood shed will be theirs. Suetonius will turn his legions on them and the Iceni will be wiped out.'

'How do you figure that?' Macro demanded. 'Suetonius is away on campaign. Every legionary who can be spared is with him. Who will protect this part of the province from the Iceni when they come hunting for Romans?'

'Suetonius will have dealt with the Ordovices and their Druid friends long before the Iceni become organised enough to present any real danger. You see, Macro, either way I have done Rome a good service. If the Iceni behave and submit to annexation, then I may release Boudica, or continue to hold her hostage for as long as it takes to ensure her people's cooperation. If they rise up, they will be crushed and there'll be plenty of spoils for the legions that do their job, and plenty of spare land for more Roman colonists to settle on. And if the Iceni do cause us sufficient trouble, there will be reasonable grounds for the emperor to withdraw from Britannia. In every event, I come out of this well.' Decianus set his cup down. 'Now, if you don't mind, I will finish my meal and go to sleep. We've an early start tomorrow if we are to get clear of Iceni territory.'

Macro was appalled by the man's cynicism, and gave an angry snarl as he moved towards the table. He grabbed the edge in one hand and placed the other on the knife an instant before he threw the table over with a roar. The cup, wine jug and bowl flew across the tent and Decianus lurched backwards with a curse, while the slave behind him cringed and half turned away. Before the procurator could respond, Macro strode out of the tent, past the sentry, who was back on his feet and breathing deeply. Further off stood some of Decianus's men, who had stirred from their places by the fire at the sound of the commotion in the tent. Macro ignored them and made for the cart containing the hostages.

Vulpinus was holding a rush torch up while Boudica and

her daughters treated their injuries. The two men assigned as guards stood to one side. As he approached, Macro slipped the knife he had taken from the table behind one of the straps of his medal harness. He grimaced at the sight of the bright red lines cut across the queen's spine. She let out a cry and then cut it off and moaned softly as Bardea dabbed a cut on her shoulder blade. Macro smelled the tang of the vinegar that had been added to the bucket of water fetched from the river. Boudica's younger daughter, Merida, was sitting further back, dressed in a clean woollen army tunic that swamped her slender frame.

'How is she doing?' Macro asked.

Boudica looked back over her shoulder. 'It feels like my back is on fire.'

Macro shook his head. 'I'm so sorry I wasn't here to protect you. Truly.'

'Protect us? You'd have probably joined in.'

Macro felt as if he had been physically struck by the accusation. He swallowed. 'You know that's not true.'

'Do I?' She glared at him a moment before sighing bitterly. 'Yes, I suppose I do. If only you were the Roman other Romans were measured against.'

'Then the Empire would be in a right bloody state.' Macro tried to jest, but she gave him a sad look.

'And who else would grieve over that?'

Bardea lowered the strip of cloth into the bucket. 'There. That's the best I can do.'

Macro nodded as Boudica picked up the tunic that had been brought to her and clenched her teeth tightly before lowering it over her head and down her body. As she settled back beside her daughters, Macro reached for one of the coiled cords at the end of the cart. 'I'll tie their hands.'

'Tie?' Vulpinus nodded towards the manacles. 'Shouldn't we put those back on?'

'Rope will do fine. Keep the torch up so I can see what I'm doing.'

Macro climbed onto the cart and crouched down. As he took Boudica's hands and crossed her wrists, he leaned forward and whispered earnestly, 'If you want to be free, trust me.'

She said nothing as he tied her hands securely in full view of Vulpinus. When he had secured the two girls and linked all three women with a short length of rope to an iron ring on the floor of the cart, he climbed back down.

'That should hold them, wouldn't you say?' He looked at Vulpinus, who nodded.

'Good, then we're done here. You can go.'

Vulpinus placed what remained of the makeshift torch on the ground, then turned and made for the veterans' campfires close to the river. Macro looked at the men assigned to protect the cart. 'No one gets close to them until you are relieved, understand? I mean no one. Not even the procurator. If he shows up, one of you is to fetch me immediately. If any more harm comes to them, you do not want me to hold you two personally responsible . . .'

He left the threat hanging. He knew what he had to do and tried to comfort himself with the thought that it was also the right thing.

Back at the veterans' camp, he found a man who still had some wine and bought it off him before settling down close to one of the fires.

He waited until most of the other men had covered themselves with their cloaks and curled up with their backs to the dying flames of the fires. A handful of others continued to talk for a while before Attalus ordered them to shut up. The veterans were the first to fall asleep, a habit they had learned from serving on many campaigns. Only Macro remained awake. As he waited for his moment, he considered the implications of setting Boudica and her daughters free. Rape was a common enough feature of the broader process of invasion, but Macro, who had a lifelong intolerance of bullying, considered it a contemptible practice. More outrageous in this case since Boudica and her daughters were supposed to be allies of Rome, entitled to protection.

If they were taken to Londinium, there was no knowing how they would be treated once Macro and his veterans left the column at Camulodunum. They might be abused again, feeding their hatred of Rome. In which case, there would be no prospect of Boudica acting as a moderating influence if she was returned to her people. The only hope of limiting the damage already caused, Macro reasoned, was to set her free now. On the basis that his actions would demonstrate that not all Romans were alike and that Decianus and his men were the aberration rather than the rule. In his heart, he wanted that to be true, even as experience frequently argued otherwise. The important thing was that Boudica had some evidence that would persuade her to try to keep the peace between her people and Rome. It was also possible, he conceded, that she might return to her tribe and stir them up into open rebellion. There was no way of knowing the consequences of what he intended to do. It appeared to be the least worst course of action and nothing more. He tried to imagine what Cato would do in his place, but found no inspiration and no other answer.

As Vulpinus rose from the ground to change the sentries, Macro went over to him. 'It's all right. I'll deal with it. Need a piss in any case.'

Vulpinus nodded gratefully and lay back down as Macro crossed the camp towards the line of carts. The men guarding the hostages and the treasure chest straightened up as they saw the dull gleam of the medals on the centurion's harness.

'Anything to report?' asked Macro.

'No, sir. Quiet as lambs. Some tears. Bad dreams maybe.'

'Very well. You can turn in now. Your replacements will be along directly. Off you go.'

The men nodded and headed off towards the glow from the embers of the campfires.

Macro stood quietly for a moment, looking around. No light showed from within Decianus's tent; the rest of the men were asleep, or tossing fitfully. There were only the men on sentry duty to contend with. The two patrolling the inside of the defence line and the four pickets beyond. The nearest sentries paced past. Macro pulled his cloak over his medallions to hide his rank and exchanged a brief greeting with them before they moved on. As soon as he judged they were far enough away, he took out the knife he had taken from Decianus's tent and crept up onto the cart. He could make out Boudica's form closest to him as she shielded her daughters, and he reached out and shook her shoulder gently.

At once she sat up, bound hands clenched into fists and raised to strike.

'Easy!' he hissed. 'It's me. Give me your hands.'

She hesitated a moment before extending her arms. Macro felt for the rope and laid the blade on it. 'Keep still.'

He began to saw, taking care not to jab or cut her. It was slow work, and the two sentries were approaching again when the rope parted. He felt for her hand and pressed the handle of the knife into it. 'Free your girls, but keep them quiet.'

He slid down and stood by the cart as the sentries passed by.

As soon as they were gone, he returned to the rear of the cart.

'Boudica?'

A dark shape sprang forward, and he felt a hand at his throat and then the prick of the knife blade under his chin.

'I would kill you. If it wasn't for . . .' She paused, glanced briefly at her elder daughter and then repeated, 'I should kill you.'

Macro kept still as he replied. 'Then you might not escape. Is that what you want? Lower the blade and listen to me.'

He could feel the trembling of her arms and the tip of the blade. Then she released her grip and lowered the knife, and he breathed deeply in relief.

'Leave the knife on the cart.'

'Why should I?' she asked suspiciously. 'I'd rather have a weapon with me.'

'The knife has to be found when they discover you are gone. I'll say that it must have come from Decianus's baggage. There's no time to explain any further. Follow me and make no sound.'

He helped them down from the cart, hearing the grunt of pain as Boudica moved. He had once received ten lashes as a young recruit for a minor offence and knew the agony she must be enduring. He indicated the bend in the river in the opposite direction to the two sentries. 'This way.'

They set off in a crouch, keeping close to the carts, and then the short stretch of abatis, before reaching the dead stalks of the reeds at the edge of the river. Macro led them through a narrow gap and along the line of the reeds for a few paces until he could make out the nearest picket, then he squatted down and whispered, 'You're on your own from here. I'm going to go ahead and distract that man. As soon as he moves away, you follow the line of the river. Keep close to the reeds but not in them, or you'll be heard. Get away from the track as quickly as you can. Understand?'

Boudica nodded.

He made to stand up, but she grasped his wrist and pulled him back down. 'Why are you doing this?'

'I need you to know that Decianus and his thugs are not Rome.'

She gave a derisive snort.

'I need you to go back to your people and persuade them against war.'

'What makes you think I'd do that, after today's outrage?'

'Hope. Nothing more. You understand what's at stake for both sides. I once knew you well, Boudica. I'm hoping, trusting, that you desire peace more than war. For all our sakes.'

She released his wrist and touched his cheek. 'It's too late, Macro. Save yourself. Take your family and leave Camulodunum. Leave Britannia and never come back. If we meet again, I fear it will be as enemies. I do not want your blood on my hands.'

Macro glanced back towards the carts, fearful that their escape might be noticed at any moment. 'Good luck!' he hissed. Then he stood and strode towards the nearest picket, coughing as he approached.

The man turned. 'Who's there?'

'Make the proper challenge!' Macro growled.

'Who goes there? Advance and be recognised.'

'Centurion Macro.'

He stood facing the river and the picket turned towards him, away from the reeds.

'Chilly night, eh?'

'Yes, sir.'

'Anything to report?'

'Nothing. Silent as the grave, sir.'

'Let's hope it stays that way. I take it you missed out on the wine that was being passed round earlier.'

'Yes, sir. Bloody shame. Could use some of that on a night like this.'

'Then you're in luck.' Macro slipped the strap of the wineskin over his head and passed it over. 'There's enough left for you and the other lads. Take it to the next man and share a swig before he passes it on. I'll cover for you here until you get back.'

'Yes, sir. Thank you, sir.' The sentry took the wineskin. 'Be as quick as I can.'

'You do that. I don't want to be kept here freezing my bollocks off.'

The man chuckled as he hurried off. Macro watched him go for a moment before looking towards the river. For a few heartbeats there was no sign of movement, then he made out three dark shapes against the backdrop of the reeds, picking their way along the bank away from the camp. A moment later, they were swallowed up by the night and were gone.

Macro ran a hand over his head and scratched his scalp. He had done the right thing, he reassured himself. In the circumstances, it had to be the right thing. But circumstances changed, he realised. Only time would tell.

# CHAPTER TWENTY-ONE

As the end of spring unfolded, the weather improved markedly and Suetonius's army advanced in bright sunshine under scattered clouds. There were occasional showers of rain, but they never lasted long, and the men marched on cheerfully, their damp kit giving off light wisps of steam. After the skirmish at the wall, the enemy seemed to have melted away. Although the Roman column was under constant observation from the high ground, there were no further attempts to block their advance. Small Ordovician warbands made harassing attacks on foraging parties but were comfortably beaten back, at some cost to the attackers.

The mounted patrols of the Eighth Illyrian rode forward to challenge the enemy observers, but the latter turned and fled each time, only to appear an hour or so later on a ridge further away. Almost every farmstead or settlement they came across had been abandoned and the animals driven off into the hills. Supplies of grain had been carried away or hidden, and everything that might have been of use to the advancing Romans was left burned or destroyed next to the empty roundhouses. Governor Suetonius had given orders that the enemy was to be swept from the path of his legions, and so the roundhouses and any other structures were torched to complete the swathe of destruction across the territory of the Ordovices. On a few occasions the enemy were surprised before they received warning, and meagre supplies of food were obtained for the army, as well as a handful of captives. But they represented scant pickings, and it soon became apparent to the men that there would be little booty to be shared out at the end of the campaign.

Cato was riding ahead with Tubero and his scouts when they came in sight of the sea. Even though the wound on his left arm was healing well, there was still some stiffness and pain in the muscle, and he was obliged to keep the reins in his good hand. Stretching out ahead of them was a long inlet, with mountains on the north side and a wide-open expanse of mostly flat country to the south, with hills beyond. There were several settlements and many farms, but already Cato could see columns of smoke rising amongst them as bands of tiny figures and animals made for the hills. A force of tribesmen, several hundred strong, guarded the end of the inlet, just over a mile below Cato and his mounted detachment.

'Should we send for the rest of the cohort, sir?' asked Tubero. 'If we can push that lot aside, there's good eating to be had amongst those herds.'

Cato understood the temptation. The cohort had found little to supplement its rations from foraging ahead of Suetonius's column. He had already given orders to cut the men's rations by a third two days before, and the same applied to the horses' feed. The men had not complained yet, but they would if they could not find enough food soon and Cato was forced to cut their rations again. It was worse for the main body of the army. They had been reduced to half-rations that morning, and Suetonius had given orders to halt the following day while the supply convoy from Viroconium caught up with the column.

It was a familiar problem, Cato reflected as he considered his subordinate's question. Roman legionaries were generally issued five days' supply of marching rations. After that, they relied on two further days of rations carried on the mules that accompanied them in terrain that was difficult for the carts and heavy wagons of the supply convoys to negotiate. At which point, unless it was possible to live off the land, they would be forced to halt until they were sufficiently replenished to continue the advance. And as the lines of communication through hostile territory grew longer, so forts would have to be built and garrisoned in the wake of the army in order to protect the supplies they depended on. The ultimate effect of which was that Suetonius's advance would be forced to slow its pace and he would have progressively fewer men available to confront the enemy when they finally turned to fight, as they must if they were going to keep Rome from taking the island of Mona.

He shook his head. 'No. But send a man to Galerius to tell him we'll be making camp here tonight. It's good ground – easy to defend, and commands all the approaches. The same man can ride on to Suetonius to let him know we've reached the sea. If the good weather holds, the navy can land supplies in the inlet. That should give the governor something to smile about.'

Tubero shot him a knowing look. Headquarters had been sending daily demands for Cato's patrols to locate stocks of Ordovician supplies and seize them, as if such things were plentiful and easy to locate. He saluted and turned his horse to assign one of the men to carry the message.

Cato looked down at the enemy force holding the end of the inlet. There were too many of them for the Eighth Cohort to take on by itself, and the main column was too far behind to summon reinforcements before the Ordovicians slipped away, having covered the retreat of their people and livestock. It was tantalising to see the animals being driven away and not be able to do anything about it.

That evening, once the cohort's defences were completed and the first watch set, Cato left Galerius in command and took a small cavalry escort with him to ride down into the valley five miles to the rear where the main column was making camp. It was almost dark when they reached the picket line that extended around the huge area being enclosed by a ditch and turf rampart, where thousands of soldiers were toiling with picks and shovels. Within, long lines of tents were being erected by their comrades. The baggage vehicles were arranged on the far side of the camp on three sides to form a giant pen for the draught animals and the horses of the two cavalry cohorts of the column. A line of stakes linked by ropes ran along the open face of the pen.

As was the custom, the headquarters tents had been set up first, in the centre of the camp, and Cato ordered his escort to wait for him at the main gate while he reported to Suetonius. A number of other officers were standing outside the governor's tent as he rode up and dismounted, handing the reins to one of the legionary handlers. The senior tribune of the Fourteenth Legion, Caius Massinus, nodded a greeting as Cato rubbed his back and buttocks, which were aching from yet another day in the saddle.

'Prefect Cato, what news from the vanguard?'

Several faces turned to him to hear his reply. Cato could see the hope in their expressions, and thought it would be useful to raise their spirits before he spoke to Suetonius.

'We're camped no more than a mile and a half from the sea.'

There were some smiles and excited murmurs before another officer asked, 'Any sign of our ships?'

'Not by the time I left camp,' Cato temporised, then indicated the governor's tent. 'Excuse me.'

He was quickly admitted by Suetonius's bodyguards and found himself in surroundings as opulent as could be managed on a campaign in Britannia. The ground was covered by wooden boards to provide flooring above the churned soil and mud. A line of collapsible tables with stools ran along one side, for the governor to confer with his senior officers. On the other side was a large bed with a down-filled mattress covered with a soft fur and thick blankets. Next to it was a small table with a silver washbowl and ewer. A cushioned couch and an ornately wrought iron brazier completed the governor's travelling luxuries. A low table was beside the couch, and a half-eaten meal of roasted pork and seeded bread lay on a platter, along with some cheese and a peeled apple. Cato could not help wondering where fresh fruit could be obtained in Britannia at this time of year, and whether it had been shipped in from one of the southern provinces of the Empire.

Suetonius was standing by the table reading a waxed slate by the light of an oil lamp stand. He greeted Cato amiably. 'I was delighted to hear that we have reached the sea. Or you have, at least. I'll enjoy the view tomorrow. No sign of the navy, I take it?'

'Not by the time I left camp, sir.'

'That would be too much to ask of Fortuna, I suppose. We'll light the signal beacons tomorrow. If the weather holds, they'll be landing supplies in a matter of days. Then I can fatten the lads up and get them back on the march. Can't be more than three or four more days after that until we reach the straits between the mainland and Mona, eh?'

'All being well, sir.'

Suetonius frowned for an instant before his expression lightened again. 'Come now, Cato. We've advanced faster than was expected, and we've met almost no resistance.'

'That is what concerns me a little, sir.'

'How so?'

'I've fought the Ordovices before, as you know. In the past, they contested us all the way. Almost every ford, mountain pass or forest track was fought over.'

'But you pushed through them all. True?'

'We did, sir, yes.'

'Then maybe they've learned the lesson from last time. Perhaps that incident on the first day we marched into the mountains taught them the futility of facing us in combat. After all, they've been withdrawing before us all the way to the sea. I'm starting to wonder if they think they can hide in the hills until we give up and return to Viroconium. If so, they are mistaken. If they won't face us in battle, we'll build forts to command the lowlands and starve them into submission. One way or another, they will be defeated.'

'Yes, sir. I hope so.'

'Sounds to me like you still have doubts. Speak freely.'

Cato paused to order his thoughts. 'It's possible that the Ordovices have resolved not to risk battle with us. In which case they might choose to go to ground until we pull out of the mountains. Or they will revert to the strategy taught to them by Caratacus and attack our supply lines and outposts. We can't be everywhere to stop them, sir. Two other possibilities occur to me. Firstly, they might be planning a trap. Lure us onto unfavourable ground, where our heavier kit and superiority in numbers will be compromised. There are plenty of bogs and marshes in these mountains where a heavily armoured man is at a distinct disadvantage. Secondly, it's possible that they know, or have guessed, that your target is the Druid stronghold on Mona and they have chosen to make their stand there to protect the sacred groves. We nearly succeeded in fighting our way across the straits the last time Rome sent an army into these mountains. I imagine that shook the Druids enough that they resolved to be better prepared if they faced a similar danger again.'

'If that's what they're up to, then why haven't they been trying to delay us and buy as much time as possible while the island's defences are made ready?'

'What if they have done that already? What if they've used the years since our last effort to make their preparations? What if they have ordered every available warrior to come to Mona to man those defences and they're lying in wait there? It would explain why we've encountered no further resistance since we took the wall.'

'Why waste those men defending the wall, then?'

'To buy a little more time. It made us advance more cautiously than we otherwise might have. The Ordovices and the Druids would have used the opportunity to stock up more supplies and bring in more men.'

Suetonius considered his subordinate's interpretation and then smiled. 'Very good. If they've put all their warriors in one place, it will save us time hunting them down. We can defeat them in one go. The enemy may have done us a favour.'

'We still have to defeat them first, sir.'

'My, but you're an amphora-half-empty sort of fellow, aren't you?'

'It has been pointed out to me before, sir. I can't help my natural disposition to speak the truth as I see it to my superiors.'

The governor stared at him. 'Well, bully for you. I prefer

my officers to be truthful, Prefect Cato. What I don't like is for them to jump at shadows. It has an unnerving effect on those around them. Better to have a more determined attitude. Like the procurator. He's only been in the province for a few months, and he's already stirring things up and getting the revenue flowing. That's the sort of attitude I need more of from my officers, particularly you, given your reputation.'

Cato was quietly seething over the accusation that he was jumping at shadows. He was minded to say that a man who jumped at shadows was hardly likely to have earned the regard of many senior army officers back in Rome, but he controlled his anger and kept quiet.

Suetonius continued in a patient tone. 'Try to look on the bright side more often, Cato. It'll do wonders for the morale of your men, not to mention your promotion prospects. Leave the cautious words to the soothsayers and oracles. Now, is there anything else to report?'

'I'll be reducing my men to half-rations in the next day or so while we wait for fresh supplies to reach us, sir.'

'Very well. Same as the main column's had to endure, then. Still, no one needs to go hungry once the supplies reach us.'

Cato could not help glancing at his superior's unfinished meal and wondering how pleasant it must be to suffer the privations of a provincial governor.

'You can call in the others now,' Suetonius continued. 'Let's hope the tone of the rest of my commanders' reports is more upbeat.'

The next day, the army camped on the open ground beside the inlet and a large beacon was lit on the cliff above the headland at first light, before the morning breeze picked up. A thick column of white smoke curled into the sky, and after an hour it was answered by another, many miles along the coast to the south, where some ships from the naval squadron had put ashore for the night. A vessel would be sent back to the fortified supply base at Leucarum to summon the cargo ships waiting there. In the intervening time, the baggage train caught up with the main body and the men rested and readied themselves for the final approach to Mona.

There was no rest for the mounted contingent of the Eighth Cohort, however. Their supplies were replenished from the small stock of rations of last resort to enable them to continue their duties. This time they were charged with scouting as far as the straits opposite Mona, where they were to assess the enemy's defences and report back to Suetonius. It was a dangerous assignment, and Cato suspected that part of the reason behind the orders was to test his nerve.

They followed the coast north as far as the bay where the shoreline turned to the west, and then struck out through the mountains, staying on a northerly course. As before, the Ordovices kept them under observation, riding their shaggy ponies along the ridges running parallel to the direction the Romans were taking. There was no attempt to attack or even harass Cato's small mounted column, and the fishing settlements and hill communities they passed were deserted as before. The first night they camped on a spit by the sea that was linked by a narrow, easily defendable strip of land to the coast. The following night's camp was in a more precarious position in the hills: an outcrop of rock with crags and scree slopes to three sides, approached by a steep slope on the only open side.

On the third morning, they were shadowed by a much stronger enemy force, which kept pace with them on the ridge to their right as the Romans picked their way along the valleys that led north through the mountains. An hour's ride further on, Tubero reined in alongside Cato and pointed to the opposite ridge.

'More of them, sir.'

Looking up, Cato saw another long line of Ordovician warriors tracking them. More than two hundred men on foot.

'What are your orders, sir?' Tubero prompted.

'We keep going.'

'Sir?'

'They haven't attacked us. Looks like they're just watching us for the present.'

'What if we're riding into a trap?'

Cato was finding the centurion's anxiety wearing. 'The difference between now and that trap you led your men into is that the enemy have made no attempt to conceal themselves this time. If there was a trap, I suspect they would be baiting it more subtly.'

It was a harsh put-down, but it did the trick of shaming Tubero into keeping his mouth shut. For his part, Cato felt strained by the need to keep calm as his men followed a gently rising track between the two enemy forces.

Just after midday, they were approaching a gentle dip where the two ridges closed in from either side when the enemy forces halted and watched the Romans in silence.

'Why don't they attack?' Cato heard one of the auxiliaries say not far behind him. He turned in his saddle.

'Quiet in the ranks! Tubero, find that man and take his name. He'll be on latrine duty for a month. Same as anyone else who speaks out of turn.'

As the centurion dealt with the man, Cato turned his attention back to the Ordovices. It was a valid question. They had a clear advantage in numbers and were on the high ground. Why stop and let the Romans advance as far as the crest? If the positions had been reversed, Cato would have charged from both flanks at the same time before the enemy got anywhere near the top of the pass. Then it occurred to him that the Ordovician forces might be under orders not to attack. That seemed to make little sense. Surely they must know that Cato and his men were far in advance of the rest of the army and beyond any help from that quarter? And yet still they stood and watched.

As the ground levelled out, he could see that the crest afforded a fine view of the landscape beyond, much gentler than the mountains they had been riding through since dawn the previous day. A little further on, the entire vista below opened up, and Cato raised his hand. 'Halt!'

Gesturing to Tubero, he trotted forward to get a better view. Below them were the straits that divided the mainland from the island of Mona. Away to the right he could see the narrowest point, where the army had tried to force a crossing last time. In the past, the enemy had defended just that strip of the island's shore. Now the defences stretched the entire length. The shore and shallows were staked, and behind the stakes was an almost continuous ditch and rampart, broken only by outcrops of rock and timber redoubts. Beyond the defences were clusters of small huts, hundreds of them stretching out amid the cleared land and copses. Many columns of smoke trailed up into the sky, and thousands of men and horses were visible amid the huts.

'Jupiter's cock,' Tubero muttered. 'How in Hades are we supposed to get through that lot?'

It was obvious to Cato why they had not been attacked. The enemy had wanted them to see their defences. To be awed by them, and the number of defenders behind them. Awed enough to realise that no assault could hope to breach them. Awed enough to turn back and leave the island of Mona in the hands of the Druids and their Ordovician allies.

Cato scrutinised the defences and the enemy's camp, and then turned to the centurion. 'Time we turned about, I think. We need to inform the general that we have found the Ordovician forces. All of them.'

# CHAPTER TWENTY-TWO

'It's going to be a tough fight before we can claim victory, gentlemen,' Suetonius announced as he stood before his senior officers gathered on a hilltop overlooking the strait. The tide was out, and mud flats extended from each shoreline. The army was concentrated on the ground below them, covering the narrowest stretch, which ran for three miles or so before broadening out north and south. Several Roman warships rode at anchor at each end, as close to the strait as was comfortably navigable. To the north, two cargo ships were anchored close to the shore and were busy unloading the components of the army's heavy catapults.

The men of the legions, under the guidance of Suetonius's engineers, were building a series of forts along the shore, linked by a palisade and ditch, to prevent any attempt by the enemy to break out of the island. Not that that was their intention, Cato surmised. The Druids and their allies had planned for this moment for years. They intended the island to be the last and greatest of the fortresses faced by the invader; a rock upon which Roman ambitions would shatter. The defences facing the strait were formidable indeed. And if the defenders had stockpiled supplies, they would have the advantage over the Roman army, which had to rely on lines of communication stretching back to Deva and Viroconium. If it became a waiting game, it was likely the defenders would outlast those who might attempt to starve them into surrender. That was the choice facing the Roman governor: attack or retreat.

Another thing occurred to Cato. The longer the army remained where it was, the more precarious the position for the troops holding down the rest of the province. His thoughts turned to the plight of the Iceni and the danger of provoking them into armed resistance once again. Boudica and her people might do some damage to Roman interests, but they would suffer the consequences of their actions, and that would sow the seeds of constant tension between Rome and the Iceni for generations to come.

Suetonius had borrowed a vine cane from one of the centurions and was using it to point out the salient features of the battlefield. As he did so, Cato was reminded uncomfortably of standing not far from this very spot when a previous commander had presented a similar briefing several years earlier. On that occasion, the Romans had failed to take Mona against a smaller number of defenders behind less impressive fortifications.

'As you can see, the enemy have planted sharpened stakes across the entire front of their position up to a depth of thirty paces. Our men can't wade across, so they'll have to land by boat at high tide or they will get caught in the mud. The boats in turn will find it difficult to get through the stakes. Some may well be holed before they reach the far shore. Any men who do land will then be faced by a steep climb before they encounter the ditch. Once they cross that, they'll have to scale the rampart and the palisade on top before they can engage the enemy. They'll be under a barrage of arrows, slingshot, javelins and rocks the moment they reach the shore. Frankly, gentlemen, a frontal assault alone is out of the question. We'd lose too many men, and any attack by the survivors of the first wave would be piecemeal and easily dealt with.'

Suetonius paused to let his assessment sink in before he continued. 'It would be best if we attacked from another direction in addition to the frontal assault. That means we'll have to land another force elsewhere. The naval squadron has reconnoitred the rest of the coast and found a number of suitable places. The problem then is that we have only eight warships, each of which can carry no more than a hundred men besides the crew if they are not to become unwieldy in the swell. If we overload them, some will founder, and once again there will be heavy casualties. Even assuming we get eight hundred men ashore, they will be unsupported for the best part of a day before the warships can return to pick up more men. I dare say the enemy would not be sitting on their hands in the meantime. They will have tracked the ships and will descend on any force we land with superior numbers, wiping them out long before the first wave ashore is reinforced.

'However, the navy did find two landing places on the south coast of Mona, a little over five miles from here. There's a spit of land that is very narrow where it joins the mainland, no more than a hundred paces, I believe. Narrow enough to defend while the first wave is reinforced. Close by is an inlet that stretches nearly two miles into the island. The warships were not able to land and test the ground due to the presence of enemy patrols, but the commander of the squadron is confident that they could get close enough to the shore to offload men directly.' Suetonius tapped the vine cane against the side of his boot as he concluded. 'If we are to avoid a frontal assault and land elsewhere, our choice is limited to the spit and the inlet. Does anyone wish to say anything?'

Cato had already thought through the timings of such a landing and had calculated that no more than four or five could be achieved in the course of a day. Even if none of the warships encountered any difficulties, four thousand men at most could be put ashore on the day of the attack. It was possible that each wave would be eliminated before the next could arrive. He cleared his throat and raised a hand. The governor looked towards him and frowned slightly.

'What is it, Prefect Cato?'

'It's going to be risky landing our men in such small numbers each time, even allowing for the ease of defending the spit. Are there no other warships available?'

'None that can reach us for at least a month. The nearest available squadron is at Gesoriacum, on the coast of Gaul.'

'What about the cargo ships?' asked another officer. 'Once they get back with the next consignment of supplies?'

'They're not much good to us. Too unwieldy and too slow. They'd only make a marginal difference to the number of men we could put ashore. Same goes for the small collapsible boats that were brought forward by the second column. They were only designed for crossing a short stretch of relatively calm water. If they were exposed to even a modest swell, they'd go down, along with the men aboard. Gentlemen, I've considered the options available to us and two attacks from two directions will give us the best chance of success. The first will be a frontal assault. We'll make a big show of it. A heavy bombardment from our bolt-throwers and catapults using incendiaries before the boats land the first wave. With luck, the enemy's attention will be fixed on that while we make the landings on the south coast.'

Cato felt a leaden despair in the pit of his stomach at the governor's announcement. If the good weather endured long enough – and they'd need it to if any landing was to be attempted – it would be easy for the enemy to spot the ruse and move its forces to deal with the landing on its flank. If the landing was to have any chance of gaining a foothold, more men would need to be put ashore more quickly than was planned so far. Cato reconsidered the craft available for the job and realised that there might be a way to give the seaborne force a better chance.

'It is possible that we could reinforce the initial waves faster,' he said.

'If you have a useful suggestion, Prefect, I'm sure we'd all be glad to hear it.'

'What if some of the reinforcements were loaded onto the cargo ships, which could accompany the warships to the mouth of the inlet at least? Once the first wave had landed, the warships could return to the cargo ships to pick up the next wave, rather than return to the mainland for them. The empty cargo vessels could then pick up more men to join those waiting to land. A sort of belt system, sir. How many men can we put on the cargo ships? A hundred? A hundred and fifty, maybe. I counted at least twenty vessels when they brought the last lot of supplies and the heavy catapults. That way we'd be able to put four thousand men ashore in a relatively short space of time.'

Suetonius was silent for a moment. 'I'm not sure how easy it would be to transfer the men between ships in a swell. Nor how long it would take.'

Cato understood his point. Transferring men between ships at sea using ladders and ramps was rarely done, and even then it was done in calm waters. But he had already considered another way of accomplishing the task.

'We can use feed nets, sir.'

'Feed nets?'

'For the horses, sir.'

'I know what they bloody well are! I just don't see what you're so excited about.'

'Sir, if we fix them to the side of the cargo ships and let them unroll to the decks of the warships, the men can climb down them. It's the quickest and easiest way.'

'You seem to have thought this through already, Prefect Cato, but I want to see it work before we attempt anything. I'll have orders drawn up for the commander of the naval squadron to give you what you need to test your idea.'

It was dusk before the two ships were anchored side by side in a small bay beyond the strait, where a headland hid the vessels from any curious lookouts on Mona. Galerius's century had been ferried out to the cargo ship on the collapsible boats intended for the assault across the shallows. A warship, one of the British fleet's biremes, lay alongside, tethered by cables fore and aft. There was a slight swell that caused the craft to move unevenly, and the woven rope fenders creaked between the two hulls when a surge brought them up against each other.

Cato was aboard the cargo ship, and had supervised the engineers as they fixed iron hooks into the ship's rail and then suspended unravelled feed nets from the hooks. Another section of engineers was adding more hooks to the deck of the bireme, where the other end of the nets was attached to give an angled descent. When the first of them was ready, he took a shield from one of the auxiliaries and swung his leg over the side rail, extending his foot to feel for one of the lengths of rope running horizontally. He was aware of the amused looks from Galerius and his men, but he had not wanted to send another man to test his idea. He needed to understand how challenging the manoeuvre was going to be before he decided whether it was practicable for a large body of men. He found his footing and eased his other leg over the rail, then reached for the next step down. The ropes sagged under his weight and the going was harder than he had anticipated. Suddenly the bireme lurched upwards, and a gap opened up between the two vessels so that he was staring down into open water. He hung on desperately with his free hand until the swell had passed, then continued descending until he reached the solid deck of the warship.

Setting the shield down, he called up to Galerius. 'Centurion, we'll try one section at a time. Send the first eight men over!'

Galerius barked the order, and the first auxiliaries began to clamber over the side, hesitating as the feed nets stretched and sagged and the sea swirled beneath them. Cato had shared their nervousness a moment earlier but had shown that it could be done. 'Don't just hang there like sides of pork in a butcher's shop!' he yelled. 'Get moving!'

The men began to scramble down, some more sure-footed and faster than others, a couple easing their way down until they reached the bireme's deck. Cato expected their confidence to grow with more practice and gave the order for the next section to descend. It was slow going, and several men encountered difficulties, getting caught in the netting or losing their footing and tumbling down the net onto the deck. All the while the sailors and marines watched the clumsy antics of their army comrades with amusement. When the last of them was down, Galerius took his turn, and Cato was slightly annoyed to see that he made it look easier than his superior had done.

He stood on the aft deck of the bireme and addressed them. 'That was ludicrous. If that's how you handle the job in a sheltered bay, then the gods only know how you will cope when we go up against the enemy. I want every man to be down that netting like a fucking monkey before we're through.

Back onto the cargo ship with you and let's do it again, by sections. And we'll keep on doing it until you get it right. Move!'

The light had almost faded by the time Cato gave the order for the exercise to end and for Galerius to return his men to the shore and march them back to camp. He made a final check of the condition of the nets and the hooks that held them in place before turning to the bireme's trierarch. 'Get these stowed for the night.'

'Yes, sir.'

'I'll want them rigged at first light when we continue the drill.'

One of the collapsible boats returned to pick him up, and he made his way back along the coast in the darkness towards the twinkling lights of the army's campfires. When he reached headquarters, he requested permission to see Suetonius. He was kept waiting until the end of the first watch before he was admitted to the governor's tent. There was no preamble. Suetonius turned as his slave undid the straps of his leather cuirass. 'Well?'

'It can be done, sir. It took the men a few attempts to overcome their nerves and get used to it, but I can train those who will be sent on the flank attack. Give me three more biremes and cargo ships and I can have them ready in three days.'

The slave slipped the cuirass off and backed away as Suetonius reached for a cup of wine. 'You've already started training them.'

'Sir?'

'I'm referring to your men. Since they have proved it's possible, you can train the rest of your auxiliaries. The Eighth Cohort will be the first wave ashore when the attack begins.

Your mounted contingent will leave their horses here and fight on foot. Eight hundred men. Let's hope it's enough to win a foothold on Mona through which we can pour the rest of the units needed to swing the fight in our favour when the flanking force falls on the enemy's rear. If all goes well, we'll crush them between the two attacks. You'll have your written orders tomorrow. In the meantime, I'm giving you command of the operation. You can select your units from the auxiliary contingent. I'm saving the legionaries for the frontal attack. The tactical decisions are for you to decide, as I suspect you already have a plan in mind.'

'Yes, sir.'

'You can let me know the details when you have refined it. Let's just hope it works when you put it into practice.'

'Hope it works, sir?' Cato gave his superior an arch look to test his sense of self-deprecation.

Suetonius regarded him without expression for a moment, then smiled. 'Your caution is contagious. All right, you've made your point. The plan will work. It has to. Dismissed.'

The next day the weather changed, and dark clouds and driving rain swept in from the sea. The preparations for the attack continued without regard for the conditions. The artillery batteries were positioned as far forward as the high-tide line along the shore, protected by substantial earthworks in case the enemy decided to risk launching raids across the strait to destroy the catapults and bolt-throwers and prevent them from wreaking destruction on the island's defences. In the drenching rain, Cato continued to drill the Eighth Cohort in using the netting to move from ship to ship, as well as training them to quickly disembark from the warships once they reached the shore. Once he was satisfied with their performance, he moved on to each of the other four auxiliary cohorts that Suetonius had placed under his command, until he was confident they were ready for the task assigned to them.

He chose the best of the other cohorts, the Tenth Gallic, to accompany the Eighth in the first wave while the rest were loaded onto the cargo transports or formed up on the coast ready to board the empty vessels on their return to the mainland. The Tenth was commanded by Prefect Thrasyllus, a dependable veteran who Cato had come to admire during the course of the campaign. His request for two of the ships to carry bolt-throwers to support the landings was approved by Suetonius. It was now a matter of waiting for the weather to improve sufficiently for the landing to be attempted at the same time as the frontal attack commenced.

After four days of rain and wind, conditions moderated enough for the next supply convoy to arrive by sea, bringing with it the last of the collapsible boats to be used to carry the legionaries across the strait. The empty cargo ships and the biremes were beached in the bay where Cato had trained his men for the attack, and the nets and bolt-throwers were fitted. Cato went over his plans for the landing, the order of units for each wave and the procedure for retreat if that became necessary.

There were many ways in which the plan could go wrong, chief amongst them being confronted with an overwhelming enemy force at the point where the Romans were aiming to establish a secure bridgehead to receive the necessary re-inforcements to launch the flank attack. From long experience, Cato was aware how often things went awry the moment contact with the enemy occurred, but his plan might fall apart even before they came face to face with the Ordovices. A sudden squall might scatter the ships or wreck them.

The army had been in position for nearly twenty days when

Suetonius summoned his officers to headquarters to announce that the assault on Mona would take place in two days' time. The skies were clear and the sea was calm. The tide would be at its highest mid afternoon, and the main assault would coincide with that.

'The artillery will commence shooting at first light,' the governor explained. 'We've stockpiled enough ammunition to last an entire day. Incendiaries will be added to the bombardment to help break down the enemy's morale as much as for any fires they might start. I've yet to face a Celt who doesn't have a disproportionate fear of incendiaries.' The officers smiled and laughed at that. For all the fearsome appearance of a flaming bundle trailing smoke as it arced across the sky, at least it was obvious and easy to avoid. The greater danger came from the blurred trajectory of the small iron-tipped shafts from the bolt-throwers or the rocks hurled by catapults, which were easy to miss amid all the frenetic movement on a battlefield.

'As soon as it's high tide, the assault will begin. The first troops across the strait will be equipped with ladders and will attempt to scale the palisade and keep the enemy occupied while the follow-up waves land. If all goes well, the entire Fourteenth Legion will be across the strait by late afternoon, with the other legionary detachments held back on the mainland as the reserve. Winning any foothold along the line of the enemy's defences is going to be difficult to achieve, and they will be able to outnumber us and overwhelm our men at any point if we do make it onto the rampart. The key to our victory is if we are able to take them from the flank and rear at the same time as the frontal attack is under way. That is where Prefect Cato's force comes into the picture. He will be commanding the bulk of our auxiliary troops as well as the marines from the naval squadron. It is no small exaggeration to say that victory tomorrow will depend on the success of the amphibious assault on the enemy's flank. So don't let us down, Cato, or we may blackball you from the officers' mess.'

There was another muted chorus of laughter, and Cato smiled, even as he felt the weight of the responsibility settle more heavily upon his shoulders. As it did so, he could not help succumbing to fresh doubt about his plan and the part he would play, even though he had considered every conceivable contingency and how they could be handled. The plan was good, he confirmed to himself forcefully.

'As soon as the bulk of Prefect Cato's force is ashore, he will march north-east to fall on the enemy's flank and rear. His men will sound their horns the moment their attack begins, and that will be the signal for the frontal assault to go all in.'

'But won't the Ordovices have lookouts watching the coast, sir?' asked one of the legionary tribunes.

'They'd be fools if they didn't. I dare say they will also have a mobile force ready to counter any landing. But it can't be everywhere at once and it won't be able to react until their scouts sight our ships and report back. I'll be using some of the cargo ships to feint around the north of the island and hopefully distract the enemy at the same time as Cato's men land on the south coast. Speaking of which, I have added a refinement to the part played by your force, Prefect. I've decided that you will begin landing at first light. That way you will not be detected until the last moment and can surprise the enemy.'

Cato straightened up on his stool. This was not part of his plan. He had briefly considered and discounted the possibility of arriving in position under the cover of darkness. There were many risks involved, however, foremost of which was the reluctance of any sailor to navigate at night unless they were familiar with the waters and there was little chance of collision or running aground. Suetonius's decision would call for more planning, and time was already short. As the governor concluded the briefing, Cato was already working out how best to achieve an approach to the correct landing place at night, as well as ensuring that the ships under his command did not become separated in the darkness. A night march and a dawn attack were difficult enough to carry out on land. A similar operation at sea was almost unheard of.

As the other officers began to leave the headquarters tent, Suetonius approached him with an apologetic expression. 'I imagine you are not too pleased by my bringing forward the timing of your attack.'

'Something like that, sir, yes.'

The governor smiled. 'I would feel the same way in your shoes. The thing is, we cannot risk alerting the enemy to your presence so that they have enough time to send sufficient forces to block your attack. You have to fall on them like a thunderbolt if the plan is to work.'

'I understand that, sir. But I've never attempted anything like this before.'

'There's always a first time, Prefect Cato. Consider it on-the-job training,' he joked weakly. 'If you succeed, Rome will never forget your achievement. If you fail, we all fail, and it'll be my head the mob will be clamouring for.'

# CHAPTER TWENTY-THREE

There was a faint mist across the surface of the sea, which had a smooth, almost glassy look to it close up, as Cato stood on the foredeck of the second bireme in the line of vessels under reduced sail. The column of ships was led by one of the biremes equipped with catapults to support the landing. From the bay where the force had embarked to the spit of land emerging from Mona was no more than ten miles, and the first of the biremes had edged out into the open sea just after midnight. A shielded lamp hung from the stern post had guided the second vessel to its station, and each ship in turn was following the lamp of the one ahead as they glided out of the sheltered waters.

The long swell rolling in from the ocean surged onto the rocks of the coast with a dull rhythmic roar and hiss that was unnerving to the landsmen, who had no experience of judging the distance from the sound. To Cato's ears it was unnaturally loud, and he feared that the ship was steering a course too close to the headland at the end of the bay. But they passed into the open sea without event, and the helmsman steadied the course so that they were following directly behind the lead warship. Behind them, one by one, came the rest of the biremes, and then the cargo ships with the follow-up unit aboard. The commander of the Tenth Gallic, Prefect Thrasyllus, was a veteran who had won Cato's respect during the course of the campaign.

Cato turned to look down the length of the deck and saw the huddled shapes of his men as they sat together along the midline to keep the slim warship's trim as even as possible. Their shields lay close to their feet to allow sufficient room for the crew to move freely around the vessel. The marines were positioned on the forecastle and at the stern, and even Cato could sense how sluggishly the ship responded with nearly a hundred extra men aboard. Under normal circumstances biremes were sleek and highly manoeuvrable vessels, capable of a fast turn of speed when under oars and a comfortable pace under sail. But now, with the need to proceed carefully and quietly in the darkness, the oars had been shipped and the rowers, many of them slaves, were sitting silently at their benches below the deck.

There was a hissed order from the navarch commanding the vessel, and a man in the bow cast his lead weight as far ahead of the warship as possible and let the line run out until the weight hit the seabed and the line went slack. As the ship glided directly over the line, he pinched it in one hand and wound it in with the other, looping the coils as he read off the marks. 'Over eighty feet, sir.'

'Very good.' The navarch nodded with relief. 'Keep your eyes and ears open. Any sight or sound of surf, you run aft and report to me.' He stepped over to Cato and saluted. 'All's well, sir. Though I have to say, I ain't at all comfortable about this.'

'I don't suppose any of us are.'

'Aye. If I could get my hands on the damned fool who dreamed this caper up . . .'

Cato was tempted to confess, but then realised the navarch did not need to worry about insulting his superior in addition to the demands of steering his ship through the darkness. They had spoken quietly, as Cato had ordered to all those aboard the ships to do. He knew how well sound carried across water, and did not want to alert any enemy sentry on Mona who was keeping watch on the approaches to the island.

The navarch went to the side and looked out over the patchy mist. 'I don't like the look of this swell.'

'Seems calm enough.'

'I've seen its like before. Always before a storm blows up. Tonight, perhaps tomorrow morning. You'll see.'

'Just as long as it doesn't reach us before my men are ashore,' said Cato.

'Aye, well . . .' The navarch spat on the deck, a regular habit that had already set Cato on edge since he had come aboard. 'I'll be at the stern, sir.'

Cato nodded, anxious to be rid of the man.

As the navarch worked his way back down the deck, Cato went to the ship's rail. The bow rose steadily and then dipped as the crest of the swell passed under the keel. At once, a wave of nausea gripped his stomach and his throat constricted as he fought the urge to retch. Some of his men, however, could not help themselves, and rushed to the side to vomit, hanging their heads over the side as they clasped the rail tightly.

There were going to be a lot of empty stomachs by the end of the day, Cato mused. They had brought no rations with them, only water in their canteens. They would eat with the rest of the army at the end of the day, provided the assault succeeded and the enemy were defeated. Otherwise . . . He smiled grimly to himself. It was pointless to dwell on that. Better to focus his mind on playing his part as well as he could.

He and his men must defeat the enemy or die in the attempt. Even though he had made plans for a retreat, he knew that falling back from a bridgehead was even more perilous than making the initial landing. He would only attempt it as a matter of last resort.

The night hours passed slowly. At times Cato could make out the third bireme, and once the warship behind that as it approached too close and was forced to spill the wind from the mainsail before it disappeared from view again. As the navarch calculated that they were nearly opposite the spit of land, he reduced sail still further and the following bireme followed suit, so that it was barely making any headway. Astern, Cato thought he could see the faintest loom from the east. A moment later, he was certain he could make out the line of the mountains on the mainland; then more of the details on the third ship, and shortly after, the one behind.

Climbing into the forecastle, he pushed past the marines and looked away to starboard. Sure enough, he could see some of the low hills on Mona. It was time to alter course towards the island.

He made for the aft deck, where the navarch was standing close to the steersman.

'It's time,' Cato announced.

The navarch nodded and gave the order to alter course. The bireme slowly eased round until the bows were in line with the distant hills, as the sailors adjusted the angle of the mainsail and the ship gently lurched to windward, further unsettling Cato's stomach. He clenched his jaw and tried to appear imperturbable. Behind them, the next bireme reached the point where Cato's warship had turned, and it too began steering towards the island.

'What in Hades is he up to?'

Cato turned to see that the vessel carrying the artillery battery was continuing out to sea.

'Bastard's not keeping an eye on us,' the navarch growled. 'Turn, damn you . . .'

Cato watched the tiny light of the stern lamp diminish into the darkness, his stomach sinking. The first and third biremes carried the batteries of bolt-throwers that were intended to cover the landings from either side of the spit. Now one of them was steadily disappearing into the distance.

'You can make more sail now,' he said. 'There'll be enough light soon for the enemy to see us coming. We need to start landing the men as soon as possible.'

'Yes, sir.' The navarch gave the order as loudly as he dared. His crew moved to the ropes, and with one calling the count, they let more of the sail out from where it hung in bulges along the spar. The deck heeled even more, and Cato had to brace his boots so that he was standing at a pronounced angle as the bireme surged forward with a hiss of spray along the sides of the vessel.

Soon there was enough light to make out some of the details on the shore, and the navarch scanned the coastline for the landmarks that would guide him in towards the spit of land. He went to the ratlines amidships and climbed up almost as high as the crow's nest. After a moment, he pointed towards a formation of hills away to the right.

'We've gone too far to the west. Helmsman, steer for the hills there.' He kept his arm extended until the bows were in line with it. 'Meet her! Steady as she goes.'

As the navarch returned to the deck, Cato noticed that the light was spreading along the eastern horizon and the outline of the mountains was sharper now. The bireme rose on a swell, and he caught sight of the spit of land no more than two miles away. Anyone looking out to sea must surely see the line of ships approaching the shore. If the alarm had already been raised, it would be a race to see who reached the landing site first.

Some of the men stood up and crossed to the rail as they became aware that they were closing on the island.

'What are you lot gawping at?' Galerius called out angrily. 'Never seen the sea before? Get your bloody arses back amidships before I toss you over the side for a closer look. Move yourselves!'

The auxiliaries hurried back to their positions, except for one youngster who had started throwing up and no longer cared about anything beyond the appalling nausea that gripped him. Cato felt his own stomach churn in sympathy. Galerius rushed over and bellowed in the lad's ear. 'What's this? Emptying your guts all over the side of this fine warship and showing us up in front of the marines? That will not do. Get back to your place and keep your mouth shut. Throw up again and I'll bloody well make you lick it up!'

The auxiliary staggered back to his place on the deck and slumped heavily, dry-heaving from time to time. Even though they were forbidden from moving from their assigned places, the auxiliaries were curious about the approaching coastline, and craned their necks to try and see over the ship's rail. Cato went forward and stood above the bows, holding on to the forestay as he scanned the coastline. He could make out forests and farming land beyond the shore, and a small collection of roundhouses on top of a hill a short distance inland. Smoke curled from the conical roof of the largest structure. Soon after that, he could pick out cattle in a pen and some goats or sheep dotted across rising ground a short distance beyond.

'Lookout!' the navarch called out to the man at the top of the mast. 'Keep an eye out for breaking surf!'

'Aye, sir!' The man leaned forward in his basket and scanned the way ahead.

Cato could make out people beside the large roundhouse, then one of them mounted a horse and spurred it into a gallop, racing in the direction of the enemy army camped on the western shore. The sight fuelled his sense of urgency, and he turned towards the stern. 'We've been sighted! We need to go faster!'

The navarch hurried forward. 'Sir, the wind is freshening. If we let out more sail, there's a danger we may capsize if there's a strong gust. This ship's not designed for sailing fast off a beam wind.'

Cato could see that the angle on the deck had increased, and he pointed to the auxiliaries. 'Get them over to the lee side. That'll help.'

The navarch opened his mouth to protest, then saw the intent expression on the face of the prefect and nodded instead. Returning to the main deck, he cupped a hand to his mouth. 'Soldiers, move to the port side of the ship!' There were looks of confusion before he shook his head and called out again. 'The left! Left! Over there, damn you!'

Each squad moved over in turn and the deck levelled out appreciably. At the same time, the sailors let out the rest of the sail. It filled with a dull slap, and the warship ploughed on, sending irregular bursts of spray onto the foredeck. Cato could see a group of figures clustering by the distant huts as the sun began to rise over the mountains, and there was a tiny metallic glint from a spear tip or helmet.

He turned and looked aft. The other ships had started to fall behind. There was an anxious delay before he saw the nearest make more sail, and then the others followed suit. Further out to sea, the sail of the first trireme shuddered, then changed aspect as the navarch grasped his mistake and began to turn. Too late to make any impact on the initial landing, though.

'Deck there!' the lookout in the crow's nest called down. 'Waves breaking ahead!'

A moment later, there was an explosion of spray half a mile ahead, where the sea was breaking over barely submerged rocks in line with the end of the spit. The navarch called an order to the helmsman and the bireme changed course to give them a wide berth. Now that there was daylight and they were closer to the island, Cato could see that the shore of the spit was made up of small beaches of sand and shingle that gave way to tufts of grass and other stunted vegetation. He made his way to the captain and pointed out the largest of the beaches, two thirds of the way along towards the island.

'Land us there.'

'I thought the plan was to land as close as possible to the base of the spit, sir.'

'We've been spotted, and we're down one floating artillery battery. We need to get ashore and formed up before the enemy can reach us. I want us on that beach. Clear?'

'Yes, sir.'

As the bireme surged past the end of the spit, the enemy huts were no longer visible beyond the slightly raised ground running down the middle of the thin strip of land. Cato looked out over the sea and noted that the surface was choppier. At least it was blowing up from the south-west and wouldn't inhibit passage to and from Mona when the remaining cohorts were picked up to reinforce the auxiliaries on the island.

Half a mile from the beach, the navarch ordered the sail to be taken in and the oars unshipped. There was a loud rumble of timber beneath the deck as the elongated blades and weathered shafts emerged from the sides and were held up above the surface of the water to prevent any drag. Like all warships operating in the heavy seas off the coast of Gaul, the lower line of oar ports had been sealed, and the bireme was propelled by one bank of oars on each side.

A drum sounded and the oars were steadied and held level. A second beat brought them splashing down together. As the blades bit into the water, another beat sounded for the pull, and then another for the lift and recovery, and so it continued in a rhythm that caused a gentle lurch underfoot with each stroke. The sailors had hauled in the mainsail and secured the sheets, and were busy coiling the slack and looping it over belaying pins to keep it from tripping the crew up. The soldiers were ordered to return to the middle of the deck as the bireme began to turn in towards the beach.

'Form up!' Galerius ordered, and they picked up their shields and stood in close formation along the centre of the warship.

The marines had untied the landing ramps and carried them forward, and opened the small gates either side of the bow rail. They ran the narrow ramps out a short distance and waited for further orders. Cato looked down. The water was clear enough to see dark and light patches on the bottom of the small bay in front of the beach.

The following bireme had also taken in its sails and was proceeding under oars straight along the length of the spit, surging across their stern as it made for a position closer to the base of the spit in accordance with its orders. Cato had a moment of self-criticism, for not accounting for the possibility of a landing further along, but consoled himself with the thought that the floating battery would be able to harass and unsettle the morale of any enemy warriors before they reached his men.

The bireme was speeding towards the shoreline, and when they were fifty paces out, the navarch barked, 'Rest oars! Brace for beaching!'

There was one last beat from the drum, and the oars rose dripping from the sea and hung six feet above the gentle swell. Cato gripped the side and bent his knees slightly as he waited. There was a gentle tremble, and then a much stronger one that caused all aboard to lurch forward and those who were unprepared to stumble and fall to the deck. Shingle ground under the prow, and the shrouds shivered as the mast creaked and shook, and then the deck was solid and unmoving beneath Cato's boots.

'Ramps down!' ordered the navarch, and the marines slid them forward before letting the ends drop into the shallows no more than a few paces from where small waves were breaking on the glistening sand of the bay.

Galerius raised his arm to draw the attention of his men. 'First Century! Forwards!'

The two lines of auxiliaries paced to the gates and shuffled down the ramps, which gave slightly under the weight of the heavily laden men struggling to keep their balance with a spear in one hand, shield in the other. Galerius splashed into the water and began to power forwards, followed by his men. Cato pushed into the line using the right-hand ramp and made his way down. The sea was bitterly cold and made him gasp as it closed round his legs. He made his way up the beach, tiny shells and sand crunching under his boots, and joined Galerius and his standard-bearer, and the men fell in, dripping seawater from the hems of their tunics as the sun rose over the spit of land and bathed them in a ruddy light.

The bireme's complement of marines, some thirty men under a decurion, formed up to the rear of the auxiliary century, and Cato gave the order to advance up the beach and onto the spine of uneven ground that ran the length of the spit. As they emerged through the high tussocks of sea grass, he was afforded a view over the surrounding terrain. He could see that the trireme carrying the small battery of bolt-throwers had shipped oars and dropped anchor nearly half a mile further along. Sailors were hauling in the stern anchor to swing the vessel side-on to the shore so that all the weapons could be easily brought to bear. Not a moment too soon, thought Cato, as he saw a band of men approaching from the direction of the settlement he had spotted earlier. They were already level with the bireme and were armed with a mix of spears, axes, a few swords and a range of other makeshift weapons. Ten or so of them led the way on ponies, followed by no more than two hundred on foot. They did not have the look of a body of hardened warriors, and Cato decided that they must be a scratch force gathered from the settlement. They still outnumbered Galerius and his marines almost two to one.

'Left flank! Face!' Galerius bellowed, and the line of auxiliaries pivoted round from the leftmost file until the century formed a new line across the highest point of the spit, facing the oncoming enemy. Galerius and the standard-bearer took up their positions on the extreme right of the line. Down on the beach, the sailors had drawn the landing ramps in and now hurried to raise the bow fractionally as the oars churned the water and the rowers thrust the vessel away from the beach. For a moment the bireme appeared stuck, but then it shifted and eased smoothly back into the shallows. The navarch shouted orders, and it turned and headed out to sea, passing the next warship as it turned in towards the shore. Soon another century and more marines would reinforce those waiting to receive the enemy.

As Cato turned to watch the tribesmen, the rider at the head of the small mounted party was struck from his horse as if he had been swatted aside by a giant invisible hand. At almost the same instant, there was a swirl of bodies close to the front of the men on foot and three or four of them were taken down. Then came the quick chorus of distant cracks from the artillery bireme, the sound carrying up the spit.

It had been an unlucky shot as far as the enemy were concerned, for their leader had been hit with the first volley. The riders halted and the men on foot looked at their stricken comrades in horror. A moment later, the second volley came, more ragged this time, as some crews loaded their weapons more swiftly than others. As the tribesmen had stopped and bunched together, they presented an easy target, and several more were struck down.

One of the riders, with more presence of mind than most of his companions, raised a horn to his lips and blew a deep note before drawing his sword and yelling out to the others, jabbing the blade at Galerius's men. His followers picked up the need to get out of range of the bolt-throwers, and the party surged forward, spilling out on either flank as they rushed through the clumps of grass growing across the sandy soil of the spit. They came straight at the line of auxiliaries, and the bireme just had time for a third volley before they were forced to cease shooting as the enemy moved out of range.

'Present spears!' Galerius called out, and the auxiliaries advanced the points of their weapons ahead of their oval shields using an overhand grip. Cato flicked the folds of his cape back over his shoulders and drew his short sword, taking up a position halfway between the auxiliaries and the small marine detachment. A quick glance to his left showed him that the second bireme to land men was still a hundred paces from the shore.

The war cries and insults screamed by the enemy filled the air as they closed in quickly in the terrifying mad rush that the Celts used to strike fear into their enemies and battle rage into their own side. They charged the Roman line in an open formation, with the swiftest reaching the shield wall first. As the fighting spread evenly along the line, the weight of numbers soon began to tell. The Roman line, two deep, was at first able to keep the enemy at bay with their spears, cutting down many of them, but soon the tribesmen pressed closer and were easily able to grab at the shafts of the spears or parry them aside. The auxiliaries in the front ranks were forced to discard their spears and draw their swords for close-up work, where such weapons excelled.

Cato could see that the flanks of Galerius's century were being steadily forced back as the auxiliaries attempted to stop their foes spilling around the ends of the Roman line. The second bireme to land men was only a short distance from the beach. He turned to the marines.

'First two sections reinforce the right flank. The rest, on me!'

The small body of marines divided and trotted towards the flanks. As they moved along the rear of the hard-pressed Roman line, an auxiliary backed out of the fight, his sword arm laid open from wrist to elbow, bleeding profusely.

'Give me your shield!' Cato called to him. He hefted the shield and made his grip as firm and comfortable as possible before they reached the left flank of Galerius's century.

Already three of the enemy had turned the flank and were attacking the auxiliary who had confronted them. He managed to block a blow from an axeman before spearing his opponent in the side. Before he could recover the spear, however, the second man had grasped the edge of the auxiliary's shield and wrenched him round, exposing his side to a blow from another axe wielded by the third man. The head of the weapon cut through some of his mail armour, but it was the force of the impact that did for the Roman. He fell to his knees, and a blow to his neck finished him before Cato and the marines could intervene. The tribesman who had struck the fatal blow let out a shout of triumph that was cut short as Cato smashed his shield into the man's back and knocked him down onto the body of the auxiliary. He stabbed his sword at the exposed flesh of the man's neck and pushed down hard to ensure it shattered the bone. The tribesman sagged forward, gasping for breath, as Cato tore his blade free.

The marines surged past him, round the end of the auxiliary line, and fell upon the enemy's own flank, carving their way into the press of tribesmen. Down on the beach, Cato saw the men of the Second Century pouring down the bireme's landing ramps. He was pleased to see that Centurion Minucius was forming his men into a column before leading them into the fight. A less experienced officer might have sent them into battle piecemeal and lost control from the outset. As they advanced at the trot, Cato ran to meet them.

'Get up there at a right angle to this end of Galerius's line and start rolling up their flank. Go!'

Minucius led his men a short distance to the left of the battle line, and the tribesmen turned to face them with anxious expressions. A handful of the more enraged charged the fresh enemy formation, but were quickly cut down. Minucius halted the column and shouted the order to turn to face the enemy. Then, with spears lowered, they marched steadily forward, careful to hold their line. The first men made contact and the Second Century began to roll up the flank and swing in towards the enemy's rear.

Fear raced from man to man amid the mass of tribesmen slowly being enveloped. While many were too busy fighting, others could see the danger and were already backing away, and then turning to flee before the trap closed. Soon almost the entire enemy force had broken and were streaming back along the spit of land towards the distant settlement. A handful, more stout-hearted than their comrades, fought on individually or in small knots, but in a short time they were all dealt with, and the auxiliaries stood panting and blood-spattered, masters of the battlefield. A few eager spirits set off in pursuit of the enemy, but were brought up as their officers bellowed at them to stop and return to the ranks.

A fresh series of cracks came from the artillery bireme, and Cato swore under his breath at the waste of ammunition. It was one thing to lay down a barrage on a dense body of men, but only the luckiest of shots was liable to find a victim amongst a dispersed group of running targets. Sure enough, he did not see one of the enemy struck down before they had fled out of range, and he resolved to have a word with the officer in charge of the battery as soon as the opportunity arose.

The two centurions ordered their men to retrieve the Roman wounded and to finish off the enemy, and then reported to Cato.

Galerius had a flesh wound on his forearm and had taken a strip of cloth from a small pouch on his belt and begun to dress the shallow cut. 'Eight dead, sir. Fourteen wounded, four seriously. The rest can fight on once they've been seen to.'

Minucius reported three dead and seven wounded. Glancing over the ground, Cato estimated that at least fifty enemy bodies lay there, in addition to those who had been hit by the bolts shot from the bireme. There would be wounded who had fallen along the path of the retreat to the settlement as well.

'First blood to us, I'd say,' Minucius concluded.

'True.' Cato nodded. 'But they were mostly farmers and hunters, not seasoned warriors. It will be a different story when we come up against those.'

He turned and scanned the bay. The errant bireme had weathered the rocks at the end of the spit and was changing course to take its place on the opposite side to the other floating battery. Away to the south-west, a band of clouds had formed and was already creeping towards the island. He noticed that the breeze had strengthened, and the sea was noticeably rougher than it had been at first light.

With the enemy alerted to the presence of his force, it was only a matter of time before they sent a powerful column of warriors to deal with the threat to their flank. Cato calculated all the elements at play and saw that it was a simple enough problem. He needed to land his troops before the sea became too rough or the enemy arrived in strength, otherwise he and the men around him would be wiped out.

# CHAPTER TWENTY-FOUR

The first two cohorts were ashore by mid morning, and more troops were being landed in a regular rhythm as the biremes unloaded and returned to the cargo ships to fetch fresh units. The two battery ships were covering the approaches to the base of the land spit, and had already seen off several cavalry patrols that had attempted to reconnoitre the Roman landings, causing several more casualties in the process.

As soon as the last hundred men of the Eighth Illyrian were ashore, Cato led his unit forward until he was between the battery ships, and then had his men seed the ground on either flank with two lines of caltrops some fifty paces apart. The small iron devices with their four sharp points could be scattered easily, as one of the points always aimed up, however the device landed. He had seen how well the defensive weapons had worked on previous campaigns, and had ensured that he had them supplied to the units he commanded.

The six infantry centuries of the cohort formed up across the open ground in two lines, each four men deep, enough to withstand an attack by any warriors sent to dislodge the Romans and hurl them back into the sea. The dismounted cavalrymen and the marine contingents formed the flanks, ready to fend off those who survived the crossing of the caltrop belt unharmed.

Satisfied with the disposition of his forces, Cato paused to consider the situation. Well over a thousand men had landed so far, and nearly three thousand were making for the beach or waiting their turn on the cargo ships that were hove to out at sea. The strengthening wind and rising sea were inhibiting the manoeuvring of the ships and the transfer of men down the feed nets, however, and the growing delays were gravely concerning. He must assemble his entire force if he was to have a chance of turning the enemy's flank and ensuring that Suetonius's frontal assault managed to overwhelm the warriors caught between the two Roman attacks.

There was also the question of timing. His troops would have to march more than five miles to reach the enemy's fortifications along the strait. With unknown country ahead of them, and the certain attempts to delay them with harassing attacks, it would take two hours or more to cover the distance. At the rate the men were being landed, it was doubtful they would be in position in time to seal the victory. If they failed to reach the defences, the main attack would surely fail, and the Ordovices and Druids would be able to turn on them with overwhelming strength and annihilate them.

If that happened, there was little hope of Suetonius taking Mona without stripping the province of all remaining soldiers and placing it at the mercy of any rebellious tribes. Alternatively, he would have to settle for starving the enemy into surrender, but there was no knowing how well the island had been provisioned in anticipation of such a siege. It might hold out for years, all the while pinning down the best soldiers in the province. Much was resting on the timely arrival of the bulk of Cato's forces.

As soon as the Tenth Gallic were formed up, Cato had them reinforce the flanks of his position at the base of the spit, opposite the settlement a mile or so further inland. He could see the remnants of the band they had fought off earlier standing in small groups as they stared back at the Romans. Behind them there was much activity as the local people gathered up their valuables, children and livestock and drove the beasts away towards the perceived safety of the interior of the island. It was an illusory safety, thought Cato. If the Romans broke through the defences along the strait, nothing would stop them from scouring the island, destroying any last pockets of resistance and pillaging every settlement as they hunted for loot. But first the defences would have to be breached, and that was by no means guaranteed given the rate at which his men were coming ashore.

'Sir!'

Cato turned to see Galerius trotting towards him. The centurion drew up and saluted with his bandaged arm. 'The lads on the right flank have spotted an enemy column moving through the trees over there.' He indicated a pine forest to the east that sprawled from the rocks above the shoreline up a gentle slope to the crest of a low hill.

Straining his eyes, Cato could just make out movement amongst the nearest of the trees, over a mile away. A moment later, the head of the column emerged from the edge of the forest. The sun glinted off the armour, helmets and spears of a large body of mounted men – as many as three hundred of them – before the first of the infantry appeared. They followed a track that wound along the path towards the settlement and the base of the spit. At length the end of the infantry column cleared the trees, and Galerius let out a low whistle.

'Over four thousand of the bastards, I'd say.'

'Closer to five thousand,' Cato estimated from long experience. 'Pass the word to the men to expect another attack. Tougher opposition this time.'

'Tough or not, they'll not get the better of the Eighth.' Galerius was grinning, and Cato saw that he was in his element, excited by the prospect of battle even if he was wounded. A man very much in the mould of Macro. For Cato, the excitement of battle was frequently sublimated by the constant need to anticipate opportunities to be exploited and dangers to avoid. He had to be alert to both at the same time.

He forced himself to smile back at the centurion. 'I don't doubt it. Tell the lads from me that we'll send them packing, the same way as the first lot.'

Galerius moved off, pausing at each century to pass on the message. Cato watched him, slightly ashamed at his own making light of the prowess of the enemy column marching towards them. Those men were no farmers or shepherds rustled up to fight the invader. They were hardened warriors, no doubt well armed with Roman equipment lost during the previous disastrous campaign. The men who would shortly be attacking the Roman line were going to be a much tougher proposition than the peasant mob that had been sent packing earlier.

The enemy halted out of range of the floating batteries and deployed in three lines, with a screen of archers and slingers spread out ahead of the main body. The Ordovician leader was easy to pick out: a nobleman in a bright red cloak, accompanied by an escort of armoured warriors, one of whom carried a green banner with some mythical red beast upon it. He rode forward as far as he dared to inspect the Roman lines, and one of the bolt-thrower crews on the bireme south of the spit tried a ranging shot, which fell a hundred paces short with a puff of sand. Encouraged by this, the enemy commander moved his men fifty paces closer. A moment after they had halted, the bireme unleashed a volley that tore through the ranks of the horsemen, and Cato saw four of them go down.

At once, the rest turned and galloped off. A loud chorus of cheers and whistles rose from the ranks of the auxiliaries and marines at the sight of the fleeing enemy leader and his retinue. Cato smiled at the neat trap the officer in charge of the floating battery had set, and made a note to commend him for it after the battle, assuming they both survived.

Once the enemy commander had returned to the main body, Cato could see him gesticulating as he issued his orders. The dense bodies of infantry opened ranks and spread out across the ground at the base of the spit. The enemy had learned a valuable lesson, Cato thought ruefully. They wouldn't fall into the same trap again, nor would they provide an easy target for the floating batteries when they attacked. However, as they approached the Roman line, the spit narrowed, the reason why Cato had chosen the spot to draw up his defence line to cover the landings. The enemy would be forced to close up, and that would result in them suffering more at the hands of the bolt-thrower crews.

A loud blaring carried across the intervening ground as a number of Celtic war horns sounded the signal to advance, and the first line, as many as two thousand warriors, Cato estimated, rippled forward. There was no mad rush, no wild shouting, just a slow, menacing movement towards the Roman line. The enemy commander was no fool, Cato realised. Moreover, he knew how to control his men and save their strength for the charge over the final distance so that the impact had the greatest effect. The men themselves were disciplined enough to maintain formation and keep their unnerving silence as the last jeers of the auxiliaries died away.

When the slingers and archers came in range of the batteries, the crews unleashed aimed shots, to little effect. Cato saw only one man taken down close to the shore. The rest of the bolts went wide. The horns sounded again and the missile troops broke into a steady trot, surging ahead of the main battle line until they drew up in range of the Romans and began to launch their projectiles. Cato saw the dark shafts of the arrows tracing a foreshortened arc towards the Roman line as the officers shouted the order to raise shields. A ragged rattle of arrows striking, piercing and shattering on the shields extended across the entire line. An overshoot struck the ground close to Cato, and he raised his own shield quickly.

The slingers were an altogether more dangerous prospect. The iron shot, the size of a small walnut, travelled in a lower, faster trajectory and was almost impossible to see. It was easy to tell when they struck the shields, as the impact caused a louder, sharper sound. As the Romans held their shields up at an angle to the arrows, they exposed their legs to the slingshot, and within a few heartbeats, three of Cato's men were struck, their limbs shattered by the ferocious impact.

He cupped a hand to his mouth and bellowed as loudly as he could above the din of the missiles striking home, 'Down! Crouch down! Now!'

The order was repeated along the line, and the auxiliaries and marines went down on one knee, resting the bottom of the shield on the ground in front of them and angling it back as they sheltered from the barrage as best they could. The damage was not all one-way, however. The floating batteries were taking their toll of the enemy, and the ground was dotted with the bodies of the dead and wounded.

The first wave of warriors began to move forward, and after a final few shots, the archers and slingers fell back. Cato waited briefly before he rose and called out, 'Stand!'

As the Romans came to their feet, the horns sounded again, and at once a great roar of war cries erupted from the enemy warriors as they charged forward, weapons raised. Cato glanced over his lines and saw that there was no sign of wavering, as was often the case with inexperienced troops. The men of the Eighth Illyrian stood firm as they waited to join battle.

'Advance spears!' Galerius ordered. Only a handful of men had not been able to recover theirs from the previous encounter, and they raised their swords along with the lethal teardrop-shaped points extended towards the enemy.

The warriors tore across the open ground, confident that they could shatter the thinner lines on the flanks and then close in to crush the auxiliaries defending the centre. The first of them pitched forward with an agonised yell. In an instant, several more impaled their feet on the vicious barbed points of the caltrops, almost invisible in the grass, and the war cries were drowned out by screams and howls of pain. The entire line wavered as the bewildered warriors tried to understand what was happening. Only those in the centre continued unimpeded, and fell upon the spears and shields of the Roman line.

As before, the spears provided a temporary advantage and caused a significant number of casualties before they were cast aside in favour of short swords as the grim, intimate struggle of close combat stretched along the centre of the line. Elsewhere the enemy were warily picking their way through the caltrop belts, only reaching the auxiliaries and marines singly and in small groups, robbed of the impetus of their initial charge.

As Cato surveyed the struggle, he saw that the Roman line held steady. When the wounded withdrew through the ranks, fresh men stepped forward into their place. The enemy were gaining no ground, and were all the while suffering disproportionate losses thanks to the thrusts of the short swords darting out from the wall of oval shields. Both sides pressed against the shields, feet braced and straining at their opponents. It was an exhausting test of strength, and it could not endure for long. Slowly the tribesmen were thrust back and the Roman line edged forward, inch by inch. Then the enemy were giving way more easily, and shortly afterwards, as if by some common decision, they pulled away, broke contact and walked, ran and limped back towards the base of the spit of land.

As before, some of the more reckless and excited of the auxiliaries chased after them and had to be recalled. One, in his eagerness, tripped and fell and was quickly dispatched by his erstwhile prey before the latter retreated with his comrades. Again the tribesmen fell victim to the floating batteries, and several more were shot down by the heavy bolts as they ran past. Soon the open ground was littered with the dead and dying, and the rest retreated to the rear of the two lines of fresh warriors.

Cato made his way through the cohort as the front line was re-formed, and offered words of praise and encouragement.

'Hot work, Centurion,' he said as he joined Galerius beside the standard.

'The lads did you proud, sir.'

'That they did.' Cato smiled briefly before looking towards the enemy position, where the leader was conferring with his entourage. Already the slingers and archers were edging forward, and shortly afterwards, the second line advanced.

'Here we go again,' said Galerius.

Cato thought a moment and then decided. 'Time for a passage of lines, Centurion. Pull the front line back and send them to the flanks. The caltrops won't be a surprise this time, and we'll need more men on the flanks. And assign a party to get our injured back to the beach and loaded aboard the ships'

'Yes, sir.' Galerius nodded and moved off to shout the orders.

The men of the second line opened ranks to let their comrades fall back, then closed up and advanced to the position that had been occupied by the first line, now demarcated by the bodies of the men who had fallen in combat, along with their weapons and shields. Some took the opportunity to loot the bodies at their feet before they were called to order and stood ready, shields and spears grounded, facing the enemy.

Once again the slingers and archers weathered the barrage from the flanks before they were close enough to pay the Romans back in kind. Cato and his men went down on one knee behind their shields as the shot and arrows struck home, clattering against the shields and tearing through any exposed flesh. Fortunately only a handful of men had been injured when the Ordovician war horns sounded the charge and the auxiliaries rose to meet it.

This time the enemy approached more warily, scanning the grass ahead of them, bending to scoop up any caltrops they found. There were still a handful of casualties, and Cato saw several of them draw up in agony before slumping to the ground to remove the iron spikes, whose barbs made extraction even more damaging and painful. When they were close enough to the Romans, they hurled the caltrops at them; some pierced and stuck to the auxiliaries' shields, while others dropped at their feet and were picked up by Cato's men before the gap closed. One of the marines was not so lucky and became a victim of his own side's weapon as he impaled his foot on a caltrop hurled back at the Romans. He had to crawl to the rear, the iron having pierced right through his boot.

The savage clatter of edged weapons on shields and the ringing clang of blade on blade and helmet filled the air once more, along with the grunts and cries of the men locked in combat, struggling to push their foe back. Cato could see the marines on the left begin to give ground, and he ran to the nearest century of the Tenth Gallic and ordered them to follow him. As they reached the position, the first of the enemy broke through the marine line: a large dark-haired warrior with wide shoulders. He was stripped to the waist and his chest was covered with swirling tattoos. He carried two bloodied axes, and as his eyes fixed on Cato, he screamed a war cry and sprinted towards him.

Cato turned to face the Ordovician, planting his feet at right angles and leaning slightly forward behind his shield as he drew his sword and held it level, ready to strike. The warrior swung with his left arm as his right drew back to cut down at Cato's exposed side the moment he tried to block the feint with his shield. Instead, Cato brought his sword up and caught the descending axe near the hilt. Sparks flew as the impact of metal on metal rang in his ears. Then, swinging his shield up, he threw his weight behind it. The warrior's right-hand axe had only travelled a short distance and was easily deflected, and the round iron boss caught the man on the chin, breaking his jaw and crushing his nose before he tumbled back senseless. The nearest of the auxiliaries from the Tenth had raced forward to assist Cato, and now plunged his spear into the warrior's chest and drove the blade home. He twisted it from side to side before pressing his boot next to the wound and tearing the weapon free as the warrior's body sagged and he bled out.

'Hold the line!' Cato called to the marines, and ordered the auxiliaries forward, throwing their weight into the fight. He pushed his shield into the back of a marine to help steady the man as he pressed against the enemy in turn, stabbing his short sword over the rim of his shield into the faces of the Ordovicians before him. A warrior fell to his knees, blinded by a thrust to the eyes, and was battered to the ground as the reinforced line forced its way forward again, winning back the ground it had given way on.

The enemy were being steadily driven back. Suddenly they were recoiling, turning for the settlement where their commander and his final fresh formation of warriors looked on. The auxiliaries and marines watched them withdraw, chests heaving from their exertions and blood dripping from grazes and minor wounds. Cato sheathed his sword and moved back to the centre of the line. This time Roman casualties had been more numerous, sprawled amongst the fallen tribesmen.

A marine came running up from the direction of the beach and stopped to salute in front of him. 'Message from the trierarch, sir.'

Cato grounded the shield and breathed deeply, licking his dry lips as he wondered what the commander of the naval squadron wanted. 'What is it?'

'The sea is rising, sir. He doesn't think it will be possible to transfer the last cohort safely. Even if it arrives.'

Cato felt his heart give a lurch. 'What's happened?'

'It's the wind, sir. It's shifting to the west. It'll be foul for the cargo ships trying to get out of the bay.'

He closed his eyes and rubbed the narrow strip of brow beneath the rim of his helmet. The last of the auxiliary cohorts to be loaded was fortunately one of the smaller infantry units. Without them, he would have a little over three thousand men with which to make his flank attack at the strait. Less than three thousand most likely, given the casualties he had suffered so far. If he ordered the naval squadron to beach their ships and leave only skeleton crews behind, he could muster a couple of hundred more. So be it. He opened his eyes and straightened up as he addressed the marine.

'Tell the trierarch that if the last cohort can't be landed, I'll go ahead with the rest of the men, as well as all the marines and sailors he can spare once he beaches his ships. Tell him to send a ship to Suetonius to explain the situation and let him know that we'll be there to play our part when the governor makes his attack. On my honour.'

# CHAPTER TWENTY-FIVE

Once the last of the auxiliaries and marines had landed, the sailors that could be spared were armed with weapons and armour taken from the dead and injured, Roman and Ordovician alike, before being formed into a unit under the command of one of the auxiliary optios. Cato decided to use them as a reserve of last resort, since they had little formal training with weapons, and none as part of an armed formation. If they had to fight, the chances were that they would be as fragile as the first body of tribesmen to confront Cato's force. Still, he mused, they would add some two hundred men to his strength, and in the absence of the auxiliary cohort aboard the cargo ships trapped in the bay, he needed every man he could find. It had occurred to him to send the biremes back for the final cohort, but they would not be able to return under sail, and if he waited for them, he would never reach the strait in time.

With his four cohorts, marines and sailors formed up, he gave the order to advance through the gap between the caltrops, and with the Tenth Gallic cohort at the head, the column marched towards the base of the spit of land. The enemy force sent to dislodge them had already retreated the way it had come, and the last inhabitants of the settlement could be seen fleeing across the rolling countryside beyond. Cato had been surprised that the enemy column had fallen back, and guessed that they had been so shaken by their losses that their commander had not been able to prevail upon them to make a third charge. It was possible that he might attempt some delaying actions to buy time while reinforcements were sent to his aid. He might not yet have been informed about the preliminary barrage on the defences of the strait before the assault began at high tide. Once he was, however, he would understand how vital it was that Cato's force was halted before it could intervene.

It was not quite midday when they reached the settlement and joined the track leading along the coast through the forest. Cato was acutely aware that he had fallen behind schedule and that his men must march five miles within the next two hours. That would have been easy under normal circumstances, but he suspected that his opponent would lay ambushes and blocking forces ahead of him. It was what he would do if their positions were reversed. As they entered the forest, he detached the leading century of the Tenth Gallic and led it at a trot a quarter of a mile ahead to scout the track. They passed some of the mortally wounded enemy, who had been left at the side of the track, and the auxiliaries finished them off with quick spear thrusts as they marched past.

The track followed the line of the coast for the first mile before it came to a fork. Both directions were clearly well used, so it was impossible to know which one the enemy that had attacked them had approached along. Cato halted his men briefly. The path to the left angled slightly upwards away from the coast, deeper into the forest. It did not appear to head directly towards the strait. Then again, there was no guarantee that the other track was the quicker route if it continued to follow the outline of the coast. He considered the opposing commander's options. He would surely have chosen the most direct route and picked a place to block the Romans where they would have to attack him on a narrow front. He would know that they were unfamiliar with the lie of the land, and that the most obvious course of action would be to follow the coastal track, where they could be more certain of their position with the sea on their right. If they chose to do that, it would be easy for him to halt their advance.

Therefore the decision Cato must make was clear. Timing was the key factor, and he could not afford to be delayed for hours fighting his way along the coast. He sent a man back to Galerius with orders to take the left fork, and then led the scouting force up the slight incline, hoping that he was going in the right direction.

The track was wide enough for three men to march abreast, and the century made good progress as it reached even ground and began to meander through denser patches of forest and gentle slopes. Three miles beyond the settlement, it entered a clearing on the crest of a low ridge, and ahead in the distance, over the treeline, Cato could see tiny glittering specks arcing through the air trailing thin streaks of smoke, and felt a surge of relief at the sight of the incendiary barrage that Suetonius had arranged to precede the assault. There were angled columns of smoke as well, proof of the damage being caused by the bombardment. It was clear now that the track would lead Cato and his men roughly where they needed to be.

'Not far now, lads,' he called out.

'Sir, look!' The centurion at his side thrust his arm out and pointed at the treeline. Cato saw movement in the shadows amid the low boughs of the pines no more than a hundred paces off, and then figures emerged raising their bows and spinning the slings up to speed.

'Rise shields! Close up!'

His men just had time to obey the order before the first volley slashed through the air and hammered at their shields. The enemy commander had been shrewd enough to set this second ambush in case the Romans defied his expectations, Cato realised.

There was a loud gasp close at hand, and he glanced round to see the standard-bearer dropping to his knees. His jaw was gone, smashed to fragments. Blood filled the ruin of his mouth, and he clawed at his throat, desperate for air. The centurion took the standard from his trembling hands and held it steady as the bearer slumped to the ground.

The enemy kept up a relentless barrage, but caused only a handful of casualties as the auxiliaries sheltered behind their shields. The rate at which the missiles were striking the formation slackened, and Cato guessed the tribesmen had expended most of their ammunition in the earlier attacks near the landing beach. He waited to be certain, then took a deep breath and called over his shoulder, 'On your feet! Form tortoise!'

The men scrambled up and there was a dull clunking as the shields closed up and those on the inside of the formation raised theirs overhead. The points of the units' spears bristled along and above the shields so that the tortoise looked more like a porcupine. As soon as the noise had stopped, Cato gave the order to advance, and called the time as the century trudged up the incline towards the archers and slingers, who were expending the last of their ammunition at a target that was impossible to miss at such short range. Within the shield wall he could hear the laboured breathing of the men around him and muttered prayers as some of them called on the gods to protect them.

A glance over the top of the shield in front of him revealed that they were within fifteen paces of the trees. He was readying himself to give the next order when an arrowhead burst through the shield just below his forearm, and splinters gouged the underside. He felt a sharp pain but there was no time to register any other reaction as he called out, 'On the command, break ranks and charge! Now!'

The formation burst apart as the auxiliaries charged the thin enemy line. Most of the Ordovicians turned and ran for the cover of the trees. Some attempted one last shot. Directly ahead of Cato, an archer nocked an arrow and was raising his bow as Cato surged towards him. He released the string almost at the same time as Cato's shield struck his bow hand and the arrow bent and snapped. Cato stabbed him in the midriff, twisted the blade both ways and ripped it out. The archer dropped his bow and hunched over, and Cato battered him to the ground with his shield before looking round for his next opponent.

A handful of the enemy who had stayed to unleash a final shot had paid the price and were cut down; the rest were fleeing up the slope through the trees as the auxiliaries chased after them. Some were caught in the undergrowth and were speared before they could free themselves, but most escaped unharmed. The going was harder for the auxiliaries, who quickly gave up the pursuit and fell back to the treeline, forming up on Cato and the standard.

The rest of the column had just reached the clearing, and Cato turned to the centurion. 'Hold this position until everyone has passed, in case the enemy comes back. Then pick up your wounded and fall in at the rear.'

'Yes, sir.'

Cato trotted to the head of the column and took his place alongside Galerius.

'Any trouble, sir?' Galerius nodded towards the auxiliaries gathered around the standard by the treeline.

'Just our friends using up the last of their ammunition. If Fortuna is kind, that's the last we'll see of them before we reach the strait.'

'What about the rest of that lot we went up against?'

'Unless I miss my guess, they're still waiting for us along the coastal path.'

Galerius chuckled. 'I'd love to see the look on their faces when they realise we got round them.'

'Very amusing, I'm sure. Let's hope the sestertius doesn't drop too soon and they don't come after us before we reach the straits.'

'Oh . . .' Galerius slowed briefly as he saw the distant display of the incendiaries bombarding the Ordovician defences. 'Wouldn't want to be the poor sod on the end of that lot.'

'Quite,' Cato agreed. 'Just as long as it distracts them long enough for us to do our job.'

The column left the clearing and marched on through the forest for another mile before the track emerged into open countryside. There were farmsteads on either side and stone pens demarcating pasture land. Some of the farmsteads were still inhabited, and animals were grazing on the fresh spring grass. As soon as the Romans were sighted, there were cries of alarm and the Ordovician farmers grabbed their families and ran from the invaders. There was no time to be spared for looting, and the column passed by without any attempt to ransack the huts or seize any livestock.

Ahead, they could hear the faint sounds of men shouting and the occasional crash as a catapult shot struck the enemy palisade. Cato felt his pulse quicken at the prospect of the decisive action of the day, though at the same time he was burdened by concern about where the track would bring them out in relation to the enemy's defences and dispositions. If they were too far north, they might come up against an Ordovician force being held in reserve. He must strike at their flank if he was to achieve the full impact of surprise and local superiority in strength. A swift attack there, driven home with determination and energy would shatter the enemy flank and roll it up. Caught between that and the frontal assault, it was likely that the morale of the Ordovician warriors and their allies would surely crumble.

They were passing another farmstead when he heard a whinny and a snort. He pulled Galerius to one side. A mile away in the direction of the strait lay a low ridge. He pointed it out.

'Keep them going. Make for the bottom of the ridge and stop there if I don't get back to you first.'

'Sir?'

'Just do as I say. You'll see.'

Cato patted him on the back, then turned to run around the cluster of huts, coming face to face with a youth about to mount a pony. He already had the reins in one hand and was about to climb onto the sheepskin saddle. Both of them froze for a beat in surprise, then Cato pounced forward.

'No you don't!' he snarled, grabbing the youth's heel and wrenching it savagely so that he tumbled to the ground. As he snatched the reins and calmed the horse, the youth sprang to his feet, fists clenched. Cato turned to him, resting his free hand on the pommel of his sword. 'If you know what's good for you, you'll just fuck right off, my young friend.'

The boy hesitated, and Cato grasped the handle of the sword and began to draw the blade. Whatever thread of courage remained in the youth snapped, and he sprinted away, hurdling the fence of a pigsty as he made his escape.

Cato mounted the pony and gave it a reassuring pat on the

neck before urging it into a walk. At first it was restless with an unfamiliar rider on its back, but it soon settled into a rhythm. He urged it into a canter as he made his way past the column, exchanging a nod with the surprised Galerius, then steered it onto the track and made for the ridge. A short distance from the foot of the slope, he looked up and saw that there was no longer any sign of the incendiaries, nor any sound of the rocks being lobbed at the enemy defences by Suetonius's catapults. He heard the distant sound of Roman trumpets and felt his guts twist with anxiety as he realised that the main attack was beginning and he and his men had not reached the position from which he was supposed to launch his flank attack.

There was a copse of yew trees to one side of the track below the ridge, and he forced his mount into a gallop as he made for them. Dismounting, he slipped the reins over the end of a broken branch before running up to the summit on foot, unfastening the straps of his helmet and removing it as he went. The crest of an officer's helmet was designed to stand out so that it could be seen and followed by Roman soldiers. It was also just as obvious to any enemy, and Cato knew that he could not afford to draw attention to himself. The tufts of grass in front of him waved in the breeze as he slowed to a walk, craning his neck. He could hear the muffled roar of cheering, like the sound of the crowd at the Circus Maximus in Rome when heard from the far side of the city. And then the sweep of the battlefield revealed itself to him.

He was off to the right of the enemy fortifications, which were over half a mile ahead. A huge camp lay between him and the defences facing the strait. Closer to the rampart there were some burning huts and log piles where the incendiaries had caused fires. Groups of warriors stood a short distance further back, out of range, ready to be called forward to reinforce their comrades facing the Romans. Thousands more of the Ordovicians were climbing the timber steps and spreading out along the walkway now that the artillery barrage had ceased. Some carried fascines to fill the gaps in the palisade smashed by the catapults and bolt-throwers. Others had baskets presumably filled with arrows, slingshot and rocks.

Beyond the defences, he could see most of the strait that divided Mona from the mainland, and on the far shore the Roman legionaries boarding the small craft that would carry them across the water to make the landing on the enemy side. He could even make out the group of figures in scarlet cloaks that must be Suetonius and his staff. To his right, the defences extended to the foot of a hill covered in the stumps of trees that had been cut down to supply the timber used in the fortifications. Near the top, trees were still growing, and the wooded area sprawled on around the south of the island. From his vantage point, he realised he could also see the empty cargo ships making their way back to the bay where they'd started the day. It seemed impossible that so much could have happened in what little time had passed since then.

His gaze returned to the forested hill. A track emerged between the trees at the base of the hill and the far end of the ridge he was standing on. The point at which it left the forest was no more than two hundred paces from where the fortifications ended, next to a rocky outcrop overlooking the shore. A perfect spot from which his men could debouch and fall on the Ordovicians' flank. He smiled briefly with satisfaction, before calculating the distance his men would have to cover. At least a mile to the ridge, and another along the bottom and into the forest before the track gave out onto open ground. He took a last look at the enemy's camp and defences, then turned and hurried down to the trees where the pony was tethered.

* * *

Once the column had been directed across the open farmland towards the forest at the far end of the ridge, Cato briefed his cohort commanders.

'The main assault is already under way. The first of the legionaries are across and they will be in the open as they wait for the next wave. Suetonius will start his attack before we can make ours. There's nothing we can do about that. It's on us now to try and make up the lost time, so we'll pick up the pace as soon as you return to your commands. Once we are in position, I'll give the men a brief rest before the Tenth Gallic leads the charge. I want you to go in like demons. Your men are to move fast and make as much noise as they can. We must hurl ourselves on the enemy. Don't stop for anything. Keep the men moving. Push forward. The priority is the rampart and palisade so the legionaries can scale it and finish the job.' He looked round. 'Any questions? No? Then good fortune go with you, and may we win a glorious victory. For the emperor and Rome!'

'For the emperor and Rome!' the officers chorused before dispersing to their cohorts.

Cato remounted the pony and trotted to the front of the column, where he swung himself down and gave the animal a grateful pat. 'Now go and find your master.'

Thrasyllus came jogging up and fell in beside him. Undoing the clasp of his cloak, Cato cast it aside to lighten his load, then nodded. 'Time to increase the pace.'

The commander of the Tenth Gallic drew a deep breath and called over his shoulder, 'At the double . . . Advance!'

The front of the column broke into a gentle run, and the pounding of boots and the clatter and patter of loose kit increased in volume as each formation in turn picked up speed.

Cato gave thanks that it was not a drier part of the year, as the dust kicked up would have given away their position, as well as shrouding the men in a choking blanket. It had been an exhausting day for those under his command. Many of them had already been in action before the forced march, and now they had to endure a swift tactical advance laden with kit and weapons. And there was still a battle to be fought at the end of it. So far during the campaign the Eighth Illyrian had proven that they deserved the reputation claimed for them by Suetonius, and today was their supreme test. Cato was grudgingly proud of them. He had served in many fine units before, and some questionable ones, and the Eighth were one of the best. He wondered what Macro would have made of them, and gave a wry smile at the thought of his friend fuming with frustration from the safety of his home in Camulodunum when he'd rather be here in the thick of it.

He sensed that his pace had fallen off, and made himself hasten. He breathed deeply in a steady rhythm as his limbs began to complain at the strain he was exerting on them. An aching weariness began to turn into a burning sensation in his calves and feet. Continuing was an act of will; he would not shame himself by revealing that he was tiring in front of his men. He breathed hard and set intermediary markers along the way ahead to keep himself going as he blinked sweat away from his eyes.

When they reached the trees, he was relieved to find that the forest floor was clear of vegetation. Even so, he was forced to slow to a fast march as they wound through the trees in the direction of the track. They encountered it after less than half a mile, and turned towards the strait. Ahead he could see the dip between the end of the ridge and the hill beyond where the enemy's fortified line began. Another half-mile to go, he calculated, and slowed the pace to a standard march, mindful of the gasps and heavy breathing of the men immediately behind him. Hard training had made them fit, and they recovered their breath quickly as they advanced along the track, which was just wide enough for four men to march abreast. The slopes began to close in on either side, and he knew that the column would be making their charge imminently. From the sounds of the battle carrying to them across the forest, he knew that the main attack was already under way.

The column tramped round a corner, and the trees parted to reveal the enemy camp ahead.

'You know what you must do, Thrasyllus. Good luck, and I'll see you after the battle.'

'Aye, sir. After the battle then.' The prefect of the Tenth Gallic drew his sword and led his men out into the open.

Cato dropped out to the right to wait for his own cohort to come up, climbing a short distance amongst the tree stumps to watch. Such was the din of the battle raging along the fortifications, and the avid attention of the defenders directed to the fight, that Thrasyllus and the first of his men had advanced fifty paces towards the end of the rampart before they were spotted by some of the enemy warriors in the camp. They froze for a few vital moments at the sight of the auxiliaries moving towards them, and then the spell was broken as they shouted and raised the alarm. Immediately Thrasyllus gave the order to charge, and his men broke into a dead run with a ragged roar of war cries. He led them straight to the rear of the rampart and up the earth slope that merged with the end of the enemy's defences before turning left onto the walkway and leading the charge at the nearest group of warriors.

Below his position, Cato saw the last men of the Tenth emerge, and he ran down to place himself at the head of the

Eighth as they strode out onto the open ground. Galerius grinned at him.

'Was worried you might lose your head and go in with the Tenth, sir.'

'That would be bad form, Centurion.' Cato drew his sword and raised it high. 'On me, lads!'

He broke into a gentle run, heading towards the nearest formation of enemy reserves, a short distance beyond the point where Thrasyllus and his men were fiercely fighting their way along the rampart. The Eighth would have to face the enemy on a wider front, and it was vital they preserve the integrity of each century if Cato was to maintain control over his section of the battlefield. For the moment the enemy was still reeling from the suddenness of the attack. It had come from a direction they must have thought they had covered by sending the force to confront and contain the Romans further along the coast.

When he was close to the foot of the rampart, he halted the cohort and ordered them to form a line four ranks deep extending from the fortifications. The following cohort formed a similar line, in echelon behind the Eighth. Then Galerius cried out, 'Let me hear you, lads, loud enough for Suetonius to hear it himself. For Rome!'

The men bellowed the cry and surged towards the nearest of the Ordovician formations as it hurriedly formed a line to face them. Beyond, Cato could see mounted men shouting orders as they tried to reorganise their forces to deal with the new danger. He could also see that many of those on the wall were looking towards the flank before their leaders pushed them back to the palisade to keep the legionaries at bay. The defenders were using every kind of missile against the men below them on the shore. Arrows, javelins, slingshot and rocks rained down on Suetonius's force as they worked their way up to the ditch under the cover of their shields and then attempted to scale the rampart and palisade.

Cato ran forward with his men, echoing the cry that Galerius raised again and again. The scattered figures of camp followers fled from their path, streaming past and through the opposing line and disrupting it as they did so. There was a sudden burst of steam ahead of Cato as one of his men knocked a cooking pot over and the contents splashed down onto the flames, and he just had time to dodge to one side.

The auxiliaries crashed into the enemy warriors with their heavy shields, their spear points darting out to pierce bodies or being wildly parried as the two sides became a heaving mass of helmets, crests, blades, spears, swords and axes, amid sprays of crimson and a cacophony of weapons clashing and thudding home on shields and limbs. Cato kept close to the cohort's standard on the right of the line so that his position would be known in case he was needed. Galerius was ahead of him, urging his men on as he pressed forward with his shield and stabbed at any enemy warrior who appeared before him.

'Stick it to 'em, boys! Kill them all!'

The men of the First Century responded to their centurion's hoarse cry with a surge that drove the enemy back before them, littering the ground with the bodies of Ordovicians and auxiliaries in their wake. The frenzied aggression of the Eighth swiftly broke the will of their foe, and most were falling back and then running towards the next body of warriors waiting to confront the auxiliaries. Their leaders and a handful of figures in dark robes were exhorting their men to fight as they brandished their weapons and hurled curses and insults at the Romans.

Some of the auxiliaries had paused to cheer their shattering defeat of the first enemy warband, and Cato called out angrily to them, 'Don't stop! Keep going!'

The centuries of the Eighth had merged into a single uneven line, but this was not the time to re-form and charge again. Victory depended upon keeping the momentum of the attack going for as long as possible before it was spent. Cato turned to the standard-bearer. 'Stay close to me, and keep the standard high where the men can see it.'

He ran forward through his men and they surged after him, pausing only to kill those of the enemy who had been wounded. Some Ordovicians turned to fight, and a running battle spilled across the enemy camp as the intermingled mass closed up on the second enemy line. As Cato had anticipated, the fleeing warriors who had been the first to face the auxiliaries had plunged heedlessly amongst their comrades, and there was no semblance of a formation. Mindful of the need not to put the standard at risk, he slowed his pace and allowed his men to flow past him and throw themselves on their opponents, shouting like madmen as they stabbed their spears and swords at the Ordovicians.

This time, despite the disruption of their ranks, the enemy stood their ground more resolutely. The moment of shock at the speed of the flank attack had passed, and now they were determined to halt the auxiliaries and force them back before the legionaries could intervene decisively. As before, there was no coherent battle line on either side, just a brawling mass of individuals duelling, and clusters of men holding their own in tight knots. Cato climbed up onto a small cart, from where he could see that the impetus of the Eighth's charge was failing, and a moment later it was clear that the advance had stalled. Moreover, many of his men were falling as they began to be forced back.

To his left, the next auxiliary cohort was feeding into the battle. The nearest century struck the enemy's flank, and the following one began to envelop it and drive the Ordovicians back. The enemy ranks compacted as they were pressed from two sides by Cato's men. As the full weight of the fresh cohort made itself felt, the enemy's morale crumbled, and soon they were attempting to break contact and back away. Tired as the Eighth were, their bloodlust was not yet sated, and they pushed forward eagerly as they sensed the failing nerve of their foe. Now was the critical moment, Cato realised, and he jumped off the cart and hurried forward with the standard at his side, pushing his way close to where the fighting was at its fiercest. As he had hoped, the sight of the standard and the crest of their commander's helmet spurred the men into renewed effort.

A short distance ahead, he saw a group of enemy warriors gathered about one of their own standards, and he thrust his sword up at an angle towards them.

'There, lads! Take that and they're finished!'

He pushed his way through the melee, blocking an axe blow with his shield before thrusting into the warrior's shoulder and battering him to the ground. The nearest of his men closed in on the ring of warriors defending their standard, and the Ordovicians prepared to go down fighting, shields linked as they swung their swords and axes at the surrounding auxiliaries.

There was a sudden swirl of bodies that carried Cato and the standard forward, and he found himself face to face with one of the warriors, a short man with dark plaits hanging either side of a bushy beard. He was holding up his kite shield with his long sword resting on the trim, the point aimed at Cato's face. Their eyes met for a beat, before Cato stepped in, raising his own shield to cover his face as the man's sword point thudded into the surface. At once he angled the shield to drive the point aside and continued forward, close enough to use his shorter blade, but his foe's body was well covered and exposed no target. He thrust his shield into that of his opponent, pressing his shoulder against the inside of it and bracing his feet squarely on the churned ground beneath. For a moment neither man gave way, and then the iron studs on the soles of Cato's boots won out over the plain leather of the warrior's, and the Ordovician began to lose his footing. With one final supreme effort, Cato thrust forward again, and his opponent stumbled back and fell at the base of the standard he and his comrades were defending. Cato almost fell with him, but managed to stay on his feet as he stuck his sword deep into the man's throat.

As he pulled the weapon free, he realised to his horror that he and the standard-bearer of the Eighth were now inside the ring of enemy warriors, and the gap through which they had plunged had closed up.

'Oh fuck.'

Going into a crouch beside the standard-bearer, he exchanged a stare with the warrior holding the enemy's standard, and neither man could help a quick grin at the wholly unexpected turn of events. Then the spell was broken as the enemy standard-bearer swung his sword. Cato managed to block the blow, but the impact was numbing, and his arm felt weak and unresponsive as he flailed at the man.

As the Ordovician stepped towards him, Cato was thrust against the back of a large warrior holding the auxiliaries away with a long-handled axe. The giant snarled angrily and glanced over his shoulder. His eyes widened as he saw the two Romans, and he turned and grabbed at their standard. The standard-bearer clung on, swinging the bottom of the shaft up between the warrior's legs as hard as he could. The giant gasped in agony, then bellowed like a bull as he dropped his axe and hurled himself at the Roman, clamping his hands around the man's neck.

Cato suddenly found himself thrust to one side, and Galerius charged past him through the gap the giant warrior had left in the Ordovician ring. The centurion hacked at the wrist of the enemy's standard-bearer, severing it so that his hand fell to the ground, still clenched around the handle of his sword. The man clasped the bleeding stump to his chest, pressing the shaft of the Ordovician standard against his shoulder as he lashed out with his remaining fist, pounding the centurion's shield and screaming incoherently. Snorting with contempt, Galerius knocked him cold with a blow from the pommel of his sword, then trapped the shaft of the enemy's standard under his boot.

As more auxiliaries pressed round them, breaking up what was left of the enemy ring, Cato battered the bottom rim of his shield on the head of the enraged warrior still trying to throttle the Roman standard-bearer. The latter's hands were clawing at the giant's fists as his eyes rolled up and his tongue protruded. The standard lay to one side, and Cato grabbed it before it could be trampled, while two auxiliaries repeatedly stabbed their blades into the muscled back of the Ordovician. Blood pulsed from the wounds torn into his flesh, but his forearms continued to strain and the veins stood out like lengths of rope. Then, with a gasp, he slumped down and his fingers slowly relaxed.

Cato helped the standard-bearer to his feet and the man croaked his thanks. The battle had passed on, and he saw that all those Ordovicians who had tried to defend their standard lay dead or dying around him. He spared a moment's admiration for the courage of his enemy. Galerius and several of his men were standing on guard, chests heaving as they looked round warily. There were smears of blood on their armour that mingled with the blood oozing from their own wounds. Far more men on both sides had been lost in the struggle for the second line of enemy warriors, and Cato could see that the remaining men of the Eighth were drawing up, too exhausted to continue pursuing the enemy as they ran to join their comrades.

The charge had brought them almost a mile from the forest track. On Cato's right, Thrasyllus's cohort had been halted a short distance further along the rampart and was now pinned against it by superior numbers as they fought to keep themselves from being surrounded. There was a glimmer of hope as he saw the first of the legionaries crossing the palisade along the stretch that had first been cleared by the Tenth. But they were too few to swing the balance of the battle in Rome's favour. Suetonius needed to get more men over before victory could be achieved. In the meantime, the enemy was gathering its strength to turn on Cato's column once more.

Cato gestured to Galerius. 'Call 'em back. I want every man who's left to form up on our standard.'

'The other cohorts as well, sir?'

'All of them, and the marines and sailors. We have to hold the enemy long enough for the Fourteenth Legion to get over the defences.'

Galerius ran his gaze over the battlefield and nodded. 'It's on us then.'

He hurried away and began to call out Cato's instructions. The men of the Eighth who were still on their feet walked and limped back towards the standard, along with those from the cohorts who had followed up the attack and taken it forward on the flank. Cato's heart ached when he saw how few of them there were. Less than half of his men, and the other cohorts had lost nearly as many. Together with the still uncommitted naval contingent, there were just over a thousand of them. The centurions and optios hurriedly did their best to re-form their units, and closed up on the other depleted cohorts to create a line to receive the enemy counter-attack when it came.

Staring across the body-strewn ground towards the Ordovicians, Cato saw that there must be at least three thousand of them. More men who had been drawn from along the rampart were trotting forward to add their strength to the charge. He realised that the enemy commander hoped to destroy the remnants of his force in one swift action before turning back to deal with the attack from the straits. He glanced back to see legionaries scaling the palisade in more places and scrambling down the earth ramp to form up on their standards. The enemy's only hope now was to crush both Cato and the legionaries behind him before too many of them had crossed into the Ordovician camp.

He bent down to pick up the enemy standard, and thrust it into the hands of one of his men. 'Keep it safe. It'll make a nice trophy when the Eighth return to barracks after the campaign is over.'

Galerius hurried over. 'Sir, they're on the move!'

Cato looked up to see that the enemy line, a quarter of a mile away, was advancing. There was no eager surge, so typical of the Celts. The Ordovician commander was conserving the energy of his men until they were close enough to charge and strike the auxiliary line with one concentrated blow. Cato's men leaned on their shields in silence as they watched the warriors approach. Some looked his way as if willing him to order a retreat, but they all knew that they had to buy their legionary comrades more time.

Cato made a show of rolling his head and stretching his shoulder muscles before calling out, 'One more fight, lads, then we're done for the day. We've earned our pay.'

Most of the men gave a weary chuckle.

'Now let's dress the line and show those barbarian bastards what proper soldiers look like!'

The officers cajoled their men into place and the auxiliaries hefted their shields and raised their weapons, though many of the spears had been damaged and discarded. Some men sheathed their swords while they took a sip of water from their canteens. Others could only lick their dry lips and cough to clear the phlegm in their parched throats. A few closed their eyes and offered a fervent prayer to their favoured gods that they might see their comrades and family again in the afterlife. The veterans amongst them stared at the enemy and tried to calculate their chances of survival.

The sun was low in the sky, and its light burnished the battlefield with a tawny glow that contrasted with the elongated shadows stretching out at an angle from the Roman line. Smoke from the dying fires started by the incendiaries still rose in thin columns and cast a pall over the battlefield.

The Ordovicians had closed the gap to a scant two hundred paces when a despairing collective cry sounded from the direction of the rampart. Cato tried to see what the cause of it was, but the fighting was hard to make out in the smoke that was billowing across the far end of the fortifications. Some of the auxiliaries seemed to be unnerved by the noise, and Galerius stepped out in front of the line and turned his back to the enemy as he addressed his men in a calm tone.

'Easy, lads. We won't let those hairy-bollocked sheep-shaggers think they have us rattled, right? We're the fucking Eighth Illyrian Cohort! If anyone does the rattling round here, it's bloody well us!'

The men cheered the centurion as he returned to his position beside Cato and the standard-bearer.

'Fine words, Galerius.' Cato smiled. 'Cicero himself couldn't have put it more appositely or succinctly.'

'If you say so, sir.'

Cato's smile faded. 'It's time.'

The two officers turned to face the enemy, swords drawn and shields raised.

The distant cries and shouts were swelling in volume, and as Cato watched, the enemy force shuffled to a halt and the warriors looked round uncertainly, staring back towards the smoke drifting across the fortifications. Figures could be seen running through it, and away to the left, more of the enemy were heading from the strait towards the centre of the island. The Ordovicians hesitated a moment before the first of them started pacing away, then breaking into a run. A group of mounted men burst round the rear of the rapidly dissolving formation and charged towards the auxiliaries before swerving away and making for the open country. The enemy's ranks were sufficiently thinned out now that Cato could see another formation emerging from the smoke in a solid line.

'There's always some who don't know when they've had enough.' Galerius shook his head wearily.

Cato felt his heart lighten, and he laughed out loud as he sheathed his sword and set his shield down. 'That's our lads over there. The Fourteenth Legion! They've done it. They've taken the rampart!'

As the sun gleamed dully between the dark clouds scudding overhead and the lingering pall of smoke hanging over the gently rolling expanse of land behind the fortifications, Suetonius and his staff officers surveyed the battlefield from the backs of their horses. The engineers had swiftly demolished sections of the rampart and filled in the ditch to permit easier passage across the defences. As soon as the gaps were opened, two cavalry cohorts went in pursuit of the enemy, while the legionaries and auxiliaries secured the bridgehead they had won on the island. The injured were being collected and stretchered to hurriedly set-up dressing stations to have their wounds seen to by the army's medics. Those Ordovicians who had surrendered had their hands bound behind their backs and were placed under guard. Those of the enemy whose wounds were mortal or deemed too serious to be treated were swiftly put to death. The Roman dead were being placed together in steadily lengthening lines, ready for identification before they were cremated the following day.

The first raindrops had started to fall before Suetonius and his staff located Cato and the remains of the Eighth Cohort. On Galerius's order, the men rose wearily from the ground and stood in their ranks as the governor approached. Cato stepped forward to salute him.

'Beg to report, the Eighth Cohort is assembled and ready for duty, sir.'

Suetonius ran his eyes along the ranks of grime-streaked and bloodied auxiliaries, many of whom had dressings on their wounds. 'You seem to be missing half your men, Prefect Cato.'

'Yes, sir.'

'A high price to pay, but one that was necessary for us to win the day. The rest of the island will be ours in a matter of days now. Your men and the other cohorts who made this possible have done fine work here.'

Suetonius paused as he spotted the enemy banner behind the cohort's standard. The folds of green cloth had started to glisten in the rain.

'A fine trophy you've won there. And it's not the only prize your men are worthy of.' He turned to one of his staff officers. 'Let me have the crown.'

The man reached into a sidebag and withdrew a small silver coronet fashioned to look like a wall with battlements. It was little bigger than an amulet. He handed it to his superior, and Suetonius walked his horse closer to Cato. Bending in the saddle, he extended the rarely presented award for the first men to breach the walls of an enemy fortification.

'On behalf of the emperor, the Senate and the people of Rome,' he declared.

Cato took the crown and bowed his head in gratitude. Then he turned and marched the few paces towards the cohort's standard. As the bearer lowered the point, he slid the crown onto the top of the shaft, then the bearer raised it up for all the men of the cohort to see as the rain hissed down around them.

Suetonius sat erect in his saddle as he ran his eyes over the auxiliaries. 'Men of the Eighth Illyrian Cohort! I salute your courage and your dedication to duty. It is because of your efforts today that we have done what no Roman army has done before. Thanks to you, the conquest of Mona is assured. The last stronghold of the Druids will be taken and destroyed in a matter of days. All hail the mighty Eighth!' He raised his hand in salute before flicking his reins and moving on to continue the inspection of the other units spread across the battlefield.

When he had gone, Cato ordered Galerius to dismiss the men to find what food and shelter there was to be had amid the remains of the enemy camp. Then he slowly removed his helmet and raised his head to the sky. He closed his eyes and relished the refreshing sensation of rain on his skin as his lips moved in a silent prayer of thanks to Fortuna. His only regret was that Macro was not here to share the honour with him.

# CHAPTER TWENTY-SIX

*June* AD *61*

Camulodunum and the surrounding countryside basked in bright sunshine. A light breeze caused silvery ripples across the cereal crops in the fields, and the trees and bushes were heavy with new leaves. The farmers were anticipating a good harvest and looking forward to rebuilding the stores of grain that had been so badly depleted after the poor crops of the previous two years. A spirit of optimism filled the greetings exchanged by neighbours in the shops and the market. There were even rumours that the members of the colony's senate were planning to celebrate a public holiday with performances of some mime plays in the newly completed theatre, as well as gladiator bouts and animal fights in the small arena outside the town that had been built for the entertainment of the men of the Twentieth Legion when they had occupied the original fortress.

Like most rumours, there was little truth to it. The members of the colony's senate were still locked in a bitter dispute over the need to pay for the restoration of Camulodunum's defences. What work was being done had slowed, as many of the volunteers had been obliged to dedicate their time to planting crops at the end of spring, while others had lost interest and ceased to turn up and collect their tools from the store Apollonius had set up in the main gatehouse. The ditch and rampart were all but completed at one end of the settlement, stretching between the two parallel rivers that ran west to east either side of the colony. The other defence line, closest to the road to Londinium, was only half complete, and Macro was growing more frustrated by the slow progress every day.

Over a month had passed since his return to Camulodunum, and there were two things weighing heavily on his mind. The first was that he had received no further word from Decianus after they had parted ways. The escape of Boudica and her daughters had infuriated the procurator, and he had demanded that they return to the Iceni capital to recapture the hostages.

'No,' Macro had said as they stood beside the empty cart. 'Enough damage has been done. Better to let the matter be until Suetonius returns from his campaign.'

'We don't have to wait until he returns,' Decianus replied. 'He delegated power to me in his absence and he placed you under my command. I am ordering you to recapture Boudica and her daughters.'

'I'm done taking your orders. You want her so badly, go back and hunt her down yourself. If you're lucky, she will have gone into hiding to evade you and your thugs. If you're unlucky, she will come and find you with her Iceni warriors at her back and they'll roast the lot of you alive. The best thing you can do now is fuck off back to Londinium and wait for Suetonius to decide what to do about it.'

'I could do that, yes. Believe me, once I tell the governor how you have defied my authority, he'll strip you of your power here in Camulodunum and banish you from the colony. Frankly, when he hears about the suspicious circumstances of the escape and the part I believe you played in it, that will be the very least of your troubles, Centurion Macro.' Decianus paused. 'I could have you arrested now and taken back to Londinium in chains to answer questions under interrogation.'

'You could try,' Macro responded. 'However, since you have fifty men of questionable quality to back up your authority, and I have a hundred seasoned veterans here who are loyal to me, that ain't going to happen. The same goes for any attempt to hunt down Boudica. So I'd suggest you cut your losses, get back to your nice cosy billet at the governor's palace and wait for his return, like I said.'

Decianus glared at him and spoke with a cold earnestness. 'I swear before Jupiter that I'll destroy you, Macro. I'll write a report for the governor the moment I reach Londinium. I'll tell him about your treachery, your refusal to obey my orders, and I'll make damn sure he knows how you aided and abetted the escape of an enemy of Rome.'

'Make sure you don't forget to tell him how you turned Boudica into an enemy of Rome while you're about it. How you had her flogged and stood by when you let your men rape her daughters. I wonder what he will make of that.'

'You think you have the upper hand here, Macro. But you haven't. It only seems that way. I've destroyed better men than you to get where I am.'

'I don't doubt it,' Macro said wearily. 'You are a greasy little weevil who connives as easily as he breathes. You seek power and riches and you don't care who you have to ruin to achieve that. You knife men in the back because you're too cowardly to challenge them fairly to their faces. You let good men die to pay for the mistakes you make. You don't serve Rome's interests, only your own, even if that means putting the Empire in danger. Cato was right about you. I should have found a way to kill you before you had a chance to humiliate the Iceni and turn them from allies into enemies.'

Decianus's sneer faded and his expression betrayed his fear. 'You would dare threaten an imperial procurator? You would dare to kill me?'

'Why not? I've killed plenty of men for Rome already. Better men than you. I wouldn't lose any sleep over it. In fact, sticking a sword in your guts might be the best thing I ever did.'

They parted company the moment Camulodunum was in sight, and since then Macro had been waiting to hear the governor's response to the report that Decianus had threatened to write. But there had been only silence.

The second concern that gnawed at his thoughts was the lack of any reaction from the Iceni to the outrage that had been perpetrated against their queen and her daughters. The horrific death of Fascus had happened before Boudica's flogging and the abuse of her daughters. It was hard to believe that an action so heinous to Icenian eyes would not have provoked a bloody response of some kind. But there had been no word of any other attacks on Romans or even their property. Much as Macro would have liked to believe that Boudica was striving to persuade her people to keep the peace, he was becoming increasingly convinced that she had other plans. So what was she up to? he wondered. What was she waiting for?

The only indication that something was amiss was the gradual disappearance of Icenians from the colony. Some had left to visit family, they said, only for them not to return. Others, including the girls who had worked as Petronella's maids, had simply packed their meagre belongings and vanished. In recent days, the same thing had begun to happen to the Trinovantians who had worked for Romans in Camulodunum or operated businesses in the colony. Even the family who had run Macro's farm had gone, taking the livestock with them. The few who remained were regarded suspiciously by the veterans, who were becoming increasingly unnerved by the absence of familiar faces they had once regarded as part of daily life, and in some cases as friends and allies.

One fine morning, Macro saddled his horse and rode out to the small settlement where Pernocatus lived. Around his neck he wore the leather thong with the boar tusks that the hunter had given him. As his horse clopped through a forest clearing, the sunlight glinted through gaps in the branches and cast a shimmering pattern of dark and light green across the forest floor. Macro reined in for a moment to try and savour the idyllic scene, and as he did so, a deer silently ambled out from between the trees ahead of him. It froze and lifted its muzzle to scent the air as its ears twitched.

'Well hello, lad,' Macro greeted it amiably.

The deer's head came up sharply as it turned to his voice, then it bounded across the clearing and disappeared amongst the trees on the far side with a faint crackle of undergrowth. Macro was about to flick the reins and make his horse walk on when he heard a stick snap on the same side of the clearing where the deer had appeared. He caught a movement at the periphery of his vision, but even as he turned to focus on the spot, it had gone. He had the impression that it was the figure of a man, but it was hard to tell. There was a rustling movement, then more silence.

He cleared his throat. 'Who's there?'

There was no reply. Suddenly the setting did not seem idyllic at all, as his soldier's instincts transformed the clearing into an ideal position to set an ambush for an unwary enemy passing through. He felt a familiar chill of fear between his shoulder blades.

The anxious feeling did not leave him until he had emerged into open countryside. Then he was angry at himself for jumping at shadows. The noise had probably been made by another creature of the forest. That was all there was to it, he told himself firmly. His nervousness was to be expected given his concerns about the growing tension in the colony.

Pernocatus's settlement lay in a hollow beside a stream. There were a handful of round huts where his family and those of two of his brothers lived. A pen held several hogs, while a small number of cattle grazed in a large fenced enclosure. Beyond, fields of wheat grew alongside the stream. Two women were sitting outside one of the huts curing some animal hides, while a group of children were splashing in the water. They stopped playing to watch Macro as he approached. He gave them a wave and received a few shy waves in response. The two women looked up from their work but did not acknowledge the words of greeting in their tongue that he had picked up.

He reined in and swung himself down from the saddle. He knew Pernocatus's hut from the handful of times he had visited the settlement in previous months. A young girl looked out at him from the entrance.

'I've come to see Pernocatus,' said Macro. When she looked at him blankly, he repeated, 'Pernocatus?'

She indicated the side of the hut, and he made his way round the daub walls to a bare patch of ground where there was a large pile of logs beside a tree stump into which an axe head was buried. Pernocatus, stripped to the waist and gleaming with perspiration, looked up as he heard Macro's footsteps, and frowned for an instant before the expression passed.

'Hello.' Macro smiled as he extended his arm.

Pernocatus stepped forward and they clasped forearms briefly before he spoke in his lilting Latin. 'You are welcome to my home, Centurion. Are you here to arrange another hunt?'

Macro knew that he must tread lightly concerning the real purpose for the visit. With the change of season and the proliferation of fresh game at this time of year, it would be a credible enough reason to seek out the hunter.

'Yes, that for the most part.'

'We can talk.' Pernocatus nodded towards the stump. 'Thirsty?'

'I could use a drink. Thank you.'

The hunter shouted in his own tongue and a girl's voice replied. A strip of woollen cloth hung from the axe handle, and he picked it up to wipe his brow before sitting down on the stump. Macro sat beside him, and they looked out over the settlement and the surrounding land.

'A fine place you have here,' said Macro.

'*Sa*,' Pernocatus agreed. 'Good land. If the Romans let us keep it.'

'Your land is safe. I have stopped our people claiming any more land they haven't a right to.'

'Safe for now. But what happens when Centurion Macro has gone? Different man in charge. What then?'

It was a fair point. He was spared having to reply as the girl approached carrying two red clay beakers containing milk. She handed them over and ran off. The hunter raised his and drained the contents in one go, a dribble of milk appearing at the corner of his mouth before he lowered the beaker and smacked his lips in satisfaction. 'Good milk!'

Macro took a mouthful and relished the creamy liquid. 'Fine milk indeed.'

'You want to hunt. When do you want me?'

'Not until next month,' Macro replied. 'I have to oversee

the completion of some work at the colony. Next month I will have time to hunt.'

'Next month,' Pernocatus repeated with a hint of sadness. 'Next month, maybe not.' Then he nodded. 'Next month, as you wish.'

'You sound like you might be busy yourself then. Did you already have something planned?'

The hunter looked away, and there was a brief silence before Macro spoke again.

'I need to ask you something. I need your help.'

Pernocatus continued to look towards the stream where the children were playing, heedless to the troubles of the world. 'What help?'

'Things have changed. The Iceni have left the colony and now your people are leaving too. I need to know why.'

'People come, people go.'

'Not like this,' Macro responded. 'Not so quickly. Something is happening. Do you know anything about it?'

'Everybody knows what happened to the queen of the Iceni and her daughters. Everyone knows that Rome wants to steal all that is hers, and all that belongs to her people. Just as it is doing to the Trinovantes. Soon there comes a time when people say enough is enough.'

'And then?' Macro prompted.

'Then . . .' Pernocatus turned to him. 'Who knows?'

'I think you know. Is that why the Iceni have gone? Is that why your people are leaving? Is there a war coming, Pernocatus?'

The hunter stared back with a troubled expression. He did not speak for a moment. 'Centurion, you saved my life. Now maybe I can save yours. Leave Camulodunum. Take your family and go.'

'Go? Go where? The colony is my home.'

'It will be your grave if you stay. Leave Camulodunum. Leave Britannia. There will be no safe place in these lands for any Roman.'

Macro felt an icy chill in his veins. 'Tell me what is going to happen.'

Pernocatus stood up and wrenched the axe from the stump. 'I have said enough. I will speak no more of it. Please go. Never come back here if you value your life. I would not harm you, but others would. Go!'

Macro rose and set the beaker down, still half-full of milk. 'I wish you peace and a long life, Pernocatus the hunter.'

The other man nodded and picked up a log. He raised the axe, then brought it down with a savage swing. The blade bit through the wood and split the log into two pieces that leaped from the tree trunk. Macro could not help wondering if he would be splitting Roman skulls with equal savagery very soon.

As he returned to his horse and rode away, he knew that he had probably seen the hunter for the last time, but that if ever they met again, it would be as enemies.

Any appreciation of the fine weather and the beauty of the landscape was absent from Macro's thoughts as he returned to the colony. He was certain that Boudica had either failed to calm her people or, more likely, had urged them to take up arms against Rome once again. A struggle that was bound to be as futile as the last attempt. One tribe alone could not hope to overcome the Roman army garrisoning the island. But what if her cause was embraced by other tribes, such as the Trinovantes? What if the tribes joined together in an alliance? Was that what Pernocatus had meant when he had said there would be no safe place for Romans?

When he arrived home, Macro dismounted and led the

horse to the stable, handing it over to Parvus to unsaddle and feed. Petronella was waiting for him in the courtyard garden, and hurried over as soon as he emerged from the passage leading through the main building.

'Thank goodness you're back.'

Macro saw her anxious expression as he eased himself down onto a bench. 'What's the matter?'

'I had some visitors while you were gone. Three of the women from the colony. They're worried about their husbands.'

'Worried? Why?'

'They said they went north six days ago to buy some cattle from an Iceni farmer near Faustinus's villa. They were supposed to be back two days ago, but there's been no sign of them, and their wives are beside themselves with worry. They came to the house to ask you to send some men to search, but you'd already left. I said I would tell you the moment you got back.'

The villa was thirty miles from Camulodunum; a day's ride, two on foot at most. Unless they had been held up by business, the men should have been back well before now. Given what Macro had heard from Pernocatus, it was possible they were already dead, along with Faustinus and his family. The first Romans to pay the price for the outrage committed against Boudica and her daughters. There was a slim chance that there was another, more innocent explanation for the delay in their return. As Macro knew, old soldiers were fond of sharing a jar or three of wine and reminiscing about their time in the army. Perhaps they were still at the villa enjoying Faustinus's hospitality.

'What are you going to do?' asked Petronella. 'What should I tell them? Are you going to send some of the veterans to look for the men?'

'No,' Macro replied firmly. 'There are any number of

reasons why they might have delayed their return. If there has been trouble, we'd only be wasting the lives of anyone sent to search for them. And I will need every able-bodied man to defend the colony.'

'Trouble?' Petronella took his hand. 'What did Pernocatus tell you?'

Macro relayed the details, and she listened with growing concern. When he'd finished, she asked, 'Do you really think the Iceni will attack us?'

'I fear so.'

'What will you say to the wives of those three men?'

'I will say that someone has been sent to look for them and report back to me.'

Her brow creased. 'But I thought you said you weren't going to send anyone.'

'None of the veterans, to be sure. They're too old and inexperienced for the kind of work that will be needed. No, I'll be sending a man who has precisely the right skills for the job.'

# CHAPTER TWENTY-SEVEN

As he rode towards the frontier that divided the Trinovantian and Icenian tribes, Apollonius was considering the mission he had volunteered for. Macro had not even had to ask him to do it. There was no question that it was dangerous, but the spy had had his fill of labouring to complete the colony's defences. He did not mind hard physical toil and discomfort. He was long since inured to both. What he could not abide was boredom. The daily grind of repetitive work. That was why he had chosen his vocation.

Spying was what suited his particular interests and skills. He lived to learn. Not just to provide intelligence to his masters – that was the least of it. He was an avid reader of philosophy, history, poetry and even works detailing the principles of mathematics and the nature of the world. He had dedicated himself to learning as many languages as his travel experiences afforded him. As for his skills, there were few men who had mastered weapons as well as he had. He could shoot a bow with the unerring accuracy of a Parthian. He could wield swords and daggers and throwing knives as well as any gladiator in the arena, and he could take the head off a rabbit with a slingshot at fifty paces.

Regarding the darker arts of spying, he had mastered the art of coding messages that could never be broken by his enemies. He knew how to kill people in such a way that an assassin would never be suspected. He knew how to kill them in ways that would make it clear that an assassin *had* carried out the killing, without anyone knowing how he had gained access to the victim. He had learned how to interrogate and torture people to get them to reveal all the information he required. He was the consummate spy of the day, and that was why his services had been so frequently sought by the most powerful figures in Roman society.

Lately, however, his interest in learning had taken a different direction. He had grown weary of the grubby morals of his masters and had wondered if it might be possible that a man of principle could rise to the heights of Roman society without compromising his integrity. It was all very well for the likes of Plato and Aristotle to talk about the pursuit of the good life, but philosophy was one thing, praxis quite another, as experience had taught him. And so he had been intrigued when he encountered Cato and Macro during a mission on the eastern frontier of the Empire.

Cato was clearly a man on the make, having risen from obscure origins to the rank of prefect at an uncommonly early age. If he lived long enough, he might become the commander of the legions in Aegyptus, the highest post available to a man who was not born into the aristocracy of Rome. Alternatively, he might one day be appointed the commander of the Praetorian Guard. Apollonius was under no illusions about the temptations open to those who held that office. After all, it was the Praetorians who had murdered Caligula and placed Claudius on the throne. It was the Praetorian commander Sejanus who had made a play for supreme power during the reign of Tiberius, and it was the current Praetorian commander who had connived to get Nero adopted by Claudius, thereby smoothing his path to the throne. If Cato was ever promoted to that post, who knew what he might do? Apollonius was keen to find out if a man of strong principles could survive the moral corruption of such power. That was why he had attached himself to Cato over the last few years.

He set aside his speculations and focused his mind on the task at hand. He had adopted the disguise of an Atrebatan trader on the road from Londinium. He had trinkets in his saddlebags of the kind he knew delighted tribeswomen in the more remote corners of the new province. Combs, brushes and mirrors of the finest polished silver. He spoke the dialect well enough to pass for a native. If he was stopped, he was confident he would pass for what he purported to be. If that failed, his weapons were concealed under the sheepskin covering his saddle.

He had not visited Faustinus's villa before, but he had been given a comprehensive description of its location by Macro and knew that he was within five miles of the place when he came across the fork in the track on the edge of a large forest that sprawled as far as he could see across the largely flat landscape. The villa was on the other side of the forest, set within a modest farming estate. Faustinus was a retired first spear centurion who had used his retirement bounty to make a small fortune brokering deals between Trinovantian and Icenian sheep and cattle farmers and the herders who bought their stock to drive down to Camulodunum, Londinium and Verulamium, the three main settlements of the province. As such, he lived on the fringe of the Roman settlement in the area, close to the frontier of the Iceni. The treaty agreed between Rome and Prasutagus had stipulated that no Icenian land was to be granted to veterans, nor permission given to Romans to settle there. Since then, the tribe had done its best to live separately from their Roman neighbours.

Apollonius planned to follow the trail through the forest before dismounting and leaving his horse some distance from the villa, then continuing on foot to investigate. If all was well, he had orders from Macro to tell Faustinus, his family and guests to leave the villa and take shelter in Camulodunum until the threat of an uprising was over, or the uprising had been quelled. If there was any sign of danger at the villa, he was to return at once and report what he had seen.

It was late in the afternoon, and the track was in the shadow of the trees to his left, whose topmost branches gleamed brightly in the slanted sunlight. Apollonius had seen ever fewer people as he travelled further away from Camulodunum. Most of the Trinovantian farms he had passed that day had been empty, and the only inhabitants had all been elderly men and women who regarded him suspiciously and refused to talk to him, waving him away as he rode past. Where everyone had gone was a mystery, but he already had some thoughts about where they might be and why. He hoped he was mistaken.

Three miles into the forest, the track curved gently to the right. He had almost negotiated the curve when he heard voices a short distance ahead. Before he could think of turning his mount and retracing his path, a blonde Iceni warrior with the swirling blue horse tattoos of his tribe came into view. He raised his spear at Apollonius and ordered him to dismount. The spy did as he was told as two more men joined their comrade, both also armed with spears. One was an older man, burly and bald, while the second was as young as the blonde warrior, though thin and spare. They were not boar spears, Apollonius noted, but the traditional weapons of war that the Romans had forbidden the Iceni to possess, along with armour and swords. That answered one of his speculations.

He opened his arms as he addressed the men in their own tongue with a heavy accent. 'My friends, why the need for weapons? I am an honest Atrebatan merchant who trades in this area. Gullabinus. Surely you have heard of me?' He took a step towards them.

'Stand still!' the first man commanded, and Apollonius raised a hand apologetically and backed off slowly to stand beside the saddle of his mount.

'What are you doing here?' asked the older man.

'I told you, I am a merchant. Here, let me show you.' Apollonius turned to his saddlebags and reached for the strap.

'Wait!' the man commanded. He indicated the side of the track. 'Stand over there. Keep still, or my friends will cut you down. Understand?'

'There's no need for that. Check my bags for yourself. You will see I am harmless and telling the truth. I'm an honest trader. I can give your women a good price on my wares. Just—'

'Keep your tongue still, Atrebatan. If you want to keep it.'

Apollonius shrugged and moved to the side of the track, folding his arms with a patient expression as the Icenian opened the saddlebags and began to take items out and toss them to the ground. He kept hold of one of the mirrors and a small pair of sprung shears as he turned to his companions.

'Looks like he's telling the truth.'

'Of course I am!' Apollonius chimed in cheerfully. 'My word is my bond. Ask any of my customers. You'll not find one who says I cheated them or sold them poor-quality items. Only the best wares.'

'That's enough!' The man who had searched his bags lowered the tip of his spear at him. 'Where are you headed?'

'Tonight? I hoped to stay at the villa owned by the Roman

on the other side of the forest, a few miles from here. After that, I will be travelling north to do business with your people. I have never before been treated with disrespect by the Icenians,' he added reproachfully.

'Are you a friend of the Roman?' asked the man.

'Friend? Who can be a friend of someone who treats a man like a trespasser in the land he once owned? There are Romans amongst my customers and I charge them prices I would never charge any friends. Do not insult me by suggesting that a man of honour like myself would call any Roman dog a friend.' He spat to one side to underline the comment.

'Fair enough. You'll have to come with us, though. There are rumours of Roman spies in the area. The chief of our warband will want to question you.'

'I would be honoured to answer any questions he asks of me.' Apollonius bowed his head. 'But first I must retrieve my wares.' He gestured at the goods scattered on the ground beside his horse.

The bald man glanced at them and nodded. 'Be quick about it.'

Apollonius began to pick up the trinkets and place them back in the saddlebags. As he worked, the thin man kept an eye on him while his companions admired the mirror they had taken. He moved round to the other side of the horse and replaced a few items in the bag on that side before reaching a hand under the sheepskin and feeling for his throwing knife and the long cavalry sword hanging from the saddle frame in two leather loops. Using the horse to hide what he was doing, he removed the blades and hefted the knife in his right hand, getting the correct grip. The thin man glanced over at his companions as the blonde warrior looked at himself in the mirror.

Apollonius moved to the rear of the horse and threw his arm forward. The knife blurred across the track and struck the thin man high on the thigh, close to the groin. He lurched and looked down in surprise, mumbling, 'Huh?'

Before he realised what had happened, Apollonius was upon him. There was a dull gleam of polished metal as the sword cut deep into his neck, and the spear fell from his fingers and thudded to the ground. Apollonius tore his blade from the wound and turned on the other warriors as they glanced round in response to the noise. The older man reacted first, lowering his spear to challenge the spy. The other man cast the mirror aside and fumbled for his own spear. Apollonius snatched up the fallen weapon from the man he had downed and hurled it at the blonde warrior, striking him in the centre of his chest. He staggered back under the impact, then slumped to the ground.

Apollonius raised his sword and smiled at the bald man. 'Just you and me now, my friend. Throw down your weapon and I will let you live.'

'Roman pig! Come and get it.'

'Greek actually,' Apollonius responded as he lowered himself into a crouch and feinted quickly to test the other man's reactions. The warrior moved swiftly to counter the threat and then recovered his poise.

'Greeks die as easily as Romans.'

Apollonius chuckled. 'Let's put it to the test, shall we?'

His opponent made a thrust. The spy parried it aside, and then cut a notch in the spear shaft before he darted out of range. 'Is that the best you can do, old man?'

The warrior's lips lifted in a snarl, and he thrust again, and again. Apollonius deftly deflected each blow. Then the older man's frustration got the better of him and he made a vigorous thrust at his opponent's throat. The spy dodged to one side, leaped forward inside the reach of the weapon and snatched the shaft with his left hand, giving it a powerful twist that tore it painfully from the other man's fingers. He hurled the weapon into the trees beside the track and jabbed the point of his sword into the man's shoulder.

'On your knees, friend.'

The warrior hesitated, and Apollonius narrowed his eyes and spoke in an icy tone. 'Now.'

The bald man went down on his knees, arms hanging at his side.

'That's better.' Apollonius spared a glance at the first man he had downed, and saw him bleeding out on the track, blood spurting from the neck wound. The blonde warrior was trying to pull the spear from his chest, his face twisting in agony. Apollonius turned back to the man on his knees. 'I'm in a hurry, so let's not waste time. You are one of Boudica's men, right?'

The man nodded.

'I take it there are more of you at Faustinus's villa. How many?'

'Thousands, Roman.' The man gave a slight smile. 'Thousands of the Iceni and the Trinovantes, and there will be many more from other tribes soon.'

'Thousands, eh? I'd be willing to wager all my trinkets that you can't even count to a hundred, let alone a thousand. What do you say?'

The warrior glared at him.

'Not a betting man, then. That's too bad. And where do your friends intend to attack next? Which villas? Which farms?'

'All of them. Wherever there are Romans to kill. And then Camulos, where we will tear down that accursed temple of yours.'

The man had used the native name for the colony, and Apollonius felt a twinge of anxiety for Macro and the others he had come to know. He raised his sword. 'We shall have to see about that.'

'Wait!' The older man raised a hand. 'You said you would let me live if I dropped my weapon.'

'You didn't drop it. I took it.' Apollonius thrust the blade into the top of the man's chest and drove it through with his full weight before twisting it violently and tearing it free. Blood poured out and the older man looked down at it, jaw slack, then fell onto his side and kicked out as his body trembled. The spy stepped past him and grasped the end of the spear in the blonde man's chest. He thrust it deeper, working it from side to side, causing more blood to flow from the wound until the young warrior's eyes rolled up and he slumped onto his back.

Apollonius dragged the bodies into the undergrowth beside the track and covered the blood trails with ferns. He broke up some soil to spread over the pools of blood on the ground and continued on his way. At some point the three men would be missed and searched for, but by that time he hoped to have found out what he needed and be on his way back to Macro to make his report and warn him of Boudica's plans.

Half a mile further on, he came to a clearing with an ancient oak tree looming over the open forest floor. Deciding that it would be an obvious landmark, even at night, he led his horse a hundred paces into the trees and left it hitched to a branch with some feed. Then he returned to the clearing and followed the track, keeping to the edge, ready to dive into cover the moment he spotted anyone. The sun had set, but there would still be enough light to see his way for at least another hour. Soon he became aware of the sound of voices, a great many of them, and as he drew closer to the edge of the forest, he could make out laughter, singing and shouts above the general hubbub of a multitude.

He left the track and began to make his way stealthily through the trees. He saw the glow of fires beyond, and figures seated and standing around them. As the trees began to thin out, he kneeled to scoop up some soil to darken his face and exposed skin, and then continued forward, slowing his pace as he lowered himself into a crouch. He stopped inside the treeline and lay on his stomach before inching forward through some ferns until he found a position from where he could survey the scene before him.

Less than a quarter of a mile away, he could see the villa of Faustinus; an imposing building with a tiled roof – proof of the affluence of the owner – surrounded by a wall and arched gateway. There were more buildings outside: stables, storerooms and what looked like a small barrack block, presumably for the slaves who worked his land. There were the remains of several pens and larger animal enclosures, all of which were empty. Any sheep, pigs or cattle had already been stolen, or were roasting over the many fires he had seen. The biggest of the blazes was a short distance from the gatehouse of the villa, though there was nothing being cooked there, nor were any people nearby, thanks to the heat it was generating.

In the dim light, he could not easily make out the number of people present, but he could estimate that there were hundreds of them. Most were men, but there were many women and children too. Any hope that Faustinus and the three veterans who had gone to do business with him were still alive seemed slim.

The last of the daylight had faded, and only the light of the fires remained, beneath the stars and a crescent moon that looked like a highly polished sickle of the finest steel. He noticed people stirring, and those on the ground hurriedly rose to their feet as all turned and began to move towards the villa. They obscured Apollonius's view, so he waited until the nearest tribespeople had moved off before he emerged from the trees and began to follow them.

As he neared the rear of the crowd, he chose a spot where he could see the gatehouse clearly. The doors had been swung open, but he could make out little in the shadows beyond. The crowd had grown quiet as they watched and waited, and Apollonius was relieved that their attention was fixed on the gatehouse so that no one was concerned to look at him too closely.

There was a movement from within the walled enclosure in front of the villa, and a moment later a chariot drawn by two black horses rumbled out through the gate and into the open ground illuminated by the largest of the fires. A brawny warrior sat astride the yoke as he steered the team. Behind him, on the bed of the chariot, stood a tall, slim woman with flame-red hair. She wore a plain green cloak over a long dark tunic, and held the side panel in one hand and a long spear in the other. Four poles had been fixed to the corners of the chariot, and on top of each was impaled a head.

The crowd burst into a wild, deafening roar as the charioteer made a slow circle of the fire before returning to the starting point in front of the gatehouse. The woman made no attempt to acknowledge them, but stared fixedly ahead, chin raised, like some statue or idol. The chariot passed close enough to Apollonius that he was able to recognise Boudica beyond any doubt. As it drew up in front of the villa, a small group of nobles and two young women emerged from the gatehouse and stood nearby.

Boudica slowly raised her arms aloft. The spear tip pointed to the stars and the teardrop head glinted red in the firelight. The crowd's fanatical cheering began to subside, and then there was silence apart from the crackle of the flames.

'Iceni! Trinovantes! Hear me! I am Boudica, wife of the late Prasutagus, King of the Iceni. I am your queen.'

Her voice, shrill but clear, carried easily, and Apollonius joined in with the cheer that greeted her introduction. She raised her hand to quieten the crowd and continued. 'For days you have travelled here to join my cause. *Our* cause. For it is not just the Iceni who have been pushed beyond endurance by the Roman dogs who call themselves our masters and treat us as their slaves. The same is true of the Trinovantes and almost every other tribe in this island of ours. We have joined together to put an end to Roman rule once and for all, and we will be free!'

She punched the spear into the air and the crowd erupted in a fresh cheer. Apollonius brandished his fist as if in approval.

'Since my warriors and I came here, took this villa and killed the Romans we found, many thousands of you have flocked to join my banner, and with each victory many more will join us, until we have such a host that no Roman army will be able to stand against us. And then we shall crush their legions, seize their standards and take the heads of their commanders for trophies. But we must not stop at that, my beloved followers. We must kill every Roman in Britannia, every man, woman and child down to the last infant. We will wallow in their blood! We will tear down their buildings and dishonour the statues they have erected to their gods. We will not rest while one Roman brick is left standing atop another. We will burn it all to the ground and remove the stain of the indignities they have imposed on us, so that a generation from now, they will be but a memory. A memory of a powerful foe who tested us and was bested by us. All glory to our people!'

Again the crowd cheered, and she indulged them for longer this time before calling for quiet. Then she lowered her voice so that all had to be still and silent to catch the words that followed.

'You must wonder where a hatred and a determination like mine came from. Why, you ask, would Boudica demand such a fate for the Romans on our shores, some of whom we counted as friends? Let me show you why . . .'

She undid the clasp of her cloak and let it drop to her feet, then slipped her tunic down to expose her shoulders and turned slowly so that the crowd could see the livid scars etched on her back. There were gasps and angry mutters, then shouts calling for revenge. Boudica eased the tunic back up and gestured to the two women. They climbed onto the back of the chariot and stood behind their mother as she addressed the crowd.

'These are my daughters, Bardea and Merida. After I was whipped, the Roman soldiers raped my daughters, my own girls. My flesh and blood.'

There were groans from the crowd and more cries of anger, and Boudica waited until the noise had died down before she pointed to the crowd and swept her arm around to embrace them all in her gesture. 'If this is how the Romans would treat the queen and the princesses of the Iceni royal household, then none of you is safe. Nor are your families, your animals, your land. Rome would take it all in a heartbeat if she so chose. Who is so craven, so lacking in honour and self-respect that they would submit to such a fate? We must show Rome what happens to those who dishonour the tribes of Britain. We must show them the fate that awaits them at our hands, just as we showed *these* Romans.'

She indicated the heads on the poles around the chariot. Then, handing her spear to one of her daughters, she clenched her fists in the hair of the nearest head, tore it free of the post and hurled it into the fire in front of the chariot. The crowd roared their approval, and then again for each of the other heads that followed.

'The war against Rome begins on the morrow!' Boudica cried out. 'At dawn we march on the colony at Camulos. We will slaughter every Roman there. Death to Rome! Death to the emperor!'

She repeated the cry again and again until it was taken up by the crowd in a deafening roar.

Apollonius had heard all he needed to. He eased his way back through the crowd and slipped into the forest to find his horse and return to Macro with news of the terrible fate awaiting all those who stood in the path of Boudica's wrath.

# CHAPTER TWENTY-EIGHT

'Thousands, you say?' asked Ulpius, rubbing his eye patch, once Apollonius had concluded his report before the members of the colony's senate. Macro had heard his account the moment Apollonius returned from his mission after midday, and immediately summoned the senate that afternoon.

'At least five thousand men,' the spy responded. 'In addition to a similar number of women, children and older folk. They had plenty of horses and wagons and carts as well to carry their supplies.'

'Five thousand,' Ulpius repeated, and exchanged glances with his faction. 'How can we be sure that your estimate is accurate? After all, you are not a professional soldier used to estimating enemy strength.'

'That's true,' Apollonius conceded. 'You could always wait until they arrive before the defences of Camulodunum and make your own expert approximation to compare with mine.'

Macro cleared his throat. 'I trust his judgement. Let's not dicker over numbers, gentlemen. Four, five or six thousand makes little difference if they are headed here to take the colony. We don't have the strength to hold the place, let alone defeat them in battle. If they set off at dawn today, it will take between two and five days before they reach us. Two if they send their fighting men ahead and let the rest catch up. Five if they go at the pace of the baggage train. Either way, there's little time and we need to take action now.'

'Action? What kind of action do you propose?' Ulpius demanded. 'You just said that we can't defend ourselves.'

'I didn't say that. Of course we can defend ourselves. The question is, for how long? The colony's defences are not yet complete, and any work we do on them now will be makeshift. We have to assume they will be breached. When that happens, we can fall back to the temple complex. It's a much smaller perimeter and easier to defend. With luck we can hold the temple long enough for help to arrive. You may have noticed that Vulpinus is not here. I sent him to the fortress of the Ninth Legion at Lindum. Six of the cohorts and some cavalry are stationed there. Over three thousand men. More than enough to swing the balance in our favour if they march at once to our aid. I've also sent a message to Londinium to ask the procurator to send us reinforcements, though I have doubts about the quality of his men. Even so, if they can wear a helmet and hold a weapon, it may help to discourage the enemy. Meanwhile, we need to prepare the defences at once, as well as taking other measures.'

'What measures?' asked Ulpius.

Macro had drawn up an initial list with Apollonius, and now gestured to the spy to proceed. They had decided it would be better for the bad news to be heard from lips other than Macro's in the first instance. Apollonius raised the wax tablets he had been carrying and began to read.

'First, messages must be sent to all outlying villas and farmsteads owned by Roman settlers. They are to be told to bring what food stocks they have, as well as animals, to Camulodunum for the use of the garrison over the duration of the siege. Anything that cannot be taken away from their properties is to be burned or spoiled. Wells are to be contaminated with dead animals and available slurry. All buildings outside the colony's defences will have to be razed to the ground to deny the enemy cover.'

Ulpius shook his head. 'You can't do that. That will mean ruin for many of our veterans. It's taken us years to build up our farms and businesses, and most of us have only just started turning a profit. We can't tell people to just abandon them.'

'Crops can be replanted, and any animals that need replacing can be purchased using the colony's reserves,' Macro countered. 'We must make it as difficult as possible for Boudica and her followers to live off the land. In any case, I am not telling people to abandon their property, I am ordering it in the name of the colony's senate. I am invoking the emergency powers of the senior magistrate. If we survive this, you can vote me out if you wish. If we don't survive, then none of us will be in a position to argue the toss about legal niceties. Continue, Apollonius.'

'Second, all but able-bodied men will be required to evacuate Camulodunum and make for Londinium at first light tomorrow. There will be an escort for the first half of the journey in case the enemy sends out advance forces. The rest of us will remain here to defend the colony. All our valuables and as much grain and livestock as can be accommodated will be secured within the temple walls. There's a good chance we can hold out until the Ninth Legion arrives to crush the enemy.'

The other men stirred uneasily as Apollonius spoke. Macro could understand their concern. It would mean upheaval and discomfort for those evacuated, and much tearful leave-taking, but it was a necessary step to ensure the safety of non-combatants. It was also necessary so that the defenders would not be encumbered by panicking civilians, nor have their morale undermined by worrying over the safety of their families. A soldier needed to focus on the job, not be distracted by the presence of those he loved.

'How many able-bodied men are available?' asked Ulpius.

'I've looked at the colony's records. Assuming all those in outlying farms and villas return to Camulodunum, we have just over six hundred able-bodied veterans and another two hundred males of military age. The latter have no training, but they can hold a weapon and we'll have to use what time we have to give them some basic training. When the fighting starts, most of them will be used to carry away and look after the wounded, as well as replenishing arrows, slingshot and javelins, and cooking. We'll only put them into action as a last resort.'

Macro paused and glanced round at the colony's senators. Most looked anxious and some afraid. No doubt they had been expecting to live out their retirement in peace.

'We don't have any choice, gentlemen. The situation is desperate. It's a shame that the decision was taken to ignore the colony's defences when we met a few months ago. We'd have been in a somewhat better position today. The responsibility for that failure is yours, and this is your chance to make up for it by doing your duty and obeying my orders until the danger has passed. If any man here is not willing to play his part, I will send him away with the evacuees. I will not fight alongside a man who hasn't the integrity to right a wrong he has done. Anyone who remains will accept my absolute authority, just as they did when they were soldiers and swore an oath to obey those placed over them by the emperor, Senate and people of Rome. Those who are unwilling to do that, kindly fuck off at once.'

Some glances were exchanged but not a single man moved, until Ulpius rose from his seat and crossed the floor of the modest senate chamber to stand in front of Macro.

'Centurion Macro, I am sure that I speak for most of the others when I say we were mistaken. We should have heeded your wishes.' He lowered himself to his knees and bowed his head as he took Macro's right hand in the ancient tradition. 'I accept you as my patron. I am yours to command until you release me from my obligation. This I swear before Jupiter, Best and Greatest, and all those present.' He released Macro's hand and stood up stiffly before returning to his seat.

'That's settled our differences, my brothers,' said Macro. 'From now until the danger is over, we're soldiers once again. We didn't survive twenty-five years in the legions by being green. We're veterans. The best of our kind. There will be little rest for us in the coming days. But when we are ready, we'll show those barbarians what real warriors can do. For now, go and make your farewells to your families and have them ready to leave for Londinium at first light. Apollonius will bring you your individual orders this evening.' He stood up and adopted his parade-ground voice. 'Dismissed!'

'You can't do this to me,' Petronella protested. 'I won't go. I won't abandon you.'

Macro put his arm round her and pulled her close as they sat on her favourite bench in the garden. 'You can't stay here, my love,' he said gently. 'I've given orders for all the veterans' dependants to be evacuated. I can't make an exception for you. I wish I could, but that's not possible. I must lead by example or the men will question my authority, and if that happens, we are doomed. Do you understand me?'

'Of course I do. I'm not stupid. I knew what I was doing when I married a soldier, and a centurion at that. I lived with the fear that you would go away to war and not return. I hardened myself to that.' She leaned into him. 'It's just that when you left the army, I believed that I no longer had reason to worry, that we could live in peace. Of course, as things turned out I was a bloody fool to think that.'

Macro laughed. 'You can take the man out of the army, but never the army out of the man, my love. That's how it is. As for what is happening now, I did not ask for this. It is not my fault.'

As soon as the words were out of his mouth, he grimaced. Petronella turned towards him with a sad expression. No words needed to be said between them. What good would recrimination do now? Macro had done the right thing in the heat of the moment and hoped that a good deed would be rewarded by a virtuous outcome. As if morality was the mechanism driving events in life. Instead he had unleashed a greater evil, and many thousands might die as a result of it. Including himself. His own death he could accept, but those of so many others weighed on his conscience unbearably. He had resolved to serve in his current role with all his strength and courage in order to win some small measure of absolution for his mistake in setting free Boudica and her daughters.

He kissed his wife on the forehead. 'I am so sorry that I have brought this on us.'

She sighed. 'What else could you have done, Macro? You are a good man. I would have expected nothing less of you.'

'Thank you,' he replied. 'For everything. For the years we have had together, and for the years we still hope to have. Now pack some things for yourself and Parvus.'

She nodded. 'Once that's done, I'll go and help Claudia and Lucius. The poor mite has had so much to endure since he was born.'

'I know. What better reason to get him out of here? When you get to Londinium, go to the Dog and Deer. My mother will take you in until the rebellion is over. Try not to argue too much, eh? There's enough trouble in the world right now without adding to it.'

Petronella squeezed his hand affectionately, then asked, 'What do you think will happen? Be honest with me.'

Macro considered the pieces in play for a moment before he replied in a matter-of-fact tone. 'It all depends on timing. If the reinforcements from Lindum and Londinium reach the colony before Boudica's force arrives, then Camulodunum will be safe, and as likely as not, her warriors will be defeated. Her host will disperse and return to their homes and there will be a price to pay once the governor returns to deal with the tribes who chose to follow her.'

'What will happen to her?'

'If she survives the battle, she will be hunted down and captured. If she is fortunate, she and her daughters will live out their days in Rome as privileged prisoners, like Caratacus. If the emperor has an appetite for revenge, they will be made a spectacle of and dragged through the streets of Rome before they are executed.'

Petronella digested the possible fates and shook her head sadly. 'I liked and admired her, you know. I would not wish her to end her life either way.'

'I know. I feel the same. I presented her with the choices she could make when I set her free. She chose war, and we must live with the consequences of our actions, me and her alike.' He sighed, then removed his arm from around his wife's shoulders and stood up. 'There isn't much time. Go and pack. Then we'll have a fine dinner, drink the last of my best wine and go to bed, eh?'

Petronella forced herself to smile. 'You really know how to show a girl a good time, Centurion Macro.'

He grinned. 'Don't I just?'

* * *

Macro was sitting by the window in his study, making the most of the last light of the day as he drew up a list of officers he had chosen to lead the veterans. There was no shortage of former centurions and optios in the colony, as well as two former first spear centurions, the most senior and respected of their rank.

With six hundred experienced men available, he divided them into six overstrength centuries. The oldest men, under the command of Ulpius, were assigned to the temple complex from the outset. They would be available as a reserve, or to cover the retreat of their comrades if the enemy broke through the colony's outer defences. Another of the centuries, commanded by a steady veteran by the name of Tertillius, would be assigned to the completed eastern rampart, while three more would man the unfinished rampart and whatever defences could be put in place to cover the gap between the restored stretch of rampart and ditch and the river to the north. The two hundred inexperienced youths and men would be commanded by an optio and a retired army surgeon and tasked with dealing with casualties and bringing forward the rations, along with other non-combatant duties. They would only be called on to fight in the most desperate of circumstances.

The final century would be commanded by Macro himself. Forty of his men would be mounted on the best horses to be found in the colony. They would be led by a former decurion of scouts by the name of Silvanus, a bald man with a neat white beard and a spare physique. Even in his sixties, he was a fine rider and the obvious choice for the position. His first task would be to take half his men out to ride round the outlying farms and villas and order their owners to join the defenders in Camulodunum while sending their families to Londinium with the others. The sixty men on foot, along with Macro and

Apollonius, would be stationed behind the wall, ready to counter any enemy effort to secure a foothold on either rampart.

He was just putting the finishing touches to the chain of command when he heard footsteps behind him. He turned to see Parvus staring at him with a hurt expression, and could easily guess at the cause.

'You're going to Londinium with Petronella. I've decided.'

'Nnnn!' Parvus clenched his fists and shook his head. 'Nai won. Nai nay hi!'

'You will, and you won't stay here.' Macro swung himself round to face the boy. 'I'd have you at my side in a heartbeat if you were four years older. Your time will come, my lad. But this is not your time.'

Parvus made a guttural protest and pointed his finger at the floor furiously.

'I'm not going to argue with you about it. My mind is made up and you have your orders. I know you want to be a soldier one day, Parvus.'

The boy nodded.

'Very well, then let me tell you what it takes to make a good soldier.' Macro counted the qualities off on his fingers. 'Courage, strength, training and discipline. I have no doubt that you possess the first two, and I know you will dedicate yourself to your training. That leaves discipline. A good soldier obeys orders. Do you want to be a good soldier, Parvus?'

The youth nodded warily, sensing where the discussion was headed.

'Then I am giving you an order. You will go with Petronella and protect her with your life. Understand me? I am asking you to keep my wife safe while I am not there to look after her. Can I trust you to do that?'

Parvus looked torn, but at length he nodded reluctantly.

'Good man!' Macro smiled and took his shoulders. 'If I had been blessed with a son, I would want him to be like you. I'd be as proud of him as I am proud of you.'

The lad flushed with embarrassment and gave a shy smile.

'That's better. Now go and help Petronella. And round up the dog. Cato will want him back when this is all over.'

Parvus left the room and Macro stared after him for a moment as he realised how fond he had grown of the mute boy, and how much he yearned for a son of his own. If he survived the siege, he would talk to his wife about adopting Parvus formally.

*If he survived . . .* Macro shook his head. He must not let himself think like that. The men would be looking to him, and he must give no sign that defeat was possible. He must believe it himself if he was to honour the responsibility the situation had forced on him.

The sun rose through a thin mist the next morning, looking like a dull disc of heated bronze amid the milky whiteness that wreathed the colony and surrounding landscape. The marketplace of Camulodunum was filled with people as the men remaining to defend their homes said goodbye to their wives and families. Some of the women and children were weeping, and were offered tender words of reassurance. Macro knew that many of the defenders would shed their own tears when they were alone.

He walked to the marketplace holding Petronella's hand and carrying her small pack containing food for the journey. Parvus accompanied them, wearing a cut-down version of one of Macro's old army cloaks and clutching Cassius's leash in one hand as the dog paced ahead of him. With the other hand he led a mule that carried a tent, spare clothes and feed on its yoke.

The other half of the mounted contingent was waiting at the end of the street leading towards the Londinium gate, and the optio in command saluted Macro as he saw him approaching.

'Ready to leave, sir.'

'Very well, Caldonius. Go with them for the first thirty miles, and then turn back and return here as quickly as you can. If the enemy have already surrounded the colony, make for Londinium and report to the procurator. No heroics. I don't want you to try and fight your way through to us. Understand?'

'Yes, sir.'

'Lead 'em off then.'

The optio returned to his men and mounted before calling across the marketplace, 'We're leaving for Londinium now. Say your final farewells.'

Macro cursed the man under his breath for his crass choice of words. Then he embraced Petronella, and they held each other tightly.

'Thank you for choosing me,' said Macro. 'You're all the woman I ever wanted.'

She held him tighter still and spoke softly in his ear. 'A simple "I love you" would have done nicely. You stay alive, you hear me. Or I'll be bloody angry with you.'

She kissed him on the neck, then pulled herself away and took the pack from him. Macro turned to Parvus, and the boy suddenly lurched forward and hugged him. Macro was surprised for a heartbeat, and then held him close.

'Take care of yourself, lad. I'll see you later.'

They stood apart, and Macro adopted a formal posture and tone as he addressed the boy. 'You have your orders. Make sure you carry them out like a good soldier.' He saluted, and Parvus smiled with delight before picking up the reins of the mule and Cassius's leash.

Petronella stood still.

'You have to go now,' said Macro. 'You have to go first to set the example. The others will follow you. Go, my love.'

She moved off towards the riders, with Parvus, the dog and the mule. More of the women and children followed. Macro waited until his wife and the boy had dissolved into the mist. Other figures faded after them. He looked round at the men watching them go and felt their grief. Then he saw Apollonius approaching with Claudia and Lucius at his side and waved a greeting. Claudia had a sling over one shoulder and a large bag hanging from a strap across the other.

'Good luck, Macro,' she said. 'May the gods protect you.'

'We'll be fine. Make sure you pass on my greetings to Cato when you next see him.'

'You can do that yourself when the time comes.'

'I will.' Macro smiled. 'Until then.'

She nodded, and a look of understanding passed between them before Macro squatted down in front of Lucius.

'Remember, lad. Keep your sword point up.'

Lucius grinned. 'I'll keep practising when we're in Londinium. You'll see how much better I am when we come back, Uncle Macro.'

'I'll look forward to it.' He ruffled the boy's hair fondly before he rose.

'And don't forget to work on your rhetoric,' said Apollonius. 'I'll be testing you when we resume our lessons.'

Claudia put her hand on Lucius's shoulder. 'Come on, let's catch up with Petronella and Parvus. I'll race you!'

Lucius gave Macro a quick wave, then darted off with Claudia trying to keep up.

For a moment the two men watched the column of evacuees trailing past, then Macro coughed and cleared his throat.

'They'll be safe in Londinium at least. We're on our own now. Let's get the men to work.'

For the remainder of the day the veterans and the other men laboured away at digging out the final stretch of the outer ditch and piling the spoil up to form a rampart. Two houses and a bakery that had been built over the ditch had to be demolished first, and the owner had been the first man to swing his axe at the daub walls before going at it in a frenzy as he destroyed his home and business rather than let the colony fall into the hands of the rebels. Another party began work on tearing down the buildings outside the defences. Ulpius led the party working on the rampart, packing the soil down into the log foundations as they built up the height before erecting a wooden palisade. Sharpened stakes were driven into the rampart, angled down as a further obstacle to attackers. More stakes were driven into the banks and beds of the rivers running north and south of the colony.

Meanwhile Apollonius was organising the defences of the temple complex, building up the wall and constructing a fighting platform running around the interior, while Macro took charge of a group of men working on a cordon of 'lilies' beyond the ditch: pits two feet deep with spikes at the bottom, which were then covered over with a lattice of twigs, leaves and loose soil to conceal the trap. He would have preferred to use caltrops, but all the province's stock of the device had been claimed for the army campaigning in the mountains.

As dusk closed in, there was a shout from the top of the gatehouse.

'Horsemen sighted to the north!' The lookout pointed his spear to indicate the precise direction.

'Is that Silvanus and his men?' asked Macro.

'Can't tell, sir.'

Running over to the gatehouse, he climbed the internal ladders and moved to the battlement. Sure enough, some two miles away, a line of riders was spread along a low ridge overlooking the approaches to Camulodunum. A moment later, a group of chariots came into view and there was no longer any doubt as to their identity. Apollonius climbed up and joined him.

'More chariots,' the spy commented. 'I only saw the one at Faustinus's villa. The Iceni have been hiding those from us, along with a great many other weapons, no doubt.'

Macro nodded. 'I had hoped for more time.'

He looked down the length of the wall and saw that there was still over a hundred feet of rampart to be completed.

'There's still time to finish the rampart if that lot is a scouting party.'

'Rather a lot of them for that,' Apollonius responded. 'What if they're the vanguard of Boudica's rebel host? Silvanus is going to be cut off.'

'If he's still alive, I hope he has the good sense to make for Londinium.'

The two men stared at the distant enemy for a moment before Macro made a decision. The rampart was the priority. He cupped a hand to his mouth and called on his work party to complete the lilies they were working on and then fall back through the gatehouse. Then he turned to the spy. 'Get your men back on it. We can't afford to rest until the job is done.'

In the dying daylight hours, progress on the rampart edged slowly towards the redoubt that was being constructed on the riverbank. Meanwhile, barricades were erected between the warehouses along the wharf to protect the bank to the north. The remaining sharpened stakes were driven into the riverbeds either side of the colony. Macro remained in the tower, watching the riders and chariots as they made their way around the colony's defences, stopping regularly to inspect certain features.

As the sun set, any hope that the small enemy force was merely a scouting party was dashed as more horsemen and chariots – hundreds of them – appeared on the ridge to the north before spilling over into the open ground of crops and pasture as they closed in on Camulodunum. Behind them marched a huge swathe of warbands, ox-drawn carts and groups of women and children. As darkness closed in, they were still coming. One by one the rebels lit their campfires, until a sea of glittering red flames extended across a front of at least two miles, all the way back to the ridge. Those veterans not engaged in work on the defences stood and regarded the extent of the enemy host in horror and awe, never having imagined that the Iceni and the Trinovantes could mass such strength. There were now at least twice as many as Apollonius had seen only a few days before.

Macro ordered that braziers be lit to illuminate the work on the ramparts as his men raced to complete the defences. Shortly afterwards, a hail of arrows and slingshot lashed the area and several men were struck down before they could scramble over the half-completed rampart to shelter behind it. After the flames in the braziers died down, Macro sent the men back to work under cover of darkness, but the enemy kept up a sporadic barrage each time they heard the sound of picks, and the work had to be abandoned. Instead, a low inner rampart was prepared during the night using the remaining carts and wagons left in the colony, lined up with timbers nailed between the wheels to block the gaps under the vehicles. As the defenders worked, they could hear the singing and laughter of the rebels beyond the river.

When the defences were as ready as they could be, Macro

had two of his centuries stand to while the others had a meal and rested.

Apollonius came to find him and reported on the progress of the defences in the temple complex. 'As good as can be, given the materials we had at hand.'

'Let's hope we can keep them out.'

'Do you think they'll breach the outer defences?'

'Given their numbers, they're bound to. Once we're forced to fall back to the temple, our only hope is that we can hold them off until the Ninth Legion arrives. We can discount any idea of help from Londinium now. It means we'll lose almost all the colony. They'll take everything they can carry and burn the rest to the ground.'

'How many days before the relief force arrives?'

Macro took a moment to estimate before he replied. 'Six days at the earliest.'

Apollonius thought about this before glancing round the tower. He waited until the lookout had moved out of earshot. 'Can we last that long?'

'Let's hope so. I'm not sure I could face Petronella if we didn't.'

They shared a chuckle before Apollonius asked, 'When do you think they'll attack? Tonight?'

'I doubt it. They've been on the march all day. Boudica and her war chiefs will want to rest their warriors before sending them into battle.' Macro looked out over the vista of campfires. 'They'll wait until daylight. We must have every one of our men in position when the attack comes. At dawn.'

# CHAPTER TWENTY-NINE

There was a thick mist as the first glimmer of daylight spread across the eastern skyline the following morning. The enemy's approach was betrayed by a flight of disturbed geese taking to the air in loud, cackling protest. The defenders of the colony had been standing since an hour or so before first light. Their cloaks and armour glimmered with dew as they manned the palisade, holding their shields and an assortment of javelins, hunting bows and spears.

Piles of flint from the building site at the temple had been placed along the ramparts. The heavier stones would cause crushing wounds, while the sharp edges of those flints that had been split would cut open a man's flesh. Two centuries were on the western defences, with two more guarding the riverbanks and a fifth on the eastern defences, which had been completed and were just over two thirds the length of the opposite rampart. Macro's century was held in reserve behind the gatehouse while he waited in the tower with Apollonius and a section of men armed with bows. Bundles of arrows stood ready in baskets at the rear of the tower. The spy had been supplied with a spare helmet and armour by one of the veterans, and another had given him a shield and sword. An optio's narrow crest rose above his helmet.

As the geese raised the alarm, Macro cupped his hands to his mouth and called out across the defences, 'They're coming!'

The first of the rebels appeared as spectral figures rushing out of the mist. As they approached the defences, Macro saw that they were armed with slings and bows, and he called a warning to the men on the palisade. 'Take cover!'

The enemy stopped fifty paces from the ditch and unleashed their missiles, and a moment later they crashed into the timbers of the palisade, splintering but not penetrating the wood. The veterans crouched down behind their shields for added protection while the din of the impacts continued. Many of the missiles overshot and plunged into the thatch of the buildings behind, or clattered into the tiles, shattering some. In the tower, one of the archers made to rise and take a shot.

'No!' Macro snapped at him. 'Save it for the assault.'

The veteran nodded and crept back two paces.

Every so often, Macro risked a quick glimpse and saw that the enemy were holding their position as they continued the barrage. Behind them he could see a solid formation of warriors emerging from the mist, accompanied by the cries of their leaders urging them on before their men chorused their various battle cries. Above them, their banners hung limply in the still air. As they neared the defences, a war horn sounded a loud, flat note that carried clearly across the battleground. The archers and slingers released their final shots and then trotted to the flanks, out of the path of the assault force.

Macro rose to his feet cautiously and glanced from side to side to ensure that none of the missile troops were taking aim at him. Reassured, he turned to the archers in the tower. 'Get ready. Make sure every shot takes one of those bastards down.'

He leaned towards the side that looked over the rampart. 'On your feet!'

A second note sounded, and there was a deep roar from thousands of voices as the rebels surged forward and then broke into a dead run towards the defences. On the far right of the Roman line, next to the river, forty men rushed up onto the uncompleted section of the rampart, some six feet lower than the rest, and prepared to defend the ground.

Apollonius was watching the enemy charge with a sinister smile. 'Be interesting to see what happens when— Ah! There we go.'

Scores of the rebels, fleeter of foot than their comrades, had outstripped the main body, and now one of them had crashed through the camouflaged screen above a lily and stumbled onto a sharpened stake that skewered his thigh. He let out a howl of agony that could be heard in the tower. More men crashed through the covers; most were injured grievously enough to be out of the fight, even if the wounds weren't mortal. The archers in the tower began to loose their shafts at the nearest of the enemy and were joined by those with bows along the palisade, and very quickly they took their toll on the rebels, particularly those with little or no armour. Bodies began to drop along the front of the enemy charge as they raced for the ditch, heedless of those who fell victim to the lilies and missiles of the defenders.

The first of the rebels reached the edge of the ditch and plunged down the slope before scrambling up the steeper incline beneath the rampart. Above them the veterans were throwing their javelins into the compacting ranks. Others hurled flints, crushing and shattering bones and tearing bloody gashes on the flesh of their victims. Macro saw the rebels scrambling up to the angled stakes and struggling to dislodge them before giving up and trying to get through and over them, all the while exposed to the arrows and stones of the veterans. Scores were falling along the ditch to lie in the bottom as their comrades stepped on and over them to get at the Romans.

Then he noticed the tied bundles of sticks being carried forward and heaped into the ditches in three places, burying alive some of the rebel wounded. Fascine by fascine the enemy were building ramps up to the pointed stakes, which they were soon able to hack through with axes or dig out to create gaps through which to scale the rampart and get to the palisade. The man-to-man fighting began, with veterans and rebels exchanging blows and blocking them with shields. It was an unequal struggle, as the defenders had the advantage of height and were not constrained by having to cling on to the palisade while trying to fight. The rebels were struck down one after another and fell back on their comrades crowding the crude ramps. All the while, the veterans' stones and arrows picked off those on the far side of the ditch.

'By the gods, there's no doubting their courage,' Apollonius commented as he witnessed the carnage below. 'How much more of this can they take?'

Macro did not answer. He had seen trouble brewing at the far end of the line, where the incomplete rampart was lowest. The rebels had placed most of their fascines there, and were engaging the defenders on more equal terms. He slapped the spy on the back. 'Come with me.'

They hurried down the ladder and picked up their shields from where they had been left inside the door of the fortified gatehouse. Running behind the wall to the century standing in reserve, Macro stopped by the officer in command, a dark-skinned man from Mauretania.

'Balbanus, your men are needed to support the right. Follow me.'

With Macro and Apollonius taking the lead, the century turned and advanced at the trot to the unfinished stretch of the rampart, surging up the inner slope to join their comrades to prevent the line buckling. The first of the rebels had already made their way onto the walkway and were fighting like maniacs as they tried to dislodge the defenders. Several of the veterans had been wounded and were falling back or crawling down the wall to the safety of the wagons that formed the inner line. Four more were lying dead on the slope.

Macro edged round the battle line until he was close to the small redoubt where archers were keeping up a steady rain of arrows on the attackers beyond the ditch. Then he shoved his way into the fight with Apollonius at his side.

'Push 'em back, lads! Camulodunum is our home. Don't give them an inch!'

A short, chubby warrior with a shaven head and wild eyes came surging up from the ditch towards him, wielding a long Celtic sword. He slashed at Macro's feet, and Macro only just managed to ground his shield in time to block the blow, which dented the trim. As the warrior drew the sword back for a second strike, Macro swung the shield up and out and slammed the bottom into the rebel's face, sending him reeling backwards into his comrades, taking another man down with him.

'Ha!' Macro exulted as he drew his shield back and readied his sword. To his right, Apollonius was duelling with a spearman who was trying without success to find a way past the spy's shield.

'Stop toying with the bastard,' Macro growled.

The next time the rebel thrust his spear, the spy stamped down on the shaft and then crouched and hacked at the man's elbow, cutting deeply and forcing him to release his weapon and slide back down the wall. Apollonius sheathed his sword and snatched the spear, reversing it and hurling it out into the mass of rebels beyond the ditch. Then he drew his blade again, ready to take on the next rebel to climb towards him.

The reinforced Roman line was holding. Try as they might, the enemy could not dislodge them, and all the time they were suffering more casualties. The mist was lifting and had almost cleared since the first of the enemy had appeared, and Macro could see a handful of chariots on a small knoll two hundred paces to the rear of the attacking force. He could even make out the red hair of the woman on the chariot in the middle as she regarded the stalled attack. The enemy's war horns sounded three notes and the host began to back off. All along the rampart and ditch the rebels disengaged, fell back and hurried away, eager to get out of range of the Roman archers, who managed to hit at least another twenty before they ceased shooting.

Macro and those about him stood their ground, chests heaving and swords raised for a moment longer. Then Macro slid his blade into its scabbard and lowered his shield before he caught his breath and turned to look at Apollonius.

'Round one to us. Balbanus!'

'Sir?' the centurion called from further along the partially completed rampart.

'Get your men back to the reserve position and take a roll call. Report your losses to me.'

As the men filed away Macro saw that the original defenders of this stretch of the defences had lost perhaps a third of their number. They couldn't hope to hold on if there was another attack. Balbanus would have to give up half of his men to support them, and at one stroke, Macro's reserve unit would be severely diminished. It was an ominous thought. He made his way along the rampart, offering quiet praise and encouragement to the veterans and noting their losses as he went. By the time he had returned to the tower above the gatehouse, he had the butcher's bill: eighteen dead, and another thirty wounded, most of whom would be able to return to their units once their injuries had been treated at the casualty station set up in a row of shops nearby.

'What do you think their next move will be?' asked Apollonius as they looked out across the bodies strewn on the ground to the enemy warriors gathered in front of the chariots.

'I doubt they'll risk another frontal assault like that now they've learned that rushing us isn't going to work.' Macro cast his gaze over the colony and its defences. 'If I was in Boudica's place, I'd try an attack on a much narrower front. Most likely the weak section of the rampart. That's where their best chance was last time. But they can see the inner line of defences from across the river, so they'll need to take that into consideration. The eastern wall is a much tougher proposition.'

'What if they attack in two places at the same time?' asked Apollonius. 'We can't reinforce both.'

'I was getting to that,' Macro said tersely. 'That's most likely to be their next move. And if they're smart, they'll wait until dark to give it a try, so we won't know how their forces are balanced and can't tell if either attack is a feint. In the meantime, we carry on with the work on the rampart. If they want to try and harass us, they'll have to run the gauntlet of our archers. The only other danger is an attack across the river, but I can't see any sign of rafts being prepared over there.' He gestured towards the vast rebel camp. The thousands of non-combatants who had lined the gentle slope leading up from the far bank of the river were starting to drift away, returning to their pitches.

'It's not that wide a river,' Apollonius observed.

'That's why we've staked the bed and the bank on our side and have men watching it. If they come in strength, I'll redeploy enough troops to deal with it. They'll be easy targets for our archers. They won't get past our defences that way.'

'I hope you're right,' Apollonius said doubtfully. 'It strikes me that we have too few men to defend such a long perimeter, even if it's smaller than that of the original fortress.'

Macro nodded.

'There are nearly six thousand men in a legion, all in the prime of life. We've got a tenth of that number, most of whom are in their fifties. No disrespect to veterans like yourself, Macro, but the situation doesn't look very hopeful to me. We'd be better off falling back to the temple and defending that.'

'I'm not giving up the rest of the colony without a fight,' Macro said firmly. 'There's a morale issue here. Any ground we give up will undermine the spirit of our lads and boost that of the rebels. For now, we stay where we are. We've showed them we can hold our ground. They've lost two, maybe three hundred. There's going to be a lot of grieving on the other side of the river when the fallen don't return to their campfires tonight.'

'But not enough to persuade them to give up and go home, eh?'

'No.' Macro turned his gaze towards Boudica and saw that she was conferring with a small group of her warriors. Presumably the senior warlords of the two tribes that formed her host. 'I think I understand her well enough to know that she cannot be persuaded to abandon her goal. She will not rest until she has swept every Roman from these shores, or perished in the attempt.'

For the rest of the day, there was no further attempt to assault the colony. At midday, a large force of men on foot crossed the river at a ford a mile or so upriver and marched round Camulodunum to take up a position facing the eastern rampart. Macro was obliged to transfer men to reinforce the fresh threat in case the next attack was made from both sides simultaneously. Another rebel party set out to retrieve the dead and wounded from the first attack, and Macro ordered his archers not to shoot at them unless they ventured as far as the ditch. Meanwhile, a group of veterans continued to raise the unfinished section of the western rampart, building up the timber framework and filling it with soil and stones. Elsewhere, the men of each century took turns to stand to, while their comrades rested and ate behind the rampart.

At dusk, Macro made the rounds of the defences and was pleased to see that the veterans were in good spirits. He ended by climbing to the top of the gatehouse once again and scrutinising the enemy's positions alongside Apollonius. As the light began to die, the two forces opposite the town's ramparts were brought food from across the river, carried in heavy carts pulled by oxen. Foraging parties roamed the forest and the nearest buildings outside the colony searching for food, loot and wood for the campfires. The main body of the rebel host remained on the far side of the river, settling down for the second night of the siege. Occasional sounds of axe blows sounded from a small forest away to the north-east.

'I'm surprised they haven't attacked again,' said Apollonius. 'Do you think they mean to starve us into surrender? After all, we're cut off on all sides now.'

'I doubt it. Boudica has too many mouths to feed. The rebels won't be able to live off the land for more than a few days. Unless they have managed to prepare a supply base and a means to reprovision – which I doubt they have – they'll need our supplies. They might try a night attack next. Most likely from both directions at once. Our lookouts will need to be on their toes, particularly in the last few hours before dawn. The initiative is with the enemy. We can't know when they will come, so they'll let us stew during the night while they rest their men. There may even be a few harassing attacks just to keep our lads on edge.' Macro glanced at the spy. 'You've been taking all this in a very different spirit to your usual demeanour.'

'What do you mean?'

'Not so much of your dry wit and sardonic comments as usual. Why is that?'

'I have a feeling I will not live to see the end of this siege. I have been in plenty of dangerous situations before, Centurion, as you well know. I took risks, but there was always a good chance of survival. This time? I'm not so sure. I've never before felt so convinced that I will die. I had thought I would live to a ripe old age, surrounded by scrolls in a comfortable villa on Ithaca.'

'I'm not sure I can picture that,' said Macro. 'You're a spy through and through. Such men usually die in a dark street with a knife in their backs. I've come to know you well enough to understand that you live for the thrill of it. I can't see you settling down anywhere.'

'You think so?' Apollonius looked at him with an amused expression. 'How little you know me. I wouldn't presume to even try if I were you.'

Macro had genuinely thought their plight had brought them closer and that a bond, which might be called friendship, had formed between them. Now that he saw the faintly mocking look on the other man's face, he realised that he was wrong and that the spy was his own man who would never let himself become close to another. He made himself smile. 'That's more like the Apollonius I'm familiar with. Keep your morbid thoughts to yourself, eh?' He gestured towards the enemy force a quarter of a mile from the western rampart. 'And keep an eye on that lot while there's still light. If they start moving, send for me.'

'Where will you be?'

'Checking on the wounded. We'll need all those who can return to duty.'

Macro climbed down the ladder and made for the row of shops taken over by the surgeon. There were several men sitting on benches along the front of the block, with dressings on their wounds. Some had splints over reset bones. There was a distracted air about them, and as Macro reached the entrance to the first shop, he smelled the wine. The surgeon had plied them with drink to help them cope with their pain.

Inside the building, a wide opening had been knocked through to link all the shops, and the walls were lined with men on bedrolls taken from the nearest houses. The surgeon, Adrastus, was hunched over a man who was pinned down by three of his medics while an incision was made to draw out a barbed arrowhead at the end of a length of shaft. Macro watched as the arrow was removed and Adrastus handed the duty of stitching the wound to one of his men. Then the surgeon stood up and rubbed the blood off his hands with an already soiled strip of cloth.

'Can I help you, sir?'

'I need to know how many of them can be sent back to their units.'

'The wounded?'

'I need every man who can hold a weapon.'

'I'll have to make an assessment. When do you need to know?'

'As soon as you can. Is there anything you need here?'

'I could use more wine, and cloth for dressings. Vinegar too, to clean the wounds.'

'My house is in the next street. I still have a jar or two of wine. Cheap stuff.'

'I doubt those who need it are going to quibble about the vintage, sir.'

'I'll be back in a moment then.'

It was dark by the time Macro left the dressing station and turned the corner into the street leading to the gate at the front of his home. There was an eerie quiet here now that most of the colony's inhabitants had been evacuated and the remainder were manning the defences. A stray dog, scavenging in the gutter, was startled at his approach and trotted off, looking back guiltily before it disappeared into an alley. Passing through the gate, Macro opened the front door. As he made his way down the corridor towards the kitchen, he heard the scrape of a bench, and stopped dead, his hand reaching for his sword. There was a metallic clatter and a faint keening noise. He drew the sword and edged towards the door as quietly as possible. It stood slightly ajar and there was a dim glow from within the kitchen. He eased it open, and as the hinge grated, he thrust it aside and stood on the threshold, sword raised.

Parvus was scraping scraps of meat onto the floor, where Cassius was eagerly snaffling them up as what was left of his tail wagged happily. Boy and dog turned towards the door in alarm.

'What the fuck?' Macro muttered, lowering his blade and sheathing it just as Cassius bounded across the room and jumped up, paws on Macro's chest as he tried to lick his face. 'Get down, you ugly brute!' he snapped, and pushed the dog away. Cassius backed off and then trotted back to finish his scraps.

Parvus was standing by the table, where an oil lamp glimmered, his eyes wide with surprise and anxiety.

'What the hell are you doing here?' Macro demanded. 'You

should be on the road to Londinium by now. More to the point, I ordered you to look after Petronella.'

Parvus lowered his head, and Macro sighed with frustration and not a little anger.

'You thought you'd come back to fight, eh? And brought Cato's bloody dog along into the bargain. You little fool, you haven't got any idea what you've got yourself into.'

Parvus looked up and nodded, miming thrusting with a sword before indicating himself and Macro. Then he waited for a response.

Macro shook his head sympathetically. 'Petronella is going to tan your hide for this. And rightly so.' He was about to castigate the boy further when another thought occurred to him. 'How in Hades did you get inside the colony's defences? When did you return?'

Parvus clasped his hands and shut his eyes.

'Last night?'

The boy nodded and then made a paddling gesture with his arms.

'You swam across, the pair of you? But that was after the rebels arrived. You must have come across the river to the south.'

Parvus smiled, but Macro's heart was beating anxiously.

'Where did you get across? You must show me, now.'

Parvus read his expression as anger, and hesitated. Macro forced himself to speak calmly. 'Show me. It's important.'

They left the house with the dog trotting beside them, and had almost reached the front gate when there was a shout of alarm from the eastern rampart.

'To arms! To arms! They're inside the colony!'

# CHAPTER THIRTY

'Stay close to me, boy.'

Before Macro could move, Parvus pointed to Macro's dagger and then himself. Macro hesitated, then unclipped the dagger sheath from his belt and thrust it into the boy's hands. 'Don't draw the blade unless I tell you to. Let's go.'

With the dog loping beside them, they ran out of the gate and turned to the eastern defence line, sprinting along the dark thoroughfare while the sounds of shouts and the clink of blades carried across the colony from somewhere ahead and to the right. As they made for the eastern gatehouse, Macro tried to work out how the rebels could have got inside the colony before the alarm was raised. Any attempt at a frontal attack or infiltration would have been detected before they penetrated the defences.

As they approached the end of the street, he could see the rampart and make out figures racing along it from left to right, towards the growing sound of fighting. At the junction, he stopped, chest heaving as he turned to take in the situation. The far end of the rampart was a dark mass of figures. The only illumination came from torches burning in brackets outside the small tower next to the river, a relic from the old legionary fortress. By their glow he could make out the enemy warriors clambering over the rampart and scrambling down the reverse slope to feed into the fight below. A cordon of veterans was struggling to contain them, while more were entering the fight along the walkway.

The gatehouse was a short distance to the right, and Macro made for it, dashing along the street. Ordering Parvus to wait with Cassius, he climbed the ladders to the top and saw an optio and four men looking towards the fight.

'Keep your damn eyes to the front!' he snapped. 'The attack could be a feint.'

While the veterans returned to their posts, Macro glanced along the rampart, but there were no other attacks under way. To the south, he could see a large body of men moving forward to cross a causeway over the ditch before they climbed ladders to the top of the rampart. He took the optio to one side. 'How in Hades did they get to the ditch and across the rampart in numbers before the alarm was raised? Were you and your men asleep?'

'There was nothing happening, sir. I swear. First thing we knew about it was when the fighting started after they got into the colony. The lads in the tower at the end never shouted a warning.'

Then they must have been silenced before the rebels rushed the rampart and got their bridge and ladders in place, Macro reasoned. The nearest lookouts on the wall must also have been silenced. The only way that could have happened was if they were dealt with from behind the rampart. The river, he realised. Just like Parvus and the dog, the enemy had somehow got across the river and marshes to the south, and through the stakes. A small group of rebels must have swum over, disposed of the veterans on watch and signalled the main force to attack.

'Take a man and go to the other side of the colony. I want two centuries sent over here at once. Go!'

The two veterans hurried away, and Macro waited a moment longer. There were still men on the northern stretch of rampart, too few to risk sending any of them to reinforce the south flank, in case a second attack was made while most of the defenders were combating the initial assault. He made his way down the ladders and grasped Parvus by the shoulders. 'Take the dog and go to the temple complex. Wait for me there.' He gave the boy a shove. 'Do as you are ordered.'

Parvus ran off, Cassius following. Macro made his way towards the fighting, and with a sickening feeling realised that his men were being forced back. Drawing his sword, he joined the line and called out over the din of battle, 'Hold on, lads! Help is coming! Hold on!'

There were two veterans in front of him, and beyond them he could see that there were already hundreds of rebels within the defences, and more crossing the palisade. The veterans had to hold their ground until reinforcements came if the attack was going to be contained and then driven back. Macro pushed through until he was one rank back and raised his voice again. 'For Rome! For our homes, boys! Stick it to 'em!'

Most of the veterans took up the cry, and there was a discernible shift forward as the rebels were pressed back into a compact mass. Macro felt his hopes rise. When the men he had sent for arrived, they would be enough to finish the job. The advance by the veterans slowed to a halt as both sides fought with desperation, shield to shield, trying to land blows through whatever gaps they could find. The superior footing of the veterans allowed them a sufficient edge to contain the greater numbers for the moment.

'Where's Macro?' a voice called out from behind the Roman line. 'Anyone seen him?'

Pushing himself back, Macro threaded his way free of his comrades. 'Over here!'

As he emerged from the rear of the line, he could make out Apollonius in the faint light from the torches burning on the nearby tower and hurried towards him.

'Where are the men I sent for?'

'They're not coming. There's an attack from the west.' Apollonius glanced round. 'Sweet Jupiter, what happened here? How did they get over the rampart?'

Macro looked past the spy. Above the clatter of weapons and cries behind him, he could hear the distant sounds of fighting from the far side of the colony.

'Where are the reserves?'

'They're already committed,' Apollonius replied. 'The rebels are contesting every inch of the line.'

'Shit.' Macro ground his teeth in anxious frustration. 'We can't hold them here for much longer. Once they get past us, they'll fall on the rear of the other centuries.' It was obvious what he had to do, even as he was reluctant to give the order. 'All right. We have to retreat to the temple complex. Get back to the other line and pass on the order. Everyone's to make for the temple. Make sure those still guarding the river lines get the word too.'

'What about those in the casualty station?' asked Apollonius.

'Have them moved first before falling back. Now go.'

Apollonius turned to run back across the colony. It was going to be a difficult and dangerous operation, Macro realised. All fighting withdrawals in the face of an enemy were fraught with danger, and he took a moment to plan his orders. Both centuries assigned to the eastern defences had become entangled, and the first step would be to try to pull one unit out and re-form ranks to cover the retreat.

'Fifth Century!' he yelled. 'Fifth Century! Disengage and fall back on me!'

He moved back fifteen paces in the direction of a street that led to the temple complex. One by one, then in small groups, the veterans of the Fifth Century trotted out of the battle line. Macro could see that some were wounded, and he ordered them to make their way to the temple. As the last of them joined him, he estimated that he had over sixty men at his command.

'Where's Tertillius? Centurion Tertillius!'

'I saw him go down, sir,' a voice called out of the darkness. 'He's done for.'

'Fifth Century . . . column of four. Close up!' Macro ordered as he took command.

The veterans shuffled into position behind him, with three men joining him in the front rank as they covered the end of the street, all but for a small gap along the side of the formation. He could see that the remaining men of the Fourth Century were giving ground. There was little time left before the rebels broke through. He turned to the men still along the rampart.

'You on the rampart! Pull back to the temple! Move it!'

They peeled away and stumbled down the reverse slope, dashing into the nearest streets as they made for the safety of the temple compound. Once the last of them had gone, Macro turned to those still fighting. 'Fourth Century! Disengage and withdraw!'

The men at the rear turned at once and ran for the street where Macro and their comrades stood ready. They passed down the line of the formation and kept going. The others fell back, covering themselves with their shields as they tried to break away from the rebels and escape. Most made it, but several left it too late and were surrounded and set upon by superior numbers, disappearing under the frenzied sword and axe blows of the enemy. When the last men had passed him, Macro extended the line to cover the width of the street, and the front rank formed a shield wall as the rebels surged towards them.

'Fall back on my time!' he called out. 'One! Two! One!'

The formation began to give ground a pace at a time. As more of the rebels pressed on, they pushed their comrades at the front hard up against the large legionary shields. It became difficult for them to wield their weapons, and they fell victim to the shorter blades of the Romans, stabbing out from between the shields. The tightly packed ranks of the rebels made for easy targets, and one man after another was wounded and fell back, impeding those behind before they were trampled into the ground.

The formation passed over the first crossroads. There were three more before they reached the open space surrounding the temple compound, and Macro knew that the enemy would realise they could use the streets running parallel to outflank the Romans. Sure enough, as they withdrew past the second junction, he glimpsed dark shapes flitting past to the left and right.

'Form box!' he ordered, and the men at the other end of the formation and those along the flanks turned their shields outwards to cover the century from all sides.

The rebels were waiting for them at the fourth junction. Macro could hear the clatter and thuds above the din at the rear of the formation. A moment later, the man to his left lunged too far and one of the rebels hacked at his wrist with an axe. The blow nearly severed his hand, and the legionary dropped his sword and groaned through clenched teeth.

'Get back,' Macro ordered him, and the man stepped aside as one of his comrades slipped round him to take his place.

Macro sensed the formation slowing behind him and realised that he needed to be at the other end to lead it forward. He called over his shoulder, 'Get ready to take my place.' He counted the next step back, then lunged with his shield, punching it into a rebel and pushing him off balance. 'Now!'

Stepping a half-pace aside, he let the man behind him move forward into the gap and drew back into the space in the middle of the formation, then worked his way through to the other end, past the handful of walking wounded and two men who needed the support of their comrades. The rebels were coming at the century from three sides now as the veterans tried to battle their way across the last junction before the wall of the temple compound.

'Keep it tight!' Macro shouted, and resumed calling the time as the veterans ahead of him thrust their shields to drive the enemy back and clear a gap for the formation to edge forward. As far as he could make out in the darkness, there was not much opposition in front of them; most of the rebels were still pressing the rear of the box as it steadily gave ground.

There was a flare of light from ahead, and he looked up to see figures on the wall heaving a bundle of burning sticks into the space between the temple compound and the nearest buildings. A moment later, a party of veterans ran past the gap, and a second group charged the rear of the enemy facing him. Caught between the two Roman forces, the rebels panicked. Most fled into the buildings on either side, though a handful fought on and paid for their courage with their lives as they were cut down. The two Roman forces met, and Macro emerged from the street to see that a line of veterans was facing off the enemy who had been attempting to get round the Fifth

Century. The blazing bundles of sticks in front of the wall lit up the scene in wavering red and flickering dark shadows.

As the veterans passed by him, Macro pointed in the direction of the temple compound gate and urged them to keep going.

'Macro!'

He looked up to see Apollonius on the wall, along with a party of men mostly armed with bows. The spy indicated the gate. 'When the last of the men are out of the street, run for it. We'll cover you.'

Macro turned to order two sections to get the wounded to safety; then, as the rear of the formation emerged into the pool of light cast by the flames, he closed them up with the men who had come from the compound to reinforce them. Apollonius shouted an order, and the men on the wall unleashed arrows and rocks onto the rebels pressed tightly together at the end of the street. Several went down quickly, and those pushing forward from behind tumbled over them until the street was blocked.

'Run!' Macro shouted. 'Into the compound, lads! Don't stop for anyone! Go!'

He let most of the veterans pass him before he joined the last of them at a dead run along the foot of the wall towards the corner, some fifty paces ahead. More of the enemy appeared individually and in small groups, rushing up the side streets, but Apollonius's men were on hand to shoot down those in the lead.

A sharp cry came from behind him, and he glanced back to see that one of the veterans had stumbled. The man threw aside his shield and limped on, but already three of the rebels had burst out from an alley and hurled themselves on him, and a final desperate cry for help was abruptly cut off.

Macro and the last men of the Fifth turned the corner and ran for the gateway a short distance ahead. The men from the western defence line were also racing for safety, and beyond them he could make out more of the rebels chasing down their prey and picking off stragglers. He drew up as he reached the gate, sweat dripping from his brow and his lungs on fire. The final veterans half ran, half staggered past him and through the gate into the compound. Macro waited a moment longer as the nearest of the enemy raced towards him. Holding his shield and sword out on either side to bare his chest, he bellowed at the rebel, 'Come on then!'

He swung his shield to the front and slapped the flat of the blade against the metal trim on the side. The rebel stopped fifteen feet away, eyeing him warily. Macro waited a beat for the man to continue his charge, then snorted with disgust and turned to march through the gates, nodding to the optio in charge of the four men standing on either side to close them.

The hinges protested as the heavy timbers swung into place with a thud and the locking bar was dropped into the iron brackets. Sturdy props were leaned up against the inside of the gates to give them more strength. Macro grounded his shield and rested his forearms along the top as he caught his breath and looked round the interior of the compound, which was illuminated by a handful of braziers. Hundreds of veterans were standing, squatting or sitting on the flagstones as they recovered from their desperate retreat through the colony. Many of them were wounded and being seen to by the surgeon and his medics. Ulpius and his men were on the narrow walkway that had been hastily constructed behind the walls, and Apollonius was with them, directing a group of archers as they shot down rebels in the open ground between the temple compound and the nearest buildings. A red glow illuminated the night sky to the north, and Macro could hear the faint roar of a large fire and the cheers of the enemy as they watched part of the colony go up in flames.

A small figure emerged between the half-completed columns. He dashed down the steps and came running through the exhausted veterans, then drew up in the loom of the nearest brazier and scrutinised Macro anxiously.

'No need to worry, young 'un. I'm fine. Where's Cassius?'

Parvus mimed tying the dog's collar to a post, before looking at Macro and opening his hands to ask him if he wanted anything.

'Water. My throat is as dry as a Vestal Virgin's . . . Never mind, just find me some water.'

Parvus ran off to one of the butts that had been set up beside the pediment. Macro forced himself to stand upright, and laid his shield down as he waited for Parvus to return with a filled canteen. He nodded his thanks as he raised it to his lips, and drank several gulps before lowering it.

'Needed that. Now you go and find the surgeon and see what you can do to help him, then get some rest. I'll find you later.'

Parvus hesitated, and Macro gave him a warning look before the boy turned and ran off.

Macro made for the nearest ladder. Climbing up onto the walkway, he moved along the wall to Ulpius and Apollonius, who were deep in discussion. Below, he could see dark figures flitting along the streets, and he could hear the cracks and crashes as the rebels began to loot the colony's buildings. Flames were already rising around the Londinium gate, and fresh glows appeared further within the colony.

'That was a close thing,' Apollonius greeted him. 'I wasn't sure you were going to make it.'

'Might not have done if it hadn't been for the men sent to clear the street ahead of us. Good work.'

'I aim to please.'

Ulpius rubbed his eye patch. 'How in Hades did the rebels get through the defences so fast? That's what I want to know.'

'Looks to me like they got some men across the river to the south and took the tower to cover an assault from outside. By the time Tertillius and his lads were on the scene, the rebels were pouring over the wall and it was too late to kick them out. All that could be done then was to get as many men back here as possible.' Macro glanced down at the veterans crowded into the open space in front of the temple. 'Looks like most of the other men made it too.'

'Not those in the casualty station, though,' said Apollonius. 'I sent the surgeon and his medics and the walking wounded here first. The order to fall back had already been given before I could get together a party of litter-bearers. We couldn't save the rest.'

Poor bastards, massacred as they lay helpless, Macro reflected bitterly. But there was no time to spare them any further thought for the present. Other matters needed his urgent attention.

'Ulpius, I want to know how many men we have. Find the remaining officers. Get them to take a roll call before they stand their men down. Your lads can take the first turn on the wall, along with Apollonius and his archers. Tell the surgeon to get the wounded into the inner sanctum. Safest place for them and they'll be out of the way. Dismissed.'

They exchanged a salute and Ulpius climbed down into the compound. Macro and Apollonius were silent for a moment as they looked out over the colony. The sounds of looting were now accompanied by cries of triumph, and over by the gate, the rebels could be seen in the lurid glare of the flames as they revelled in the blaze. Some of them brandished the heads of fallen veterans that they had taken for trophies.

'We've lost the colony already,' said Macro. 'I had counted on holding them off for a few more days at least. I doubt we'll last long enough for the Ninth Legion to reach us.'

'You can't shoulder the blame for that,' Apollonius countered. 'The defences were in poor shape. Things might have been different if the senate had stepped up when there was still time to make a difference. Besides, we had too few men to cover the perimeter. The rebels were always going to breach the defences.'

Macro reluctantly conceded the point, but it had been important for the morale of the men that they were fighting to protect their homes. From now on, they would be fighting for their lives.

# CHAPTER THIRTY-ONE

As the rebels looted the colony throughout the rest of the night, the defenders made their preparations for their final stand. Macro had little doubt about the outcome, and kept his weary mind focused on his duty to hold out for as long as possible and make the enemy pay a high price for their victory. Once the roll call had been taken, the defenders were left with fewer than four hundred able-bodied veterans and a hundred and fifty of those who had no military training. The supplies that had been gathered within the compound were more than adequate to sustain them for a month. Macro smiled ruefully as he reflected that they would be unlikely to survive for a fraction of that time.

The compound wall was a smaller perimeter to defend than that of the colony, but there was no ditch beyond, and even though the height of the wall had been raised, it was still only ten feet or so. In addition, it had never been designed as a fortification, merely as a boundary to mark out the sacred ground of the temple once it had been completed. A sturdy battering ram could create a breach with a few blows. It had been reinforced with blocks of stone and other building materials used to create the walkway, but it was still incapable of withstanding a determined assault.

It was inevitable that the wall would be breached. After that, the last line of defence would be the hastily built breastwork between the uncompleted pillars running around the pediment, itself scarcely six feet above the ground. The front of the pediment was the weakest point, as it faced a wide flight of steps and the defenders would have to hold a line of forty feet protected only by the breastwork.

Once the injured had been carried inside the inner sanctum and the men had been fed, Macro assigned Ulpius to take the first watch while he went to snatch some rest. Before that, though, there was one last matter to be seen to.

He found Parvus curled up on his side not far from the entrance to the inner sanctum. Cassius lay beside him, head resting between his large paws, jowls puffing as he whimpered his way through a dream. Macro regarded them fondly as he undid his chin strap and removed his helmet and padded skullcap. He ran a hand through his hair before he eased himself down as quietly as he could and rested his back against the breastwork. Despite all his concerns, and the hopelessness of their situation, he fell asleep swiftly and deeply, his chin resting on his chest as he snored.

The early hours of the following day were cold when Apollonius came to find Macro with a mess tin filled with hot stew. He hesitated before deciding not to wake the centurion. Setting the mess tin down, he went to find two of the spare cloaks that were being stored in the sanctum and covered Macro and Parvus. Cassius stirred and stood, wagging his stumpy tail, and Apollonius raised a finger. 'Shh. If you keep quiet, you can share the stew. Over here.'

The spy sat cross-legged a short distance away and made the dog sit before he fished out a piece of meat and held it up between two fingers. 'Gently now.'

Cassius craned his head forward and took the proffering carefully, before gulping it down.

'My turn.' Apollonius managed a couple of spoonfuls before the dog pawed his arm.

They took it in turns until the mess tin was empty and Cassius was allowed to lick out the dregs. Then he sat next to the spy, resting his head in Apollonius's lap as the latter stroked his head and neck and mused softly, 'What I would give to trade places with you. It must be comforting to live from one meal to the next and have little else to worry about, eh, boy?'

Leaning his head back, Apollonius looked up at the sky. There were no clouds above, and the stars and a half-moon gleamed serenely amid the velvet darkness. Like Macro, he entertained little hope for their survival. He had faced great danger before and lived through it by virtue of his quick wits and handiness with weapons. But this time there would be no escape. The odds were stacked against them so completely that hope was a pointless luxury. And so he set hope aside and stared up at the heavens and savoured the chilly edge of the night air and the distant hoot of an owl in one of the fields outside the colony. He could hear the faint sounds of merry-making from the vast enemy camp beyond the river. Even though he knew the rebels were celebrating the destruction of the colony and the coming slaughter of the defenders, there was something reassuring about the sound. Life would go on for some, even as his own was snuffed out. But that was not yet, and he had these few hours of bittersweet peace to savour by himself.

Macro had stopped snoring. He pulled the cloak over himself as he muttered, 'Please go to sleep, spy. Your thinking is keeping me awake.'

Apollonius chuckled lightly. 'As you command, my centurion.'

He took one last look at the moon before closing his eyes, emptying his mind and breathing in an easy rhythm until sleep came.

Macro shook his shoulder and Apollonius blinked his eyes open. There was enough light to see by, and he realised that the dog had left him while he was asleep and moved back to the side of Parvus, who slept on. Apollonius stood up and looked out over the breastwork. The dark figures of the century on watch paced along the compound wall as their comrades slept below. Those who had not been able to sleep had kept the braziers going to warm themselves through the night. There was an acrid odour of smoke in the air that caught in his throat, and he saw several columns of smoke rising from the buildings surrounding the compound. There was no sound from the enemy camp, and the only noises from beyond the walls were the faint crackle of flames and the dawn chorus of birds.

'Come on,' said Macro. 'Let's see the lie of the land.'

Leaving Parvus and Cassius to sleep on, they descended the steps of the pediment and crossed the compound to climb one of the ladders onto the walkway to the left of the gate. The duty centurion, a slim man with wrinkled skin, approached them.

'Morning, sir.'

'Anything to report, Venutius?'

'The enemy have gone quiet since my lads took the watch. Seen a few of them in the streets, but they've left us alone. Been too busy helping themselves to our property.' He pointed towards the nearest buildings beyond the wall, and Macro saw smashed pottery and broken and discarded furniture in the streets. Doors hung open in most of the buildings. Further off, a number of fires were still spreading across the colony, and elsewhere, thin trails of smoke rose from those buildings that were no more than smouldering ruins now. He felt his heart sink as he realised that where his own home had once stood there was now a blackened tracery of charred timbers and dirty grey wisps curling into the dawn sky.

On the far side of the river, the enemy was also now stirring, as warbands gathered and made for the upriver ford to cross over and join their comrades occupying the colony. The sounds of sawing and hammering carried from the far end of the colony, as the rebels who had slept outside began to file through the ruined defences and disappear amid the buildings.

'There's going to be no rest for us today,' Venutius muttered.

'Come now.' Macro grinned. 'You didn't really believe that nonsense about joining the army's reserves and never having to fight again?'

'I had hoped—'

'Macro,' Apollonius interrupted. 'Look there, opposite the gate.'

A party of burly rebels emerged from the end of a street. Their swords were sheathed and they carried large woven baskets covered with scraps of cloth. There was no sense of urgency or threat in the casual way they approached the gate.

'What are they up to?' Venutius mused. 'Shall I have the archers loose a few shafts at them, sir?'

'Not just yet. Let's see how this plays out.'

The rebels placed their baskets a short distance from the gate and trotted back to the shelter of the street they had emerged from. Macro and the others looked down curiously.

'What's that all about?' asked Venutius. 'Some kind of a trick?'

'Only one way to find out,' said Macro as he turned to one of the veterans nearby. 'Get me a ladder.'

'You aren't serious?' Apollonius challenged him, but the veteran had already returned with the nearest of the walkway ladders and Macro ordered him to lower it over the front of the wall.

He took a quick look around and saw that the enemy were hanging back in the shadows and making no attempt to approach the temple complex. Swinging his leg over the parapet, he climbed down and approached the baskets. He stopped by the nearest, grasping a fold of the cloth and lifting it. Inside were several heads. It took him an instant before he recognised the face of one of the mounted escorts that had accompanied the colony's evacuees. Dread chilled his heart and he felt nausea clench his throat. He went from basket to basket, tearing the cloth away and hurriedly inspecting the identities of the heads within. All were men from the escort, including Caldonius. He threw down the last piece of cloth in disgust, then strode back to the ladder and climbed back onto the wall before two of the veterans hauled the ladder up and lowered it into the compound.

Venutius rounded on him anxiously. 'Who are they? Silvanus and his men?'

Macro shook his head. 'It's Caldonius and his lads.'

'Caldonius?' Venutius's expression suddenly changed into a look of horror. 'What about our women and children?'

'I didn't see any of them down there.' Macro nodded towards the baskets. 'He must have got them far enough down the road before turning back to rejoin us.'

'You ordered him to make for Londinium if the rebels reached Camulodunum before he could return,' Apollonius pointed out.

'Then he and his men must have been ambushed on the way back,' Macro responded tersely before lowering his voice so that only the other two men could hear him. 'That's the story we tell the lads here. They need to believe their families are safe. I can't afford to have them distracted by grief. Besides, there's every chance that Caldonius did get the families away safely and was only ambushed on the way back here, like I said. That's what I want to believe. I need to believe my Petronella is alive.'

'So whose heads do we say they are if – when – we are asked?' Venutius demanded.

'Silvanus and his party. That's what you tell the men,' Macro said firmly.

Apollonius nodded, and Venutius looked away and hissed, 'Shit.'

'Venutius, that's an order, do you understand?'

The centurion was still for an instant, and then nodded.

'Good. Let's make sure the men are fed before they go onto the wall. We know what the enemy are up to.' Macro gestured in the direction of the sawing and hammering. 'They'll be bringing up ladders and rams as soon as they're ready. I'll hold Ulpius and his lads in reserve to plug any breaches, or counter-attack any footholds they get on the wall.'

He looked over the weary veterans stirring within the compound and tried to think of some words of encouragement to offer his subordinates. Cato would have found something to say. The right phrases to lift other men's spirits, no matter what the odds against them. Macro reached out to clasp their forearms in turn. 'May the gods look out for us, and if they don't, then fuck the gods. We'll look out for ourselves.'

'Spoken like a true philosopher.' Apollonius gave a weary grin before they parted to take their positions along the wall.

* * *

The rebels continued to mass in the streets surrounding the temple compound for the rest of the morning. They began to chant and cheer as their leaders moved amongst them, rousing the warriors' spirits for when the attack began. Shortly before noon, the cries rose in intensity and merged into a deafening roar of acclaim.

Macro climbed onto the top of the temple compound gatehouse so that he could get a good view along the wide thoroughfare that led to the charred remains of the Londinium gate. The ruins had been cleared to allow easy access across the ditch. A crowd of rebels filled the surrounding area, cheering wildly as they brandished their weapons and held up the heads of the veterans they had taken as trophies. In the middle of the throng was a body of horsemen with green cloaks, gleaming helmets and chain-mail vests. Standing proudly on the chariot in the centre of them was the unmistakable figure of Boudica. She too wore a mail vest and carried a spear, which she raised as she basked in the adulation of her followers. The chariot halted, and she spread her arms to call the crowd to order. Gradually the cheering subsided and the rebels looked towards her in silence. She began to speak, punctuating her words with gestures aimed at the temple compound.

Macro turned to see Apollonius climbing up to join him. A moment later, they stood side by side looking on as Boudica roused her people's passions.

'Three hundred paces, give or take,' said Apollonius. 'I could try a shot from here. If I can strike her down, it might put a dent in their morale.'

'It might just as easily inflame it further,' Macro responded. 'Leave it be. You'll have plenty of easier targets soon.'

They continued to watch before Apollonius spoke again. 'The hammering has stopped.'

'They'll be coming soon. I've seen enough. Let's prepare.'

They returned to the wall and separated again, standing with the other veterans. All over the compound there was a stillness and a silence as they waited. The only sign of nerves was amongst the civilians who had remained in Camulodunum to defend their homes. They were now all armed and spread out along the wall so that they might be encouraged by the steady resolve of the professional soldiers on either side. Some were clearly terrified, and Macro could see the tips of some of their spears trembling. Elsewhere a man turned away from the wall and vomited into the compound before he was turned back to face the enemy by the veteran standing beside him.

No more than half an hour had passed by Macro's reckoning when the first of the enemy's war horns sounded, swiftly followed by others from the buildings around the compound. Wild cheers rose as the first of the rebels broke from cover and surged across the open ground towards the wall. There was no need to raise the alarm or issue orders. The archers unleashed their shafts into the dense masses racing towards them. The small supply of javelins was quickly expended, and the only other missiles were the rocks and stones hurled by the defenders.

Amongst the rebels were small parties carrying ladders, which they hurriedly raised against the walls and began to scale to get at the veterans. As Macro looked on, he saw that the entire perimeter was swiftly enveloped. The defenders were using their swords and spears to keep the rebels from reaching the top of the wall. Some were struggling to push the ladders away or to the side, and where they succeeded, the enemy warriors tumbled onto their comrades and a brief respite was won for that stretch of the line.

The first of the Roman casualties were those who were struck down by rebel archers shooting over the heads of their comrades, or by attackers who scooped up rocks to throw back at the defenders. The wounded sank onto the walkway, or toppled back and crashed onto the ground at the foot of the wall, where the civilians assigned as litter-bearers hurried forward to pick them up and carry them up the stairs to the temple's inner sanctum for the surgeon and his medics to deal with as best they could.

Macro had anticipated that the main attack, using a ram, would be made against the reinforced gates, traditionally the weakest part of a fortification's defences. But there was no sign of any men carrying a ram across the open ground below him, nor in the streets beyond.

The top of a ladder slapped against the wall in front of him, and he readied his sword and shield. The point of a long Celtic blade appeared above the edge of the breastwork, and he battered it to the side and leaned forward to stab down into the rebel's shoulder, the point jarring as it struck bone. He pulled the sword back and raised his shield just as a stone rattled off the surface. There was a pause before he saw the top of the ladder twitch as the next man scaled the rungs. The veteran next to him was armed with a spear. He raised it overhead to stab at an angle, and the point pierced the next rebel's side.

Seizing his chance, Macro crouched and set his shield and sword down before rising quickly and grabbing the top of the ladder. With a powerful jerk, he pulled it up and over the wall and dumped it inside the compound, then retrieved his blade and shield. He had won a brief interval for the veterans on either side of him. He looked along the wall. The defenders appeared to be holding their ground, with the loss of only a handful of their number. The civilians, who had been so nervous shortly before, were fighting well alongside their veteran companions, to the point where it was hard to distinguish them. Nowhere had the enemy managed to get onto the wall. Then he heard a shout from his right.

'Ram!'

He turned to see a veteran thrusting his sword out over the wall to indicate the direction, and a moment later, Apollonius shouted an order for the nearest archers to target the rebels carrying the ram.

'Make way!' Macro ordered as he hurried along the walkway to the corner and down the longer side wall towards the threatened spot.

A warrior suddenly appeared to his left, boosted up by his comrades below; a blonde bearded man with a bare chest. He quickly swung a leg over the wall and sat astride it as he swung an axe at the sword arm of the veteran close by, who was duelling a rebel at the top of a ladder. The axe blade landed on the veteran's wrist, driving it down onto the wall before cutting through flesh and bone to sever the hand. It fell over the wall, still clutching the veteran's sword. As blood spurted from the stump, Macro pushed past the injured man and drove his shield into the rebel's torso, unbalancing the man so that he could not use his weapon. A second blow was enough to finish the job and knock him off his perch, and he fell backwards onto his comrades. The veteran was clutching his stump to his chest as he dropped his shield and climbed unsteadily down into the compound.

Macro was close enough now to look down and see the party carrying the ram reach the wall five paces from his position. Before they could ready the weapon, two of them were struck by arrows and another was hit on the head by a rock that drove him to his knees before he toppled to the side, senseless.

'Kill 'em!' Macro shouted. 'Don't let them use the ram!'

A concentrated barrage of arrows and rocks continued to strike the rebels as they tried to raise the ram by its rope handles. Now Macro could see how the enemy had fashioned the weapon. It was made from a long beam that had been taken from one of the colony's larger buildings. A section near the end had been shaped by an adze so that an anvil could be fastened to it, and the pointed iron end was now poised a short distance from the foot of the wall. A large warrior with a round shield and a helmet with a white flowing crest shouted orders to those around him, and a party of men covered the ram and its bearers with their shields to protect them from the missiles raining down from above. Some still found their target, but the stricken rebels were instantly replaced by their comrades. The ram was raised and drawn back as the warrior called the time, and then the first blow was struck.

Macro felt the shock of the impact through his feet and saw the dark crack that appeared above the walkway. Further along the wall, Apollonius called out, 'There's another ram coming! And another!'

The first ram continued to batter the wall in a steady rhythm. The crack widened, and then another appeared. It was obvious to Macro that the wall would not withstand the battering for long. A moment later, a section at the top tumbled down, just as the second ram came into action a short distance further along the line.

Macro turned towards the small force of reserves down in the compound. 'Ulpius! Get your lads over here!'

The centurion relayed the order to his men, and the formation trotted over to the vulnerable section of the wall just as another stretch of masonry crumbled and fell away. A few more blows created a gap three feet across, and the second and third rams extended the damage. It was clear that the rebels intended to create a single wide breach through which to mount their assault. The attack on the rest of the perimeter continued unabated, so that there was no chance to pull men off the wall to defend the breach. It was a cleverly executed attack, Macro conceded. No doubt the enemy had been well informed about the details of the temple's construction by those tribesmen who had been forced to labour on the site.

More of the wall fell away, and a section of the walkway collapsed, sending two veterans crashing into the compound along with the debris. Macro climbed down to join Ulpius. Through the gap, he could see the shields covering the enemy wielding the ram.

'Why don't they come?' Ulpius asked. 'The breach is practicable.'

'They want it wider before they attack.' Macro indicated the damage being done by the other rams nearby. A stretch of about thirty feet was being targeted, and it was clear that the enemy would soon achieve a breach wide enough to serve their intention.

He looked round the interior of the compound and saw that scores of his men had fallen along the wall. Already, in the far corner beyond the gate, several warriors had gained a foothold on the walkway and were fighting to hold the veterans off as more of the rebels climbed up to reinforce them.

The sound of falling masonry drew his attention back to the breach, and he saw that the gap was now some six feet wide. Through the swirl of dust, the first of the rebels appeared, a large dark-haired man whose face, chest and arms were festooned with blue tattoos. He carried a spear and at once turned to the side to thrust the point into the thigh of a veteran still fighting to hold his stretch of the wall. Driving the spear in, he forced his victim into the side of the Roman next to him. More of the enemy appeared through the gap, just as a section further along came down, creating a second, smaller breach.

Macro saw that the fight for the compound was lost. In a matter of moments the enemy would have widened the breach enough to pour through in sufficient numbers to overwhelm the reserve force with which he had hoped to block their way.

'Ulpius, you and your men must hold them here for a moment.'

The one-eyed veteran faced the breach as Macro turned to shout across the interior of the compound. 'Those on the wall, fall back! Fall back to the temple!'

# CHAPTER THIRTY-TWO

The remaining men who were not engaged hurried down the ladder and ran across the inside of the compound as they made for the temple stairs. Those still fighting tried to disengage and follow suit. Some managed to strike down their opponents and get away, while others were forced to fight on until they were overwhelmed and killed.

Macro stood in front of the breach with Ulpius and his men. 'We have to hold them back, lads,' he called out steadily. 'Buy time for our comrades.'

A few more blows from the second ram caused the stretch of wall between the two breaches to collapse and create a gap some twenty feet wide. A roar of triumph swelled from the throats of the rebels, and the Romans could hear feet scrambling over loose masonry, then the enemy burst through the billowing dust and charged at the waiting veterans. Swords, spears and axes thudded on the large curved surfaces of the Roman shields as the veterans braced against them and stabbed at any enemy that came within striking range. The first of the rebels fell at their feet, and those behind crowded forward but could find little purchase on the rubble from which to push the Roman line back.

Macro and Ulpius fought side by side, thrusting and cutting

at the enemy with a proficiency born of many years of training and battles fought with enemies across the Empire. The rebels were now packed tightly, unable to advance or to wield their weapons effectively, and all the while more were pressing forward from behind, pushing the foremost onto the blades of the Romans. As he tore his sword free from the guts of a rebel, Macro glanced quickly over his shoulder to see that the last of his men were climbing down from the wall and already the first of the enemy were dropping down into the compound. A crash came from his right as the third ram took its toll on the wall. It was time for the veterans of the reserve force to withdraw to the temple.

'Rear ranks! Fall back!'

The men at the back turned and ran along the foot of the pediment towards the steps. The men who had already made it to the temple were lining the breastwork, and Macro waited a few heartbeats longer before he gave his next order.

'On my command . . . Break contact and withdraw!'

The short line of veterans blocking the press of rebels struck out one last time, then turned to flee. Macro and Ulpius were the last to go, running after their comrades as the first of the rebels forced their way clear of the packed mob in the breach and set off in pursuit. They had only gone a few paces before they were struck by stones thrown from the defenders lining the pediment, and those that came after them raised shields or ran along the base of the pediment out of sight of the Romans above.

Macro was slightly ahead of Ulpius as he reached the corner of the pediment. He heard a sharp cry behind him, and turned to see Ulpius on the ground, his leg pierced by a spear. Surrounding him were three rebels desperate to claim the honour of killing a Roman officer. Ulpius held up his shield and sword to defend himself as he called out to Macro, 'Run, brother!'

There was no chance of saving him, so Macro hurried on to the temple steps and bounded up them two at a time, making for the narrow gap in the barricade running along the top. Behind him he could hear the rebels racing across the compound as they tried to catch up with him. An arrow splintered as it struck the riser to one side of him, and he weaved to the side and back again as he ran up the final few step and sprinted through the gap.

Apollonius shouted an order, and four men heaved a heavy set of shelves across the gap, then piled slabs of stone onto the shelves to prevent the enemy from shifting them. On either side the defenders readied their spears and swords to stab down at the rebels when they reached the top of the stairs. Macro stumbled on a few steps and leaned his shield up against one of the columns, bending over as he fought for breath. The sounds of the enemy's triumphant cries and the clash of weapons and the grunts of men filled his ears. Straightening up, he saw that the defenders were engaged all along the barricade, striking at the rebels on the other side. Apollonius stood amongst them, wielding his blade and shield as well as any of the veterans.

Still straining for breath, Macro made a circuit of the pediment. The enemy had brought several ladders in through the breach and were setting them against the pediment and the barricade above, ready to scale the Romans' last refuge. There were more than enough of the veterans left to defend every foot of the perimeter, and each rebel who tried to get over the barricade was run through and shoved back onto his comrades. Reassured that the enemy would not overwhelm them for the moment, he completed his circuit. He estimated that no more than two hundred of his men remained along the barricade, including the armed civilians. A glance inside the inner sanctum revealed that it was packed with wounded men, propped up against the walls and lying on the ground as the surgeon and his medics did their best to deal with the wounds. Parvus was sitting in the far corner, using Macro's dagger to tear strips of material from a heap of old clothes to serve as dressings. Cassius sat on his haunches nearby, his good ear twitching anxiously.

Returning to the fighting raging along the top of the stairs, he saw that a handful of veterans had been wounded or killed, and the injured were waiting between the bases of the columns to be carried into the inner sanctum. The survivors of Ulpius's century stood ready to fill the gaps. Macro retrieved his shield and selected ten veterans to stand with him to counter any breakthrough in the defences.

'Macro!' Apollonius called out. He had taken a step back from the barricade and one of Ulpius's men went forward to take his place. 'Over here!'

Macro trotted over, and the spy gestured towards the gatehouse of the compound. Between the men fighting along the barricade, he caught glimpses of the enemy warriors pulling the props away from the rear of the gates and dragging aside the building materials that had been used to reinforce them. A moment later, the locking bar was raised and dumped on the ground and the gates were hauled open. More rebels burst into the courtyard, and then a short distance behind them, Macro saw what he had anticipated. A team of men moved into the compound carrying one of the battering rams. Behind them he could see carts piled with bundles of sticks and thatch torn from the roofs of the colony's buildings.

'They're bringing up a ram,' he said. 'If that doesn't work, they mean to burn us out.'

Apollonius risked a quick glance over the barricade. 'The

ram's the most immediate danger. We can't let them get it to the top of the stairs.'

Macro looked round. He pointed to one of the piles of rock that had been placed at points around the inner sanctum. 'Take six of the reserves and have them target the men carrying the ram as soon as it starts up the stairs.'

Apollonius set his shield down and called to the nearest of Ulpius's men. Meanwhile, Macro climbed onto a block of stone in front of one of the pillars and looked down over the enemy pressing forward against the barricade. Several men were clearing a path through the packed ranks of rebels to make way for the party carrying the ram. He saw them reach the bottom of the flight of stairs and begin their ascent towards the reinforced wooden shelves in the middle of the Roman line. He indicated their direction with his sword.

'Ready your men, Apollonius.'

The veterans hefted their rocks as Macro watched the rebels carrying the ram labour up the steps. When they were halfway up, he shouted the order. 'Now!'

The spy and his veterans hurled the stones over the defenders so that they inscribed a shallow arc down towards the approaching ram. Several of the enemy were struck down, including three men at the front. As they released their hold on the rope handles, the front of the ram dropped onto a step and jarred to a halt against the riser.

'Keep it up!' Macro urged Apollonius and his men. 'Pour it on the bastards!'

The rocks continued to strike the men on the ram, and those who went to replace the wounded. Then the inevitable happened as the rebels started to scoop up the rocks and throw them back at the defenders. There was a sharp cry as one of the veterans was struck in the face, crushing his nose and shattering his cheekbone in a welter of blood. Another man was hit on the side of his helmet as he stooped to pick up some more rocks, and he swayed before sinking to his knees and throwing up.

'Raise your shields!' Apollonius ordered, and his men continued the exchange of missiles with the enemy.

As before, the rebels sent their own shield-bearers forward to cover the warriors carrying the ram, and it came on again. Macro could see there was no point in continuing the barrage, and shouted the order for Apollonius's men to rejoin the reserve line.

There was a brief delay before one of the enemy warriors began to call the time. As he reached three, the heavy oak timbers of the bookcase shuddered under the first blow of the ram. Macro and those that remained of Ulpius's century stood a short distance back, ready to advance and defend the breach once the ram had done its work.

The second blow stove in two of the planks, scattering splinters over the paving slabs on the shelves. The third dislodged some of the slabs and shattered more of the oak. Several more blows reduced the makeshift barricade to ruins, and then the enemy lowered the ram and began to tear away at the broken timbers and smashed slabs of stone. It was the work of a few heartbeats to clear a gap wide enough for three men to pass through at a time.

Macro tightened his grip on the handles of his shield and sword and braced his feet as he made ready to defend the breach. The first of the rebels clambered through the rubble and broken timber and charged the line of shields before them. Two were stabbed at once, while the third managed to burst through the line before he was set upon by Apollonius and one of the veterans. Sword thrusts pierced his back, and he collapsed onto his front and lay gasping for breath as blood filled his lungs. But more of the enemy swept through the gap and pressed themselves against the Roman line, which was steadily pushed back, half a pace at a time. So tightly compacted were both sides that neither could wield their weapons, and it became a desperate test of strength that the outnumbered veterans could not hope to win.

'They're coming over the side!' a voice cried as the ladders of the rebels proved their worth once more against the lesser challenge of the pediment and the breastwork on top. As more warriors climbed onto the pediment, they divided the defenders, driving them around the rear of the temple while forcing those closest to the steps towards Macro and the veterans slowly losing ground around the breach.

Macro backed out of the fight and the men on either side closed up to fill the gap. He needed to take stock. Running to the side where the enemy were scaling the ladders, he saw that at least a hundred of them were on the pediment and driving the Romans back in both directions. The pediment was lost, he conceded with a bitter hiss of frustration. The end was near. All that mattered now was to hold out and kill as many of the rebels as possible before the last of the veterans were overwhelmed. Running across the entrance to the inner sanctum, he looked down to see that the other side of the temple was also being assaulted by rebels carrying more ladders. Even as he watched, he saw a group of enemy warriors surge round the rear of the sanctum and charge down the length of the pediment howling their war cries. They drove into the Roman flank, giving the defenders no chance to check the impetus of their charge. In moments they would reach the front of the pediment.

Macro knew that there was one last hope of refuge where the survivors could make their final stand.

'Fall back into the sanctum!' he called out.

The men who were not yet engaged retreated first, filing through the narrow gap of the open door. It was one of a pair, twice the height of a man and constructed from oak reinforced by straps of iron and studs. Enough to withstand a ram for long enough for the defenders to catch their breath. As the last of those veterans who were not committed to the fight reached the door, there was a cry of alarm from the left as the enemy came round the corner of the pediment.

Apollonius was still with the men who had attempted to delay the ram with a rock barrage. 'Follow me!' he cried.

The small party charged the enemy and slammed their shields into the rebels, driving them back on those behind them. The spy and his companions stabbed and slashed furiously as they bought time for Macro and the others to form a steadily shrinking shield wall around the doorway of the inner sanctum. One man after another peeled off and fell back. Macro turned to Apollonius.

'Get over here! Now!'

The three men still fighting alongside the spy stepped back together and merged with the tight knot of Romans defending the doorway. At that moment, a lithe rebel who had climbed onto the barricade took aim with his bow and released a shaft. The arrow struck Apollonius high on the chest, just below his neck, and the point burst out through the muscle above his left shoulder blade. His left arm spasmed and went limp, and the shield slipped from his fingers. Blood drenched his tunic and spread across his chest as he continued to stab and slash at the enemy.

'Fall back, Apollonius!' Macro ordered.

There were only five Romans outside the door now. Macro filled his lungs and roared with battle rage as he slammed his shield into a rebel and then swung his sword in a frenzied arc to buy time for his comrades.

'Inside! Now!'

The three veterans darted through the gap, then Macro felt a hand on his harness as Apollonius swung him round and thrust him through. The last thing he saw as the men behind the door slammed it closed was the spy flailing with his sword as he was driven to his knees by the blows of the rebels surrounding him. The bar was dropped into its brackets and the veterans quickly began to pile slabs of stone and roof tiles against the rear of the doors as the rebels pounded the other side with their weapons.

Only the section of the roof closest to the entrance of the inner sanctum had been constructed, and the sky was clearly visible through the beams and rafters for most of its length. Even so, the interior was gloomy, and for a moment no one spoke as they caught their breath and listened to the challenges and jeers of the rebels outside the final refuge of the colony's defenders. The sanctum was no more than fifty feet long and thirty feet wide, and the rear was packed with wounded and dying men being ministered to by the surgeon and his medics. Parvus was still with them, handing out the dressings from a large bag at his shoulder. Cassius had retreated to a corner and sat trembling. Of the veterans, no more than thirty were still standing, gathered about the doorway, waiting for Macro to give his orders.

He licked his dry lips and cleared his throat. 'We'll take a quick breather before we counter-attack, lads.'

The comment drew smiles and a few wry chuckles. None of the veterans had any doubt what lay ahead, and he could see that they shared his wish to die on his feet, sword in hand, facing the enemy.

'What now? What are we going to do?'

Macro turned to see one of the civilians who had remained to defend the colony. A rotund man in his early fifties whom he recognised as the owner of one of the colony's inns.

'Do?' He shook his head. 'This is where we go into the shadows, friend.'

'No. There has to be another way.' It was clear what the man meant, though he did not want to be the one to suggest it out loud.

'Surrender?' Macro spoke for him. He pointed to the door. 'You hear that? I don't think they're in the mood for taking prisoners. Even if we did surrender, what do you think they would do to us then? You must have lived in Britannia long enough to know about the human sacrifices they offer their gods.'

He let his words sink in before continuing. 'Like I said, this is where we die. We do it like men – like Apollonius, on our feet – or like slaughtered cattle. Either way we die. But at least we can choose *how* we die.'

The innkeeper grimaced and drew a deep breath before he nodded. 'On my feet then.'

'That's the spirit.' Macro offered a reassuring smile. 'We'll make a soldier of you yet, my friend.'

The futile beating against the outside of the door quickly subsided, and the cheers of the rebels died away as their leaders gave fresh orders. Macro's weary mind tried to anticipate the enemy's intentions. The obvious approach would be to bring up the ram. The doors of the sanctum would present a greater challenge than the barricade or even the compound wall, but they would give way in the end. And then the defenders would be cut down one after another before the wounded were slaughtered. On the other hand, the rebels might content themselves with starving the defenders to death, or waiting until the water ran out. However, their blood was up, and Macro did not believe they were patient enough to pursue such a course of action. Whatever their intentions, it was clear that he and his comrades were not likely to see another dawn.

He sheathed his sword and lowered his shield as he ordered the other veterans to stand down, then made for the rear of the sanctum, stepping over the wounded until he reached the surgeon. Adrastus wore a bloodstained leather apron over his tunic as he rose from stitching the thigh wound of one of his patients.

'A quiet word with you,' said Macro. He lowered his voice so that no one would overhear the exchange. 'We'll not be able to keep the enemy out for long. When the doors go, we'll be overwhelmed in short order. We have to think about what they will do to the injured if they take them alive.'

'I understand,' the surgeon responded.

'Good. If there's a way you can make it easy for the men with the worst injuries, then do so. For the others, give them a blade and they can make their own decision. You'll need to explain it to your lads. I expect most will want to go down fighting, but if they want to take their lives, I'll not stand in their way.'

Adrastus glanced round at the men dealing with the wounded packed against the walls and across the flagstones. 'Most of them will fight.'

'What about you?'

'I'll deal with the badly wounded first. There are some blood vessels that can be cut relatively painlessly and they'll bleed out quickly. It's as merciful as it can be in the circumstances. Once I've seen to the last of them, I'll find a sword to fight with.'

Macro nodded. 'You've done yourself proud. You and your men. I'd be honoured to fight to the end with you at my side.'

Adrastus smiled grimly. 'That's an honour I'd sooner avoid.'

'As would I. No offence.'

They shared a dry chuckle before the surgeon nodded towards Parvus, who was squatting beside Cassius and stroking the dog's head. 'What about them? Do you want me to deal with it?'

Macro's stomach lurched. 'No. I'll speak to the boy. He wants to fight, but I don't think he understands what is at stake if he is taken alive. I can't let that happen to him.'

They were interrupted by a loud crash. The ram had arrived. At once Macro turned and rushed back to join the veterans re-forming their line behind the door. Each blow shook a small wave of dust from the door frame, and once more the enemy's voices rose in a cheer. Macro cleared his mind of all thought save what he must do when the doors gave way. He was aware of the acrid scent of smoke, a gust from those buildings of the colony that were still burning, he surmised.

There was a cry of alarm from behind him, and he glanced over his shoulder just as a blazing faggot crashed down amongst the injured towards the rear of the sanctum. Then another appeared at the top of the wall, and more, already alight before they tumbled inside, bursting into sparks and flame as they fell on the flagstones or the bodies of the wounded and those who were treating them. Macro saw the surgeon look up anxiously, a scalpel in his gory hand as he prepared to carry out the mercy killing of the man lying beside him. Then both were wreathed in fire as they were struck by a large bundle of blazing sticks and thatch coated with pitch. The walls of the sanctum echoed with the roar of flames and cries of terror and agony. Some of the men were already alight, shrieking figures in frenzied motion as they tried in vain to beat the blaze out.

'Parvus,' Macro muttered. He glanced frantically towards

the last place he had seen the boy, but he was no longer there. Then he spotted him, across the flames, trapped in the opposite corner with Cassius cowering at his side. Their eyes met for an instant, but before Macro could react, both boy and dog were struck down by a flaming bundle of sticks. He heard Cassius let out an agonised howl before the beast fell silent. There was no hope of fighting through the blaze to try and save them. Despair tightened round his heart like a fist.

Macro coughed violently as smoke filled the confined space and it became a churning mass of flame, swirling black clouds and the brilliant flares of more faggots dropping from above. All the while, the piteous screams of the dying filled the ears of those by the door, driven back by the blistering heat of the inferno.

'We can't stay here,' he called out. 'We'll burn to death. One last charge, my brothers!'

In desperation, he began to clear away the tiles and masonry that had been used to reinforce the doors. When only the locking bar remained, he realised that the rebels were no longer using the ram. He detailed two of the veterans to raise the bar on his order, while the others recovered their shields and readied their swords. Behind them the screams had almost died away, with only one voice still shrieking.

'Now!' Macro choked, tears streaming from his eyes so that he could hardly see.

He heard the bar clunk on the flagstones as it was heaved aside, and then the doors opened and a blinding shaft of daylight pierced the swirling inferno inside the sanctum. He made to give a defiant war cry as he burst out, jumping over Apollonius's body, but his lungs were too full of smoke, and he staggered on coughing and half blinded. He felt his shield being torn from his grip, then his sword arm was seized and the blade twisted from his fingers. More hands grabbed at him. He tried to tear himself free and lash out, but his arms were pinioned behind him and he was forced down the stairs and dragged across the flagstones of the compound, accompanied by the kicks and jeers of the dense press of rebels surrounding him. He was forced onto his knees and his helmet was removed. A rope was laced around his neck before his wrists were bound tightly behind his back.

As his vision cleared, he saw the other veterans who had survived the blaze, their faces blackened and streaked and their wrists similarly tied. A space opened around them as a group of warriors in chain mail and green cloaks pushed the crowd back. Twisting painfully to look back towards the temple, he saw thick smoke billowing from the open doors and the unfinished roof of the sanctum. A moment later, the stretch that had been tiled collapsed with a shattering roar, and the crowd let out a deafening cheer of triumph. The cheering continued for a while before rising in intensity, rippling outwards from the direction of the compound gatehouse, and he saw Boudica approaching, smiling to both sides as she brandished her spear and called out to her followers.

She stopped at the edge of the open space and lowered the butt of the spear as she beheld the grimy faces of the twenty or so Romans, who had been stripped of their weapons and bound, and who now regarded her anxiously from their kneeling position. The expression of triumph that had lit up her features an instant before now resolved itself into a mask of hatred and cruelty.

Macro raised his chin as he stared back defiantly, doing his best to meet his end with courage and dignity. His heart was filled with sorrow for Parvus, Apollonius and the comrades who had died defending their homes. He even felt the loss of

Cassius for his fierce loyalty and unconditional affection for those who had adopted him. His feelings shifted to anxiety for the fate of Petronella, his mother, Lucius and Claudia, now placed in great peril by the rashness of Decianus. He closed his eyes and mouthed a prayer to Jupiter, Best and Greatest.

'I have always served Rome with loyalty and courage. I have shed my blood for Rome. For the sake of that I ask the gods to spare my family and those close to me. I ask that the procurator meets the fate he deserves and I pray that Cato lives to avenge me, my brothers and Parvus. This I ask in return for my service to Rome. Please grant my dying wish.'

He opened his eyes and breathed in deeply as Boudica slowly paced towards him. He met her gaze steadily, and then looked over her shoulder to a white gull hovering in the distance, aloof from the horrors of the world, as he braced himself to meet his end.

'You,' the Iceni queen said quietly. 'Macro.'

There was a pause as he waited for the killing blow. Then she snapped an order, and Macro was grasped by the arms and dragged away from the burning temple.

# CHAPTER THIRTY-THREE

## *The Island of Mona*

It was late in the afternoon, and the stench of death and charred wood hung over the scene like a veil. The last Druid stronghold had been taken three days earlier, and the ancient circle of trees that surrounded the grove had been cut down and burned. The large stone altar that had stood in the centre was smashed and the fragments scattered across the site. Every stone in the avenue that approached the grove had been pulled down by teams of prisoners, while the surviving Druids had been bound and forced to witness the destruction. Afterwards, the Druids were nailed to the limbless trunks of the oak trees that had once shaded the grove. The same oaks from which their own grisly trophies and divine offerings had once hung.

As the survivors of the Eighth Illyrian Cohort marched past on their way to the nearby camp, Cato steered his horse to the side of the rutted track to regard the scene. The destruction wrought by the soldiers of the Fourteenth Legion was a fitting conclusion to the savagery of the month since Suetonius and his army had landed on Mona. After their failure to prevent the Romans taking the island, the Druids and their allies had retreated to the interior to defend the sacred groves and their hill forts, while small parties of horsemen had harassed the Roman columns that had spread out from the beachhead to hunt down and destroy any who resisted the invaders. Governor Suetonius had issued orders that those who surrendered were to be rounded up, put in chains and marched to the strait, where they were to be held before being sold into slavery. Once they had been looted, every village was put to the torch and the livestock driven off to feed the army.

Following the battle, Suetonius had briefed his commanders to destroy all trace of the cult they found on Mona. Every Druid was to be executed, along with those who served them, down to the last woman and child. Mona was to be turned into a wasteland. Every building was to be razed, every hill fort levelled and its ditches filled in. Every grain store was to be seized and any supplies that could not be carried away were to be burned.

Although obliged to obey his orders, Cato had not agreed with them. Suetonius was going too far. The object of the campaign had been to defeat the hill tribes and crush the Druid cult once and for all. It was not necessary to annihilate or enslave the inhabitants of the island, who might otherwise have been pacified and left to farm their crops and pay their taxes to Rome. It was possible that they might even have been grateful to be relieved of the burden of being forced to support the Druids, who had dominated the island since fleeing there after the Roman invasion of the mainland.

Once word of the devastation of Mona reached those tribes in Britannia who still refused to accept Roman rule, or chafed under it, the lesson learned might go either way, Cato reflected. Some might regard the island's fate as something to be avoided at all costs and would accept their subjugation, while others – more proud and defiant – might hold it up as a warning to their people of the price of defeat and therefore the need to resist Rome's encroachment to the last. Either way, it was a wasteful excess of destruction. There was more to be lost than gained through Suetonius's treatment of the inhabitants of Mona, Cato decided.

Since the landing, Cato's cohort had been tasked with scouting ahead of the main column to locate the enemy strongholds, then wait for the artillery and heavy infantry to come up and destroy the fortifications and crush those inside them. None lasted more than a few days, and then the Eighth Cohort would march on and find the next target to eliminate. And so it had gone on. An endless cycle of scouting and scouring of the countryside until Cato's men had grown numbed by the slaughter and fervently wished to quit the island and return to the peace and comfort of garrison duty.

The sour odour of decaying flesh mixed with the acrid tang of charred timber was foul. Cato tugged the reins and turned his horse towards the track, trotting back to the head of the column, where the denuded ranks of the mounted contingent led their weary horses. He had received fresh orders from Suetonius two days ago, announcing that the last of the Druid strongholds had been taken and the campaign was over. Every unit was to concentrate on the main column to celebrate the victory before the army marched back to its base at Deva, where it would disperse to garrison duties and await replacements for those lost in the campaign.

In the case of the Eighth Cohort, less than half of those who had begun the campaign remained. It would be some months before they were ready for action again. The new men would have to be trained, remounts acquired, wills resolved and each man's share of the loot determined and allocated according to the shares associated with each rank. More than enough work to keep Cato busy for the rest of the year. But first he would take some leave and return to Camulodunum to see his son and

Claudia and regale Macro with the details of the campaign over a jar of wine. He smiled at the thought, before recalling the prospect of the discontent the procurator might stir up regarding Boudica and her tribe. With luck, Macro would have been able to curb the man's callous zeal in extracting the outstanding tribute owed by the Iceni. In any case, the gods had been kind. Suetonius's campaign had ended more quickly than Cato had anticipated. The army would return from Mona in time to discourage any hotheads from considering taking advantage of its absence from the rest of the province.

The stink of the grove faded behind them as the cohort marched down the gentle incline towards where Suetonius's column had constructed a marching camp large enough to contain the entire army. From the vantage point of the slope, Cato could see the long lines of tents and the wide thoroughfares that demarcated the areas assigned to each of the legionary and auxiliary cohorts. Preparations for the army's victory celebration were already under way. There were large pens filled with livestock, and he could see a group of men busy butchering cattle, while others built up cooking fires in long, shallow trenches close by. In the heart of the camp, several long tables had been set up with benches on either side as the headquarters clerks and Suetonius's personal slaves prepared fires for the senior officers' banquet.

As Cato and his cohort descended towards the southern gate of the camp, he saw a small party of riders galloping in from the east. They barely paused at the gate before racing through the camp towards the headquarters tents. Cato could not help wondering about the urgency that caused them to ride so fast. A moment later, he lost sight of them as the track dipped down to the final stretch of the approach to the camp.

Even though the campaign was over, the enemy defeated

and any danger vanquished, the optio in charge of the section of legionaries on the gate halted Cato to identify his unit and query his orders before allowing the cohort into the camp. There they were met by a headquarters clerk who directed them towards the space reserved for their tent lines. Cato ordered Galerius to take charge of setting up the tents and arranging feed and space for the horses to be tethered.

'I'll be back once I've reported to headquarters,' he concluded. 'Have my servant ready a fresh change of clothes for me. Tunic, cloak and boots. All clean. Wouldn't want Suetonius to disapprove of my appearance.'

Galerius smiled and nodded. 'I'll see to it, sir.'

They exchanged a casual salute, and Cato turned his mount towards the cluster of large tents at the heart of the camp, walking the horse through the encampment where some of the legionaries and auxiliaries were already in their cups, having looted the stocks of ale and wine that the Druids had amassed for the use of their inner circles. The early-evening air was filled with singing, laughter and the hubbub of happy conversation. He felt the last of his concerns ebb away as he looked forward to the coming feast. He had not eaten since dawn, and was already savouring the prospect of roast meat, fresh bread and wine when the governor's victory dinner began.

Turning onto the broad, muddy avenue that ran across the camp, he could see the tents of the army's headquarters. A small party of horsemen stood by their mounts a short distance away, and he guessed they must be the riders he'd seen shortly before. He stopped at the tethering rail next to theirs and dismounted wearily, rubbing his back and rump vigorously to ease out the aches from the day's ride. There were a number of centurions and tribunes sitting on the benches either side of the long tables that the engineers had constructed earlier that day, drinking from the jars placed along them. Cato approached a group of tribunes he had met earlier in the campaign, nodded a greeting and accepted the goblet of wine one of them held out to him. Before he could take a sip, however, a voice called out from the direction of Suetonius's command tent.

'All senior officers! Report to the governor at once!'

He set the goblet down. 'Look after that for me. I'll be back in a moment.'

He trudged across the worn grass towards the largest of the tents, along with the auxiliary prefects and senior centurions from the legionary cohorts who had also been drinking at the long tables. The bodyguards either side of the tent flaps had drawn them open to admit the officers, and they passed inside. Cato saw Suetonius in urgent conversation with a man in a mud-spattered cloak in the far corner of the tent. Looking round, he saw Thrasyllus nearby and made his way over.

'Any idea what this is about?'

'I heard there's some news from Londinium.'

'What news?'

'No idea. But we'll know soon enough.'

Cato glanced round to see that Suetonius was leading the man to the middle of the tent.

'Gentlemen! Quiet!' The tone of his voice was harsh and commanding, and he communicated a sense of urgency to the officers surrounding him. He waited until there was silence in the tent before he continued, indicating the muddy individual at this side. 'This is Marcus Verno from the procurator's staff. He left Londinium less than six days ago, bearing a message for me. Decianus reports that there has been an uprising amongst the Trinovantes and Iceni, led by the queen of the Iceni, Boudica.' He hesitated before he went on. 'According to the procurator, there is a large host following her; thousands of warriors armed with weapons they had hidden from us. I regret to inform you that eight days ago, the colony at Camulodunum was burned to the ground. A scout party sent by Decianus saw smoke covering the colony and a vast army of rebels encamped around the walls. The scouts witnessed the last stand of the veterans from a hill overlooking the colony. We must assume that those who remained to defend it have been wiped out.'

Cato felt his heart lurch at the governor's words. What had become of all those he knew and loved at the colony? What had happened to Lucius and Claudia? Macro and Petronella? Apollonius? Cassius? A nausea born of dread and exhaustion made him feel light-headed, and it took a supreme effort of will to force himself to continue listening to Suetonius.

'There is worse to come, gentlemen. The rebels will surely turn on Londinium next, destroying everything in their path. There are twenty thousand people there, protected by a small garrison. However, the town has no defences worth speaking of. I will do my best to prevent Londinium sharing the same fate as Camulodunum. To that end, the army is to prepare to march at first light and make for Deva to await my orders. Meanwhile, I will take the cavalry and ride ahead to see what can be done to prepare Londinium's defences. There is no time for any questions at this moment. You must return to your men and prepare them for the march of their lives. We must reach Londinium before the rebels do. Thousands of lives and the riches of the biggest settlement in the province depend on it. I'll have my staff draft your orders at once.'

Suetonius looked round at his officers before he spoke again. 'The province's darkest hour has come, and it could not be at a worse time, with the army so far from where it is needed. The very future of Britannia hangs by a thread. If we are to survive this and save the honour of Rome and the lives of all our people in the province, we will have to march and fight as no Roman army has ever done before. This is the great test of our age, gentlemen. We must meet and defeat the rebels before Britannia goes up in flames and these lands are drenched with the blood of Romans. Now go to your men and order them to prepare to march at first light. There are only two paths open to us now. Victory or annihilation. Dismissed.'

As the officers streamed from the tent, Cato's heart was filled with dark resolve. If his family and friends had escaped the conflagration at Camulodunum, he must race to save them before such a fate caught up with them at Londinium. He and the rest of the army must march as swiftly as if they were pursued by ravening demons. They must save Londinium and her people from the barbarian horde bearing down on them, determined to burn and slaughter every person or object that bore the stamp of Rome.

# AUTHOR'S NOTE

The Boudican revolt is one of the most celebrated events in the history of the British Isles. Its leader is one of the modern nation's foremost icons. A huge monument depicting Boudica atop a fanciful war chariot stands opposite the Palace of Westminster in London. She brandishes a spear as she beckons to her followers, while her two daughters kneel at her feet. Boudica has frequently appeared in fiction, historical periodicals and on screens small and large. You might be forgiven for thinking that her legendary status has been a constant fixture of our history since the time of the bloody rebellion she fronted.

And yet the truth is that she all but disappeared from history for many centuries until, so the story goes, a monk looking for some spare writing materials happened upon a trove of Roman histories in the cellars of Monte Cassino. These documents were read by an Italian chancer, who included them in a historical work concerning the great queens of England at the time when Elizabeth I was on the throne. The tale of Boudica caught the attention of certain poets and dramatists, via various corruptions of her name – the most popular of which was Boadicea (an error that persisted until comparatively recently).

The high point of her legend occurred during the reign of

Victoria, when once again the status of a female monarch needed some burnishing. This was when the monument to Boudica was funded by public subscription and erected opposite the seat of Britain's government. Which is an odd thing when you consider that she and her followers were responsible for the razing of the town of Londinium and the atrocities committed against its inhabitants. It's about as historically insensitive as erecting a monument to Osama bin Laden opposite the site of the Twin Towers. But there we are: history is a twisted thing.

The historical context of the rebellion is rather more interesting and complicated than the freedom-fighter legend would have us believe. The Roman conquest of Britain was motivated by political concerns rather than strategic necessity. It coincided with the early years of the reign of Emperor Claudius. His predecessor had been assassinated by senior officers of the Praetorian Guard, and Claudius owed his position to the support of those Praetorian Guards who realised that they were on to a good thing under the emperors and that a return to the days of the Republic would leave them short-changed. The reader can easily imagine how the legitimacy of Claudius might well be viewed with scepticism under the circumstances. Therefore, he needed to win over the Roman people by taking credit for some military success that would add the necessary lustre to his reputation.

He was fortunate that the previous emperor, Caligula, had been tempted by the same political expedient and had concentrated an army and fleet on the coast of Gaul in readiness to invade Britannia. Using these forces, Claudius gave the go-ahead, and even made a brief appearance during the early part of what turned into a long, grinding campaign in order to take the credit for the swiftly announced conquest of Britannia. The celebration of a triumph in Rome might have impressed the mob, but for the Roman soldiers in Britannia, many more years of bitter fighting lay ahead.

The task of the Romans was made somewhat easier by the endemic divisions between the tribes inhabiting the main island. Some of these tribes were suborned in advance of the Roman invasion. We are told that twelve delegations presented themselves to Claudius during his brief visit to pledge their loyalty to Rome. No doubt some of these tribes were pleased to settle scores with long-standing enemies amongst the tribes that resisted the invaders. Indeed, Boudica's rebels wreaked their havoc on Romans and tribal enemies alike. The rebellion was as much about settling scores with traditional enemies as it was a conflict against an imperial invader. A pattern that has played out across history in many locations. Stuart Laycock's excellent *Britannia: The Failed State* highlights the importance of tribal divisions and the problems this caused for Roman governance very persuasively.

The compounded difficulties of establishing the new Roman province and the constant drain of military resources in exchange for meagre progress in subduing the tribes who continued to resist prompted second thoughts in Rome. Any hopes that Britannia would yield sufficient treasure and spoils to justify the cost of invasion and occupation were soon dashed. However, the prestige of Rome and Emperor Claudius was at stake, and the ongoing conflict became justified by political necessity. Rather like many more recent examples of invasions initiated by overoptimistic dictators that soon became bogged down by stubborn resistance.

The situation changed with the death of Claudius and the accession of Nero. At this point there was an opportunity to reassess the justification for maintaining the new province. Despite the considerable investment of resources in Britannia, there were many in Rome who questioned whether it might be better to call it a day and withdraw from the island. Of course, that would entail a blow to Roman prestige, but there were other uses the four legions and attached auxiliary units could be put to. It was a very large garrison to support in view of the paltry revenues Britannia generated. Accordingly, those who had invested in Britannia and made loans to some of the tribal rulers began a scramble to get their money out of the island before any decision was made about its future. The calling-in of loans hit the Britons at a time when there had been a sequence of poor harvests. To make matters worse, the Romans were gouging the locals for taxes and, in the case of the veterans settled at Camulodunum, helping themselves to the lands of the local people. At the same time, young Britons were being forcibly conscripted into Roman auxiliary units. It is not difficult to imagine the tensions this created between the occupied and the occupiers.

As the saying goes, no society is ever more than a few square meals away from rebellion. The increasing grievances of the tribes simmered away until matters came to a head around 60–61 CE, when Prasutagus, the king of the Iceni, died. The cavalier treatment of the will he left behind and the brutal outrages committed against his widow and daughters provided the spark that ignited open rebellion and the horrors that were to follow.